Winter Solstice

Also by Rosamunde Pilcher

The Carousel

Voices in Summer

September

The Blue Bedroom and Other Stories

Flowers in the Rain and Other Stories

Coming Home

Wild Mountain Thyme

Under Gemini

Sleeping Tiger

The Empty House

The End of Summer

Snow in April

The Day of the Storm

Another View

The Shell Seekers

WINTER SOLSTICE

ROSAMUNDE PILCHER

THOMAS DUNNE BOOKS
ST. MARTIN'S GRIFFIN
NEW YORK

This is a work of fiction. All of the characters, organizations, and events portrayed in this novel are either products of the author's imagination or are used fictitiously.

Thomas Dunne Books.
An imprint of St. Martin's Press.

www.thomasdunnebooks.com
www.stmartins.com

St. Martin's Press gratefully acknowledges the permission of David Higham Associates on behalf of Macmillan Press Ltd. to excerpt from Charles Causley's poem "The Seasons in North Cornwall."

The Library of Congress has cataloged the hardcover edition as follows:

Pilcher, Rosamunde.
Winter solstice. / Rosamunde Pilcher.—1st ed.
p. cm.
"Thomas Dunne Books."
ISBN 978-0-312-24426-2 (hardcover)
ISBN 978-0-312-27771-0 (e-book)
1. Country life—Fiction. 2. Winter—Fiction. 3. Scotland—Fiction. I. Title.
PR6066.I38 W56 2000
823'.914

00031713

ISBN 978-1-250-07746-2 (trade paperback)

First St. Martin's Griffin Edition: December 2015

10 9 8 7 6 5 4 3

ACKNOWLEDGMENTS

There were times during the writing of this book when my lack of knowledge on certain aspects precipitated a bad case of writer's block. Therefore, I must thank those who gave liberally of their time and expertise, and helped me get going again.

Willie Thomson, who put me in touch with James Sugden of Johnstons of Egin, and so got the whole show on the road.

James Sugden, for sharing with me his vast knowledge and experience of the Woollen Trade.

My neighbour, David Tweedie, for his legal advice.

David Anstice, the clock man of Perthshire.

The Reverend Dr. James Simpson, for his constant interest and wise guidance.

And finally, Robin, who paid back a debt by digging his mother out of a literary hole.

ELFRIDA

Before Elfrida Phipps left London for good and moved to the country, she made a trip to the Battersea Dogs' Home, and returned with a canine companion. It took a good—and heart-rending—half-hour of searching, but as soon as she saw him, sitting very close to the bars of his kennel and gazing up at her with dark and melting eyes, she knew that he was the one. She did not want a large animal, nor did she relish the idea of a yapping lap-dog. This one was exactly the right size. Dog size.

He had a lot of soft hair, some of which fell over his eyes, ears that could prick or droop, and a triumphant plume of a tail. His colouring was irregularly patched brown and white. The brown bits were the exact shade of milky cocoa. When asked his ancestry, the kennel maid said she thought there was Border collie there, and a bit of bearded collie, as well as a few other unidentified breeds. Elfrida didn't care. She liked the expression on his gentle face.

She left a donation for the Battersea Dogs' Home, and her new companion travelled away with her, sitting in the passenger seat of her old car and gazing from the window in a satisfied fashion, as though this were the life to which he was happy to become accustomed.

The next day, she took him to the local Poodle Parlour for a cut, shampoo, and blow-dry. He returned to her fluffy and fresh and smelling sweetly of lemonade. His response to all this sybaritic attention was a show of faithful, grateful, and loving devotion. He was a shy, even a timid, dog, but brave as well. If the doorbell rang, or he thought he spied an intruder, he barked his head off for a moment and then retreated to his basket, or to Elfrida's lap.

It took some time to decide on a name for him, but in the end she christened him Horace.

Elfrida, with a basket in her hand, and Horace firmly clipped to the end of his lead, closed the front door of her cottage behind her, walked down the narrow path, through the gate, and set off down the pavement towards the post office and general store.

It was a dull, grey afternoon in the middle of October, with nothing much to commend about it. The last of autumn's leaves fell from trees, with an unseasonably icy breeze too chill for even the most ardent of gardeners to be out and about. The street was deserted, and the children not yet out of school. Overhead, the sky was low with clouds, that shifted steadily and yet never seemed to clear. She walked briskly, Horace trotting reluctantly at her heels, knowing that this was his exercise for the day and he had no alternative but to make the best of it.

The village was Dibton in Hampshire, and here Elfrida had come to live eighteen months ago, leaving London forever and making for herself a new life. At first she had felt a bit solitary, but now she couldn't imagine living anywhere else. From time to time, old acquaintances from her theatre days made the intrepid journey from the city and came to stay with her, sleeping on the lumpy divan in the tiny back bedroom that she called her work-room, which was where she kept her sewing machine and earned a bit of pin money making elaborate and beautiful cushions for an interior decorating firm in Sloane Street.

When these friends departed, they needed reassurance: "You're all right, aren't you, Elfrida?" they would ask. "No regrets? You don't want to come back to London? You're happy?" And she had been able to set their minds at rest. "Of course I am. This is my geriatric bolt-hole. This is where I shall spend the twilight of my years."

So, by now, there was a comfortable familiarity about it all. She knew who lived in this house, in that cottage. People called her by her name. "Morning, Elfrida," or "Lovely day, Mrs. Phipps." Some of the inhabitants were commuting families, the man of the house setting out early each morning to catch the fast train to London and returning late in the evening to pick up his car from the station park and drive the short distance home. Others had lived here all their lives in small stone houses that had belonged to their fathers and their grandfathers before that. Still others were new altogether, inhabiting the council estates that ringed the village, and employed by the electronics factory in the neighbouring town. It was all very ordinary, and so, undemanding. Just, in fact, what Elfrida needed.

Walking, she passed the pub, newly furbished and now called the Dibton Coachhouse. There were wrought-iron signs and a spacious car-park. Farther on, she passed the church, with its yew trees and lych-gate, and a notice-board fluttering with parish news. A guitar concert, an outing for the Mothers and Toddlers group. In the churchyard, a man lit a bonfire and the air was sweet with the scent of toasting leaves. Overhead, rooks cawed. A cat sat on one of the churchyard gate posts, but luckily Horace did not notice him.

The street curved, and at the end of it, by the dull bungalow which was the new Vicarage, she saw the village shop, flying banners advertising ice-cream, and newspaper placards propped against the wall. Two or three youths with bicycles hung about its door, and the postman, with his red van, was emptying the post-box.

There were bars over the shop window, to stop vandals' breaking the glass and stealing the tins of biscuits and arrangements of baked beans which were Mrs. Jennings's idea of tasteful decoration. Elfrida put down her basket and tied Horace's lead to one of these bars, and he sat looking resigned. He hated being left on the pavement, at the mercy of the jeering youths, but Mrs. Jennings didn't like dogs in her establishment. She said they lifted their legs and were dirty brutes.

Inside, the shop was bright with electricity, low-ceilinged and very warm. Refrigerators and freezers hummed, and it had strip lighting and an up-to-date arrangement of display shelving which had been installed some months ago, a huge improvement, Mrs. Jennings insisted, more like a mini-market. Because of all these barriers, it was difficult to know at first glance who was in the shop and who wasn't, and it was not until Elfrida rounded a corner (instant coffee and teas) that she saw the familiar back view, standing by the till and paying his due.

Oscar Blundell. Elfrida was past the age when her heart leaped for joy, but she was always pleased to see Oscar. He had been almost the first person she met when she came to live in Dibton, because she had gone to church one Sunday morning, and after the service the vicar had stopped her outside the door, his hair on end in the fresh spring breeze, and his white cassock blowing like clean washing on a line. He had spoken welcoming words, made a few noises about doing flowers and the Women's Institute, and then, mercifully, was diverted. "And here's our organist. Oscar Blundell. Not our regular, you understand, but a splendid spare wheel in times of trouble."

And Elfrida turned, and saw the man emerging from the darkness of the interior of the church, walking out into the sunshine to join them. She saw the gentle, amused face, the hooded eyes, the hair which had probably once been fair but was now thickly white. He was as tall as Elfrida, which was unusual. She towered over most men, being five feet eleven and thin as a lath, but Oscar she met eye to eye and liked what she saw there. Because it was Sunday, he wore a tweed suit and a pleasing tie, and when they shook hands, his grip had a good feel to it.

She said, "How clever. To play the organ, I mean. Is it your hobby?"

And he replied, quite seriously, "No, my job. My life." And then smiled, which took all pomposity from his words. "My profession," he amended.

A day or two later, and Elfrida received a telephone call.

"Hello, Gloria Blundell here. You met my husband last Sunday after church. The organist. Come and have dinner on Thursday. You know where we live. The Grange. Turreted red brick at the end of the village."

"How very kind. I'd love to."

"How are you settling in?"

"Slowly."

"Splendid. See you Thursday, then. About seven-thirty."

"Thank you. So much." But the receiver at the other end of the line had already been replaced. Mrs. Blundell, it seemed, was not a lady with time to waste.

The Grange was the largest house in Dibton, approached by a drive through hugely pretentious gates. Somehow none of this exactly fitted in with Oscar Blundell, but it would be interesting to go, to meet his wife and see his background. You never really got to know people properly until you had seen them within the ambiance of their own home. Seen their furniture and their books and the manner of their life-style.

On Thursday morning she had her hair washed, and the colour given its monthly tweak. The shade was officially called Strawberry Blonde, but sometimes it came out more orange than strawberry. This was one of the times, but Elfrida had more important things to worry about. Clothes were a bit of a problem. In the end she put on a flowered skirt which reached her ankles and a long cardigan-type garment in lime-green knit. The effect of hair, flowers, and cardigan was fairly dazzling, but looking bizarre was one of Elfrida's best ways of boosting her confidence.

She set out on foot, a ten-minute walk, down the village, through the pretentious gates, and up the drive. For once, she was dead on time. Never having been to the house before, she did not open the front door and walk in, calling "Yoo-hoo," which was her normal procedure, but found a bell and pressed it. She could hear its ring coming from the back of the house. She waited, gazing about her at well-tended lawns which looked as though they had just had their first cut of the year. There was the smell of new-cut grass, too, and the damp scent of the cool spring evening.

Footsteps. The door opened. A local lady in a blue dress and a flowered apron, clearly not the mistress of the house.

"Good evening. Mrs. Phipps, is it? Come along in, Mrs. Blundell won't be a moment, just went upstairs to fix her hair."

"Am I the first?"

"Yes, but not early. Others'll be here soon. Want me to take your coat?"

"No, I'll keep it on, thank you." No need to enlarge on this, to explain the little silk blouse beneath the cardigan had a hole under the sleeve.

"The drawing-room . . ."

But they were interrupted. "You're Elfrida Phipps. . . . I am sorry I wasn't here to greet you. . . ." And looking up, Elfrida saw her hostess descending the wide staircase from a balustraded landing. She was a large lady, tall and well-built, dressed in black silk trousers and a loose, embroidered Chinese jacket. She carried, in her hand, a tumbler half-full of what looked like a whisky and soda.

". . . I got a bit delayed, and then there was a telephone call. Hello." She held out her hand. "Gloria Blundell. Good of you to come."

She had an open, ruddy face with very blue eyes, and hair which, like Elfrida's, had probably been tweaked, but to a more discreet shade of soft blonde.

"Good of you to invite me."

"Come along in by the fire. Thank you, Mrs. Muswell; I expect the others will just let themselves in . . . this way. . . ."

Elfrida followed her through into a large room, much panelled in the style of the thirties, and with a vast red brick fireplace where burnt a log fire. In front of the hearth was a leather-padded club fender, and the room was furnished with hugely padded and patterned sofas and chairs. Curtains were plum velvet braided in gold, and the floor was closely carpeted and scattered with thick, richly coloured Persian rugs. Nothing looked old or shabby or faded, and all exuded an air of warmth and a cheerful masculine comfort.

"Have you lived here long?" Elfrida asked, trying not to appear too inquisitive.

"Five years. The place was left to me by an old uncle. Always adored it, used to come here as a child." She dumped her glass onto a handy table and went to hurl another enormous log onto the fire. "I can't tell you the state it was in. Everything threadbare and moth-eaten, so I had to have a really good refurbish. Made a new kitchen as well, and a couple of extra bathrooms."

"Where did you live before?"

"Oh, London. I had a house in Elm Park Gardens." She picked up her glass and had a restoring swallow, and then set it down again. She smiled. "My dressing drink. I have to have a little boost before parties. What would you like? Sherry? Gin and tonic? Yes, it was a good place to be and marvellously spacious. And Oscar's church, Saint Biddulph's, where he was organist, only ten minutes or so away. I suppose we'd have stayed there forever, but my old bachelor uncle was gathered, as they say, and the Grange came to me. As well, we have this child, Francesca. She's twelve now. I've always thought it better to bring a child up in the country. I don't know what Oscar's doing. He's meant to pour drinks. Probably forgotten about everything, and reading a book. And we have other guests to meet you. The McGeareys. He works in the City. And Joan and Tommy Mills. Tommy's a consultant in our hospital at Pedbury. Sorry, did you say sherry or gin and tonic?"

Elfrida said gin and tonic, and watched while Gloria Blundell went to pour her one from the well-provided table at the far end of the room. She then replenished her own glass, with a generous hand for the Scotch.

Returning, "There. Hope it's strong enough. You like ice? Now, sit down, be comfortable, tell me about your little cottage."

"Well . . . it's little."

Gloria laughed. "Poulton's Row, isn't it? They were built as railway cottages. Are you frightfully cramped?"

"Not really. I haven't got much furniture, and Horace and I don't take up much room. Horace is my dog. A mongrel. Not beautiful."

"I have two Pekes, which are. But they bite guests, so they're shut in the kitchen with Mrs. Muswell. And what made you come to Dibton?"

"I saw the cottage advertised in *The Sunday Times.* There was a photo. It looked rather dear. And not too expensive."

"I shall have to come and see it. Haven't been inside one of those little houses since I was a child and used to visit the widow of some old station porter. And what do you do?"

"Sorry?"

"Garden? Play golf? Good works?"

Elfrida hedged slightly. She knew a forceful woman when she met one. "I'm trying to get the garden straight, but it's mostly shifting rubbish so far."

"Do you ride?"

"I've never ridden a horse in my life."

"Well, that's straightforward anyway. I used to ride when my sons were boys, but that's a long time ago. Francesca's got a little pony, but I'm afraid she's not all that keen."

"You have sons as well?"

"Oh, yes. Grown up now and both married."

"But . . . ?"

"I was married before, you see. Oscar's my second husband."

"I'm sorry. I didn't realize."

"Nothing to be sorry about. My son Giles works in Bristol and Crawford has a job in the City. Computers or something, totally beyond me. Of course, we had known Oscar for years. Saint Biddulph's, Raleigh Square, was our church. He played divinely at my husband's funeral. When we married, everybody was astonished. *That old bachelor,* they said. *Do you have any idea what you're taking on?*

It was all marvellously intriguing. "Has Oscar always been a musician?" Elfrida asked.

"Always. He was educated at Westminster Abbey Choir School, and then went on to teach music at Glastonbury College. He was choirmaster and organist there for a number of years. And then he retired from teaching, moved to London, got the post at Saint Biddulph's. I think he'd have continued there until they carried him out feet-first, but then my uncle died and fate decreed otherwise."

Elfrida felt a little sorry for Oscar. "Did he mind saying goodbye to London?"

"It was a bit like pulling an old tree up by the roots. But for Francesca's sake, he put a brave face on it. And here he has his music room and his books and scores, and he does a little private coaching, just to keep his hand in. Music is his life. He loves it when there's an emergency and he can play for morning service in the Dibton church. And, of course, he's always sneaking over to have a little quiet practice all on his own." Behind Gloria, quietly, the door from the hall had opened. Talking away, she was unaware of this, but, realizing that Elfrida's attention had strayed, turned in her chair to peer over her shoulder.

"Oh, there you are, old boy. We were just talking about you."

All at once, and all together, the other guests arrived, letting themselves in and filling the house with the sound of their voices. The Blundells went out to welcome them, and for a moment Elfrida was alone. She thought it would be rather nice to go home now and have a solitary evening mulling over all she had learned, but of course this was not to be. Almost before she could put the shameful thought out of her mind, her hosts were back, their guests surged into the room, and the dinner party was on its way.

It was a formal evening, lavish and traditional, with excellent food and a great deal of splendid wine. They ate smoked salmon and a beautifully presented crown of lamb, and there were three puddings, and bowls of thick cream, and then a creamy blue-veined Stilton. When the port was handed around, Elfrida noticed with some amusement that the ladies did not leave the room, but stayed with the men, and although she was now on to copious glasses of water, which she poured for herself from a cut-glass jug, she saw that the other women enjoyed their port, and Gloria, perhaps, most of all.

She wondered if Gloria, sitting in state at the head of the table, had slightly overdone her alcoholic intake, and if, when the time came for them to leave the table, she would heave herself to her feet and fall flat on her face. But Gloria was made of tougher stuff, and when Mrs. Muswell put her head round the door to say that coffee was all ready in the drawing-room, she led the way with a steady step, out of the dining-room and across the hall.

They gathered around the fire, but Elfrida, lifting her cup of coffee from the tray, saw through the uncurtained window a sky of deep sapphire blue. Although the spring day had been fitful, with showers and glimpses of sunshine, while they sat over dinner the clouds had dispersed, and a first star hung in the heavens over the top of a distant budding beech. There was a window-seat and she went to sit on it, cradling the cup and saucer in her hands and watching the stars.

Presently she was joined by Oscar. "Are you all right?" he asked her.

She turned to look up at him. So busy had he been through dinner, pouring wine, clearing plates, handing around the delectable puddings, that she had scarcely addressed him all evening.

"Of course. Such a lovely evening. And your daffodils will very soon be in bud."

"You like gardens?"

"I've not had much experience. But this one looks particularly inviting."

"Would you like to take a little stroll and be shown around? It's still not dark."

She glanced at the others, settled down in the deep chairs around the fire and in full flood of conversation.

"Yes, I would like that, but wouldn't it be rude?"

"Not at all." He took her cup from her hand and carried it back to the tray. He set it down. "Elfrida and I are going to have a stroll around the garden."

"At this hour?" Gloria was astounded. "It's dark and it's cold."

"Not so dark. We'll be ten minutes."

"Right, but make sure the poor girl's got a coat. It's chilly and damp . . . don't let him keep you too long, my dear. . . ."

"I won't. . . ."

The others went back to their discussion, which was about the iniquitous price of private education. Elfrida and Oscar went out through the door. He closed it quietly behind him and then lifted from a chair a thick leather coat lined in sheepskin. "It's Gloria's . . . you can borrow it," and he draped it gently over Elfrida's shoulders. Then he opened the half-glassed front door, and they stepped outside into the chill and purity of the spring evening. Shrubs and borders loomed in the dusk, and underfoot the grass was wet with dew.

They walked. At the far end of the lawn was a brick wall, fronted by borders and broken by an archway with an imposing wrought-iron gate. He opened this and they went through and were in a spacious walled garden, neatly divided into geometrical shapes by hedges of box. One quarter was a rose garden, the bushes pruned and richly composted. Clearly, when summer came, there would be something of a display.

Faced with professionalism, she felt inadequate. "Is this all your work?"

"No. I plan, but I employ labourers."

"I'm not much good at flower names. I've never had a proper garden."

"My mother was never lost for names. If someone asked her the name of a flower, and she had no idea what it was, she simply said, with much authority, *Inapoticum, Forgetanamia*. It nearly always worked."

"I must remember that."

Side by side, they strolled down the wide gravelled pathway. He said, "I hope you didn't feel too distanced at dinner. I'm afraid we're something of a parochial lot."

"Not at all. I enjoyed every moment. I like to listen."

"Country life. It teems with intrigue."

"Do you miss London?"

"From time to time, enormously. Concerts and the opera. My church. Saint Biddulph's."

"Are you a religious person?" Elfrida asked impulsively, and then wished that she hadn't. Too soon for such a personal question.

But he remained unfazed. "I don't know. But I have spent the whole of my life steeped in the sacred music, the liturgies and magnificats of the Anglican Church. And I would find it uncomfortable to live in a world where I had no person to thank."

"For blessings, you mean?"

"Just so."

"I understand, but even so I'm not a bit religious. I only went to church that Sunday because I was feeling a bit isolated and I needed the company of other people. I didn't expect the lovely music. And I'd never heard that setting of the Te Deum before."

"The organ is a new one. Paid for by countless Bring and Buy sales of work."

They trod in silence for a moment. Then Elfrida said, "Do you count that as a blessing? The new organ, I mean."

He laughed. "You are like a little dog, worrying a bone. Yes, of course I do."

"What else?"

He did not immediately reply. She thought of his home, his wife, his enormously comfortable and lavish house. His music room, his friends, his obvious financial security. She thought it would be interesting to know how Oscar had come to marry Gloria. Had he, after years of bachelordom, small boys, meagre salaries, and dusty academic rooms, seen, looming in the future, the emptiness of an elderly bachelor's old age, and taken the easy way out? The wealthy, forceful widow, the capable hostess, good friend, competent mother. Or perhaps it was she who had done the stalking, and she who had made the decision. Perhaps they had simply fallen madly in love. Whatever, it seemed to work.

The silence lay between them. She said, "Don't tell me if you'd rather not."

"I was simply trying to decide how to explain. I married late in life and Gloria already had boys by her previous marriage. For some reason it never occurred to me that I should have a child of my own. When Francesca was born, I was amazed, not simply that she was *there,* a tiny human being, but so beautiful. And familiar. As though I had known her always. A miracle. Now she is twelve and I am still astounded by my good fortune."

"Is she here at home?"

"No, at a weekly boarding-school. Tomorrow evening, I fetch her for the weekend."

"I would like to meet her."

"You shall. I like to think that you'll be charmed by her. When Gloria inherited this pile of a house, I kicked against leaving London. But for Francesca I went with the tide and complied. Here, she has space and freedom. Trees, the smell of grass. Room to grow. Room for the rabbits and the guinea pigs and the pony."

"For me," said Elfrida, "the best is bird-song in the morning and big skies."

"You too, I believe, have also fled from London?"

"Yes. It was time."

"A wrench?"

"In a way. I'd lived there all my life. From the moment I left school and left home. I was at RADA. I was on the stage, you see. Much to my parents' disapproval. But I didn't mind about disapproval. I never have, really."

"An actress. I should have known."

"And a singer, too. And a dancer. Revues and big American musicals. I was the one at the back of the chorus line because I was so dreadfully tall. And then years of fortnightly Rep, and then bit parts on television. Nothing very illustrious."

"Do you still work?"

"Heavens, no. I gave it up years ago. I married an actor, which was the most dreadful mistake for every sort of reason. And then he went off to America and was never seen again, so I kept myself by doing any sort of job that came my way, and then I got married again. But that wasn't much use either. I don't think I was ever a very good picker."

"Was number-two husband an actor as well?" His voice was amused, which was exactly the way Elfrida wanted it to be. She seldom talked about her husbands, and the only way to make disasters bearable was to laugh about them.

"Oh, no, he was in business. Terribly expensive vinyl flooring. One would have thought I would have been marvellously secure and safe, but he had that disagreeable Victorian conviction that if a man feeds and houses his wife, and doles out some sort of a housekeeping allowance, then he has kept his share of the marital bargain."

"Well," said Oscar, "and why not? An old-established tradition, going back for centuries. Only then it was called slavery."

"How nice that you understand. Turning sixty was one of the best days of my life, because I got my old age pension book, and knew that I could walk down to the nearest post office and be given money, cash in hand, for doing nothing. I'd never in my life been given something for nothing. It was like a whole new world."

"Did you have children?"

"No. Never children."

"You still haven't explained why you moved to this particular village."

"A need to move on."

"A big step."

It was nearly dark now. Turning, Elfrida looked back towards the house, and saw, through the lace-work of the wrought-iron gate, the glow of the drawing-room windows. Somebody had drawn the curtains. She said, "I haven't talked about it. I haven't told anybody."

"You don't need to tell me."

"Perhaps I've talked too much already. Perhaps I drank too much wine at dinner."

"I don't think so."

"There was this man. So special, so loving, funny, and perfect. Another actor, but successful and famous this time and I won't say his name. Brilliant. We lived together for three years in his little house in Barnes, and then he got Parkinson's disease and it took him another two years to die. It was his house. I had to leave. A week after his funeral I saw an advertisement for the cottage in Poulton's Row. In *The Sunday Times.* And the next week I bought it. I have very little money, but it wasn't too expensive. I brought my dear dog, Horace, with me for company, and I have my old age pension, and I have a little job making cushions for a rather snob interior designer in London. It's not very arduous and it keeps me busy and my head above water. I always liked to sew, and it's good to work with lovely, expensive materials, and each project is different." It all sounded very trivial. "I don't know why I'm telling you all this. It's not very interesting."

"I find it fascinating."

"I don't see why you should. But you're very kind." It was dark now. Too dark to see into his face, or read the expression in his hooded eyes. "I think perhaps it's time we went back to the others."

"Of course."

"I love your garden. Thank you. Sometime I must see it in the daylight."

That was Thursday. The following Sunday morning, it rained, not a spring shower, but regular rain drumming down against the windows of Elfrida's cottage and darkening the tiny rooms, so that she was forced to switch on all the lights. After she had put Horace out into the garden for his morning wee, she made a cup of tea and took it back to bed with her, intending to spend the morning warm, comfortable, and idle, reading yesterday's newspapers and struggling to finish the crossword.

But, just after eleven, she was interrupted by the ringing of the front-door bell, a jangling device operated by a hanging chain. The noise it made was like nothing so much as an emergency fire alarm and Elfrida nearly jumped out of her skin. Horace, lying across the foot of the bed, raised himself into a sitting position and let out a couple of barks. This was as much as he was prepared to do in the cause of protecting his mistress, for he was of a cowardly nature and not in the habit of snarling, nor biting intruders.

Astonished, but not alarmed, Elfrida climbed out of bed, pulled on her dressing-gown, tied the sash, and made her way down the steep and narrow staircase. The stairs descended into her living-room, and the front door opened straight onto the miniature front garden. And there she found a small girl, in jeans and sneakers and a dripping anorak. The anorak had no hood, so the child's head was wet as the coat of a dog that had just enjoyed a good swim. She had auburn hair, braided into plaits, and her face was freckled and rosy from the chill, damp outdoors.

"Mrs. Phipps?"

There were bands on her teeth, a mouthful of ironmongery.

"Yes."

"I'm Francesca Blundell. My mother said it's such an awful day, would you like to come for lunch? We've got an enormous bit of beef and there's heaps—"

"But I've only just been to dinner—"

"She said you'd say that."

"It's terribly kind. As you can see, I'm not dressed yet. I hadn't even thought about lunch."

"She was going to phone, but I said I'd bicycle."

"You biked?"

"I left it on the pavement. It's all right." A douche of water from an overflowing gutter missed her by inches.

"I think," said Elfrida, "you'd better come in before you drown."

"Oh, thank you." Briskly, Francesca accepted the invitation and stepped indoors. Hearing voices, and deciding that it was safe to appear, Horace, with dignity, descended the stairs. Elfrida closed the door. "This is Horace, my dog."

"He's sweet. Hello. Mummy's Pekes always yap for hours when there's a visitor. Do you mind if I take off my anorak?"

"No, I think it would be a very good idea."

This Francesca proceeded to do, unzipping the jacket and draping it over the newel-post at the bottom of the banister, where it dripped onto the floor.

Francesca looked about her. She said, "I always thought these were the dearest little houses, but I've never been inside one of them." Her eyes were very large and grey, fringed with thick lashes. "When Mummy said you were living here, I couldn't wait to come and look. That's why I biked. Do you mind?"

"Not a bit. It's all rather cluttered, I'm afraid."

"I think it's perfect."

It wasn't, of course. It was cramped and shabby, filled with the few personal bits and pieces Elfrida had brought with her from London. The sagging sofa, the little Victorian armchair, the brass fender, the battered desk. Lamps, and worthless pictures, and too many books.

"I was going to lay and light a fire as it's such a grey day, but I haven't got around to it yet. Would you like a cup of tea or coffee or something?"

"No, thank you, I've just had a Coke. Where does that door go?"

"Into the kitchen. I'll show you."

She led the way, opened the wooden door with the latch, and pushed it ajar. Her kitchen was no larger than a boat's galley. Here a small Rayburn simmered away, keeping the whole of the house warm; a wooden dresser was piled with china; a clay sink stood beneath the window; and a wooden table and two chairs filled the remainder of the space. Alongside the window, a stable door led out into the back garden. The top half of this was glazed in small panes, and through this could be seen the flagged yard and the narrow border, which was as far as Elfrida had got in the way of making a flower-bed. Ferns thrust their way between the flags, and there was a honeysuckle scrambling over the neighbour's wall.

"It's not very inviting on a day like this, but there's just room to sit out in a deck-chair on a summer evening."

"Oh, but I love it." Francesca looked about her with a housewifely eye. "You haven't got a fridge. And you haven't got a washing machine. And you haven't got a freezer."

"No, I haven't got a freezer. I have a fridge and a washing machine, but I keep them in the shed at the bottom of the yard. And I do all my dishes in the sink, because there's no space for a dishwasher."

"I think Mummy would die if she had to wash dishes."

"It's not very arduous when you live on your own."

"I love all of your china. Blue and White. It's my favourite."

"I love it, too. None of it matches, but I buy a bit whenever I find something in a junk-shop. There's so much now, there's scarcely space for it."

"What's upstairs?"

"The same. Two rooms and a tiny bathroom. The bath is so small I have to hang my legs over the side. And a bedroom for me and a work-room where I do my sewing. If I have a guest, they have to sleep there, along with the sewing-machine and scraps of material and order books."

"Daddy told me you made cushions. I think it's all exactly right. For one person. And a dog, of course. Like a doll's house."

"Have you got a doll's house?"

"Yes, but I don't play with it any more. I've got animals. A guinea pig called Happy, but he's not very well. I think he'll have to go to the vet. He's got horrible bare patches all over his fur. And I've got rabbits. And a pony." She wrinkled her nose. "He's called Prince but he's a bit nappy sometimes. I think I'd better go now. Mummy said I had to muck Prince out before lunch, and it takes ages, 'specially in the rain. Thank you for letting me see your house."

"A pleasure. Thank you for bringing that kind invitation."

"You'll come, won't you?"

"Of course."

"Will you walk?"

"No, I'll bring my car. Because of the rain. And if you ask me where I keep my car, I'll tell you. On the road."

"Is it that old blue Ford Fiesta?"

"It is. And 'old' is the operative word. But I don't mind provided the wheels go round and the engine starts."

Francesca smiled at this, revealing, unembarrassed, her wired-up teeth. She said, "I'll see you later then." She reached for her anorak, still dripping, pulled on the sodden garment, and tossed free her plaits. Elfrida opened the door for her.

"Mummy said, a quarter to one."

"I'll be there, and thank you for coming."

"I'll come again," Francesca promised, and Elfrida watched her go splashing down the path and through the gate. A moment later, she was off, on her bike, with a wave of her hand, pedalling furiously down through the puddles and along the road, out of sight.

Oscar, Gloria, and Francesca were Elfrida's first friends. Through them, she met others. Not just the McGeareys and the Millses, but the Foubisters, who were old-established and held the annual summer church fête in the park of their rambling Georgian house. And Commander Burton Jones, Royal Navy Retired, a widower and immensely industrious, labouring in his immaculate garden, Chairman of the Public Footpath Association, and principal chorister in the church choir. Commander Burton Jones (*Bobby's the name*) threw racy little drinks parties and called his bedroom his cabin. Then there were the Dunns, he an immensely wealthy man who had bought and converted the old Rectory into a marvel of space and convenience, complete with games-room and a covered and heated swimming-pool.

Others, humbler, came into her life one by one, as Elfrida went about her daily business. Mrs. Jennings, who ran the village shop and the post office. Mr. Hodgkins, who did the rounds, once a week, with his butcher's van, was a reliable source of news and gossip, and held strong political views. Albert Meddows, who answered her advertisement (a postcard stuck up in Mrs. Jennings's window) for garden help, and tackled, single-handed, the sad disarray and crooked pavings of Elfrida's back garden. The vicar and his wife invited her to a fork supper, in the course of which he repeated his suggestion that she join the Women's Institute. Politely declining—she did not enjoy bus trips and had never made a pot of jam in her life—she agreed to involvement with the primary school and ended up producing their annual pantomime at Christmas.

All amiable enough and welcoming, but none of them Elfrida found either as interesting or stimulating as the Blundells. Gloria's hospitality was without bounds, and scarcely a week went by when Elfrida was not invited to spend time at the Grange, for lavish meals or some outdoor occasion like a tennis party (Elfrida did not play tennis, but was happy to observe) or a picnic. There were other, more far-flung, occasions: the spring point-to-point at a nearby farm, a visit to a National Trust garden, an evening out at the theatre at Chichester. She had spent Christmas with them, and New Year's Eve, and when she threw her first little party for all her new friends (Albert Meddows having resuscitated her garden, levelled the flagstones, pruned the honeysuckle, and painted the shed), it was Oscar who volunteered to be her barman and Gloria who produced copious eats from her own spacious kitchen.

However, there were limits and reservations. There had to be if Elfrida was not to be absorbed by, and beholden to, the Blundells. From the very first, she had recognized Gloria as a forceful woman—with, possibly, a ruthless streak, so determined was she always that things should go her way—and was more than aware of the dangers of such a situation. She had left London to make a life of her own, and knew that it would be only too easy for a single and fairly impoverished female to be swept along (and possibly drowned) in the churning wake of Gloria's social energy.

So, from time to time, Elfrida had learned to step back, to keep to herself, to make excuses. A work overload, perhaps, or a prior engagement, which could not possibly be broken, with some imagined acquaintance whom Gloria did not know. Every now and then, she escaped from the confines of Dibton, packing Horace into the passenger seat of her old car and driving far out across country, to some other county where she was not known, and where she and Horace could climb a sheep-grazed hill, or follow the path by some dark flowing stream, and find at the end of it a pub full of strangers, where she could eat a sandwich and drink coffee and relish her precious solitude.

On such occasions, distanced from Dibton, and with perceptions sharpened by a sense of perspective, it became possible to be analytical about her involvement with the Blundells, and to catalogue her findings, impersonal and detached as a shopping list.

The first was that she liked Oscar immensely; perhaps too much. She was well past the age of romantic love, but companionship was another matter. From their first meeting outside Dibton church, when she had been instantly taken with him, she had come to enjoy his company more and more. Time had not proved that first impression wrong.

But the ice was thin. Elfrida was neither sanctimonious nor a lady with enormously high moral standards; indeed, all the time she lived with him, her dear dead lover had been the husband of another woman. But Elfrida had never met his wife, and the marriage was already on the rocks by the time he and Elfrida found each other, and for this reason she had never been consumed by guilt. On the other hand, there was another and not nearly so harmless scenario, and one which Elfrida had witnessed more than once. That of the single lady, widowed, divorced, or otherwise bereft, being taken under the wing of a loyal girl-friend, only to scarper with the loyal girl-friend's husband. A reprehensible situation and one of which she strongly disapproved.

But in Elfrida's case, it was not about to happen. And she knew that her awareness of danger and her own common sense were her greatest strengths.

Second was that Francesca, at twelve years old, was the daughter whom, if she had ever had a child, Elfrida would have liked to call her own. She was independent, open, and totally straightforward, and yet possessed of a sense of the ridiculous that could reduce Elfrida to helpless laughter, and an imagination that was fed by voracious reading of books. Into these, Francesca became so absorbed that one could go into a room, switch on the television, hold loud discussions, and Francesca would not even raise her head from the printed page. During the school holidays, she frequently turned up at Poulton's Row, to play with Horace or watch Elfrida at her sewing-machine, at the same time asking endless questions about Elfrida's theatrical past, which she clearly found fascinating.

Her relationship with her father was unusually close and very sweet. He was old enough to be her grandfather, but their delight in each other's company went far beyond that of the normal parent and child. From behind the closed music-room door could be heard the two of them playing duets on his piano, and fumbling mistakes brought not recrimination, but much laughter. On winter evenings he read aloud to her, the two of them curled up in his huge armchair, and her affection for him was manifested in frequent hugs and loving physical contact, thin arms wound about his neck and kisses pressed onto the top of his thick white hair.

As for Gloria, Gloria was a man's woman, and so closer to her grown-up and married sons than her lately conceived daughter. Elfrida had met these sons, Giles and Crawford Bellamy, and their pretty, well-dressed wives, when they turned up at the Grange for a weekend, or drove down from London for Sunday lunch. Although not twins, they were strangely similar—conventional and opinionated. Elfrida got the impression that neither of the brothers approved of her, but as she didn't much like either of them, that was not bothering. Their mother doted on them, which was far more important, and when the time came for them to leave for London or Bristol or wherever they lived, the boots of their expensive cars loaded down with fresh vegetables and fruit from Gloria's kitchen garden, she would stand, waving them away, like any sentimental mother. It was patently clear that in her eyes neither son could do wrong, and Elfrida was pretty sure that if Gloria had not approved of their chosen brides, then both Daphne and Arabella would have got short shrift.

But Francesca was a different cup of tea. Deeply influenced by Oscar, she went her own way, followed her own interests, and found books and music a good deal more alluring than the local Pony Club gymkhana. Even so, she was never rebellious or sulky, and with good grace cared for her bad-tempered little pony and exercised him regularly, riding around the paddock that Gloria had set aside for equestrian activities, and taking him on long hacks down the quiet tracks by the little river. Often, on these occasions, Oscar accompanied her, mounted on an ancient sit-up-and-beg bicycle, relic of schoolmaster days.

Gloria let them be, possibly, Elfrida decided, because Francesca was not that important to Gloria; not as absorbing or fulfilling as her own hectic life-style, her parties, her circle of friends. Important, too, was her position as social mentor, and sometimes she reminded Elfrida of a huntsman blowing his horn for attention and whipping in his hounds.

Only once had Elfrida fallen from grace. It was during a convivial evening with the Foubisters, a dinner party of great formality and style, with candles lit and silver gleaming and an aged butler waiting at table. After dinner, in the long drawing-room (rather chilly, for the evening was cool), Oscar had moved to the grand piano to play for them, and after a Chopin étude, had suggested that Elfrida should sing.

She was much embarrassed and taken aback. She had not sung for years, she protested, her voice was hopeless. . . .

But old Sir Edwin Foubister added his persuasions. *Please,* he had said. *I've always liked a pretty tune.*

So disarming was he that Elfrida found herself hesitating. After all, what did it matter if her voice had lost its youthful timbre, she wobbled on the high notes, and was about to make a fool of herself? And at that moment, she caught sight of Gloria's face, florid and set like a bulldog in an expression of disapproval and dismay. And she knew that Gloria did not want her to sing. Did not want her to stand up with Oscar and entertain the little group. She did not like others to shine, to steal attention, to deflect the conversation away from herself. It was a perception of total clarity and somewhat shocking, as though she had caught Gloria in a state of undress.

In different circumstances Elfrida might have played safe, gracefully declined, made excuses. But she had dined well and drunk delicious wine, and emboldened by this, a tiny flame of self-assertion flickered into life. She had never allowed herself to be bullied, and was not about to start. So she smiled into Gloria's threatening frowns, and then turned her head and let the smile rest upon her host. She said, "If you want, I should like to, very much. . . ."

"Splendid." Like a child, the old man clapped his hands. "What a treat."

And Elfrida stood, and crossed the floor to where Oscar waited for her.

"What will you sing?"

She told him. An old Rodgers and Hart number. "Do you know it?"

"Of course."

A chord or two for introduction. It had been a long time. She straightened her shoulders, filled her lungs. . . .

"I took one look at you . . ."

Her voice had aged to thinness, but she could still hold, truly, the tune.

"And then my heart stood still."

And she was all at once consumed by reasonless happiness, and felt young again, standing by Oscar, and, with him, filling the room with the music of their youth.

Gloria scarcely spoke for the rest of the evening, but nobody endeavoured to coax her out of her black mood. While they marvelled and congratulated Elfrida on her performance, Gloria drank her brandy. When it was time to leave, Sir Edwin accompanied them out to where Gloria's highly powered estate car was parked on the neatly raked gravel. Elfrida bade him good night, and got into the back of the car, but it was Oscar who slipped in behind the driving wheel, and Gloria was forced to take the passenger seat of her own vehicle.

Heading home, "How did you enjoy your evening?" Oscar asked his wife. Gloria replied shortly, "I have a headache," and fell silent once more.

Elfrida thought, no wonder, but prudently didn't say it. And that was perhaps the saddest truth of all. Gloria Blundell, hard-headed and with a stomach like a tin bucket, drank too much. She was never incapable, never hung over. But she drank too much. And Oscar knew it.

Oscar. And now, here he was, in Mrs. Jennings's shop on a grey October afternoon, picking up his newspaper and paying for a bag of dog meal. He wore corduroys and a thick tweedy-looking sweater, and sturdy boots, which seemed to indicate that he had been gardening, remembered these necessary errands, and come.

Mrs. Jennings looked up. "Afternoon, Mrs. Phipps."

With his hand full of change, Oscar turned and saw her.

"Elfrida. Good afternoon."

She said, "You must have walked. I didn't see your car."

"Parked it round the corner. That's it, I think, Mrs. Jennings."

He moved aside to make space for Elfrida, and stood, apparently in no sort of hurry to go. "We haven't seen you for days. How are you?"

"Oh, surviving. A bit fed up with this weather."

"Dreadful, isn't it?" Mrs. Jennings chipped in. "Chilly and muggy all at once, doesn't make you feel like doing anything. What have you got there, Mrs. Phipps?"

Elfrida unloaded the contents of her basket, so that Mrs. Jennings could price them, and put it all through her till. A loaf of bread, half a dozen eggs, some bacon and butter, two tins of dog food, and a magazine called *Beautiful Homes*. "Want me to charge them?"

"If you would; I've left my purse at home."

Oscar saw the magazine. He said, "Are you going to go in for some domestic improvements?"

"Probably not. But I find reading about other people's is therapeutic. I suppose because I know I haven't got to get my paint-pot out. A bit like listening to somebody else cutting the grass."

Mrs. Jennings thought this was very funny. "Jennings put his mower away, back of September. Hates cutting the grass, he does."

Oscar watched while Elfrida reloaded her basket. He said, "I'll give you a ride home, if you like."

"I don't mind walking. I've got Horace with me."

"He's welcome to join us. Thank you, Mrs. Jennings. Goodbye."

"Cheerio, Mr. Blundell. Regards to the wife."

Together, they emerged from the shop. Outside on the pavement, the youths still loitered. They had been joined by a dubious-looking girl with a cigarette, raven-black hair, and a leather skirt that scarcely reached to her crotch. Her presence seemed to have galvanized the young men into a pantomime of joshing, insults, and meaningless guffaws. Horace, trapped in the middle of such unseemly behaviour, sat and looked miserable. Elfrida untied his lead, and he wagged his tail, much relieved, and the three of them made their way around the corner and down the narrow lane where Oscar had left his old car. She got into the passenger seat, and Horace jumped up and sat on the floor, between her knees, with his head pressed onto her lap. As Oscar joined them, slammed the door, and switched on the ignition, she said, "I never expect to meet anyone in the shop in the afternoons. Mornings are the social time. That's when you get all the chat."

"I know. But Gloria's in London, and I forgot about the papers." He turned the car and nosed out into the main street. School for the day was over, and the pavements were busy with a procession of tired and grubby children, trailing satchels and making their way home. The man in the churchyard had got his bonfire going, and grey smoke streamed up into the still, dank air.

"When did Gloria go to London?"

"Yesterday. For some meeting or other. Save the Children, I believe. She took the train. I've got to meet her off the six-thirty."

"Would you like to come back and have a cup of tea with me? Or would you prefer to return to your gardening?"

"How do you know I've been gardening?"

"Clues dropped. Woman's intuition. Mud on your boots."

He laughed. "Perfectly correct, Mr. Holmes. But I wouldn't say no to a cup of tea. Gardener's perks."

They passed the pub. Another moment or so, and they had reached the lane that ran down the slope towards the railway line and the small row of terraced cottages that was Poulton's Row. At her gate, he drew up, and they decanted themselves; Horace, freed of his lead, bounded ahead up the path, and Elfrida, lugging her basket, followed him. She opened the door.

"Don't you ever lock it?" Oscar asked from behind her.

"Not for a village shopping spree. Anyway, there's little to steal. Come along in, shut the door behind you." She went through to the kitchen and dumped the basket on the table. "If you feel very kind, you could put a match to the fire. A day like this needs a bit of cheer." She filled the kettle at the tap and set it on the stove. Then she took off her jacket, draped it over the back of a chair, and began to assemble a few items of mismatched china.

"Mugs or teacups?"

"Mugs for gardeners."

"Tea by the fire, or shall we sit in here?"

"I'm always happier with my knees under a table."

Without much hope, Elfrida opened cake-tins. Two were empty. The third contained the heel of a gingerbread. She put this on the table, with a knife. She took milk from the fridge and emptied the carton into a yellow pottery jug. She found the sugar-bowl. From the other room could now be heard crackling sounds and the snap of hot twigs. She went to the doorway and stood, leaning against the lintel, observing Oscar. He was placing, with some care, a couple of lumps of coal on the top of his small pyre. Aware of Elfrida's presence, he straightened and turned his head to smile at her.

"Blazing nicely. Properly laid, with plenty of kindling. Do you need logs for the winter? I can let you have a load, if you'd like."

"Where would I store them?"

"We could stack them in the front garden, against the wall."

"That would be marvellous, if you could spare a few."

"We've more than enough." He dusted his hands on his trouser legs and looked about him. "You know, you have made this little place very charming."

"It's a muddle, I know. Not enough space. Possessions are a quandary, aren't they? They become part of you, and I'm not very good at throwing things away. And there are one or two little bits and pieces I've been carrying about with me for years, dating back to the giddy days when I was on the stage. I was like a snail with its shell on its back. A silk shawl or the odd knick-knack rendered theatrical lodgings a little more bearable."

"I particularly like your little Staffordshire dogs."

"They were always part of my luggage, but they're not, actually, a pair."

"And the little travelling clock."

"That travelled, too."

"It appears well-worn."

"'Battered' would be nearer the truth. I've had it for years; it was left to me by an elderly godfather. I . . . I have one thing which I think might be very valuable, and it's that little picture."

It hung to one side of the fireplace, and Oscar found his spectacles and put them on, the better to inspect the painting.

"Where did you get this?"

"A present from an actor. We were both in a revival of *Hay Fever* at Chichester, and at the end of the run he said that he wanted me to have it. A leaving present. He'd picked it up in a junk-shop and I don't think paid all that much for it, but was excited, because he was sure that it was a David Wilkie."

"Sir David Wilkie?" Oscar frowned. "A valuable possession. So why did he give it to you?"

But Elfrida would not be drawn. "To thank me for mending his socks?"

He returned his gaze to the painting. It took up little space, being only about eleven inches by eight, and depicted an elderly couple in eighteenth-century dress sitting at a table on which lay a huge leather Bible. The background was sombre, the man's clothes dark. But the woman wore a canary-yellow shawl and a red dress, and her white bonnet was frilled and ribboned.

"I would say she's dressed for some celebration, wouldn't you?"

"Without doubt. Perhaps, Elfrida, you *should* lock your front door."

"Perhaps I should."

"Is it insured?"

"It *is* my insurance. Against a rainy day. When I find myself on the streets with only a couple of plastic bags, and Horace at the end of a piece of string. Then, and only then, will I think about selling it."

"A hedge against disaster." Oscar smiled and took off his spectacles. "Whatever. It is the manner in which you have put your possessions together that melds into such a pleasing whole. I am sure you own nothing that you do not think to be beautiful or know to be useful."

"William Morris."

"And, perhaps, the measure of good taste."

"Oscar, you say the nicest things."

At this moment, from the kitchen, Elfrida's kettle let out a startling toot, which meant that it was boiling. She went to retrieve it, and Oscar followed, and watched while she made the tea in a round brown teapot, which she set upon the wooden table.

"If you like builders' tea, you'd better wait for a moment or two. And if you'd rather, you can have lemon instead of milk. And there's some stale gingerbread."

"A feast." Oscar pulled out a chair and settled himself, as though relieved to get the weight off his legs. She sat, too, facing him across the table, and busied herself cutting the gingerbread. She said, "Oscar, I am going away."

He did not reply, and she looked up and saw, on his face, an expression of horrified astonishment.

"Forever?" he asked fearfully.

"Of course not forever."

His relief was very evident. "Thank God for that. What a fright you gave me."

"I'd never leave Dibton *forever.* I've told you. This is where I'm going to spend my twilight years. But it's time for a holiday."

"Are you feeling particularly exhausted?"

"No, but autumn always depresses me. A sort of limbo between summer and Christmas. A dead time. And I'm going to have another birthday soon. Sixty-two. Even more depressing. So, time for a change."

"Perfectly sensible. It will do you good. Where will you go?"

"To the very end of Cornwall. If you sneeze you're in danger of falling over a cliff into the Atlantic."

"Cornwall?" Now he was astounded. "Why Cornwall?"

"Because I have a cousin who lives there. He's called Jeffrey Sutton and he's about three years younger than me. We've always been friends. He's one of those nice people one can telephone, without reservations, and say, 'Can I come and stay?' And you know he'll say yes. And, moreover, sound pleased. So, Horace and I will drive down together."

Oscar shook his head in some bewilderment.

"I never knew that you had a cousin. Or any sort of relation, for that matter."

"The product of an immaculate conception, you mean?"

"Hardly that. But, admit, it is surprising."

"I don't think it's surprising at all. Just because I don't rabbit on all the time about my family." Then Elfrida relented. "But you're not far wrong. I am a bit denuded. Jeffrey's a special person and we've always kept in touch."

"Has he a wife?"

"Actually, he's had two. The first was a pain in the neck. She was called Dodie. I suppose he was charmed by her pretty looks and sweet air of helplessness. Only to discover, poor man, that he had tied himself to a woman of such self-absorption as to beggar belief. She was, as well, idle and undomestic, and most of Jeffrey's hard-earned salary went on paying the wages of cooks, cleaners, and au pairs in the faint hope of keeping some sort of an establishment going for his two daughters."

"What happened to the marriage?" Oscar was clearly fascinated.

"He remained constant and enduring, but finally, when both the girls were grown and educated and earning, he walked out. There was this girl, Serena, much younger than Jeffrey, and perfectly sweet. She was a gardener and ran a nice little business doing flowers for parties and looking after other people's window-boxes. He'd known her for years. When he walked out on his marriage, he walked out on his job as well, wiped the dust of London from the soles of his shoes, and moved, with Serena, as far away from London as he could possibly get. When the very acrimonious divorce was over, he married Serena and almost at once started another little family. A boy and a girl. They live on a shoestring, keeping hens and doing bed and breakfast for summer visitors."

"Happy ever after?"

"You could say that."

"What about his daughters? What happened to them?"

"I've rather lost touch. The eldest was called Nicola. She married some man, and had a child, I think. She was always dreadfully disagreeable, dissatisfied and perpetually complaining about the unfairness of life. I think she was always terribly jealous of Carrie."

"Carrie being her sister."

"Precisely so. And a darling. Jeffrey's nice personality all over again. About ten years ago, when I had to have some female operation, upon which, at this moment, Oscar, I shall not enlarge, she came to take care of me. She stayed for six weeks. I was on my own at the time, living in a grotty little flat in Putney, but she took it all in her stride and we got on like a house on fire." Elfrida frowned, grappling with mental arithmetic. "She must be about thirty now. Aged. How time flies."

"Did she marry?"

"I don't think so. Like I said, I've rather lost touch. Last time I heard, she was working in Austria for some big tour company. You know, being a ski rep, and making sure every tourist was in the right hotel. She always loved skiing more than anything. Whatever, I'm sure she's happy. I think your tea will be black enough now." She poured his mug—it was satisfactorily dark—and cut him a slice of the crumbling gingerbread. "So you see I do have a family, if not a particularly close one." She smiled at him. "How about you? Confession time. Do you have any dotty relations you can boast about?"

Oscar put up a hand and rubbed it over his head. "I don't know. I suppose I do. But like you, I haven't much idea where they are or what they're up to."

"Tell."

"Well. . . ." Thoughtfully, he ate a bit of gingerbread. "I had a Scottish grandmother. How's that for starters?"

"Hoots toots."

"She had a great big house in Sutherland, and a certain amount of land, and a farm."

"A lady of property."

"I used to spend summer holidays with her. But she died when I was sixteen and I never went back."

"What was her house called?"

"Corrydale."

"Was it enormously grand?"

"No. Just enormously comfortable. Huge meals, and gumboots and fishing-rods lying around the place. Good smells; of flowers and beeswax polish, and grouse cooking."

"Oh, delicious. Mouth-watering. I'm sure she was heaven."

"I don't know about that. But she was totally unpretentious and enormously talented."

"In what way?"

"I suppose a talent for living. And for music. She was an accomplished pianist. And I mean, really accomplished. I think I inherited my small talent from her, and it was she who set me on the road to my chosen career. There was always music at Corrydale. It was part of my life."

"What else?"

"Sorry?"

"What else did you do?"

"I can scarcely remember. Go out in the evenings and pot rabbits. Fish for trout. Play golf. My grandmother was an avid golfer, and she tried to get me going on the links, but I was never a match for her. Then people came to stay, and we played tennis, and if it was warm enough, which it mostly wasn't, I might bicycle to the beach and fling myself into the North Sea. At Corrydale, it didn't matter what you did. It was all very relaxed. Good fun."

"So what happened?"

"My grandmother died. The war was on. My uncle inherited and went to live there."

"Didn't he invite you for summer holidays?"

"Those days were over. I was sixteen. Into music. Taking examinations. Other interests, other people. A different life."

"Does he still live there? Your uncle, I mean."

"No, he's in London now, in a mansion flat near the Albert Hall."

"What's his name?"

"Hector McLennan."

"Oh, splendid. All kilts and a red beard?"

"Not any more. He's very old."

"And Corrydale?"

"He made it over to his son, Hughie. My cousin. A feckless fellow, whose one idea was to live a grand life and do things in tremendous style. He filled Corrydale with all his rather degenerate friends, who drank his whisky and behaved badly. To the despair of all the respectable old retainers who had worked in the house and on the estate for years. It was all something of a scandal. Then Hughie decided that life north of the border was not for him, so he sold up and scarpered off to Barbados. As far as I know, he's still there, on to his third wife, and leading the life of Riley."

Elfrida was envious. "Oh, he *does* sound fascinating."

"No. Not fascinating. Boringly predictable. We used to put up with each other, but we were never friends."

"So everything's sold up, and you'll never return?"

"Unlikely." He leaned back in his chair and crossed his arms. "Actually, I could go back. When my grandmother died, she left Hughie and me a house. Between us. But it's been rented for years to some old couple. Every quarter I get a trickle of rent, posted from the factor's office. I suppose Hughie gets the same, though it's scarcely enough to pay for a couple of planter's punches."

"Is it a big house?"

"Not particularly. It's in the middle of the little town. It used to be estate offices, but then it was converted to a dwelling-house."

"How too exciting. I wish I had a house in Scotland."

"Half a house."

"Half a house is better than half a loaf. You could take Francesca for half a holiday."

"Never thought of it, to be truthful. Never think about the place. I suppose one day Hughie will either offer to buy me out or suggest that I buy him out. But it's not something I worry about. And I prefer not to precipitate any action. The less I have to do with Hughie McLennan, the better."

"I think you're being frightfully feeble."

"Just keeping a low profile. Now, when are you off?"

"Next Thursday."

"For how long?"

"A month."

"Will you send us a postcard?"

"Of course."

"And let us know when you return?"

"At once."

"We shall miss you," said Oscar, and she felt warmed.

The house was called Emblo Cottage. It stood with its granite face to the north wind and the Atlantic, and on this side, the windows were small and few and deep-set, with windowsills wide enough for the potted geraniums and scraps of driftwood and the shells that Serena loved to collect. Once, it had been part of Emblo, a prosperous dairy farm, and the dwelling of the resident cowman. But the cowman retired and then died, mechanization took over the milking parlours, agricultural wages soared, and the farmer cut his losses and sold the cottage. Since then, it had belonged to three different owners, and had come on the market for the last time just as Jeffrey had made the great decision to cut loose from London, Dodie, and his job. He saw the advertisement in *The Times,* got straight into his car, and drove through the night in order to view the property before any other person had time to put in a bid. He found a dank little place, dismally furnished for holiday letting, crouched in an untended garden, and set about by stunted sycamores leaning at right angles, away from the prevailing wind. But there was a view of the cliffs and the sea, and on the south side a sheltered patch of lawn, where wisteria climbed the wall and there still flowered a camellia bush.

He telephoned his bank manager, got a loan, and bought the place. When he and Serena moved in, there were birds' nests in the chimneys, old paper peeling from the walls, and a smell of damp and mould that hung over every room. But it didn't matter. They camped in sleeping bags and opened a bottle of champagne. They were together and they were home.

That was ten years ago. It had taken two of those years to get the place in order, involving much hard physical labour, dirt, destruction, inconvenience, and a succession of plumbers, builders, tilers, and stonemasons, who trod around the place in mud-caked boots, boiled up endless cups of tea, and indulged in long conversations as to the meaning of life.

From time to time, Jeffrey and Serena became exasperated by their slowness and unreliability, but it was impossible not to be beguiled by these amateur philosophers, who seemed to know no sense of hurry, content in the knowledge that tomorrow was another day.

Finally, all was done. The workmen departed, leaving behind them a small, trim, solid stone house, with kitchen and sitting-room downstairs and a creaking wooden stair leading to the upper floor. At the back of the kitchen jutted out what had once been a wash-house, slate-floored and airy, and here waterproofs and rubber boots were dumped, and Serena kept her clothes washer and her deep freeze. There was as well a huge clay sink, which Jeffrey had found abandoned in the ditch of a field. Restored, it was constantly in use, for washing eggs and mud-caked dogs, and for the buckets of wild flowers which Serena loved to pick and arrange in old-fashioned pottery jugs. Upstairs were three white-painted bedrooms with sloping ceilings, and a small bathroom, which had the best view of all from its window, looking south, over the farmers' fields and up the slope of the hill to the moor.

They were not isolated. The farmhouse, with its considerable outbuildings, stood only a hundred yards or so away, so that there was a constant coming and going of traffic up and down the lane and past their gate. Tractors, milk lorries and cars, and small children who, dumped by the school bus at the end of the road, walked their way home. The farmer had a family of four, and these children were Ben and Amy's best friends. With them, they rode bicycles, went blackberrying, and walked down to the cliffs with haversacks slung from their inadequate shoulders to swim and picnic.

Elfrida had never seen this house, had never been to visit them. But now she was coming, and Jeffrey was filled with an old sensation, almost forgotten, but which he finally acknowledged to himself, was excitement.

Elfrida. He was now fifty-eight, and Elfrida was . . . ? Sixty-one, sixty-two? It didn't matter. As a boy, he had always thought the world of her, because she was fearless and she made him laugh. As an adolescent, trapped in the inky disciplines of boarding-school, she had been like a light in his life. Gloriously attractive, admirably rebellious, fighting parental opposition, and finally going on the stage and becoming an actress. Such determination, bravery, and achievement had filled Jeffrey with admiration and devoted attachment. Once or twice, she had actually come to his boarding school and taken him out for an exeat Saturday or Sunday, and he had boasted about her a little to his friends, and kept her waiting at the ghastly pseudo-Gothic red brick front door, because he wanted others to see her there, sitting in her little red sports car, with her dark glasses and her pineapple-coloured hair tied about with a chiffon scarf.

"My cousin. She's in some show or other. In London," he said, with marvellous casualness, as though it happened to everybody, every day. "They brought it over from New York."

And finally he would go out to meet her, apologizing for his lateness, climbing into the tiny bucket seat beside her, being driven away with an impressive roar of the engine and a lot of flying gravel. And when he got back to school, he remained determinedly blasé. "Oh, we just went to the Roadhouse. Had a swim in the pool and a meal."

He was enormously proud of her and more than a little in love.

But time went by, they grew up, lost touch, and made their own lives. Elfrida married some actor or other, and it all fell apart and then she married another dreary character, and finally ended up with her famously successful lover. All seemed set for lifelong happiness, and then the alliance was stunned by tragedy, his struggle with Parkinson's disease and eventual death.

The last time Jeffrey had seen Elfrida it was in London, just after she had met this exceptional man, whom she always referred to as Jimbo.

"Not his real name, darling, but my own name for him. I never thought it could be like this. I never thought one could be so close, and yet so different to a single human being. He is everything I've never been, and yet I love him more than any person or anything I've ever known."

"What about your career?" Jeffrey had asked.

"Oh, bugger my career," Elfrida had said, and collapsed into laughter. He had never seen her so happy, so beautiful, so utterly fulfilled.

When his own unhappy marriage was falling to bits, Elfrida was always there at the end of the telephone, ringing him up, ready with all sorts of advice, both good and bad, but, most important, endlessly sympathetic. Once he took Serena to meet her, and she rang the next evening and said, "Jeffrey, darling, she is too sweet . . . cut your losses and concentrate on *her*."

"What about my daughters?"

"Grown up and self-supporting. You must think of yourself. Bite the bullet. Don't dither. There's not time. Only one life."

"Dodie . . . ?"

"She'll manage. She'll bleed you white for alimony. She's not going to give up her creature comforts. Let her have the lot and go and be happy."

Go and be happy. He had done just that.

Five o'clock on a grey October evening. The wind was getting up. He had done the hens, gathered in the eggs, shut away the clucking creatures in their small domestic wooden houses. It was growing dark. Inside Emblo Cottage, Serena had turned on the lights, and small yellow windows glowed out into the dying light. It was a Thursday, the day when the wheelie bin had to be trundled down the lane in order for the weekly dustbin lorry to empty it in the morning. A wind had got up, blowing in from the sea with an edge to it that tasted and smelt of salt. In this wind, the gorse-bushes jigged and rustled along the tops of hedges. Over its whine, he could hear the water of the stream bubbling its way down the hill and along the edge of the lane. Because it felt cold, he went indoors to get a thick jacket. Serena was stirring something at the stove and the children were busy with their homework at the kitchen table.

He said, "Wheelie bin."

"Oh, clever man, to remember."

"Back in five minutes."

"I shall watch out for Elfrida."

He trundled the bin down the rutted lane and set it in its place on the verge of the road. Across the road was a wooden gate which led into another field, and Jeffrey went to lean against this. Like any old countryman, he felt for his cigarettes, and lit one with his old steel lighter. The day was dying. He watched the sky darken, thick with cloud. The sea was the colour of slate, flecked with foam. A rough evening. Breakers boomed at the foot of the cliffs and he could feel the damp of sea mist on his cheeks.

He thought of a poem once read, long forgotten.

My room is a bright glass cabin,
All Cornwall thunders at my door,
And the white ships of winter lie,
In the sea roads of the moor.

He stayed until his cigarette was finished, then threw away the stub and turned to go home. And, at that moment, saw the headlights, approaching from the east, blinking as the road twisted. He leaned against the gate and waited. After a bit, an old blue Fiesta appeared, cautiously taking the last narrow bend before the Emblo turning. He knew, instinctively, that it was Elfrida. He stepped into the road, waving his arms, and the car stopped, and he went and opened the door and got in beside her. He smelt her familiar perfume, the scent that she had always used, that was part of her.

He said, "You mustn't park here. This is the main road. You will be struck by a tractor or a German tour bus. Turn into the lane."

Which she did, and then stopped again.

She said, "Hello."

"You made it."

"Five hours."

"Found the way?"

"Such a splendid map you drew for me."

"Who's this in the back?"

"Horace, my dog. I told you he had to come."

"How wonderful that you are here. I kept steeling myself for a telephone call to say that you'd changed your mind."

"I'd never do that," Elfrida told him. And then became practical. "Is this your front drive?"

"It is."

"Dreadfully narrow, darling."

"Wide enough."

"Forward, then."

He began to laugh. "Forward."

She put the car into gear, and they lurched forward up the narrow tunnel that was the lane.

"What sort of a journey did you have?" Jeffrey asked.

"All right. I was a bit nervous. It's years since I've done such a long drive; unknown motorways and thundering lorries I find a little unnerving. This car isn't exactly a Ferrari."

"Good enough."

As they approached the cottage, an outside light came on. Serena, clearly, had heard them grinding up the lane. The light illuminated an open space backed by a tall granite wall. The road continued towards the distant farm, but Jeffrey said, "Park here," and so she did. At once two sheep-dogs appeared from nowhere, bounding towards them and barking their heads off.

"Not to worry," Jeffrey assured her, "they're mine. Tarboy and Findus, and they don't bite."

"Not even Horace?"

"Least of all Horace."

They climbed out of the car and let Horace free, and there was the usual small skirmish as the three strange dogs met and circled and smelt, and then Horace disappeared into the thicket of a handy bush and, gratefully, lifted his leg.

Jeffrey was amused. "What breed of a dog is Horace?"

"Unknown. But loyal. As well, trouble free and clean. He can sleep with me. I've brought his basket."

He opened the boot of her car and heaved out a battered suitcase and a large bulging paper carrier-bag. "Have you brought your own supplies?"

"That's Horace's food and his bowl and stuff." From the back seat of the car she hauled his basket and another bulging carrier-bag. Doors were slammed shut, and Jeffrey led the way up a slate path and around the corner of the house. The wind from the sea pounced upon them, and yellow squares of light, from windows and a half-glassed door, lay upon the cobbles. Jeffrey set down Elfrida's suitcase and opened the door. She went through into the kitchen, and the two children looked up from the table. Serena turned from the stove and came, aproned and open-armed, to greet them.

"Jeffrey, you actually *found* her. So clever, he went down with the wheelie bin and came back with you. What a perfect bit of timing. Did you have a frightful drive? Would you like a cup of tea and something to eat? Oh, and you haven't met the children, have you? Ben. And Amy. This is Elfrida, ducks."

"We know," said the boy. "You've been talking about her for ages." He was dark and his younger sister blonde. He got up from the table and came to shake hands, his eyes scanning Elfrida's luggage with some interest. He was expecting a present but had been told not to mention this fact in case none was forthcoming. He had his father's eyes and olive skin, and a thatch of heavy dark hair, and Elfrida guessed that in a few years' time, there would be a clutch of broken girlish hearts in the surrounding neighbourhood.

His father came through the door behind Elfrida and dumped the suitcase at the foot of the stairs. "Hi, Dad."

"Hi, Ben. Finished your homework?"

"Yep."

"Good man. And Amy. You done, too?"

"I finished mine ages ago," Amy told him smugly. She was shy. She came to her father and buried her face in his leg, so that all that showed of her was her long flaxen hair, pale as milk, and the faded blue of her dungarees. Elfrida had always known about Ben and Amy, but, seeing them now, marvelled that they were actually the children of Jeffrey, although young enough to be his grandchildren. She decided that they were beautiful. But then Serena was beautiful in her own individual way. Her hair was pale as Amy's but twisted up into a chignon and fastened with a tortoiseshell clip. Her eyes were a brilliant blue, and her thin face dusted with freckles. She wore slender jeans, which made her legs look endless, and a blue pullover, and she had knotted a silk scarf around her neck. Because of the cooking, she had tied the striped apron around her waist, and now made no effort to remove it.

"What's the form?" Jeffrey asked, and Serena told him. "I'll make a cup of tea for Elfrida if she wants one. Or she can sit by the fire; or go up to her room and unpack; or have a bath. Whatever she wants."

"When's dinner?"

"Eight, I thought. I'll feed Ben and Amy first."

Amy emerged from her father's legs. She said, "Sausages."

Elfrida frowned. "Sorry?"

"Sausages for our tea. And mashed potatoes and baked beans."

"How delicious."

"But you're having something else. Mum's been making it."

"Don't tell me, and then it will be a wonderful surprise."

"It's chicken and mushrooms."

"Amy!" her brother yelled at her. "Don't *tell*."

Elfrida laughed. "It doesn't matter. I'm sure it will be delicious."

"Now," said Serena, raising her voice slightly over the squabblings of her offspring, "would you like a cup of tea?"

But other treats that had been mentioned were more tempting. "What I'd really like is to go upstairs and unpack and have a bath. Would that be inconvenient?"

"Not a bit. We only have the one bathroom, but the children can go in after you. There's plenty of hot water."

"Bless you. Then that's what I'll do."

"How about Horace?" Jeffrey asked. "Does he need to be fed?"

"Yes, of course he does. Are you offering to do it for me? Two scoops of biscuits and a half-tin of meat. And a bit of hot water."

"Is Horace a dog?" asked Ben.

"Well, he's certainly not my husband."

"Where is he?"

"Outside. Making friends—I hope—with your dogs."

"I want to go and see. . . ."

"I do, too. . . . Wait for me. . . ."

They were away, out into the dark garden, without extra sweaters, gumboots, or any wails of protest from their mother. The door was left swinging open, letting in gusts of cold air. Jeffrey went quietly to shut it, and then once more picked up Elfrida's suitcase.

"Come," he said, and led the way up the creaking wooden stair.

He showed her round, said, "See you in about an hour. I'll give you a drink," and left her, closing the door behind him. The door had a wooden latch. Elfrida sat on the bed (a double one) and realized, all at once, that she was dreadfully tired. She yawned enormously, and then looked about her at the charming room, minimal to the point of sparseness but marvellously tranquil. A bit like Serena. White walls, white curtains, rush matting on the floor. A pine chest of drawers, draped in white linen and lace. Wooden pegs and a clutch of colourful hangers for a wardrobe. The duvet cover was blue gingham, and there were books on the bedside table and new magazines and a blue pottery mug in which sat a single hydrangea head, blotting-paper pink.

She yawned again. She was here. She had not lost the way or broken down, nor been involved in any accident. And Jeffrey had been out there to meet her at the end of the lane, leaping out from the side of the road like a footpad and waving her to a halt. If he hadn't been so instantly recognizable she could well have been frightened out of her wits, but there could be no mistaking that tall, lanky figure. Still lithe and active, despite his advancing years, and in all likelihood kept that way by the company of his youthful wife and little children. Most important, he looked content. He had done the right thing. His life seemed to have worked itself out, which was exactly what she had always wished for him.

After a bit, she got off the bed, unpacked, and set about the place her few belongings, turning the simple room into her own. Then she undressed, wrapped herself in her old robe, and went next door to the little bathroom, where she soaked for a little in a scalding bath. When she got out of the bath she had stopped yawning and felt tired no longer, but active and cheerful and all ready for the evening ahead. She dressed again, in velvet trousers and a silk shirt, gathered up her carpet-bag, which was filled with presents, and went downstairs, feeling like a sailor descending a gangway onto a lower deck. In the kitchen she found the children eating their sausages, while their mother whipped up egg whites in a bowl with an electric beater. As Elfrida appeared she looked up to smile, and said, "Go and be with Jeffrey . . . he's in the sitting-room. He's lit a fire."

"Can't I help? I'm not much of a cook, but a dab hand at scouring saucepans."

Serena laughed. "Not a saucepan to be scoured."

"Will I see Ben and Amy again?"

"Of course. They'll come and say good night after their bath."

"I had a wonderful bath. Rejuvenating."

Ben said, "What does rejuvenate mean?"

"It means make younger," Serena explained.

"She doesn't look any younger."

"That's because I'm so old," Elfrida told him. "Be sure to come and say good night, because I've got something for you"— she raised the carpet-bag—"in here."

"Can we look now?"

"No, you can look later, by the fire. A bit like Christmas stockings."

She found Jeffrey in the little sitting-room, ensconced like any old gentleman by the fire, and reading *The Times.* As she appeared, he tossed this aside and rose cautiously to his feet. Cautiously because in this room, for some reason, the ceiling was exceptionally low, and Jeffrey was clearly aware of the dangers of bashing his head on one of the white-painted beams. He was particularly vulnerable because he was bald, his head burnt chestnut-brown by the sun; but the remaining hair which circled his collar was still as dark as it had ever been. Laughter lines fanned out over his thin cheeks, and he wore a navy-blue sweater with a red bandanna knotted around his neck in lieu of a tie. Elfrida had always had an eye for a good-looking man, and it was gratifying to discover that her cousin Jeffrey was as toothsome as ever.

He said, "How dashing you look."

"Clean, at least. Heavenly bath." She dumped down her carpet-bag, lowered herself into the other armchair, and looked about her appreciatively, seeing pictures that were familiar, others that were not. A blazing fire, jugs of dried grasses, family photographs in silver frames, a few pieces of pretty old furniture. There wasn't room for much more. She said, "You have made an enchanting house here."

"No credit to me, Elfrida. All Serena. A glass of wine?"

"Delicious, thank you. It's like another world, isn't it, from the way you used to live. The house in Campden, and flogging off to the City every day, and formal entertaining, and knowing all the right people?"

He was on the other side of the room, pouring her wine. He did not immediately reply to her remarks, but seemed to be considering them. Returning, he gave her the wineglass, and sat again in his wide-lapped chair. Across the hearthrug, their eyes met.

She said, "I'm sorry."

"Why sorry?"

"Tactless. You know I've never thought before I spoke."

"Not tactless. Just truthful. You're right. Another world and one not mourned. Chasing after money, sending the girls to the right, and so appallingly expensive, schools. Hiring a butler every time we had a dinner party. Redesigning the kitchen because the Harley Wrights on the other side of the square had redesigned theirs and Dodie couldn't stand to be left behind. Perpetually worried about the cash flow, the state of the stock market, the demands of Lloyds, the possibility of being made redundant. Sometimes I went through the whole night without sleeping. And all about nothing. But I had to walk out to discover that."

"You're all right now?"

"In what way?"

"I suppose, financially."

"Yes, we're fine. Even keel. We haven't got much, but we don't need it."

"What do you live on? Your hens?"

He began to laugh. "Scarcely. But they provide an occupation and a tiny income. Bed and breakfast helps in the summer, but we only have one room, which is yours, and the shared bathroom, so we can't charge too much. There's a derelict outbuilding between us and the farm, and from time to time we think of putting in an offer and converting it into an annex for paying visitors, but it's such an undertaking that we keep putting it off. But Serena still works, doing flowers for weddings and parties and such, and Ben and Amy are getting an excellent education at the local school. To me it's been a revelation, how simply one can live."

"And happy?"

"Happier than I ever thought possible."

"What about Dodie?"

"She's living in a flat near Hurlingham, very desirable, with a view of the river. Nicola's living with her. Nicola's marriage fell to bits, so the two of them are shacked up together, doubtless getting on each other's nerves."

"And Nicola's child?"

"My granddaughter. Lucy. She's fourteen now. Poor kid, she's living there, too. Can't be much fun for her, but there's not much I can do about it. I've tried asking her to come down to us and stay for a bit, but Nicola has labelled me as a villain, and Serena as a witch, and refuses to let her visit."

Elfrida sighed. She could understand perfectly the hopelessness of the situation. She said, “How about Carrie?”

“Still in Austria or wherever. She’s got a good job with a travel company, quite a responsible position.”

“Do you see her?”

“Last time I was in London we had lunch together. But our paths seldom cross.”

“Not married?”

“No.”

“Does *she* come here?”

“No, but for the best of reasons. She doesn’t want to intrude, to make things awkward for Serena and Ben and Amy. Anyway, she’s nearly thirty now. Not a child. She leads her own life. If she wanted to come to Emblo, she knows she only has to pick up the telephone.” He paused, to set down his glass and reach for a cigarette and light it. Elfrida said, “You haven’t given up smoking?”

“No, I haven’t given up and don’t intend to. Does that offend you?”

“Jeffrey, nothing in all my life has ever offended me. You know that.”

“You look wonderful. How are you?”

“Wonderful, perhaps.”

“Not too lonely?”

“Getting better.”

“It was cruel, what happened to you.”

“Jimbo, you mean? Darling man. It was crueler for him than for me. A slow degeneration of a wonderful, brilliant man. But no regrets, Jeffrey. I know we didn’t have very long together, but what we did have was special. Not many people achieve such happiness, even for a year or two.”

“Tell me about your Hampshire hideaway.”

“Dibton. The village is rather ordinary and dull. But somehow that was what I wanted. The house is a tiny railway cottage, one in a row. All I need.”

“Nice people?”

"Ordinary again. Kind and friendly. I think you could say I've been made welcome. I couldn't stay in London."

"Any special friends?"

She started telling him about the old Foubisters and Bobby Burton Jones, the vicar and his wife, and the Sunday school pantomime. She told him about Mrs. Jennings and Albert Meddows and the fabulously wealthy Mr. Dunn with his indoor swimming pool and immense conservatory filled with red-hot geraniums and rubber plants.

Finally, she told him about the Blundells. Oscar and Gloria and Francesca. "They've been truly, enormously kind. Taken me under their wing, one might say. Gloria is wealthy and generous. The two don't always go together, do they? She owns the house they live in, it's called the Grange and is perfectly hideous, but frightfully warm and comfortable. She was married before, so she's got two grown-up married sons, but Francesca is so original and funny and sweet. Gloria is an avid hostess, scarcely a day passes when she isn't organizing some party or picnic, or a get-together or committee meeting. She's rather horsy and loves gathering a great gang of friends and setting off for some point-to-point, with a bar in the boot of her car, and her Pekingeses tied to the bumper barking their heads off at anyone who passes."

Jeffrey was clearly amused. "And does Oscar enjoy such occasions?"

"I don't know. But he's a gentle, amiable man . . . a charmer, really . . . and he and Francesca go off together, and put bets on unlikely horses and buy themselves ice-creams."

"What does he do? Or is he retired?"

"He's a musician. An organist. A pianist. A teacher."

"How clever of you to find such an interesting couple. They clearly adore you. Probably because you've always had the effect of a good strong gust of fresh air."

But Elfrida voiced her reservations. "I have to be quite careful and strict with myself. I do not intend to become absorbed."

"Who wouldn't want to absorb you?"

"You mustn't be partisan."

"I was always on your side."

In later years, looking back to those weeks she spent at Emblo, the thing that Elfrida most clearly remembered was the sound of the wind. It blew perpetually; at times shrunken to a lively breeze, at others pounding in from the sea at gale-force strength, assaulting the cliffs, howling down chimneys and rattling at doors and window-panes. After a bit, she became used to its constant presence, but at night the wind was impossible to ignore, and she would lie in the dark, hearing it sweep in from the Atlantic, stream up across the moor, send the branches of an elderly apple tree tapping like a ghost at her window.

It was—this wind made very clear—summer no longer. October moving into November and the nights drawing closer every evening. The farmer's cows, his handsome Guernsey dairy herd, trod down from the fields, for the morning and evening milking, and churned to mud the lane that ran between Emblo and the farmhouse. After the evening milking, they were turned out into the fields again, and were adept at seeking shelter in the lee of a wall, or behind a tangle of thicket and gorse.

"Why can't they spend the night indoors?" Elfrida wanted to know.

"They never do. We have no frosts, there's plenty of grass."

"Poor things." But, she had to admit, they looked sleek and happy enough.

The daily routine of the little household took her over, and she slowed herself to its pace. There was always washing to be pegged out, shirts to be ironed, potatoes to be dug, hens to be fed, and eggs washed. After the first week, she realized with some surprise that for seven days she had neither read a newspaper nor watched television. The rest of the world could have blown itself to pieces while all Elfrida worried about was whether she could get the sheets off the line before the next shower of rain.

Some evenings, she took over the kitchen and cooked supper for Ben and Amy, so that Jeffrey and Serena were able to grab the chance of a dinner out by themselves or a visit to the nearest cinema. And she taught the children to play rummy, and mesmerized them with stories about the old days, when she was in the theatre.

One weekend, the fickle weather turned warm as spring, and the wind dropped and the sun shone from a cloudless sky. Determined to make the most of the benevolent day, Serena gathered up the farmer's four youngsters, packed a picnic, and they all set out to walk across the fields towards the cliffs, a straggling party consisting of six children, three adults, and three dogs. Amy and Elfrida, side by side, brought up the rear. The footpath crossed stone stiles and snaked down between the gorse- and bramble bushes.

Elfrida spied blackberries. "We should pick them," she told Amy. "We could make blackberry jelly."

But Amy was wiser. "No, we can't. We can't pick blackberries after the beginning of October, because that's when the Cornish witches do wees on them."

"How extraordinary. How do you know that?"

"Our teacher told us. But she didn't say wees, she said 'urinated.'"

They reached the edge of the cliff and the whole breadth of the ocean was revealed, extravagantly blue and glittering with sunshine. The path trickled on, a precipitous and dangerous-looking descent into a secret cove. It was low tide, and so there lay a tiny sickle of sand, and rock-pools gleaming like jewels.

With some difficulty they all scrambled down, the dogs bounding fearlessly ahead. On the rocks, Amy left Elfrida and went to join the others on the sand, where Jeffrey had already started everybody digging a mammoth sand castle, and Serena searched for shells and pebbles with which to decorate this edifice.

Now midday, there was a real warmth in the sun, so Elfrida shed her jacket and rolled up the sleeves of her sweater. Rugs and baskets and haversacks had been dumped on a smooth flat rock, and she sat beside them watching the restless sea, and felt mesmerized by its sheer size and magnificence. The colours of the water, the clearness was breath-taking. Streaks of blue, green, turquoise, purple, all laced and streaked with white surf. A heavy swell was running, and the breakers formed far out, moving in and gathering height and weight before finally crashing against the jagged granite coastline, sending up great fountains of sizzling spray. Overhead the gulls wheeled, and out towards the horizon, a small fishing boat butted its way through the turbulent water.

Staring, bewitched, she lost all sense of time, but after a bit was joined by Serena, come to unpack the picnic. From the haversacks she produced bottles, plastic cups, paper napkins, a bag of apples. As well there emanated the warm, mouth-watering smell of hot pasties.

Elfrida was amazed. "Whenever did you make pasties, Serena? They take forever."

"I always keep a dozen or so in the deep freeze. The children love them."

"Me, too."

"I took them out last night. I had a feeling it was going to be a good day. How about a drink? You can have lager or wine. Or lemonade, if you're feeling abstemious."

"Wine would be perfect."

The bottle was wrapped in a wine cooler, and drunk from a plastic glass tasted better than any wine had ever tasted before. Elfrida turned back to the sea.

She said, "This is heaven."

"In the summer we come most weekends. It's easier now that both children can do the walk themselves."

"What a happy family you are."

"Yes," said Serena, and smiled. "I know. So fortunate. But I do *know* that, Elfrida. I really do know. And every day I say thank you."

From time to time, Elfrida left Emblo and took herself off on her own, driving her little car and leaving Horace behind in the company of Jeffrey's sheep-dogs. She found herself amazed that such a small tract of country could be so wild, so remote, and yet so varied. Roads, freed of the summer tourist traffic, were narrow and winding, but all she ever met was the occasional bus or butcher's van or tractor. And she would cross an empty moor, and the road would slip down into a tiny valley thick with rhododendrons, where enviable gardens were still verdant with hydrangeas and the dangling ballerina blossoms of fuchsia.

One day, she made the trip into the neighbouring town, where she parked her car and walked down into the warren of baffling lanes and alley-ways that led to the harbour. On the harbour road were restaurants and gift shops and many small galleries displaying every kind of art and sculpture. She found a bookshop and went in and took some time choosing two books for Ben and Amy. And so delightful was this that she browsed on and, thinking of Francesca, bought a book for her as well. She found it in the second-hand section, *The Island of Sheep,* by John Buchan, and she remembered reading it at school and becoming totally caught up in the adventure. This was a story Oscar and Francesca could read together, the two of them squashed into a single huge armchair by the flickering log-fire.

She had the books wrapped and went out into the street again, continuing on her way. In a craft-shop, she found brilliantly patterned hand-knitted sweaters, and chose two. One for Jeffrey and one for Serena. She bought postcards and a bottle of wine, and by now considerably laden, set out once more walking away from the harbour and into a maze of cobbled streets where washing hung, and window-boxes were brilliant with nasturtium and pink petunias. Another gallery. Unable to resist, she paused to look in its window and saw a little abstract painting, its frame bleached like driftwood, with all the colours of Cornwall set into shapes that represented exactly her own impressions and feelings about this ancient land.

Elfrida craved it. Not for herself, but as a present. She thought that if Jimbo were still alive, she would have bought it for him, because it was exactly the sort of image that he would have loved beyond anything. She imagined giving it to him, bringing it to his house in Barnes where they had been so unimaginably happy together. Watching him strip off the wrappings, watching his face, knowing that his reaction would be one of delight and pleasure . . .

The picture wavered and became watery. She realized that her eyes had filled with tears. She had never cried for Jimbo, simply grieved and mourned privately to herself, and tried to learn to live with the cold loneliness of an existence without him. She had thought that she had achieved this, but it could not be so. She wondered if perhaps she was a woman who could not live without a man, and if this was true, then there was nothing she could do about it.

The tears receded. Ridiculous. She was sixty-two, snivelling like a young girl who has lost her lover. But still she stayed, staring at the picture, wanting it. Wanting to share her pleasure. Wanting to give.

The idea occurred to her that she could buy it for Oscar Blundell. But Oscar was not simply Oscar. He was one half of Oscar and Gloria, and Gloria would be completely bewildered by such a gift. . . . In her head Elfrida could hear Gloria's voice. *Elfrida! You can't be serious. It's just a lot of shapes. A child of four could do a better job than that. And which way up is it meant to be? Honestly, Elfrida, you are a hoot. What possessed you to put down good money for a thing like that? You've been robbed.*

No. Not a good idea. Reluctantly, she turned from the window of the gallery and walked on, and left the streets behind her, and set out on a path that climbed, in zigzags, to the top of the grass promontory that divided the two beaches. As she climbed, the wind became blustery, and when she reached the shallow summit, she found herself surrounded by ocean and sky, the whole blue curving rim of the horizon. It felt a bit like being at sea. And she came to a bench and sat upon it, huddled in her sheepskin jacket and with her packages set about her, like any old pensioner exhausted by shopping.

But she was not any old pensioner. She was Elfrida. She was here. She had survived. Was moving on. But to what? A sea-gull, scavenging for crusts or some edible picnic titbit, swept down out of the air and landed at her feet. His eyes were cold and acquisitive, and his aggression made her smile. And she found herself longing for company. Specifically, for Oscar. She wanted him to be with her, just for a single day, so that when she returned to Dibton, they could talk about the wind and the sea and the gull, and remember, and marvel at the magic of a special moment.

Perhaps that was the worst of all. Not having someone to remember things with.

When the day came to return to Dibton, Elfrida could scarcely believe that she had been at Emblo for a month, so swiftly had the weeks sped by. They tried to persuade her, of course, to stay. "You are welcome for as long as you like," Serena told her, and Elfrida knew that she was totally sincere. "You've been the best. A lovely mixture of mother, sister, and friend. We'll miss you so dreadfully."

"You're sweet. But no, I must get back. Pick up the thread of life again."

"You'll come again?"

"Try and stop me."

She had planned to set off as early as possible, so that she could reach Dibton before darkness fell. At eight in the morning she was out of doors, with Jeffrey loading her car. The little family stood about her, and Amy was in tears.

"I don't want you to go. I want you to stay."

"Guests don't stay forever, Amy, my pet. It's time to leave."

Horace, too, showed a disloyal reluctance to depart. Every time he was put into the car, he jumped out again, and finally had to be dragged by his collar, deposited on the back seat, and the door shut behind him. He gazed from the window, his furry face doleful and his dark eyes agonized. "I think," Ben observed, "that *he's* probably going to cry as well."

Neither Amy nor Ben was yet dressed, and they looked bizarre with padded jackets and gumboots pulled over their pyjamas. When her brother made this remark, Amy's tears welled up once more, and her mother stooped and picked her up and held her on her hip. "Cheer up, Amy. Horace will be fine once he's on his way."

"I don't want *anybody* to leave us."

The parting had gone on for long enough. Elfrida turned to Jeffrey. "Dear man, thank you a thousand times." He had not yet shaved, and her cheek grated against the stubble of his dark beard. "And Serena . . ." A swift kiss, a hand over Amy's flaxen head, and she got firmly in behind the driving wheel, slammed the door, turned on the ignition, and drove off. They stood and waved until the car was lost to view, but she had a pretty good idea that they didn't go back indoors until the little Fiesta had turned out onto the main road and she and Horace were truly on their way.

Not the time to feel lonely and bereft. The goodbye was not forever, because she could return to Emblo any time she wanted. In a year, maybe, or sooner. Jeffrey and Serena would always be there, and Ben and Amy. But that was the poignant bit, because Jeffrey and Serena would remain more or less unchanged, while Ben and Amy would be taller, thinner, fatter; growing street-wise, losing front teeth. She would never know Ben and Amy again as the small children she had come to love during this particular period of their lives. Like the holiday that was over, those children would be gone forever.

To cheer herself up, Elfrida looked ahead, in positive fashion, which she had always found a reliable method of dealing with a sense of loss. She was going home. To her own little nest, filled with her own possessions. The small and humble refuge that she shared with Horace. She would open doors and windows, inspect her garden, put a match to the fire.

Tomorrow, perhaps, she would telephone the Grange and speak to Gloria. And there would be cries of delight that she was back again, and an instant summons to come and see them immediately. And when she went Elfrida would take the book with her to give to Francesca. *The Island of Sheep.* I chose it specially, because I loved it so much when I was your age, and I'm sure you'll love it, too.

But first, of course, before even reaching Poulton's Row, Elfrida knew that she must do some shopping. There was no food in the cottage, and she had cleaned out the refrigerator before she left. So her first port of call must be Mrs. Jennings's mini-supermarket. She began to make a mental list. Bread and milk. Sausages, eggs, and butter. Coffee. Biscuits and some tins for Horace. Perhaps a tin of soup for her supper. Something sustaining, like Cullen Skink . . .

Half an hour later, she joined the motorway that led up-country. She switched on her car radio and settled to the long drive.

The Dibton church clock stood at half past two as she drove into the main street of the village. Outside Mrs. Jennings's slouched the usual gang of louty youths, and a little farther on, she spied Bobby Burton Jones trimming his privet hedge with a pair of shears. Nothing much seemed to have changed, except that most of the trees had shed their leaves and there was a definite wintry feel to the air.

She parked the car, found her bag, and went into the shop. It seemed to be empty. She picked up a wire basket and moved up the aisles, taking what she needed from the shelves. Finally, she presented herself at the counter, where Mrs. Jennings was doing sums on the back of an envelope and had not heard her come in.

But now she looked up, saw Elfrida, laid down her pencil, and took off her spectacles.

"Mrs. Phipps. Well, what a surprise. I haven't seen you for weeks. Have a good holiday, did you?"

"Wonderful. Just back. Haven't even been home yet, because I had to buy some provisions." She put the wire basket on the counter and reached for a *Daily Telegraph*. "You won't believe this, but I haven't read a newspaper for weeks. To be truthful, I didn't miss it."

Mrs. Jennings made no comment on this. Elfrida looked up and saw that Mrs. Jennings was staring at her, biting her lip and looking much troubled. Elfrida put the newspaper on top of the basket. After a bit, she said, "Is anything wrong, Mrs. Jennings?"

Mrs. Jennings said, "You don't know?"

"Know what?"

"You haven't heard?"

Suddenly Elfrida's mouth was dry. "No."

"Mrs. Blundell."

"What about her?"

"She's dead, Mrs. Phipps. A car smash at Pudstone roundabout. She was bringing the little girl home from a fireworks party. November the fourth, it was. A lorry. Heaven knows how it happened. She couldn't have seen it. It was a dreadful night. Pouring with rain . . ." Elfrida, stunned by shock, said nothing. "I'm sorry, Mrs. Phipps. I thought you might have heard."

"How could I have heard? I never read a paper. Nobody knew where I was. Nobody knew my address."

"A tragedy, Mrs. Phipps. We couldn't believe it. None of the village could believe it."

"And Francesca?" She made herself ask the question, dreading the answer.

"She died, too, Mrs. Phipps. And the two little dogs who were in the back. You couldn't believe the photograph in the paper. That great car, smashed and flattened to bits. They didn't stand a chance. Only good thing was the police said it was instant. They couldn't, any of them, have known a thing." Mrs. Jennings's voice shook a little. She clearly found it almost impossible to speak of what had taken place. "You hear of things like this happening, but when it happens to folk you know. . . ."

"Yes."

"You've gone white as a sheet, Mrs. Phipps. Would you like me to make you a cup of tea? Come into the back shop. . . ."

"No, I'm all right." Which she was, because she was numb, quite calm and cool, shocked beyond horror. She said, "A funeral?"

"A couple of days ago. Here in the village. A huge turnout. A real tribute."

So she had missed even that chance to mourn and comfort. She said, "And Oscar. Mr. Blundell?"

"Hardly seen him. At the funeral, of course, but not since then. Kept to himself. Poor gentleman. It doesn't bear thinking what he's been through. What he's going through."

She thought of Francesca, laughing and teasing her father, playing duets with him on the piano, curled up in his big armchair and the two reading a book together. And then blotted the image from her mind, because it was unbearable to remember.

She said, "Is he at the Grange?"

"Far as I know. The boy's been delivering milk and papers and so forth. Suppose he's just gone into himself. Natural, really. The vicar went to call, but he didn't even want to see the vicar. Mrs. Muswell goes up to the Grange each day, just like she always did, but she says he just stays in his music room. She leaves a tray for his supper on the kitchen table, but she says most times he doesn't even touch it."

"Do you think he would see me?"

"I wouldn't know, Mrs. Phipps. Except that you and them were always friends."

"I should have been here."

"Not your fault, Mrs. Phipps." Someone else had come into the shop. Mrs. Jennings put her spectacles on again, in a brave attempt to be business-like. She said, "I'll put these things through the till, shall I? It's nice to see you back. We've missed you. I feel I've spoilt your homecoming. I'm sorry."

"Thank you for telling me. I'm glad it was you and not anybody else."

She went out of the shop and got back into her car, where she sat for a moment, feeling as though the day, her life, had been snapped into two pieces; it could never be repaired and would never be the same again. She had moved from the laughter and happiness of Emblo into a place of loss and unthinkable pain. And what upset her most was the fact that she had had no knowledge of the tragedy, no inkling, not a suspicion. For some reason, this made her feel guilty, as though she had reneged on responsibilities, stayed on at Emblo when she should have been here. In Dibton. With Oscar.

After a bit, heavy-hearted, she started up the engine and moved on.

Bobby Burton Jones had finished clipping his hedge and disappeared indoors, which was a relief because she didn't want to stop and talk to anybody. She drove down the main street of the village, passed by her own turning. As the houses thinned out, she came to the great gates of the Grange, the house that had been Gloria's. She turned in, up the drive, and around the curve where grew the huge cedar tree. She saw the elaborate face of the house, and outside the front door, a large black limousine upon the gravel.

She parked a little way off and got out, and saw that behind the wheel of this impressive vehicle there sat a uniformed driver, wearing his cap and reading a newspaper. Hearing her, he glanced up, acknowledged her presence with a nod of his head, and then went back to his racing results. He clearly was not expecting conversation. She left him there and went up the steps, and through the open doorway into the familiar tiled porch. The half-glassed door was closed, and she did not ring the bell, but opened this and went inside.

It was tremendously quiet. Only the tock of the long case clock, snipping away at the passing seconds. She stood for a little, listening. Hoping for comforting, domestic sounds from the kitchen, or a thread of music from upstairs. Nothing. The silence was suffocating, like a fog.

To her right, the drawing-room door stood open. She crossed the hall, thick carpets blanketing her footfall, and went through. At first she thought the room was empty, and she alone. And then saw that a man sat in the wing-chair by the empty fireplace. Tweed trouser-legs, polished brogues. Not much else was visible.

"Oscar," she said softly, and moved forward, to look down at him, and experienced the second stunning shock of that dreadful day. For here was Oscar, aged beyond belief, all at once an old man, bespectacled, wrinkled and hunched in the padded chair, a gnarled hand clenched over the ivory handle of an ebony stick. Instinctively, her hand went to her mouth, to stop a scream, or perhaps to conceal her despair.

He looked up at her and said, "My word," and instantly such relief flooded through her that she thought her legs were going to give way. Swiftly, before they did this, she sat with a thump on the padded leather seat of the club fender. They stared at each other. He went on, "I never heard you coming in. Did you ring a bell? I'm a bit deaf, but I'd have heard the bell. I'd have come to the door. . . ."

He was not Oscar, aged beyond belief, just another person resembling him. Maybe twenty or so years older than Oscar. An old gentleman well into his eighties, and speaking most courteously with a strong Scottish accent. His voice reminded her of a well-loved old doctor who had looked after Elfrida when she was a small child, and for some reason this made everything much easier to deal with.

"No," she told him. "I didn't ring the bell. I just walked in."

"You'll forgive me not getting up. I'm a bit stiff and slow these days. Perhaps we should introduce ourselves. I am Hector McLennan. Oscar is my nephew."

Hector McLennan. Who had once owned Corrydale, but now lived in London, and whose son Hughie had wiped the dust of Britain from the soles of his shoes and gone to live in Barbados.

She said, "Once, Oscar told me about you."

"And you, my dear?"

"Elfrida Phipps. I have a house in the village. I live on my own. Gloria and Oscar were endlessly kind to me. I'm sorry I was so rude when I first came in. I thought you were Oscar, and then of course I realized my mistake."

"Oscar, aged by grief?"

"Yes. I suppose so. You see, I haven't seen him yet. I've been in Cornwall for a month with cousins, and only just heard about everything from Mrs. Jennings in the village shop. I went in to buy bread . . . and things. She told me."

"Yes. A ghastly accident."

"What happened?"

The old man shrugged. "Gloria drove her car onto the roundabout, right into the teeth of this great articulated lorry."

"You mean, she never saw it?"

"It was very dark. It had started to rain."

"Mrs. Jennings said she'd been to a party with Francesca. Fireworks and such."

"That's so."

Elfrida bit her lip. After a little, she said, "Sometimes, at the end of a party, she'd have a strong drink." And immediately wished she hadn't said such a thing. But the old man was unfazed. "I know, my dear. We all knew. Sometimes she overdid it a wee bit. A dram too many at the end of a convivial evening. Hard to say no, perhaps. And then to drive home. Oscar knows this, better than any of us. He is consumed with guilt because he didn't take Francesa to the fireworks party himself. I think it never occurred to him that it was anything more than a children's party, that Gloria wouldn't bring Francesca straight home. But I suppose there were other parents there, and it just went on. The rain started just before they set out. And then, a momentary lapse of concentration, a confusion of lights, a heavy vehicle, a wet road . . ." He spread his hand in a gesture that said it all. "Finished. All over. Lives wiped out."

"I've even missed the funeral."

"I missed it, too. I had a touch of flu, my doctor forbade it. This is my first visit, though of course I wrote my letter of condolence, and have been in touch over the telephone. It was while I was speaking to him that I became aware of his situation. So as soon as I could, I made the journey down from London to talk things through. I am aged, but I am still his uncle. No doubt you saw my car and driver at the door."

"Yes." Elfrida frowned. "You said 'his situation.' Does that have special meaning?"

"It most certainly does."

"Am I allowed to be told?"

"No secret, my dear. Gloria has left everything, including this house, to her sons. The day after the funeral they presented themselves and told Oscar he could no longer live here, because they intended selling."

"And where do they imagine Oscar's going to live?"

"They suggested some old folks' home. The Priory, I think it is called. They had brochures for him to read." He added with gentle irony, "They had clearly thought of everything."

"You mean, they're throwing him out? Into an old folks' home? *Oscar?* They must be mad."

"No. I don't think they're actually insane. Just avaricious and without heart. And they've got two hard wee wives as well, probably pushing from the back line to get every brass farthing they can lay their hands on."

"Then Oscar must buy another house."

Hector McLennan lowered his head and regarded Elfrida over the top of his spectacles. He said, "Oscar is not a man of means."

"You mean he has no money?"

"A pension, of course. And a little put by. But not enough to buy a decent house at these days' inflated prices."

"Gloria's sons, Giles and Crawford, must know that." Another thought occurred to her. "And Gloria must have known, too. Surely she could have left Oscar *something.* She was so generous, so giving of worldly goods."

"Maybe she intended to. She was a relatively young woman. In all likelihood, it never occurred to her that she would die before Oscar. Or perhaps she simply never got around to making a new will, or even adding a codicil. We shall never know."

"But he can't go and live in an old folks' home." The very notion was an affront. Oscar, of all people, bundled in with a lot of old incontinent geriatrics, eating milk puddings and being taught to make baskets. Elfrida's vision of an old folks' home was a little fuzzy, on account of her never having been in one. She said firmly, "I won't let it happen."

"What will you do?"

"He can come and live with me." But even as she said it she knew that this was an impractical suggestion. There was scarcely space for one at Poulton's Row, let alone two. And where would she put his grand piano? On the roof or in the garden shed? "That's stupid. No, he can't."

"My notion," said the old man, "is that he should move away. This house, this village is too filled with poignant memory. I think he should cut loose. That's why I drove down today to see him. Mrs. Muswell gave us lunch, and I put forward my suggestion. But he seems unable to make any sort of decision. Doesn't seem to care what happens."

"Where is he now?"

"He was called to the garden. Some problem with the greenhouse heating system. I said I would wait until he returned, and then start back for London. Which is why you found me sitting here in my nephew's chair, and looking, doubtless, like an old ghoul."

"You don't look like an old ghoul, and what was *your* suggestion?"

"That he goes back to Sutherland for a bit. Corrydale, and the wee Estate House. Half of it belongs to him anyway, and my Hughie, who is the co-owner, lives in Barbados and is likely to stay there."

"I thought it was let. The house, I mean. Occupied."

"No. At the moment, it's standing empty. An elderly couple, called Cochrane, were living there, but the old man died, and the wife has gone to stay with her daughter. I discovered this from our erstwhile factor, Major Billicliffe. He's retired now, but he still lives on the Corrydale estate. At the time of Hughie's big sale, he bought his house. I gave him a telephone call, and we spoke at length. He says the place is in good condition, maybe needs a lick of paint, but otherwise sound and dry."

"Is it furnished?"

"It was a furnished let. There will be no frills, but the essentials of day-to-day living should be there."

Elfrida thought this all over. Sutherland. She imagined it: peat bogs and sheep. Remote as the moon. She said, "It's a long way for Oscar to go all on his own."

"He's known at Corrydale and Creagan. He's family. His grandmother's grandson, and my nephew. People are kindly, and he will be remembered, even though he's not been back for fifty years."

"But is he up to such an uprooting? Such upheaval? Why not return to London, and be near the church where he was organist? Wouldn't that be more sensible?"

"A regression. And one haunted, I should think, by memories of his child."

"Yes. You're right."

"And, saddest of all, he has abandoned his music. It's as though the best part of him has died."

"How can I help?"

"That's up to you. A little gentle persuasion, perhaps?"

"I can try." But she wondered where she was going to find the strength.

They fell silent, gazing sadly at each other. This silence was disturbed by the sound of approaching footsteps, the slow tread of a person crossing the gravel in front of the house. Elfrida raised her head and watched Oscar pass by the long window. All at once she was nervous. She got to her feet. "He's coming now," she said.

The front door opened and closed. They waited. A long pause. Then the drawing-room door swung open, and he was there, surveying the pair of them across the expanse of the thick carpet. He wore old corduroys and a heavy sweater, knitted and flecked like tweed. His thick white hair fell across his forehead, and he put up a hand to push it aside. She had imagined him diminished, felled by tragedy. But heartbreak is a hidden thing, and Oscar was a private man.

"Elfrida. I knew you had come because I saw your little car."

She went to meet him, and he took her hands in his own and leaned forward to kiss her cheek. His lips were icy against her skin. She looked into his eyes. "Dear Oscar. I'm home again."

"How long have you been here?"

"About fifteen minutes. I drove up from Cornwall this morning. I went into the shop, and Mrs. Jennings told me. I hadn't known. I haven't read a newspaper for a month. So I came straight here and walked in on your uncle."

"I see." He let go of her hands and turned to Hector, who sat in his chair and watched their reunion. "I am sorry I kept you waiting, Hector. There were complications. Something to do with a trip-switch. But you have had Elfrida for company."

"And very pleasant it has been, too. Now I must be on my way." Which entailed something of a struggle, the old man leaning on his stick and endeavouring to rise from the chair. Oscar moved forward to lend a hand, and after some effort on both their parts got his uncle to his feet, supported by his stick, and prepared for departure.

They all moved, at the old gentleman's pace, across the big room and through to the hall. There, Oscar helped him into his old-fashioned overcoat and handed him his aged brown trilby. Hector put this on at a rakish angle.

"It was good of you to come, Hector, and I really appreciate it. Splendid to see you."

"Dear boy. Thank you for lunch. And if you're in town, drop in."

"Of course."

"And give thought to my suggestion. It may seem a little drastic, but it would at least give you a breather. You mustn't stay here." It was then that he remembered something, and began groping in the pocket of his overcoat. "Nearly forgot. Wrote it down for you. Billicliffe's telephone number. All you have to do is give him a ring; he's got the key of your house." He withdrew from the pocket a scrap of folded paper and handed it over. "Only thing is," he added, with a dry twinkle in his rheumy old eyes, "don't leave it too late in the day. He's inclined to hit the whisky bottle, and doesn't make much sense after that."

But Elfrida was concerned by other, more practical, matters. "How long has the house stood empty?"

"Couple of months. But there's a Mrs. Snead who's been going in and out. Keeping the place cleaned and aired. Billicliffe arranged that, but I've been paying her wages. Doesn't do to let property disintegrate."

"You seem," Elfrida told him, "to have thought of everything."

"Haven't much else to think about these days. Now I must be off. Goodbye, my dear. I have much enjoyed meeting you. I hope one day we'll be able to renew our acquaintance."

"I hope so, too. We'll come with you to the car."

Oscar put a hand beneath Hector's elbow, and they all proceeded out through the front door and down the steps onto the gravel. The afternoon had turned chilly, and a thin rain threatened. The chauffeur, seeing them, got out of the big car and went around to hold open the door of the passenger seat. With some effort on all sides, Hector was loaded into this, and his safety-belt fastened.

"Goodbye, Oscar, dear boy. My thoughts are with you."

Oscar embraced the old man. "Thank you again for coming, Hector."

"I only hope I've been a wee bit of comfort."

"You have." He stepped back and slammed shut the door. The car started up. Hector waved a bent old hand, and they stood and watched him go, borne off to London at a suitable and dignified pace. They stayed until the car was out of sight and they could no longer hear the engine. The ensuing silence was filled by the cawing of rooks. It was cold and damp. Elfrida shivered.

Oscar said, "Come indoors."

"Are you sure you don't want me to leave as well?"

"No. I want you to stay with me."

"Is Mrs. Muswell here?"

"She leaves each day after lunch."

"Would you like me to make us a cup of tea?"

"I think that would be an excellent idea."

"May I bring Horace indoors? He's been shut in the car all day."

"Of course. He's safe now. There are no Pekingeses to attack him."

Elfrida thought, oh, God. She went across the gravel to where her little car was parked, and set Horace free. Gratefully he leaped out and shot off across the lawn to a handy laurel bush, beneath which he relieved himself at length. When he was done with this necessary operation, he scratched about for a bit, and then returned to them. Oscar stooped and fondled his head, and only then did they all go back into the house. Oscar closed the door behind them and led the way into the kitchen, where it felt comfortingly warm. Gloria's kitchen, large and efficient, from which such hospitable meals and copious amounts of delicious food had appeared to sate the appetites of her many relations and friends.

Now it was empty, and very neat, and Elfrida saw that Mrs. Muswell had left a tray, with a single mug and a milk jug and a tin of biscuits, on the table. She was clearly doing her best to feed and care for her solitary employer.

She found the kettle and filled it from the tap, and put it on the Aga to boil. She turned to face Oscar, who was leaning against the comforting warmth of the stove. She said, "I wish I was articulate and brilliant at thinking of things to say. But I'm not, Oscar. I'm sorry. I just wish I'd known. I would have come back from Cornwall. I would at least have been at the funeral."

He had pulled out a chair and sat now at the kitchen table, and as she spoke he put his elbows on the table and buried his face in his hands. For a dreadful moment, she thought that he was weeping. She heard herself rabbiting on. "I had no inkling. Until today . . ."

Slowly, he drew his hands from his face, and she saw that he did not weep, but his eyes were filled with an anguish that was almost worse than tears.

He said, "I would have been in touch, but I had no idea where you were."

"That was because I had no idea that you might need to know." She took a deep breath. "Oscar, I *do* know about loss and bereavement. All the time that Jimbo was so ill, I knew it was terminal, that he would never recover. But when he died, I found myself quite unprepared for the pain, and the terrible emptiness. And I know, too, that what I went through then is simply one tiny fraction of what you are going through now. And there is nothing I can do to help, to ease you."

"You are here."

"I can listen. If you want to talk, I can listen."

"Not yet."

"I know. Too early. Too soon."

"The vicar called, very soon after the accident. Very soon after I had been told that both Gloria and Francesca were dead. He tried to comfort, and mentioned God, and I found myself wondering if he had taken leave of his senses. You asked me once if I was religious, and I don't think I was able to answer your question. I only knew that my music and my work and my choirs meant more to me than any churchly dogma. The 'Te Deum.' Do you remember, that first day we met, outside the church, and you said that you had particularly enjoyed a certain setting to the 'Te Deum.' The words, and that music, once filled me with a certainty of goodness, and perhaps eternity.

"We praise thee, O Lord.
We acknowledge thee to be the Lord.
All the earth doth worship thee, the Father Everlasting.

"Thundering away on the organ, pulling out all the stops, hearing the boys' voices soar to the rafters. That was when I truly believed, when I knew a faith that I thought nothing could rock."

He fell silent. She waited. After a bit, she said, "And now, Oscar?"

"It was all to do with God. And I cannot believe in a God who would take Francesca away from me. I sent the vicar home. He departed, I think, in some umbrage."

Elfrida was sympathetic. "Poor man."

"He will, no doubt, survive. The kettle's boiling."

It was a welcome interruption. Elfrida busied herself finding the teapot and the tea, spooning tea, pouring the boiling water. She found another mug for herself, and carried everything over to the table and sat facing Oscar, just as they had sat that day, an eternity ago, before she went to Cornwall. In her little house in Poulton's Row, and Oscar with gardening mud on his boots.

"You like builders' tea, don't you?"

"Strong and black."

She poured her own mug and left the pot to stew. She said, "Hector told me about your stepsons and the house. About selling it, I mean."

"They think that I should book into the Priory, a Victorian mansion converted for the benefit of desiccated gentlefolk."

"You won't go there."

"I admit, I would rather not."

"What do you want to do?"

"I would like to be left alone, to lick my wounds. But I can't be left alone *here,* because Giles and Crawford want me out of the way, so that they can put the house on the market as soon as possible."

"Brutes." She poured his tea, black as ink, and pushed the mug towards him. He reached for the jug, added some milk, and drank.

She said, "Hector McLennan told me his suggestion."

"I had a suspicion that he might have."

"Is it such a bad idea?"

"Elfrida. It's mad."

"I don't see why."

"Then I'll tell you why. Because Sutherland is the other end of the country. And I haven't been there for fifty years. For all Hector's optimism, I should not know a single soul. The house will be half empty, and hasn't been lived in for weeks. I am not a naturally domesticated animal. I wouldn't know how to start to make it habitable. And who would I turn to?"

"Mrs. Snead?"

"Elfrida." It was a reproach, but Elfrida persisted.

"Is it very isolated? Your house, I mean."

"No. It's in the middle of Creagan, the little town."

It sounded to Elfrida perfectly suitable. "Is it horrid?" she asked.

"Horrid," he repeated. "What words you use. No. It's simply a large, square, undistinguished Victorian dwelling. Not actually ugly. But not blessed with redeeming features. And it has a garden, but that's not much joy in the middle of winter."

"It won't always be winter."

"It's just that I can't imagine what the hell I would do with myself."

"Well, one thing's for sure. You can't stay here, Oscar. And you go into the Priory over my dead body. So you must consider any available alternative. You could come and live with me at Poulton's Row, but as you know there is scarcely space for me and Horace in that little cottage." Oscar made no comment on this wild suggestion. "I thought perhaps you'd like to go back to London, but Hector said no."

"He's right."

"Scotland," she mused. "Sutherland. It would at least be a fresh start."

"I am sixty-seven, and at the moment in no shape to start anything. And although I can scarcely bear to speak to any person, I still dread being alone. Solitary. Living alone is the worst. Empty rooms. Even before I married Gloria, there were always colleagues, choristers, schoolboys—a whole world of lively company. My life was full."

"It can be again."

"No."

"Yes, Oscar, it can. Never the same, I know. But you have so much to give people. A generosity of spirit. We mustn't waste it."

He frowned. "You said 'we.'"

"A slip of the tongue. I meant *you*."

Oscar had finished his tea, and the mug stood empty. He reached out for the teapot and poured himself a refill, the tea blacker than ever and singularly unappetizing.

"Supposing I went to Scotland. How would I travel so far?"

"There are planes and trains."

"I would want my car."

"Then drive. You're in no hurry. Take it in stages. . . ." Elfrida heard her voice drift into silence, and found herself unable to finish her sentence. Because the image of Oscar setting off by himself on such a journey into the unknown filled her with desolation. Gloria should be there beside him, to share the driving, Francesca in the back, with her computer games and her ingenuous chat. In the boot of the big car, the two yapping Pekes, included in the holiday, along with golf clubs and fishing-rods. . . .

All gone. Dead. Never again.

He saw her distress, and put out his hand and laid it over her own. "You have to be brave, Elfrida, otherwise I shall go to pieces."

"I'm trying. But I can't bear it for you."

"Suppose . . . suppose we discuss your idea? Suppose I went. Drove to Scotland, to Sutherland. If I made that journey, would you come with me?"

She was silenced; could think of nothing to say. She stared into his face, wondering if she had heard aright; if he really had made that extraordinary proposal, or whether, confused by shock and sadness, her imagination had made it all up.

"Come with you?"

"Why not? Is it such a bad idea? To go together? Somehow we'll get there. We shall collect the key from Major Billicliffe, and find my house, and take possession and spend the winter there."

"Christmas?"

"No Christmas. Not this year. Would that be so bad? It's so far north that the days will be short and the nights long and dark, and I probably won't be a very lively companion. But, by spring, perhaps, I shall be stronger. Time will have passed. Here, as you so clearly stated, I have no future. Giles and Crawford want the house, so I shall let them have it. With all convenient speed."

"And my house, Oscar? What should I do with my little cottage?"

"Let it. Or shut it up. It will be safe. Your neighbours, I am sure, will keep an eye on it."

He meant it. He was asking her to go away with him. He wanted her company. Needed her. She, Elfrida. Eccentric, disorganized, not beautiful any longer; even a little raffish. And sixty-two years old.

"Oscar, I'm not sure that I'm that good a bet."

"You underestimate yourself. Please come, Elfrida. Help me."

How can I help? she had asked Hector as they waited for Oscar to return from the glasshouse. And now it was he who answered the question.

She had been impulsive all her life, made decisions without thought for the future, and regretted none of them, however dotty. Looking back, all she regretted were the opportunities missed, either because they had come along at the wrong time or because she had been too timid to grasp them.

She took a deep breath. "All right. I'll come."

"Dear girl."

"I'll come for *you,* Oscar, but I owe it to Gloria as well. I shall never forget her kindness and generosity to a stranger. You and Gloria and Francesca were my first friends when I came to Dibton. . . ."

". . . Go on."

"I feel ashamed. We've been talking, and this is the first time I've said their names to you. In Cornwall I spoke about you so much. Telling Jeffrey about you all, telling him how good you'd been to me. I went shopping and bought Francesca a book, and I very nearly bought a picture for you and Gloria, but then I thought that Gloria wouldn't really like it."

"Would I have liked it?"

"I don't know." A lump had swelled in her throat, and it became difficult to talk. She was crying and could feel her mouth trembling, but the tears, strangely, were something of a relief, warm and wet, rolling down her cheeks. Old people, she told herself, look dreadful when they cry. She tried to wipe the tears away with her fingers. "I . . . I've only been to Scotland once. To Glasgow, ages ago, with a touring company. We had pathetic audiences and it never stopped raining . . ." Fumbling up her sleeve for a handkerchief, she found one and blew her nose. ". . . and I couldn't understand a single word anyone said to me."

"There's a Glaswegian for you."

"It wasn't funny at the time."

"It's not funny now, but as always you've made me smile."

"Like a sort of clown?"

"No. Not a clown. Just a dear, funny friend."

SAM

At seven o'clock on the first dark Friday morning of December, Sam Howard wheeled his trolley of luggage out into the Arrivals hall of Heathrow Airport. Beyond the barrier crowded the usual confusion of people come to meet the plane. Elderly couples, youths in trainers, and tired mothers humping toddlers. As well, uniformed drivers for the VIPs—of which Sam was not one—and unidentified men holding up mysterious notices, labelled in capitals. MR. WILSON was one; and ABDUL AZIZ CONSOLIDATED TRADERS another.

There was nobody to meet Sam. No wife, no driver. No welcome, however tame. He knew that outside the heated terminal building it would be very cold, partly because they had been warned of the temperature in London before the plane landed, but also because everybody was bundled up in padded jackets, gloves, and scarves and woollen hats. It had been cold in New York, but a dry crisp cold that stimulated, with a bitter wind blowing up the East River, and all the flags at mast-heads flying stiff and square in the teeth of its blast.

His trolley was awkward, laden with two suitcases, a huge American golf bag, and his brief-case. He manoeuvred it towards the automatic exit doors and out into the wet black cold of an English winter morning. There, he joined the queue for taxis. He had only to wait five minutes or so, but even that was long enough to freeze the soles of his feet. The taxi was covered, for some reason, in simulated newsprint, and the driver a morose man with a walrus moustache. Sam hoped that he was not a talker. He was not in the mood for conversation.

"Where to, guv?"

"Wandsworth, please. SW17. Fourteen Beauly Road."

" 'Op in."

The driver did not stir himself to help with luggage, apparently having decided that Sam was young and fit enough to deal with it himself. Accordingly, he humped it aboard, stowed the golf clubs on the floor, shoved the empty trolley out of the line of trouble, and climbed in, slamming the door shut behind him. The taxi, windscreen wipers going full-tilt, trundled forward.

The short wait had chilled him. Sam turned up the collar of his navy-blue overcoat and leaned back against the fusty plastic of his seat. He yawned. He felt tired and unclean. He had travelled Club Class, with a number of other business men, but before landing, they had made discreet trips to the lavatory, to wash, shave, knot ties, and generally freshen themselves up. Probably, poor sods, they had early meetings. He did not have an early meeting and was grateful for this. His first appointment was for Monday at twelve-thirty, when he had to present himself at Whites for lunch with Sir David Swinfield, Chairman of Sturrock and Swinfield, and Sam's ultimate boss. Until then, his time was his own.

He yawned again, and ran a hand over the raspy stubble of his chin. Perhaps he *should* have shaved. He would have felt a little less like a vagrant. It occurred to him that he probably looked like one, too, dressed as he was in elderly and casual clothes: a thick pullover, a pair of worn jeans, boat shoes. His eyes were dry and gritty from lack of sleep, but that was because he had spent the short night reading his book. And his stomach was slightly queasy, but that was doubtless the result of eating a huge dinner at two o'clock in the morning UK time.

The taxi drew up at a red traffic light. Suddenly the driver spoke, flinging the question back over his shoulder.

"Been on 'oliday?"

"No," Sam told him.

"Fort . . . you know . . . the golf clubs."

"No, I haven't been on holiday."

"On business, then?"

"You could say. I've worked in New York for six years."

"Blimey. 'Ow do you stand the pace?"

"It's okay. Good. You get used to it."

Rain streamed down. "Not much of a mornin' for comin' 'ome." Green light. They moved forward again.

"No," Sam agreed. He did not add, *And I'm not coming home.* Because right now, he did not have a home. Which seemed to figure with the vagrant image. For the first time in his life, and he was now thirty-eight, he found himself without bricks and mortar to call his own.

Bundled gloomily in his overcoat, cocooned in the back of the taxi, he thought of homes, remembering to the very beginning. Yorkshire and Radley Hill, where, an only child, he had been born and brought up. A large, solid, and comforting family home, filled with the smell of wood-smoke and spring flowers and cakes baking. The house was surrounded by four acres of land, and it had a tennis court and a little wood, where on autumn evenings he would stand with his gun, waiting for the pigeons to fly in from the stubble fields. To Radley Hill he had returned from day-school, and then boarding-school, usually with a friend in tow, come to spend the holidays. It was a place comfortable as an old tweed jacket, which he had thought would never change, but of course it did. Because, during his last year at Newcastle University, his mother died, and after that nothing was ever quite the same again.

The family business was a small woollen mill, in a small Yorkshire town. After Newcastle, Sam had intended to spread his wings, perhaps get a job abroad, but with his mother gone, he hadn't the heart to abandon his father, and, with a degree in engineering under his belt, he went home to Yorkshire, to Radley Hill, and the mill. For a few years, father and son boxed along happily together, and business boomed. But then, recession hit, and the mill, which specialized in fine worsteds and lightweight tweeds, came up against sophisticated competition from Europe, an influx of imports, and a cash flow problem. At the end of the day, Sturrock and Swinfield, the huge textile conglomerate, based in London, moved in. The little mill was taken over. Sam was given a job under the new umbrella, but his father, too old a dog to learn new tricks, took early retirement. But digging his garden and playing the odd game of golf was not enough to fend off the stress of loneliness, boredom, and enforced inactivity, and he died twelve months later of a massive heart attack.

Radley Hill was left to Sam. After some heart-searching, he put it on the market. It seemed the only sensible thing to do, for he was now London-based, still working for Sturrock and Swinfield, and wise to all the ups and downs of fluctuating markets and the business of woollen brokering. With the money he got for Radley Hill, he was able to buy his first property, a garden flat in Eel Park Common, so close to the tube station that at night he could hear the rattling of the trains. But it had a scrap of garden that caught the evening sun, and once he had furnished it with some of the smaller stuff from the old house in Yorkshire, it felt familiar and homely. He had been happy there, living a carefree bachelor life, and in memory it was always sunlit and filled with friends. Countless impromptu parties, when the rooms overflowed and guests ended up sitting on the tiny terrace. Crowded winter weekends, when old colleagues from the North came down for rugger matches at Twickenham. And, of course, a number of poignant love affairs.

He was in the throes of one of these when, out of the blue, came a summons from Sir David Swinfield. There, in the prestigious high-rise office, far above the maze of the City of London, Sam was told that he was being transferred to the United States, to New York. The head of the New York office, Mike Passano, had particularly asked for him. It was promotion, responsibility, a rise in salary.

"No reason not to go, Sam?"

New York. He said, "No, sir," which was true. No family ties, no wife, no children. Nothing that could not be abandoned. "No reason." It was the opportunity that he had subconsciously yearned for ever since University. A new job, a new city, a new country. A new life.

He took the current love affair out to dinner and tried to explain, and she cried a bit and said that if he wanted, she'd come to New York with him. But he knew that wasn't what he wanted. Feeling a heel, he told her this, and she cried some more, and when it was time to go he found a taxi for her and watched her drive away. He never saw her again.

He was equally ruthless about material possessions. A chunk of his life was over, and he had no idea when, if ever, he would return to London. Accordingly, he sold his car and his flat, putting only a few favorite pieces of furniture, pictures, and books into store. At the office, he cleared his desk. Someone threw a leaving party, and he was able to say goodbye to all his friends.

"Don't stay too long," they told him. "Come back soon."

But New York waited, and once arrived, he was seduced by all he found. He took to the place like a duck to water, relishing every aspect of the stimulating, cosmopolitan melting pot that made up the city. Home, there, was a walk-up in Greenwich Village, but after he married Deborah, she persuaded him to move and they ended up in a fancy duplex on East Seventieth Street. He had always enjoyed the challenge of a new home, new surroundings. Doing a bit of painting, shunting furniture around, and hanging pictures. But Deborah didn't much want any of the old Greenwich Village stuff in her beautiful new apartment, and anyway, she had engaged the services of an interior designer, who would *die* if that sagging old leather sofa were integrated into his string-coloured décor. There were a few spats, but not too many because Sam usually gave in, and he was quite happy to have the old leather sofa in his den, where he kept his computer and his fax machine. It felt friendly there, and sometimes, on weekends, when Deborah thought he was working overtime, he could lie on the leather sofa and watch football on television.

Homes. East Seventieth Street had been the last, and that, too, had gone. Along with Deborah.

She had never been a moral coward. She told him, face-to-face, that she was leaving. She was tired of playing second fiddle to Sturrock and Swinfield, and tired of being married to a workaholic. There was, of course, another man, and when she told Sam his name, he was both appalled and filled with anxiety for her future. He said as much, but Deborah was adamant. It was too late. Her mind was made up. He could not persuade her.

He was furious, but he was hurt, too, bewildered and abased. He thought of that old-fashioned word, *cuckold. I am a cuckold. I have been cuckolded.*

And yet, in a way, he understood.

The morning after her departure, he walked into the office and was met with covert glances and sympathetic faces. Some colleagues were over-hearty, slapping him chummily on the shoulder, letting him know they were his buddies. There if he needed them.

Others, who had never particularly liked Sam, the Limey, showed signs of snide amusement, resembling cats that had got at the cream. He realized then that probably they had all had a fair idea of what was going on, and Sam, the leading actor in the drama, had been the very last to know.

During the course of the day, Mike Passano appeared, breezing through the open door, and coming to perch on the edge of Sam's desk. For a bit they talked day-to-day business, and then Mike said, "I'm sorry. About Debbie, I mean. Just wanted to let you know."

"Thanks."

"It's no comfort, but at least you haven't got kids to complicate matters."

"Yeah."

"If you want to come over for dinner one evening . . ."

"I'm okay, Mike."

"Right. Well. You can always take a rain-check."

He soldiered on for six weeks. At the office he found every excuse to stay at his desk long after others had left, returning late to an empty apartment and no food. Sometimes he stopped off at a bar and had a sandwich and a Scotch. Or two Scotches. For the first time in his life he suffered from insomnia, and during the day found himself pervaded by an unfamiliar restlessness, as though not only his marriage but everything else had gone stale.

Mike Passano said, "Take a vacation," but that was the last thing Sam wanted. Instead, it slowly became clear to him that he had had enough of New York. He wanted England. He wanted to go home. He wanted misty skies and temperate green fields and warm beer and red buses.

And then one evening, at the nadir of his despair, the telephone rang in the apartment, and it was Sir David Swinfield from London.

"Is this a good time to talk, Sam?"

"As good as any."

"Hear things aren't running too smoothly for you."

"Bad news travels fast."

"Mike Passano told me. Had a word this morning. I'm sorry."

"Thank you."

"Do you feel like a change?"

Sam was cautious. "What did you have in mind?"

"New idea. New project. Right up your street. Might be interesting."

"Where?"

"UK."

"You mean, leave New York?"

"You've had six years. I'll square it with Mike."

"Who'd take over?"

"Lowell Oldberg?"

"He's inexperienced."

"So were you."

He had to get it right. "Is this a demotion?" Sam asked bluntly.

"No. Just a shunt. Upwards and onwards." A pause. "I want you back, Sam. I need you. I think it's time."

The house in Beauly Road was a semi-detached three-storey Victorian villa, set back from the pavement by a front garden which had been turned into a paved carport. The rest of the quiet residential road was lined on both sides with cars, an indication of the affluence of the district. There were as well trees, bare now, but which in summer and in full leaf would give a country illusion, suggesting a pleasant suburb far from the city of London.

On that black morning, it was still dark. As Sam, surrounded by his baggage, paid off the taxi, the front door of the house opened, letting forth a stream of light, and a masculine, burly figure appeared. "Sam." Semi-prepared for his day in the City, Neil Philip wore the trousers of a business suit and an enveloping navy-blue polo-neck sweater. He came down the path and through the gate. "God, it's good to see you."

And Sam felt himself swept up into a huge and masculine embrace, because Neil had never been a man to be shy about showing emotion. It was a bit like being hugged by a bear. The taxi driver, still expressionless, trundled away, and Neil stooped, scooped up the two enormously heavy suitcases, and charged back towards the open door, leaving Sam to hump the golf clubs and his brief-case.

"Janey's just getting the kids organized, she'll be down in a moment. Did you have a good flight? Bloody exhausted, probably." He dumped the suitcases at the foot of the stair. "The kettle's on; would you like a cup of coffee?"

"Love one."

"Come on, then."

Sam shed himself of his overcoat and draped it over the banister. From upstairs he heard a child's voice complaining about something. A pair of small gumboots and a toy lorry sat side by side on one of the stairs. He followed Neil down the passage into a spacious family kitchen, with a skylight and windows over the sink. The curtains of these were still closed, but overhead he could see the dark clouds, stained with reflected light. There were pine cupboards and a humming fridge, and the table was set for breakfast. A checked table-cloth, packets of cereal, a milk jug, egg cups.

Neil spooned coffee into a jug and poured on boiling water. The delicious, fresh aroma filled the room.

"Do you want something to eat?"

"No, just coffee."

Sam pulled out a chair and took the weight off his feet. He could not imagine why he felt so weary, considering the fact that he had been sitting down for at least seven hours. "You're looking terrific, Neil."

"Oh, not so bad. Surviving family life." He found bread and put two slices into an electric toaster. "You've never seen this house, have you? We bought it a couple of years after you went to New York. Upgrading, Janey called it. And we needed a garden for the children."

"Remind me."

"Sorry?"

"Ages. Daisy and Leo. One loses track."

"Daisy's ten, Leo six. They're wildly excited about you staying. Been talking about it ever since your phone call. How long can you stay?"

"It's not a holiday, Neil. Business. I've been summoned by the Chairman. Some new project."

"Goodbye to New York?"

"For the time being."

"Sam, I'm so sorry about Deborah, and everything."

"We'll talk about it, but not now. There's too much to say."

"Let's weave our way down to the pub this evening, and you can spill it all out over a pint. But remember, you're welcome here for as long as you like."

"You're more than kind."

"It's my nature, old boy, it's my nature."

The toast popped and Neil removed it from the toaster and put another couple of slices in. Sam watched him, the neat and precise movements of a large and apparently ungainly man. Neil still had a head of thick dark hair, but there showed a sprinkling of grey. He had put on weight as well, as athletic men tend to do, but otherwise nothing else much seemed to have changed.

Neil Philip was part of Sam's life. They had been friends ever since they met, on their first day at boarding-school, two apprehensive new boys feeling their way into the system. Neil was one of the regular visitors invited to Radley Hill for the holidays, and Sam's mother had ended up calling him her second son. When Sam went to Newcastle, Neil went to Edinburgh University, where he played Rugby like a fanatic and spent one brilliant season as fly-half for Scotland. After University, meeting up again in London, in the Eel Park Common days, it was just as though there had simply been a pause in the conversation. When Neil married Janey, at Saint Paul's, Knightsbridge, Sam had been their best man. And when Sam married Deborah, in the garden of her grandparents' house in East Hampton, Neil and Janey had flown out to be with him, so that Neil could be best man to Sam. Sam was deeply grateful, because otherwise the bridegroom would have been sadly short of family or friends.

Neil poured coffee and put eggs on to boil. From upstairs, voices grew louder, and then there were scurrying feet on the stairs, and the two children erupted into the kitchen, Daisy dressed in her school uniform, and Leo wearing jeans and a pullover. They stood staring at the stranger.

Sam said, "Hi."

They stared, silent, all at once overcome.

"Say hi back," Neil told them.

Leo said, "I fort you'd be wearing a cowboy hat."

"They don't wear cowboy hats in New York, silly," his sister squashed him.

"Well, what do they wear?"

"They probably don't wear anything."

"Who doesn't wear anything?" Janey came through the door,

dressed much as her little son, and her arms were held wide, all ready for her welcome. "Oh, Sam, it's been too long. It's so heavenly to see you." He stood, and she hugged and kissed him. "God, you haven't shaved, you brute."

"I was too idle."

"It's been such ages since we saw you. I do hope you can stay forever. Daisy, you're never going to eat all those Cocoa Puffs, put some of them into Leo's bowl."

The house was quiet, its owners all gone. Neil to his daily grind, Janey to take the children to school. Sam had been shown his bedroom and his bathroom. He had a relaxing bath and shaved, and then, bundled into the towel robe he had found on the back of the bathroom door, fell into bed. It was light now. Through the window he could see the lacy branches of a plane tree. Cars passed, swishing down the road. Far overhead, a jet moved across the sky. He slept.

It rained for most of that weekend, but Monday morning was dry, with even a few clear patches of sky blinking in and out beyond the sailing clouds. After watching a soggy football match on Saturday, organizing a long wet walk in Richmond Park on Sunday, and playing a Monopoly marathon after tea-time, Neil inspected the clear morning, said, with faint bitterness, "Sod's law," and left for work.

The children were next to go, picked up by a neighbour and taken to school. A wonderfully black Jamaican lady appeared to push the vacuum cleaner around the house, and Janey went off to shop.

"Do you want a key?" she asked Sam. "I'll be in after four o'clock."

"In that case, I don't need a key."

"When will you be *back*?"

"No idea."

"Well." She smiled up into his face, gave him a quick kiss. "Good luck."

Sam was not far behind her, suitably attired for the important occasion, buttoned into his overcoat and armed with an umbrella of Neil's, in case of unexpected downpours. He closed the front door on the strains of the Jamaican lady singing hymns as she scoured the bath. At twenty-five past twelve, he walked up Saint James's Street, presented himself to the porter at Whites, and asked for Sir David Swinfield. Sir David was in the bar, he was told, and expecting a guest.

It was three-thirty before they emerged from the club, descending the steps to the pavement where Sir David's car and driver waited. Sir David offered a lift, which Sam politely refused. They parted, and he stood and watched as the great black saloon slid out into the stream of traffic and disappeared in the direction of Piccadilly.

Sam turned and set out to walk, at least part of the way, back to Wandsworth. He went by way of Green Park, and Belgrave Square, Sloane Street, and the King's Road. By now, the day had died and the street lights had come on. Shop windows shone and glittered with all the paraphernalia of Christmas decoration and seductive consumerism. He found himself astonished by this. He had been so turned in upon himself that he had forgotten about Christmas. The months, lagging in some respects, had shot past in others. Christmas. He had no idea where he would be for the holiday, and could think of no person who would be expecting a present from him, which was a bleak truth and brought no credit upon himself. However, the thought of presents galvanized him into action, and he went into a flower shop and bought a huge bouquet of white lilies for Janey; a little farther on, he paused at a wine shop and purchased there brandy and a bottle of champagne for Neil. Burdened, he thought about the children, Daisy and Leo. They should have presents, too, but he couldn't think what on earth they would like. He would have to ask them. Having already spent two days in their company, he was pretty sure they would know.

By World's End, he had expended his energy and it had started to rain again. It was now nearly five o'clock and the traffic at its most dense, crawling along at the pace of a snail, but after five minutes or so he picked up a cab and gave the driver the address. It took an incredibly long time to get across the Wandsworth Bridge, and when they finally trundled up the length of Beauly Road, he saw the lights shining from behind the drawn curtains of number fourteen and felt welcomed, as though he were coming home.

When he rang the bell, Janey came to let him in.

"There you are. I thought you'd got lost."

She wore her jeans and a red pullover and her dark hair was bundled up and fixed with a tortoiseshell clip.

"I've been taking exercise."

Janey closed the door. "One would have thought a wet Sunday in Richmond Park might have lasted the week. How did you get on? Lunch with the Chairman, I mean."

"It was all right. I'll tell you but not at this moment." He handed her the lilies. "These are for you. A house present for a kind hostess."

"Thank you. You didn't have to bring me flowers, but I'm glad you did. And lilies. They make the whole house smell like heaven. Come into the kitchen and I'll make you a cup of tea."

Pausing to take off his coat and hang it up on a peg along with a lot of small overcoats and anoraks, he followed her, hefting the carrier-bag with the bottles. He put the brandy into Neil's wine cupboard and the champagne in the fridge.

"Champagne." Janey was filling the kettle, plugging it in. "Does that mean a celebration?"

"Maybe." He pulled out a chair and sat with his elbows on the table. "Where are Daisy and Leo?"

"Upstairs, watching television or playing computer games. They're allowed to, once they've done their homework."

"Delicious smells in this kitchen."

"It's dinner. I have gloomy news. We have another guest."

"What's so gloomy about another guest?"

"This one's a pain."

"Why ask him?"

"I didn't. He asked himself. He's an old acquaintance of my parents, and he's in London on his own and he's at a loose end. He telephoned and sounded pathetic, so I felt I had to invite him. I'm really sorry, because I wanted it to be just us three. I've already told Neil. I rang him at the office, and he's livid, but he's going to try to get home a bit early, to do the drinks and lay the table and light the fire."

"I could do all that for you."

"You're the guest. You have to go and have a shower and a rest and make yourself beautiful."

"I suppose, to impress your unwanted friend." Janey made a face. "Come on, what's so gruesome about him?"

She had found a large flowered ewer, filled it with water, and was now engaged in arranging her lilies.

"He's not *really* gruesome. Just a bit boring. Likes to be thought of as an old roué. When he's around, one instinctively whisks one's behind out of reach of his fingers."

Sam laughed. "One of those."

"You could say so. He's been married three times, but he's on his own right now."

"Where does he come from?"

"I think he was at school with my pa. But now he lives in the Bahamas or Barbados or somewhere. He's been out there for ages."

"What's he doing in London?"

"Not sure. En route for France, I think. He's going to spend Christmas in Nice."

"He sounds interesting."

"He isn't. There. Those look lovely. Thank you again. I'll put them, pride of place, in the sitting-room." The kettle boiled and she reached for the teapot. "I'm longing to hear about today, but I can't concentrate when I'm cooking, and I've still got to make a pudding."

"It can wait."

"It was all right, Sam? It was good?"

"Yes. *I* think so."

"Too exciting. I am pleased."

He drank his tea, and then, shooed out of her kitchen by Janey, went upstairs. He found Daisy and Leo in their playroom. They had switched off the television and were sitting at a battered table littered with sheets of paper, which they seemed to be in the process of cutting up. As well as scissors, they had assembled tubes of glue, felt pens, a ball of coloured string, and a few scraps of gauzy ribbon. Some form of handcraft was clearly taking place.

They looked up. "Hello, Sam."

"Hi. What are you up to?"

"We're making Christmas cards," Daisy told him importantly. "My art teacher showed us today, and I'm teaching Leo. You paint glue, and then spill glitter and it sticks. But we've got to draw something first."

"Like what?"

"Well, a Christmas tree. Or a stocking. Or a house with lighted windows. The only thing is it's a bit messy, and the glitter gets everywhere. Leo calls it tinkle. Now, Leo, you fold the paper like this, very neatly. . . . It mustn't be all skew-wiff. . . ."

It was made obvious that they were in no need of his help. He left them and went to his room, stripped off his clothes, and took a shower.

Have a shower and a rest and make yourself beautiful. He had brought *The Times* upstairs with him, and after his shower he put on the towelling robe and collapsed on his bed, intending to read it. But concentration drifted, and he let the paper slip to the floor and simply lay, staring at the ceiling. Sounds emanated from beyond the closed door. The children's voices; a telephone ringing; Janey's footsteps as she went to answer it. "Hello," he heard her say. He caught the mouth-watering smell of dinner being prepared, and later heard taps turned on for the children's bath.

It was a long time since he had been embraced into the bosom of a proper family, and felt so cherished and wanted. Investigating this line of thought, he realized that Deborah's withdrawal had started months before her announcement that she was leaving, but Sam had been too preoccupied to notice the gradual erosion of their relationship. The breakup of a marriage, he knew, could never be one partner's fault. The other half, one way or another, had to shoulder some part of the blame.

He found himself remembering Radley Hill, because the atmosphere of this ordinary London house, where Neil and Janey were raising their children, brought back secure and comforting memories of the place where Sam had spent his boyhood. Always the welcome, the lighted fire, the scent from the kitchen of delicious and robust food. Boots on the porch, tennis rackets littering the hall, the voices of the youngsters who were his friends, the sound of their footsteps clattering down the stairs. He wondered if he would ever achieve such a haven of family life. Up to now, in that respect, his efforts had met with failure. He and Deborah could have had children, but she had never been particularly keen on the idea, and he was reluctant to force the issue. Which, the way things had turned out, was just as well. But the house on East Seventieth Street, with just the two of them, had never been more than simply a place to live. True, the living-room had been the envy of all their friends, so immaculately decorated in cream and beige, with modern sculptures and cunningly lighted abstracts on the walls. And the kitchen was a marvel of modern convenience, but nothing much had ever emerged from it except a slice of melon or a microwaved pizza. Deborah, partying, preferred to entertain in restaurants.

Radley Hill. Looking back across the frantic, pressurized years of urban life—the wheeling and dealing, the late nights, the long days, the smells of subways and car fumes—he remembered Yorkshire, saw the solid stone unpretentious house, the terrace, the lawns, his mother's rose borders. He thought of the little town where stood his father's mill, where the wind swept aslant the smoke of chimneys, and the river, flowing down from the hills, slipped along between the tree-shaded streets and under curved bridges. The sound of water running over rocks was so familiar, so part of his life that one simply stopped hearing it. He thought of the surrounding countryside, and long Sunday hikes with his father; of fishing in the remote dark tarns that lay cupped in the moors, where the air was cold and clean, and the empty spaces were pierced with the cry of curlews. . . .

Outside, in the street, a car drew up beneath his window. The front door was opened and slammed shut. He heard Janey's voice. "Neil? Hi, darling." And he knew that his friend was home.

He heaved himself off the bed, shucked off the towel robe, and proceeded to dress himself in a suitable fashion for the evening which lay ahead. Pressed chinos, a clean shirt, a navy-blue cashmere sweater, no tie. Cream socks, polished loafers. He brushed his hair, splashed on a bit of aftershave, went downstairs. The sitting-room door stood open, and he went in and found Neil, in shirt-sleeves, engaged in polishing up some glasses to set out on the drinks table. The room looked festive, prepared for entertaining. Magazines and books squared off, cushions fattened, the fire lighted. The lilies Sam had given Janey stood in their jug on a round, polished table, surrounded by an arrangement of Battersea boxes. Their scent, in the warmth, already filled the air. The clock in the middle of the mantelpiece stood at a quarter past seven.

He said, "Hi."

Neil turned from his task. "There you are. Did you have a good kip?"

"I should have been beavering away, helping you."

"Not at all. Sneaked home early to perform my hostly tasks."

"I gather we have company for dinner."

Neil pulled a face. "Stupid old bugger. Janey should have put him off, but she's got too kind a heart." He gave a final swipe at the last glass, set it neatly down, and tossed the tea-towel aside. "There, that's it. All done and dusted. Let's have a drink, and sit down for a peaceful moment. I want to hear all about everything before our guest arrives and we have to start listening to him. Scotch? Soda or water? Or on the rocks? You see, I have all the right phraseology, in case you've forgotten how to speak the language."

"Soda sounds good. Where's Janey?"

"Whipping cream."

"And the kids?"

"In bed, I hope. Reading books. If not, there'll be trouble." He poured their drinks, added ice, and brought the tumbler over to Sam. Then, with a relieved sigh, he thumped himself down into one of the comfortable chairs that stood at either side of the fire. "So, tell me, how did the lunch go?"

Sam sat himself down in the opposite chair. "All right, I suppose."

"Nothing gruesome? No kindly suggestion of redundancy?"

Sam laughed. It was a good feeling to have someone come straight to the point, to be with a man he had known for most of his life, and from whom he had never had a single secret.

"The very opposite."

"Really? A new job, then?"

"Yeah."

"In the States?"

"No. Here. UK."

"Whereabouts?"

Sam did not answer at once. He took a slug of his drink, cold and crisp and smoky on his tongue, and then set down the glass on the low table alongside. "Ever heard of McTaggarts of Buckly?"

"What—the tweedy people in Sutherland?"

"Yeah, that's right."

"Well, of course. Any country gentleman worth his salt wears a shooting suit made of Buckly tweed. My father had one, or should I say *has*. Built like a bloody suit of armour." He chuckled at the thought. "Don't tell me they're in trouble."

"Have been. But Sturrock and Swinfield bought them out a few months ago. I'm surprised you didn't pick it up, but perhaps you don't read *The Financial Times*."

"Every day, but I missed that one. Textiles don't come into my line of business. Extraordinary, McTaggarts going down the drain." He twisted his mouth into a rueful smile. "Mind you, probably the eternal-light-bulb scenario. Can't expect to make money on a product that lasts forever."

"That, of course, was one of their problems. And they never diversified. I suppose, an old-fashioned set-up, and saw no need. But even for the classic tweeds, the market has shrunk. Great estates sold up, and shooting-lodges standing empty. No longer a call for tweeds for the gamekeepers and the foresters. But they've had other setbacks as well. Old McTaggart died a couple of years ago, and his two sons weren't interested in the business. One was already into computers and the other running a huge garage on the outskirts of Glasgow. They had no desire to return. I suppose life in the Far North had lost its appeal."

"How extraordinary." Neil let out a sigh. "Oh, well, I suppose everyone has different aspirations. So what happened then?"

"Well, first the sons did a bit of asset-stripping, selling off all the mill houses; then they put the whole place on the market. When there wasn't much interest forthcoming, the work-force approached the local Enterprise Company and together they undertook a management buy-out of the business. Problem is, there's not a bottomless source of employment in that area, as you can well imagine. Anyway, they're all skilled workers, they've been in the trade father and son—weavers, spinners, dyers—you name it." Sam drained the last drops from his glass. "So, they were ticking along all right, getting a few new orders, exports to the States, that sort of thing—then, bang, disaster struck. It rained non-stop for two months; the river broke its banks and flooded the mill to the height of a man's head. They lost everything—their stock, their computers, most of the machinery. And that was it. The banks foreclosed, the LEC got their fingers burnt, and the work-force faced up to a future without employment."

Neil got to his feet and came over to Sam and took his glass. "God, that was really hard luck."

"I know. So, in desperation, they approached Sturrock and Swinfield. David Swinfield carried out a fairly extensive feasibility study on the place, and it was duly rescued. The mill's still in a hell of a mess, though. It hasn't been in operation since the flood, and all but three of the workers are laid off."

Neil handed him his replenished glass. "So, what's your part?"

"I'm to go and get it back on its feet again. Run the place."

"Just like that? Straightaway?"

"Not quite. Even before the flood, the mill was pretty run-down. Most of the machinery was probably put in at the time of the Ark. So it'll be a year before it's all up and going again."

"I'm surprised that Swinfield's feasibility study showed that there was any financial viability at all in the place. I mean, do you think it's still possible to make something of an industry in such a remote location? To be quite honest, I wonder if it's really worth the hassle."

"Oh, I think so. Of course, we'll have to diversify, but remember, the name of McTaggarts has terrific good will throughout the world. It's worth a hell of a lot if we're to look closer at the luxury markets."

"What? Not the end of the good old heavyweight thornproofs for 'countrywear,' surely? That would be tragic. You'll have to keep making those."

"Of course we will—and tartans too. Those are McTaggarts' stock-in-trade. Tradition. But they'll form only a part of our production. We'll be concentrating more on lighter, more colourful textiles. Jacketing fabrics for the Italian market, for instance. Shawls, scarves, throws, sweaters. You know, the fashion industry. Both expensive and expendable."

"Cashmere?"

"Of course."

"So, forays into darkest China are on the cards?"

"David Swinfield already has agents in Manchuria."

"And what about machinery?"

"Probably source it in Switzerland."

"Which will mean a total retraining programme for the work-force."

"Yeah, but it'll be carried out on-site by the supplier's commissioning team. What unfortunately it will mean is a reduced work-force."

Neil was silent, assessing all this. Then he sighed and shook his head, looking a little bemused. "It sounds exciting, but it's hard to see you settling down to life in a peat bog. After London and then New

York. It sounds on a par with being posted as British Vice-Consul to the Andaman Islands. Hardly a leg up."

"It's what I know about and what I can do."

"Salary?"

"Upped."

"Bribery."

Sam smiled. "Not at all. Simply a bonus."

"And what will you do with yourself? Your leisure time? When you're not working flat out on the mill floor, or trying to get books to balance. I hardly think Buckly is going to be a hive of local gaiety. You may well be forced to take up bingo."

"I shall fish. Remember fishing with my father? And I shall play golf. There are at least five wonderful links in the neighbourhood. I shall join clubs and make friends with old gentlemen in soup-stained pullovers."

"More likely to be all kitted up by Nick Faldo."

"Whatever."

"So you don't feel all this is a bit of a regression?"

"I'm going back to my roots, if that's regressing. And oddly enough, I relish the prospect of being a trouble-shooter. As well, I know about running a small mill. I learned it all from my father. And he truly loved the business. He loved his machines the way other men loved their cars. And he used to touch great bales of tweed as though he were caressing them, for the pleasure of feeling the woven wool beneath his fingers. Perhaps I'm the same. I only know I've had enough of marketing. I can't wait to get back to the factory floor, back to the start of it all. Right now, I feel it's exactly what I need."

Neil eyed him across the hearth. He said, "Don't be offended, but I am not sure whether your chairman isn't being paternalistic."

"You mean because my personal life has fallen apart."

"Frankly, yes."

"Don't worry. I asked him the same question over the Stilton. But I'd been earmarked for the Buckly Mill job long before he heard about Deborah."

"Of course. Silly question, really. Sir David Swinfield didn't get where he is by having a soft heart. When do you go?"

"Soon as possible. But there's a lot of planning and thrashing-out to be done before I take off. A meeting's set up for tomorrow morning with the financial chaps. A time schedule of reinvestment. That sort of thing."

"Where are you going to live once you get there? I thought you said that the McTaggart sons had sold off all the houses."

"Yeah, you're right. But that's just a small matter. I'll probably stay in a pub or rent a house. Never know, I might even shack up with a raven-haired lassie with a turf-roofed cottage."

Neil laughed. "And hoots, mon, to you!" He glanced at the clock, shifted his considerable weight in the chair, and yawned enormously, running his fingers through his hair. "Well, all I can say is best of luck, old boy."

"It just needs a good kick-start to get it going again."

Neil grinned. "In that case, you'd better buy yourself a good pair of football boots, because you're going to need them. . . ."

He got no further for, at that moment, the doorbell rang.

Neil said, "Oh, hell," set down his glass and got to his feet. "That'll be the old bore now." But before he got any farther, they heard the kitchen door open and Janey's swift footsteps pass down the hall. Then, her voice. "Hello. How are you? How lovely to see you." And she sounded nothing but delighted, and Sam thought, not for the first time, what a wonderfully kind girl she was. "Come along in." Murmurs of a male voice. "Oh, chocolates. How kind. I'll have to keep them out of the way of the children. Did you walk from the tube, or were you able to get a taxi? Give me your coat, and I'll hang it up. Neil's in here. . . ."

The door opened. Both men by now were standing, and Neil went forward to greet his guest, who was being ushered into the room by his hostess.

"Hello, there . . ."

"Neil. My word! Good to see you. It's been too long. This is enormously kind of you."

"Not at all . . ."

Janey said, "And look what he's brought me." She had changed for the evening into black velvet trousers and a white satin shirt, but over these still wore her red-and-white-striped cook's apron. She held up a modest box of After Eight mints. "Divine chocolates."

"Just a token. Trying to remember how many years it is since I've seen you both. When was it? A lunch with your parents, Janey. Too long ago. . . ."

Standing with his back to the mantelpiece, Sam eyed the newcomer. He saw a man well into his sixties, but with the bearing and mannerisms of a young blade from forty years ago. He had probably once been attractive, in a David Niven-ish sort of way; but now his features were blurred, his cheeks veined, and his trim moustache, like his fingers, stained with a lifetime of tobacco. His hair was white, thinning, but worn long on his collar, his eyes gleaming and very pale blue, and his face and hands deeply tanned, and smudged with age-spots. He wore grey flannel trousers, brown suede shoes, a navy blazer, brass-buttoned, and a blue-and-white-striped shirt. From the high, stiff collar streamed a silk tie of great flamboyance, striped in startling shades of red, yellow, and peacock green. His wrist-watch was gold and there were gold links in the cuffs of his shirt. He had clearly made much effort with his appearance, and smelled strongly of Eau Sauvage.

". . . yes, ages," said Janey. "It must be seven years. When they were still living in Wiltshire. Now, I must introduce you. This is Sam Howard, who's staying with us for a few days. And Sam, this is Hughie McLennan."

"How do you do?"

"Good to meet you." They shook hands.

"Sam and Neil have been friends forever . . . since they were at school."

"No friend like an old friend. God, the traffic in London is ghastly.

Never seen anything so chock-a-block. Took me fifteen minutes to get a taxi."

"Where are you staying?" Neil asked.

"Oh, my club, of course, but not what it was. Primed the porter, but might just as well have saved myself a gold sovereign. And the trouble."

"Let me get you a drink, Hughie."

Hughie visibly brightened. "Good suggestion." He glanced at the table upon which stood the bottles and glasses. "Gin and tonic, if I may." He patted pockets. "You don't mind if I smoke, do you, Janey?"

"No. No, of course I don't. There's an ashtray somewhere." She searched, found one on her desk, emptied it of paper-clips, and set it down on the table by the sofa.

"Hell, these days, nobody smokes. New York is a nightmare. Light up, and a guy comes and shoots you dead." He had taken from his blazer pocket a silver case and extracted a cigarette, which he now ignited with a gold lighter. He blew out a cloud of smoke, immediately looked much more relaxed, and put out a hand to take his glass from Neil.

"Bless you, dear boy. Happy days."

"Do you want a drink, Janey?"

"I've got my cook's drink in the kitchen. A glass of wine. Talking of which, Neil, could you come and open a bottle for dinner?"

"Of course. Sorry. I should have done it before. Would you excuse me, Hughie, just for a moment? Sit down, make yourself comfortable. Sam will keep you company. . . ."

When they had gone, and the door closed, Hughie proceeded to do as he had been invited. With his drink and his ashtray conveniently to hand, he settled himself in a corner of the sofa, one arm outflung, resting on the deep cushions.

"Charming house, this. Never been here before. Last time I was over, they were still living in Fulham. Known Janey since she was a child. Parents are old friends."

"She told me. You've come from Barbados, I believe."

"Yes, I've got a house in Speightstown. Come back to London every now and then, just to keep the old finger on the pulse, check up on my stockbroker, get my hair cut, visit my tailor. Sad thing is, friends are getting a bit thin on the ground; every time I come, some other old mucker has popped his clogs. Sad, really. Still, the truth is we're all getting older." He stubbed out his cigarette, took another long swig of his gin and tonic, and fixed Sam with a speculative eye.

"You're on holiday?"

"You could say that. Just for a few days."

"What line of business are you in?"

"Wool-brokering." And then, because he did not want to talk about himself, Sam carried on: "How long have you lived in Barbados?"

"About thirty years. Ran the Beach Club for fifteen of them, but chucked it in before I became a raving alcoholic. Before that, I had a place in Scotland. It was handed over to me by a parsimonious father who had no intention of paying death duties."

A mild interest stirred. "What sort of place?" Sam asked.

"Oh, a sizey estate. Farms, land, that sort of thing. A Victorian pile of a house. Shooting, good fishing."

"Did you live there full time?"

"Tried to, old boy, but the winters at that latitude are not a joke. And to appreciate life to the full in the back of beyond, it's necessary to have a bit of backup. It was all very well for one's grandparents, with servants and staff, and cooks and keepers, slaving away for incredibly modest wages. When I came along, it cost an arm and a leg just to heat the bloody place. Not to say . . ." He cocked an eyebrow and gave a sly smile. "Not to say that we didn't have a good time. My first wife was a manic hostess, and she made certain that Corrydale was always bulging with house guests. I used to say she had house guests the way other people had mice. Food for an army and drink for a drunken army. Memorable days." As he talked, recollecting his apparently halcyon past, Hughie fondled his silken tie, stroking it, letting it slip through his fingers. "Of course, they couldn't last forever. Then Elaine ran off with a commodity broker, and after that there didn't seem much point soldiering on. As well, half the staff had left, and the bank manager was making disagreeable noises. . . ."

Sam listened to all this with a curious mixture of irritation and compassion. Here was a man who had been handed treasure on a silver plate, and squandered the lot away. It was hard to be sympathetic, but Hughie's bravura made him a sad character.

". . . so I sold up and that was it. Moved to Barbados. Best thing I ever did."

"Sold up. Just like that? Lock, stock, and barrel?"

"Well, hardly. The property went in lots. The farm was bought by the sitting tenant, and one or two of the cottages went to faithful old retainers who'd been living in them. What remained—the house, stables, land—was sold to a chain who run country hotels. You know the sort of thing. Fishing available and the odd pot at a pheasant or grouse."

Hughie knocked back the last of his gin and tonic and then sat gazing thoughtfully at the empty glass.

"Can I get you the other half?" Sam asked.

Hughie brightened. "What a good idea. Not too much tonic." Sam took the tumbler from his hand, and Hughie reached once more for his cigarettes.

Fixing the drink, "How long are you staying in London?" he asked.

"As short a time as possible. Flew in about four days ago. Leave on Wednesday. Headed for Nice. I've got an old friend there, Maudie Peabody, perhaps you know her? No? Oh, thank you, old boy. Kind of you. Maudie's an old acquaintance of my early Barbados days. American. Rich as Croesus. Got a divine villa in the hills above Cannes. Spending Christmas with her, and New Year. Then back to Barbados."

Sam returned to his position by the fire. "You seem very well organized."

"Oh, not too bad. Do one's best. But lonely now, living on my own. Rather unsuccessful in the marriage stakes. And *that's* bloody expensive. All my ex-wives want a cut of the lolly. What's left of it!"

"Do you have children?"

"No. No children. I had mumps when I was at Eton and that put paid to procreating. Bloody shame, really. I'd have liked kids to look after me in my old age. Truth to tell, I'm a bit short of relations. Got my father, but we're only just on speaking terms. He blew a fuse when I sold the place up, but there wasn't a mortal thing he could do about it. There's a cousin as well, a dull fellow. Lives in Hampshire. Tried to phone him, but there was no answer."

"Where does your father live?"

"In solitary and comfortable state in a mansion flat near the Albert Hall. Haven't got in touch yet. Putting it off. Probably drop in on my way back from France. Courtesy visit. We never find much to talk about. . . ."

It was something of a relief to Sam when once more they were joined by Janey and Neil. Janey, apparently done with her cooking, had removed her apron. She looked aglow with pleasure, and came instantly across the room to put her arms around Sam's neck and kiss him soundly. "Neil's told me. About the new job. I'm thrilled. You don't mind my knowing, do you? So exciting, a real challenge. I'm *really* pleased for you. I can't think of anything more exciting to take on."

Across her head, Sam caught Neil's eye. Neil looked a bit abashed. "You didn't mind me telling her?"

"Of course not." He gave Janey a hug. "Saved me the trouble."

"What's this?" Hughie pricked up his ears.

Janey turned to him. "It's Sam's new job. He heard today. He's going to the very north of Scotland to restart an old woollen mill."

"Really?" For the first time Hughie's attention and interest were caught by something and somebody other than himself. "Scotland, eh? Whereabouts?"

Sam told him. "Buckly. Sutherland."

Hughie gaped. "For God's sake. *Buckly.* Not McTaggarts?"

"You know them?"

"Dear boy, like the back of my hand. Buckly's only a few miles from Corrydale. Used to have all my shooting suits made of Buckly tweed. And Nanny used to knit my shooting stockings with McTaggarts' wheeling. Old family firm. Been going for at least a hundred and fifty years. What the hell happened?"

"Old McTaggart died. Sons weren't interested. They ran out of money, and the mill was finally finished off by a flood."

"What a tragic story. Like hearing an old friend has died. And you are going to take over! When do you go north?"

"Soon."

"Got a place to live?"

"No. All the mill's domestic property has been sold off. I'll camp in a pub, and look around for something to buy."

Hughie said, "Interesting." They all looked at him, but he did not enlarge on this, simply concentrated his attention on carefully stubbing out his cigarette.

At last, "Why interesting?" asked Janey.

"Because *I* have a house."

"Where do you have a house?"

"Not Corrydale, but Creagan. Even closer to Buckly."

"Why do you have a house in Creagan?"

"It was the old estate office, and where the factor's family lived. Quite large, solid, Victorian. With a garden at the back. But my grandmother decided it was too far from Corrydale, for day-to-day convenience, and she put the factor and his family into more suitable accommodation, within the walls of the park. The old Estate House she left to me. And to my cousin. We are joint owners."

Neil frowned. "So who lives there now?"

"It's standing empty. An old couple called Cochrane have been renting it out for the past twenty years, but one has died, and the other gone off to live with some relation. To be truthful, one of the reasons I'm in London is to put it on the market. I could do with a bit of the old ready. Tried to ring Oscar . . . he's the other owner . . . to talk things over, but couldn't get hold of him. He's probably died. Bored himself to death, no doubt."

Janey ignored this little spurt of malice. She said, "Would he be willing to sell out his half of the house?"

"Can't imagine why he shouldn't. No earthly use to him. I have, in fact, a date with Hurst and Fieldmore tomorrow morning, thought I'd sound them out, see if they'd handle a sale."

"But your cousin . . ."

"Oh, I can square things off with him when I get back from France."

"So what are you saying, Hughie?"

"That your friend Sam needs a house and I have one for sale. Suit him down to the ground, I should reckon. Short commute to business, close to the shops, championship golf course. No man could ask for more." He turned his head to look at Sam. "No harm done, going to cast your eye over the place. We could come to some arrangement. A private deal would suit me very well."

Sam said cautiously, "How much are you asking?"

"Well, there's been no valuation, for obvious reasons. But . . ." Hughie dropped his eyes, brushed a little cigarette ash from the knee of his trousers. "A hundred and fifty thousand?"

"Between you and your cousin?"

"Exactly so. Seventy-five each."

"How soon can you get in touch with him?"

"No idea, old boy. He's being elusive. He could be anywhere. But there is no reason why you shouldn't go and have a look at the place."

"Is there some agent or person I should get in touch with?"

"No need." Hughie heaved himself sideways and felt in his trouser pocket. From this he withdrew a large old-fashioned key, attached to a red label upon which was written in large capitals, ESTATE HOUSE. He held it up like a trophy.

Janey was amazed. "Do you carry it with you *all* the time?"

"Silly girl, of course not. Told you, I was going to see Hurst and Fieldmore tomorrow, was going to hand it over then."

Sam took the key. "How do I get in touch with you?"

"Give you my card, old boy. You can fax me in Barbados. And Maudie's telephone number in the south of France, just in case you make a snap decision."

"I'll certainly look at the house, and thank you. But of course nothing can be official without your cousin's approval."

"Course not. No underhand shenanigans. Everything above-board, cut and dried. But still, a viable proposition."

There fell another pause. Then Janey said, "It is the most extraordinary coincidence. I'm *sure* it's an omen. A marvellous omen. Of everything going right, and everything going well. Shouldn't we celebrate? Sam gave us a bottle of champagne. Why don't we open it and drink a toast to Sam, McTaggarts, and happy days in his new house?"

"Splendid idea," said Hughie. "But if you don't mind, I'd much prefer another gin and tonic."

Carrie

That night, Carrie dreamed of Austria and Oberbeuren. In the dream, the sky was a deep blue and the snow so dazzling that every frozen flake glittered like a jewel. She was skiing. An empty *piste.* Floating down through the white fields that spread to infinity on either side. There were black pine trees, and the *piste* ran between these trees, and she was alone. And then, emerging from the pines, she realized that she was not alone, because, far ahead, she saw another lone skier, a black silhouette, hurtling away from her, down the slope, dancing Christianias in the snow. She knew that the skier was Andreas, and she wanted him to know that she was there, so that he would wait for her. She called his name. *Andreas. Stop and let me be with you. Let us ski down together.* She could hear her voice blown away by the wind, and the sound of her skis on the beaten surface of the *piste. Andreas.* But he was gone. And then she topped a rise and saw that he had heard her call and was waiting. Turned, leaning on his sticks, watching for her. His head tipped up, his dark goggles pushed to the top of his head.

He was smiling. White teeth in a deeply tanned face. Perhaps his flight had been just a tease. Andreas. She reached his side and stopped, and only then saw that it was not Andreas at all, but another man, with a wolfish grin and eyes hard as grey pebbles. And the sky was not blue any longer but storm-dark and she was afraid. . . .

The sense of fear awoke her, eyes flying open to the darkness. She could hear the beating of her heart. Disoriented, she saw a strip of uncurtained window, the street lights beyond. Not Austria, not Oberbeuren, but London. Not her pine-scented apartment with the balcony beyond the windows, but Putney, and the spare bedroom of her friends, Sara and David Lumley. Not frosty, starlit skies, but the drip of grey rain. The dream receded. Andreas, who had never been truly hers, was gone. It was all over.

She reached out a hand and found her watch on the bedside table. Six o'clock on a dark early-December morning.

The empty bed felt desolate. She found herself overcome with a physical yearning, a desperate need for Andreas, for him to be there, his smooth and muscular body close to her own. To be back where they both belonged, in the huge carved bed beneath the sloping beams: lovers, bundled in goose-down and bliss. She turned on her side, hugging herself for comfort and warmth. It will be all right. It's like an illness, but I will recover. She closed her eyes, turned her face into the pillow, and slept again.

At nine o'clock she awoke once more, and saw that the gloomy winter morning had begun to lighten. By now, David and Sara would already have departed, set off for work, and she knew that she was alone in their house. Already, she had been there for a week, and in that time had accomplished little; seen nobody, done nothing about finding herself a new job. Sara and David, infinitely understanding, had left her alone, and Carrie's only contact with her family had been to call her father in Cornwall and have a long and comforting conversation with him, lasting almost an hour. "You will get in touch with your mother, won't you?" he had said, and she had promised that she would, but kept finding good reasons for putting off this course of action. But a week was too long, and she knew that it could be postponed no longer. Today, this very morning, she would telephone

Dodie. *Surprise,* she would say, sounding cheerful. *I'm back. Here. In London.*

And there would be astonishment, and explanations and excuses, and then arrangements made for their reunion. She did not dread this, but neither did she much look forward to seeing either her mother or her sister, Nicola. She knew that they would have much to tell her and none of it would be good news. However, blood runs thicker than water, and the sooner it was done, and over with, the better.

She got out of bed and pulled on her dressing-gown and went downstairs. The kitchen was neat and shining. Sara was an exemplary housekeeper, despite a full-time job. She had even found time to leave a note for Carrie, propped against the pot plant that stood in the middle of the table.

> *Have a good day. There's bacon in the fridge and orange juice. David has a late meeting, but I'll be home the usual time. If you go to Safeway, could you buy a veg. for supper. Cauliflower will do. And some Lapsang Souchong tea-bags.*
>
> *Love X Sara*

Carrie boiled a kettle, made coffee, put bread in the toaster. She drank the coffee but didn't eat the toast. The telephone sat on the dresser and looked at her, like a bad conscience. By the time she had drunk three cups of coffee, it was a quarter to ten. Surely, even Dodie Sutton would be up and about by now. She reached for the receiver and punched the number. The rain dripped against the window. She heard the ringing tone. She waited.

"Hello."

"Ma."

"Who's that?"

"Carrie."

"*Carrie?* Are you ringing up from Austria?"

"No. London. I'm here. Home."

"At Ranfurly Road?"

"No. Ranfurly Road's been let for three years. Three months' notice on either side. I'm homeless."

"Then where are you?"

"In Putney. With friends. Just across the river from you."

"How long have you been back?"

"About a week. But there's been a lot to do, otherwise I'd have called before."

"A *week*? Is this a holiday?" Dodie's voice was querulous, as though in some way her daughter had pulled a fast one on her.

"No, not a holiday. I chucked my job in. Decided I'd done it for long enough."

"I always imagined you were there for good. We haven't seen you for years. What happened?"

"Nothing happened. Just a whim."

"Will you get another job?"

"Have to. Look, Ma, I thought I'd come and see you. Are you going to be in today?"

"I'm in this morning. This afternoon I have to go and play bridge with old Leila Maxwell. She's got cataracts, poor thing, and can scarcely see the cards, but it's the least one can do."

Carrie persisted. "How about lunch, then?"

"Here, you mean?"

"I'll take you out if you'd rather."

"No. I can manage. Soup and pâté or something. Would that be all right?"

"Perfect. How's Nicola?"

"Oh, my dear girl, such drama."

Carrie's heart sank. "Drama?"

"I think she's gone mad. I'll tell you all about it when you come." A pause, and then Dodie added, some bright idea having obviously just occurred to her, "Actually, all this might be rather fortuitous.

You coming home, I mean. She'll be back for lunch, but perhaps you could get here a bit earlier and we can have a private chat about it all."

Carrie began to wish that she hadn't telephoned after all. She said, "And what about Lucy?"

"Lucy's here, too. She's got a morning off school, something to do with the boiler being replaced. She's in her room, swotting for some exam or other. She spends most of her time in her room, so she won't disturb us."

"I'd like to see her."

"Oh, you will, you will. What time will you be here?"

"Eleven-thirty? I'll probably walk."

"Haven't you got a car?"

"Yes, but the exercise will do me no harm."

"It's a vile day."

"I'll survive. See you later then, Ma."

"I'll expect you." And Dodie rang off. After a little, Carrie put the receiver down, sat and looked at it for a moment, and then found herself laughing. Not from joy, but wryly, because her mother's chill and ambiguous welcome was exactly what she had both dreaded and expected.

It had always been thus. A lack of communication, an antipathy, perhaps, that Carrie had come to terms with and learned to accept even before she entered her teens. Being with other families, seeing how they behaved with each other, had compounded her perception, and had it not been for the presence of her father, she could well have grown up with no knowledge of loving or being loved.

She had never quite worked out why Jeffrey Sutton had married Dodie in the first place. Perhaps because she was pretty, flirtatious, and engaging, and as a young woman had the ability to turn herself into exactly the sort of companion any potential husband would wish to spend his life with. Only to discover, too late, that it was all a calculated act. On Dodie's side, in Jeffrey she saw not only an attractive and virile man, but security as well, for his job as a City broker was sound, his career climbing steadily, and his colleagues were blessed with the social background that Dodie had always craved.

Nicola was their first child, and then, five years later, Carrie arrived. So different were the sisters, so little did they have in common, it seemed that each belonged solely to a single parent. As though Dodie had produced Nicola without co-operation from Jeffrey, and Jeffrey had fathered Carrie, in some miraculous fashion, entirely by himself.

He was her father, her friend, her ally . . . the strong partner of a marriage that could only be called a misalliance. It was Jeffrey who drove his daughters to school, while their mother lay in bed, sipped China tea, and read novels. Carrie remembered him returning home from work, the sound of his latchkey in the door, and running downstairs to welcome him, because Dodie hadn't returned from her bridge game, and only the au pair clashed about in the kitchen. Grubby and exhausted after a demanding day at his work, he would dump his briefcase and shuck himself out of his overcoat, and come upstairs to help with homework, or listen to piano practice. It was Jeffrey who brought fun into family life, always ready with a spontaneous idea for a picnic, an outing, a holiday. It was he who had first taken Carrie skiing at Val d'Isère when she was only ten, to stay in a rented villa and be part of a cheerful house party consisting of two other families. It was one of the best holidays of Carrie's life, and the start of a passion that had never left her, but Nicola had turned down the invitation, partly because she was hopelessly unathletic, but also because she liked being on her own with Dodie, so that the two of them could go shopping together, and buy new dresses for Nicola to wear to all the Christmas parties to which she had been invited, and had no intention of missing.

Clothes, boys, and parties were Nicola's passionate interests, and it surprised nobody when she became engaged, and then married, when she was twenty-one. The young man in question was called Miles Wesley and was all that Dodie had ever dreamt of for her elder daughter. He had a grandmother called Lady Burfield, parents with an enviable property in Hampshire, had been educated at Harrow, and held a respectable job with Hurst and Fieldmore, an old-established property agent with branches all over the country. Miles was in the head office, in Davies Street, learning the ropes of selling huge sporting estates, grouse moors, and tracts of expensive fishing rights. No mother could have wished for more, and Dodie had a lovely time planning a wedding that would be the envy of all her friends, and a talking point for some years to come.

Carrie was not a bridesmaid at this wedding because she refused to be. Now fifteen, she was tall, lanky, and working passionately at her lessons, because she wanted, above all else, to get a place at University. Her general appearance was the despair of her mother, who abhorred the worn jeans, heavy boots, and baggy T-shirts that Carrie favoured, and nearly fainted away when Carrie brought back from the Oxfam shop a leather jacket that looked like nothing so much as a dead sheep.

When the word "bridesmaid" was mentioned, Carrie made her position instantly clear.

She said no.

There were terrible rows.

"How can you be so selfish?" Dodie wanted to know.

"Easily."

"You only have one sister; you could think of her."

"Look, Ma, I wouldn't do it even for the Queen. I'm five feet nine inches tall, and I'm just not bridesmaid material. And I'm not walking down any aisle looking like a great pink taffeta meringue. A complete idiot."

"You know perfectly well it won't be pink taffeta. Nicola and I have chosen deep-rose chiffon."

"Even worse."

"You never think of anybody but yourself."

"This time, that's just what I'm doing. Nicola won't mind. She's got masses of pretty girl-friends just dying to be bridesmaids. Anyway," Carrie yawned, "I'm not all that dotty about church weddings." She found it amusing, sometimes, to wind her mother up a bit. "Why can't they just nip round the corner to the Registry Office? Just think of the money you'd save. On the other hand, that would mean no wedding presents and yummy cheques."

"That is the most unkind thing to say."

"Just practical."

Dodie took a deep breath and kept her voice low and even. "If people wish to give Nicola a cheque for a wedding present, then I know it will be gratefully received. They have, after all, got to furnish their new flat. Refrigerators, lamps, carpets. Nothing's cheap, you know."

"Or they could put all that lovely lolly into a special account, and use it to pay for the divorce. . . ."

Dodie left the room, slamming the door behind her. The subject of bridesmaids was not mentioned again.

Carrie was the first person Jeffrey confided in. She was nineteen now and at Oxford University, reading English and philosophy, and relishing every moment of her new life. One Sunday morning, he telephoned from London.

"You doing anything today?"

"Nothing special."

"I thought I might give you lunch."

"What a treat."

"Your mother's with Nicola. Lucy's running a temperature, so there was a cry for help. I'll be with you around twelve."

Carrie was thrilled. "I'll be ready."

It was a golden day in October, and when he had collected Carrie from outside her residence, he drove her out into the country and stood her lunch at Le Manoir de Quatre Saisons. An enormous and expensive treat. After lunch, they wandered into the garden and sat in the benign Indian summer warmth, and there was bird-song and leaves drifted down, like copper pennies, onto the grass.

It was then that he told her about Serena, about meeting her, and seeing her, and falling in love. ". . . I have known her for five years now.

She is young enough to be my daughter, but she means everything to me, and I don't think I can live without her any longer."

Her father with a lover. Another woman. And Carrie had never had the faintest suspicion. It was hard to come up with something to say.

"Are you shocked, Carrie?"

"Of course I'm not. Just taken unawares."

"I am going to leave you all and be with her." Carrie looked at him, and saw the pain in his dark eyes. "This is a terrible thing I am doing to you."

"No. Just telling me the truth."

"I would have gone before, taken Serena with me. But I couldn't leave until I felt that both you and Nicola were . . . settled, I suppose. Adult. I had to be around while you needed me, while I could still be of use to you. Now, it's different. You, I am pretty sure, can stand on your own feet. And Nicola is a married woman with a little girl of her own. I can only hope that she is content. Miles has always seemed a decent sort of chap, if a bit wet. I think she probably runs rings around him, but that's his look-out."

"Poor man." She thought of his own marriage to Dodie. She said, "All these years, have you been very unhappy?"

Jeffrey shook his head. "No. There have been moments of great joy, mostly when I was with you. But I'm worn out of keeping up appearances, and making the best of things. I'm exhausted by the grind of trying to make enough money, struggling on, working flat-out. I need a different life. I need warm love and companionship and laughter, and Dodie is incapable of letting me experience any of these things. As you probably realize, we haven't shared a bed for years. I want a home where friends drop in and sit at the kitchen table, and share spaghetti and a bottle of wine. I want to open the front door at the end of a day and hear someone call my name. In the mornings I want to shave and smell bacon and eggs cooking, and coffee perking. And it's not just the male menopause, it's a deep need that's been simmering for years."

"I wasn't going to say male menopause."

"I know you weren't."

Another family had come out of the hotel into the warm afternoon sunshine. A young mother and father and a little boy. The little boy found a croquet mallet and a ball and was attempting to hit the ball with the mallet. After three misses, his father came to stand behind him, his hands wrapped around his son's, to show him how.

Carrie said, "You've done everything you could for us all. No man could have done more. If you feel this way, you must go."

"What about your mother?"

"She'll be devastated, of course, and her pride will be bruised. But I know she's never put much into your marriage, and perhaps, at the end of the day, she's a person better on her own." Carrie sighed. "You have to be realistic, Dad. She'll get a good divorce lawyer and make you pay."

"I know that. A price I'll have to pay."

"What about your job?"

"I shall chuck it in."

"Won't you miss the cut and thrust?"

"No. I've got as high up the ladder as I ever will. And I'm tired of the rat race, and the anxiety and the perpetual driving competition to keep up front. Perhaps I was never a very ambitious animal. And now I'm selfish. Do you think it's wrong, at my great age, to want to be happy?"

"You know what I think."

For a bit they didn't say anything, simply sat there in a sort of silent harmony. Then Jeffrey spoke again. "This is about *you*, now. There's a trust fund for you; I set it up when you were born. Nicola, too, but hers has mostly gone on that ridiculous wedding. The point is, it's sitting in the bank, breeding a bit of interest, and I think it would be sensible if you cashed it in and used it to buy yourself a house. In London, or somewhere. Property is always a good investment; I like to think of you being independent. . . . It's not a great deal of money, but it would pay for a fairly modest house. What do you think?"

"I think I like the idea." Carrie leaned forward and kissed her father's cheek. "You're sweet. Thank you. We won't lose each other, will we? We'll write letters and faxes and telephone, wherever you end up. We'll keep in touch."

He smiled, and looked less stressed than she had seen him look for a long time. He had, clearly, had a lot on his mind. He said, "Next Sunday, if I come back to Oxford and bring Serena with me, would you like to meet her?"

"Of course I would. But she mustn't think I'm too important, that I'm ever going to come between you. I don't want to be a reason for Serena to feel guilty or remorseful. This must be where old responsibilities end, and your new life begins. Just make sure, this time, that it's all happiness."

"And you, my darling? What about you? Have you a love in your life?"

"Dozens," she teased. "Safety in numbers."

"No chance of another top-heavy wedding?"

"Not a ghost. Not for years. I have far too many other things to do with my life. And now, on top of everything else, I've got to go and buy myself a house. What a lot of plans we've laid and what a lot of things we've discussed."

"Don't be too light-hearted. We're in for a traumatic time."

She took his hand in hers. She said, "Allies, Dad. Shoulder to shoulder."

Jeffrey was right. They were in for a traumatic experience, and sounds of resentment and recrimination were to echo for a long time. At the end of the day, though, most people had to agree that Dodie had done very well for herself and made the best of a sorry situation. As Carrie had foreseen, she let Jeffrey get away with nothing, and ended up with the family house in Campden Hill, her car, most of Jeffrey's worldly goods, and much of his money. He contested nothing, and could scarcely have done more to make amends.

As soon as she heard that Carrie had bought herself a small terrace house in Ranfurly Road, Dodie put the Campden Hill house on the market (swearing dramatically that it was too filled with unhappy memories for her to be able to stay there), sold it at a socking profit, and moved herself into a charming old-fashioned apartment in Fulham, looking south over the river to Putney, and with private gardens alongside Hurlingham.

"My little lonely nest," she told her friends, sounding both wistful and plucky, and everyone said she was marvellous, but in truth she was as content as she had ever been, with her bridge, and her little drinkie parties, and the unfailing panacea of shopping and returning home with designer bags and boxes stuffed with tissue paper and goodies. With friends, she began to take holidays abroad, cushioned in Club Class to Paris, or Mediterranean cruises in immaculately run liners, where there was every opportunity to dazzle in a newly acquired wardrobe of clothes. On one of these cruises she met Johnnie Struthers, a retired Group Captain and a widower. He clearly fancied Dodie, and from time to time, when he was in London, telephoned and took her out to dinner.

She was happy. And then, seven years after Dodie's own divorce, Nicola Wesley discovered that the mild-mannered Miles was having it off with another woman, and grabbed this opportunity to flounce out of a marriage that had become both predictable and boring. She flounced, of course, to her mother, and her mother's spacious and pretty apartment. All of which might have been quite fun and companionable, had not Nicola brought with her seven-year-old Lucy, and Dodie knew that her halcyon days were over.

The coffee-pot was empty, the dregs of her cup grown cold. Carrie got to her feet, threw the uneaten toast into the trash-bin, rinsed out the pot, put the cup and saucer into the dishwasher. She went upstairs, took a shower, washed her short hair, and dressed. Lately she had not bothered too much about how she looked, simply slopped around in old jeans and with no make-up on her face, but this morning she knew that the time had come to take a bit of trouble, if only for Dutch courage.

So, slim camel-coloured trousers, a cashmere polo-neck sweater, polished boots. Gold earrings, gold chains around her neck. She sprayed scent, checked her leather shoulder bag, took her coat from the wardrobe, went downstairs.

The front-door keys lay in a brass bowl on the chest in the hall, alongside a blue bowl of white hyacinths. Over this chest was a long mirror, and as she pulled on her coat and did up the buttons, her reflection gazed back at her. She paused, regarding herself. Saw a tall, slender, dark-haired girl . . . or perhaps, more accurately, a tall, slender, dark-haired woman. After all, soon she would be thirty. Chestnut-brown hair shone with cleanliness, a lock like a bird's wing swept across her forehead. Her eyes, accentuated by shadow and mascara, were large and dark as coffee, and her face still tanned from the reflected sunlight of the snow-fields. She looked all right. Confident. Not a person to be pitied.

She did up the buttons of the coat, a dark-grey loden piped with forest green, that had been bought, a year ago, in Vienna. And Andreas had been with her, and helped to choose the coat, and then insisted on paying for it.

You will wear it forever, he told her, *and you will always look a million dollars.*

It had been a day of bitter cold and thin snow, and after they had bought the coat, they had walked through the streets, arm in arm, to Sacher's and there lunched in some style, and . . .

Don't think about it.

Dodie had been waiting for her. She was there almost at once, dealing with the double lock, and flinging the door open.

"Carrie!"

She looked much as she always had—no older, no thinner, no fatter. Small and trim, with dark, neatly dressed hair flashed with a streak of white which was entirely natural, and so enviable. She wore a little cardigan suit, the skirt fashionably short, and court shoes decorated with square gold buckles. A still-pretty woman, with apparently everything going for her. Only her mouth gave her away, moulded by the years into an expression of constant discontent. Carrie had always been told that the eyes are the mirror of the soul, but had long ago decided that a person's mouth is the true giveaway of character.

She stepped through the door, and Dodie closed it carefully. There were to be no outflung arms then, no hugs, no exclamations of motherly delight.

"Hello, Ma. How are you?" she asked, shedding her coat. "You're looking marvellous."

"Thank you, dear. You're looking well, too. So brown. As though you'd just returned from a holiday in the sun. Put your coat on the chair. Do you want coffee or anything?"

"No, I've just finished breakfast." Now they kissed, formally, touching cheeks. Dodie's cheek was soft and fragrant. "I didn't get up till nine."

"Lovely to have a lie-in. Come along. . . ."

She turned and led the way into her sitting-room. The clouds on this wintry day all at once parted, and for an instant the room was filled with dazzling winter sunshine. It was a pleasant room, with large windows facing south onto a balcony, and beyond, the view of the river. Alongside it, divided by a double door which always stood open, was Dodie's dining-room. Carrie saw the mahogany table, the pretty sideboard, all part of her childhood, and come from the family house in Campden Hill. There were a great many flowers about the place and the air was heavy with the heady scent of white lilies.

"Where is everybody?" she asked.

"I told you. Lucy's in her room, and—"

"Is she not very social?"

"Not noticeably so. She's quite happy there. She's got her desk and her computer and a little television."

In the white marble fireplace, there flickered a small mock-coal electric fire. Dodie settled herself beside this, in her own chair. She had been reading the newspaper when Carrie rang the bell, and now reached for it, with a delicate pink-nailed hand, folded it, and set it on the coffee-table.

Another cloud rolled in and the sunshine was gone.

"It was good of you to come so promptly. I wanted to tell you about everything, this ridiculous drama that's suddenly blown up."

"Nicola?"

"She'll be back soon."

Carrie lowered herself into the chair on the other side of the white sheepskin hearthrug.

"Where's she gone?"

"Travel agent."

"Is she planning a trip?"

"I think she's gone mad. I said that, didn't I, over the telephone. She's met this man. He's an American. She met him at some party a few weeks ago, and they've been seeing each other ever since."

Carrie thought it sounded quite hopeful, and not at all as though her elder sister had gone mad.

"What sort of American?" she asked cautiously.

"Oh, quite presentable. A business man. Railways, or steel or something. He's based in Cleveland, Ohio, wherever that is. He's called Randall Fischer. And now he's gone back to America, and he's invited Nicola to go and spend Christmas with him."

"In Cleveland, Ohio?"

"No, he's got a place in Florida. Apparently he always spends Christmas there."

It all sounded so reasonable that Carrie could not imagine what the drama was about. "Is he married?"

"He *says* he's divorced."

"In that case he probably is. Have you met him?"

"Of course I have. Once or twice she's brought him here for a drink, and one night he took us both out to dinner. To Claridge's. He was staying there."

"In that case, he must be loaded." Carrie frowned. "Don't you like him, Ma?"

"Oh, he's all right, I suppose. About fifty. Not particularly attractive."

"Does Nicola think he's attractive?"

"I suppose she does."

"So what is so dire?"

"I think she's being foolhardy. She really knows nothing about the man."

"Ma, she's thirty-five. Surely by now she can look after herself, make her own mistakes if she wants to."

"That's not the point."

"Then what is the point? Enlighten me."

"Don't you see, Carrie? It's Lucy."

"You mean Lucy is not included in the invitation?"

"She most certainly has been included, but she refuses to go. She says she doesn't want to go to Florida, she won't know anybody, there won't be anything for her to do, and Randall doesn't really want her anyway. He's only asked her because he feels he has to."

Carrie was sympathetic. "I see her point. What age is she? Fourteen. She'd probably feel like a fish out of water, and I'll admit it's a bit embarrassing watching your own mother in the throes of a love affair."

A faint flush was creeping up Dodie's neck, a sure sign that she was becoming rattled. She disliked any form of disagreement, and hated being put in a position where she had to argue her point.

"It's such a wonderful opportunity for Lucy. To travel. See another bit of the world."

"Not if she doesn't want to."

"But what will she *do*?"

Now, thought Carrie, *we're getting to the nub of the matter.*

"For Christmas, you mean? Stay with you, I suppose. After all, this seems to be her home for the time being. It's been her home since her parents divorced. Where else would she go?"

Dodie did not at once reply. Instead, restless, she got to her feet and walked away from Carrie and stood at the window, gazing down at the river. Carrie waited. Then her mother turned. "I can't deal with her on my own. I have a life to lead. I have plans made, invitations. . . . I may go down to Bournemouth and stay there with the Freemans. They go every year to the Palace Hotel. They've invited me to join them." Her tone of voice made it perfectly clear that Lucy was not included in this giddy scheme. "I'm not as young as I was, Carrie. My child-caring days are over. And I'm not going to change my plans for a stubborn little girl."

No, Carrie thought, *I don't suppose for a moment you'd even contemplate such a thing.*

After a bit, she said, "What about her father? Miles. Can't she go and spend Christmas with him and his new wife? Or does she never see him now?"

"Oh, yes, she sees him." Dodie came back to her chair and sat again, perched forward, tense. "Every now and then, she spends a Sunday with them, but without noticeable enthusiasm."

"They don't have children, do they?"

"No. And I doubt if they ever will. She's a career woman." Dodie spoke the words with a curl of her lip. "Babies won't ever interfere with *her* life."

"So they wouldn't have Lucy for Christmas?"

"As a matter of fact, in desperation, I telephoned Miles and put the idea to him. I had to do it, because Nicola refuses to speak to him or even say his name. But Miles and his wife are going to Saint Moritz to ski for Christmas, with a grown-up party. Lucy's never skied and she's hopeless with people she doesn't know. Miles said it was out of the question, and she'd just spoil it for everybody."

Carrie began to feel desperately sorry for the child, slung in limbo between two feuding and unsympathetic parents. She said, trying not to sound too cool, "In that case, you seem to have come to a deadlock."

"Nicola is absolutely determined to go to Florida. She can be very selfish, you know. And after all I've done for her. . . ."

"Perhaps she just wants to grab the chance of a bit of fun."

"A bit of fun." Bitterly, Dodie repeated the words, making them sound almost indecent. Carrie watched her. All at once, it seemed, Dodie did not want to meet her daughter's eyes. She glanced down, fiddled with the cuff of her little jacket, adjusted a gold button. She said, "That's what I meant when I spoke to you on the telephone. About your abrupt return from Austria coming at a fortuitous time."

"You mean *me. I* take Lucy off your hands."

Dodie looked up. "Have you plans laid?"

"Ma, I'm only just back from Austria. I haven't had time to lay a plan. I haven't even got a house, and won't get Ranfurly Road back until the end of February. I'm living out of a suitcase. I'm really not in a position to have someone to stay."

"I didn't mean that. I thought maybe . . . your father . . ."

"Jeffrey?"

"You call him Jeffrey now?"

"I've called him Jeffrey ever since the divorce. He's my father, I know, but he's also Serena's husband, and my friend."

As she spoke their names, Dodie flinched delicately, but Carrie, knowing that she was being cruel, ignored this. "And I don't think that's a viable idea, either."

"But he's Lucy's grandfather. Surely . . ."

"Look, Ma. I've already spoken to Jeffrey. I called him the day after I got back. We had a long conversation. We talked about Christmas then, but he's got Serena's brother and his wife and baby coming down to spend the holidays with them. Emblo is going to be bursting full, not an inch for two more people."

"You could suggest . . ."

"No. It's not fair to Serena. She can't have us, and she'll be riddled with guilt *because* she can't have us. I'm not going to ask."

"Oh." Dodie let out a sigh and sat back in her chair, as though at the end of her tether, and looking like a balloon that has had all the air let out of it, shrunken and suddenly older. "I really can't go on like this much longer. It's too unsettling. No co-operation from anybody, least of all my own family."

"But, Ma . . ."

She did not finish. There came the sound of a key in the lock of the front door, and then the door opening and shutting again.

"Nicola's back," Dodie said unnecessarily, and she pulled herself together and put a hand to her hair, and was sitting, brightly expectant, when Nicola came into the room. Carrie got up and turned to face her sister.

She said, "Hi."

"Carrie!" Nicola's jaw dropped in astonishment. "What on earth are you doing here? I thought you were in Austria."

"I was," Carrie told her, "but I'm back now."

The sisters eyed each other. They had never been close, never been friends, never shared secrets. And it occurred to Carrie that Nicola, as she matured, was growing to look even more like their mother. The same height, the same neat figure, thick dark hair. The same small, mean-tempered mouth. Put side by side, and they could easily have been mistaken for a pair of cross little twins.

Whenever she thought of Nicola, Carrie always had a mental picture of her wearing some little outfit. Skirts and sweaters coordinating. Shoes matching handbags, a silken scarf toning exactly with her lipstick. A bit like one of those cardboard cut-out dolls they used to dress in paper outfits with folding tabs to fix them in place. A paper sun-dress for the beach, a furry-collared coat for a winter walk, a crinoline and poke-bonnet for the fancy-dress party. Now, Nicola did not let her down, for there was the immaculately tailored trouser suit, beneath a car coat of faux leopard. Her sack bag was of chocolate-brown suede and the suede was exactly the same shade as her high-heeled boots.

Nicola laid down her handbag on the seat of a chair that stood against the wall. She began to unbutton her jacket.

"Back for good?" she asked.

"I don't know. I'll have to see." Carrie moved forward and gave her sister a kiss, which Nicola, perfunctorily, returned.

"But when did you get home?" She shrugged out of her jacket and tossed it down on top of her bag.

"About a week ago. But I've been fairly occupied, so I didn't ring Ma till this morning."

"Well, I never did." She gave Dodie a cold look. "I suppose Mother's been telling you about all the drama. Getting you on her side." Dodie and Nicola were clearly, at this moment, on the worst of terms. Carrie decided that Lucy must have been having a hellish time between the pair of them.

Dodie looked hurt. "Nicola, that's not fair," she protested.

"No, but I bet it's true." Nicola settled herself with a thump in the middle of the sofa. "Anyway, it's too late now. I've booked my flight. I'm going on the eighteenth of December. For two weeks."

A pregnant silence followed this defiant announcement. Dodie turned her head away and stared at the flickering electric coals. Disapproval emanated from every bone in her body. Nicola caught Carrie's eye and made a face, as if the two of them were in alliance against their mother. Carrie did not return her glance, because, at that moment, she didn't like either of them very much.

But it was no good getting caught up in the ongoing row. She said, as evenly as she could, "There seems to be a problem with Lucy."

"She was asked to Florida, but she refuses to come with me."

"I do see her point."

"Oh, you would."

"Ma suggested that I look after her for Christmas."

"You?" Nicola made the word insulting. And then she thought for an instant, and said it again, and this time it didn't sound insulting at all, but quite different. A brilliant notion that had not previously occurred to her. "*You.*"

"But I can't."

"Why not?"

"No house. No home."

"Ranfurly Road?"

"Still let."

Dodie now chose to chip in to the conversation. "I thought Carrie might have taken Lucy to stay with your father. In Cornwall. But apparently that's out of the question as well."

"Why?" Nicola demanded.

Carrie told her. "A dearth of space."

"And bloody Miles and his bloody wife won't have her, the selfish sods. Excuses, excuses on all sides." She chewed her thumb-nail. "Anyway, I'm going. I'm going to Florida with Randall, and nobody's going to stop me. I haven't had a holiday forever, and I'm going."

Carrie, sympathetic in a way, but thinking of Lucy, tried reasoning. "But, Nicola . . ."

She got no further. Nicola rounded on her. "It's all very well for you." Carrie wondered how many thousands of times in her life she had heard that familiar wail. *It's all very well for you.* "You've never had a family, you don't know what it's like being tied, day in, day out, to a child. Term time, and holidays. Keeping Lucy amused, dealing with problems at school. All on your own. As far as I can see, your life has been one long holiday. Nothing but skiing, and having a good time. Mountains and young people and glühwein parties. And never coming back from Austria. It's years since we set eyes on you. Not a care in the world."

Carrie, with some difficulty, kept her voice even. "Nicola, you clearly haven't the faintest idea what I've been doing. My job was public relations officer for a prestigious travel firm, and each morning nine people had to report in to my office. I had a secretary, and an apartment of my own, and in high season, I very often worked seven days a week. So let's hear a little less about irresponsibility."

"It's not the same." Mulish, Nicola stuck to her grudge. "Not the same as bringing up a child."

Carrie gave up. "Look, this isn't getting us anywhere."

Nicola ignored her. "It's up to you, Mother. You'll have to forget about Bournemouth for the moment. . . ."

Dodie, not unnaturally, became incensed. "I shall do no such thing."

"You can scarcely leave Lucy here on her own. . . ."

"And why should *I* be the one to make the sacrifice . . . ?"

Carrie suddenly knew that she could listen to this pointless sniping no longer. The two of them were entrenched, and all the argument in the world was not going to come to any sensible conclusion. "Do *stop,*" she told them sharply.

Rather surprisingly, they did. After a bit, Nicola said, "So, have *you* got any bright suggestions, Carrie?"

"I don't know. I only know that we're talking about your daughter, not about a dog that has to go into a kennel. If you don't mind, I'd like to go and have a chat with her, since she couldn't talk less sense than either her mother or her grandmother."

"Thank you *very* much."

"Where's her room?"

"Next to the kitchen." Nicola gave a jerk of her head. "At the back . . ."

Carrie went to the door. As she opened it, her mother spoke again. "See if you can persuade her to be a good girl and simply . . . go."

Carrie did not reply. She went from the room and closed the door gently behind her.

LUCY

Farnham Court had been built at a time when middle-class families were still expected to employ resident servants. Therefore each apartment had been designed with a small and undistinguished room for a housemaid or a hard-worked cook-general. Lucy Wesley, when she came to live with her grandmother after her parents' divorce, had been given this room, and did not really care that it was both cramped and sunless because it was her own.

The window, veiled in folds of white voile, looked out onto the well in the centre of the building, at the bottom of which was a paved courtyard with a few tubs containing shrubs and bulbs which the hall porter was meant to keep trim and watered, so there was virtually no view. But the walls were yellow, which imparted the illusion of sunlight, and Lucy had her bed, piled with teddies, and a large table with drawers for doing her homework, and lots of shelves for her huge collection of books. Her computer sat on the table, and there were lamps and a small television set, and a sheepskin rug on the blue carpet. When her schoolfriends came to visit, they were always loud with envy and admiration, mostly because the space belonged to Lucy only, and she didn't have to share it with some tiresome younger sister and a clutter of sibling's possessions.

It was a very tidy room because Lucy was an extremely tidy person.

On the shelves, her books stood in straight and regimented lines; her bed was smooth, her clothes folded. At school, her desk was the same, with pencils sharpened and exercise books squared and neatly stacked. Once a week, Mrs. Burgess, who came to clean for her grandmother, went through Lucy's room with Hoover and duster and left it smelling strongly of lavender polish. But from time to time, driven by a sort of housewifely compulsion, Lucy cleaned it again herself, polishing the mirror of her dressing-table and the silver frame that held the photograph of her father.

She missed him dreadfully, not simply as a person, but because, like a piece of furniture that had lost a leg, with his going all sense of family had collapsed, fallen sideways, crooked and useless; and Lucy knew that it was unmendable and would never be the same again. She had been seven years old at the time of her parents' divorce. A bad age (though could there possibly be such a thing as a *good* age?). Still a small child, but old enough to know exactly what was happening. Which was that the fabric of existence had come apart, and that she and her mother were left to put together the detritus of all that remained. They had moved in with Gran, and Lucy had thought for a bit that this was a temporary arrangement, but slowly accepted the fact that it was for good. For some reason, despite disagreements and occasional rows, it seemed to suit both women, and as nobody ever bothered to ask Lucy's opinion, she kept it to herself.

From time to time, she saw her father, but his new wife, who was called Marilyn, was wary of involvement, and clearly had no interest in children or stepdaughters, or anything except her absorbing job; otherwise, surely, she would have had babies of her own by now. She and Miles did not even have a proper house with a garden, but a flat, and it was the sort of flat that, if you couldn't be bothered to cook dinner, you telephoned and a snacky sort of meal was delivered at the door, on a trolley.

Marilyn was certainly not the sort of person one could confide in, and Lucy felt she could no longer confide in her father, because of divided loyalties on both their parts. Sometimes she felt that she would burst if she didn't find someone adult to talk to. Her headmistress, Miss Maxwell-Brown, was exactly that sort of a person, and had, every now and then in the course of a private interview, intimated quite clearly that if Lucy had something to say, then Miss Maxwell-Brown was more than happy to listen. But Lucy's reserve, and that same tiresome loyalty, got in the way. And she was terrified of anybody being sorry for her, as though she were some sort of orphan. So, "No, I'm all right," she had insisted. "Really, everything's all right." And, reluctantly, Miss Maxwell-Brown would let her go.

Now, at a quarter to twelve on a Friday morning, she had finished her homework (it had taken since after breakfast) and was writing in her diary. The diary was fat as a little Bible, leather-bound, and with its own tiny lock and key. It had smooth thick paper that was a pleasure to write upon, and had been a present from Cornwall. *Happy Christmas, Lucy,* was written upon the flyleaf, *from Grandfather, Serena, Amy, and Ben.*

They never forgot Christmas and birthdays, which was good of them, because Lucy had been a baby when *that* particular marriage broke up, and she had no memory of Jeffrey Sutton, and of course had never met Serena, or Amy or Ben. Sometimes, when life felt really bleak, she lay in bed and wove fantasies about them, about being asked to go and stay and—even less likely—being allowed by Mummy and Gran to make the trip. She planned it all in her mind. A taxi to Paddington and then the train, and being met somewhere with a palm tree and a blue sea, being taken to a house in a wonderful garden, close to a beach, perhaps, and where the sea winds would blow in through the open window of her bedroom. And having Ben and Amy would be like having brothers and sisters of her own.

Lucy had kept up the diary ever since the day she had received it. It wasn't so much a diary as a notebook, because there were no dates, just lovely clean pages, which meant that you wrote the date yourself, and then the day's doings underneath. Sometimes, there was little to record, but other days, if she had been to the cinema or to a concert with the rest of her class, there was quite a lot to remember, and she could use up two or three pages. She got a lot of satisfaction writing, with her best pen, on the thick creamy paper. She had a passion for notebooks, paper, pens, the smell of ink, all the tools of writing. Stationery shops were her most favourite, and she seldom emerged from one without a little box of coloured paper-clips, a packet of postcards, or a new red-ink Biro.

She wrote:

Mummy has gone to the travel agent this morning. She went right after breakfast. She and Gran are scarcely speaking to each other because of Christmas and Bournemouth and Florida. I wish they would understand how I would hate Florida. You can't swim all day in a pool, and I don't like Randall that much, or ice-cream, or watching videos.

The diary was better than having nobody to confide in, but a person would be better. She laid down her pen and gazed out at the grey morning beyond the floaty, white voile curtains. She thought about Carrie, Mummy's younger sister, and a splendid aunt. Carrie would be perfect, because she talked to you as though you were a grown-up, and yet was always prepared to do exciting and innovative things. Before she disappeared to Austria and never came home again, Carrie had been Lucy's saviour, the giver of special treats, like going to see *La Fille Mal Gardée* at the Opera House, or outings to Kew on the first warm spring days. Carrie made even the National History Museum fun and interesting; and once they had gone down the river together in a boat, all the way to Tower Bridge, and had lunch on board. All of London, seen from the water, had become a foreign city, unfamiliar, with towers and spires washed in sunlight.

She picked up her pen again.

I wouldn't have minded spending Christmas with Dad and Marilyn, but they're going away to ski. Marilyn says it's a long-standing engagement. I'm sure Daddy would have put it off but of course she wouldn't let him. I don't know what has to be so special about Christmas anyway, and why everybody makes such a fuss. Anyway, this afternoon I'm going to the pictures with Emma Forbes and then back to tea with her.

While Lucy sat in her bedroom, doing homework and now writing in her diary, beyond the closed door, Gran was living her own tidy life. Every now and then during the course of the morning, Lucy had heard the telephone ring, and Gran's low voice, chatting away. And, about an hour ago, someone had rung the bell and come to visit, and as Lucy finished her French, she was aware of the soft murmur of conversation from behind the drawing-room doors at the end of the passage. She had no idea who it could be, and did not particularly care. Some boring friend of Gran's. But now, she heard the whine of the ascending lift, and then the rattle of a latchkey in the front door, and knew that her mother had returned, back from the travel agent.

The awful thing was that, despite Lucy's insistence that she wasn't going to go to Florida, she couldn't be too sure that, in desperation, Mummy might not have booked two flights, and Lucy, willy-nilly, would be dragged along with her. After all, at fourteen, there wasn't much one could do, except sulk for two weeks and loathe every moment of it, and hopefully spoil it all for everybody. She was perfectly capable of all this, and her mother knew that she was perfectly capable, but still, there remained the daunting possibility. She raised her head, like an alert dog, to listen. But the footsteps passed her door and went down the passage, towards the sitting-room. The door opened and shut. Voices again. She closed her eyes and wished that she could close her ears as well.

Small comfort, but at least the third person, whoever the visitor was, would preclude another row, anyway, for the time being. She waited for what was going to happen next. Which was nothing for about five minutes. And then, once more, the drawing-room door opened and closed, and somebody was approaching. Lucy shut her diary and leaned on it, her head turned to watch the doorknob. Her mother, come to impart the latest news about plans for Florida. Lucy, all at once, felt almost sick with apprehension. But then, there was a soft knock, and she knew it wasn't Mummy, because Mummy never knocked, just barged in, invading privacy, disrupting whatever Lucy happened to be doing.

At a knock, Miss Maxwell-Brown always called out, "Come in," but before she could bring herself to say this, the door opened slowly, and a head came around the edge of it.

"Am I interrupting?" She was smiling. Not her mother. Not Gran. Not some boring acquaintance of Gran's. But . . .

Carrie. Carrie? She'd only just been thinking of Carrie and now she was here, at the door, and not in Austria where Lucy thought she was, living a glamorous life of skiing holidays and luxury hotels. Carrie. And she used to have long hair, but now it was short and she was very thin, very tanned, and just as tall as Lucy remembered.

Carrie. Lucy found herself dumbfounded, without words. A turmoil of mixed emotions. Astonishment and incredulous delight that such a marvellous and unforeseen event was actually taking place. Carrie. She felt the warm blush of sheer pleasure creeping up into her cheeks. Things like this didn't happen very often, and she couldn't think of a word to say. Her instinct was to leap to her feet and fling herself into Carrie's arms, but perhaps Carrie would think this dreadfully babyish. Perhaps . . .

Carrie said, "Don't goggle. It's really me."

Slowly Lucy got to her feet. She said, "Goodness."

Carrie came into the room and gently closed the door behind her. "Surprised?"

"Yes. I'd no idea. Have you been here ages?"

"About an hour. Chatting to Ma."

"No. I mean in London."

"A week."

"I didn't know."

"Nobody did. Never mind, you know now." She stooped and planted a kiss on Lucy's cheek. She smelt gorgeous. "You've grown. Stupid thing to say. I used to bend double to kiss you." She looked about her. "What a pretty room. It used to be very gloomy. And how tidy. Have you been giving it a spring clean?"

"Not this morning. And Gran did it up for me. She let me choose the colours."

"Perfect. All sunny." There was a small blue armchair by the bed, and Carrie sank into this, long legs stretched out, her neatly booted feet crossed at the ankles. "Have you been working?"

"Yes. Homework." Lucy picked up her diary, stowed it away, privately, in a drawer, and then sat again, swivelling her typist's chair around so that she faced her aunt. "When did you get back?"

"I said. A week ago. I would have let you all know I was coming, but it was all a bit precipitant."

"How long are you home for?"

"Indefinitely. Chucked the ski job in. At the moment, I'm both homeless and unemployed, but it doesn't matter. How's everything with you?"

Lucy shrugged. "All right."

"There seems to be a certain crisis looming. Or perhaps it's already loomed. Poor child, you must be wondering what on earth is going to happen next."

This was in character, and Lucy was grateful. Carrie had always been completely direct, never avoiding awkward questions and coming straight to the point of any dilemma. Suddenly, Lucy felt much better, and even strong enough to ask, "Mummy didn't buy *two* air tickets for Florida, did she?"

"Would you have minded?"

"Dreadfully."

Carrie laughed. "Don't worry, she's going on her own. So that little battle you've actually won. It must have been something of a fight."

"Do you think I'm being *really* stupid, not wanting to go with her?"

"No, I think you're absolutely right. You'd be like a sore thumb, a green gooseberry. Much better for Nicola to be on her own. But it does pose problems."

"You mean Christmas?"

"No, I don't mean Christmas. I mean you. What do *you* want to do? I bet you anything nobody's even asked you that."

"Not really."

"I suggested you go to your father, but apparently he and Marilyn are off to the ski slopes with a lot of their friends."

"I wouldn't want to go with them. Marilyn doesn't like me much and I've never been skiing, so I don't suppose it would be all that much fun."

"You haven't got cosy schoolfriends with cosy mothers you'd want to go and be with?"

Lucy felt a bit abashed, because she hadn't. She had schoolfriends, of course, lots of them, but nobody special, nobody with a motherly mother. Emma Forbes was about her closest friend, and *her* mother was the editor of a magazine and always dashing off to meetings. Lucy scarcely knew her, and Emma had to be tremendously independent and organize her own social life with the help of a latchkey and a Swedish au pair. So far, for all their chat and giggles and time spent together, Emma had not even mentioned Christmas.

Carrie was waiting. Her dark eyes watched, and were filled with kindness. Lucy said, "I did think perhaps I could go to Cornwall. To Grandfather. The only thing is that I've never been and I can't even remember him, and I've never met Serena, or Ben, or Amy. And Gran's always horrid about him and won't talk, or say their names, but I thought perhaps if she didn't have any alternative, they might let me go."

"Would you like that?"

"Yes, I think I would. The only thing is, I've never been. . . ." Her voice trailed away. "And perhaps they wouldn't want me anyway."

Carrie said, "I think it's a wonderful idea, and I think one day you should go. But not this Christmas, because I spoke to Jeffrey when I got back from Austria, on the telephone, and I know they've got a houseful. Their house isn't very big anyway, tiny, in fact, and it's going to be stuffed to the gunwales with visitors."

Hope died. "Oh, well. It doesn't matter. . . ."

"But you should certainly go one day. In the spring, perhaps. They'd love it, and you'd love all of them. So we'll have to come up with something else."

We was significant. "We?"

"Yes. You and me. Orphans of the storm together. What shall we do?"

"You mean, for Christmas?"

"Of course, for Christmas."

"In London?"

"I think London would be rather dull, don't you? Perhaps we should go away."

"But where?"

There seemed to be no answer to this. They gazed at each other, and then Carrie got to her feet and went to the window, raising the voile curtain and staring down into the cheerless area three floors below. She said, "I've an idea. I just had it, this moment." She dropped the curtain and turned, and came to perch on the edge of Lucy's desk. She said, "Have you ever heard of Elfrida Phipps?"

Lucy shook her head, wondering what was coming next.

"She's heaven. A cousin of Jeffrey's. Your gran could never stand her, because she was rather wild and louche and an actress, and always had lots of boy-friends and husbands. They never had, what you might call, a lot in common, and your gran thoroughly disapproved of Elfrida. But I always loved her, and when I was at Oxford I started seeing her again, and we made terrific friends."

"How old is she?"

"Oh, ancient. Over sixty. But more fun than anyone you ever knew."

"Where does she live?"

"She used to live in London, but then her . . . well, he wasn't her husband, but she adored him . . . he died and she moved to the country.

Once, ages ago, she was ill after an operation, and I stayed with her until she was better, and we've always kept in touch. Now, she's living in a little village in Hampshire; she says the house is weeny. But there'd be space for you and me. And if there isn't space, Elfrida will make it. Would that be a good idea, do you think? Shall we give it a try?"

"You and me?"

"And Elfrida."

"For two weeks?"

"Of course."

"Would she mind?"

"I would bet my bottom dollar that she'll jump at it."

"How will we ask her?"

"I'll ring. I've got her number."

"Now?"

"No, not now. When I get back to Putney. We don't want the others to know our plans until they're all cut and dried. Then we'll present them as a *fait accompli*."

"If she *doesn't* have us for Christmas . . . ?"

"We mustn't think so negatively. We must be positive. And at the moment, don't say a word. It shall be our secret." Carrie pushed back the cuff of her cashmere sweater and looked at her watch. "Heavens, it's nearly one o'clock. I'm starving, aren't you? Your gran said she'd give us soup and pâté, but I'm not sure if that's going to sustain me. Why don't I take all four of us out to lunch. Is there somewhere cheap and cheerful not too far away?"

"There's Rosetti's. It's a five-minute walk."

"Italian?"

"Spaghetti and stuff."

"My favorite food. What do you say? Shall we go and round up our mothers and tell them they're in for a treat?"

Lucy remembered Emma. "I'm going to the cinema this afternoon with a girl-friend. I have to meet her at two-thirty."

"How do you get there?"

"Tube."

"No problem. We'll have lunch, and then I'll stand you a taxi. You won't be late."

It was getting better and better. Restaurant lunches and taxis. Lucy wondered if Carrie, returned from Austria, was now rich. She certainly looked rich, in her beautiful clothes and with her shining locks of hair and her glamorous make-up . . . just as good as the attenuated models who posed in leather and fur between the glossy pages of Gran's favourite, *Vogue*. She felt as though, suddenly, she had walked from a dark and cold corner into a blaze of warm sunshine. All part of being relieved, shed of worry, and having Carrie back again, a benevolent presence who was making everything all right. To her horror, emotion caused Lucy's eyes to mist over with ridiculous tears and she felt her face begin to crumple, like a baby's. "Oh, Carrie . . ."

"Hey, don't cry. There's nothing to cry about. We're going to have a great time." And she opened her arms, and Lucy stood, and leaned against her aunt, and pressed her cheek into the soft cashmere of her sweater, smelling her scent again. She was really here. Mercifully, before they could fall, the stupid tears receded, and in a moment she was able to find a handkerchief and lustily blow her nose. "I'm sorry."

"Nothing to be sorry about. Now, wash your face and find a jacket or something, and I'll go and break the happy news to the others."

"Just about lunch?"

"Just about lunch. We won't say a word about our plans until we've got them all cut and dried. A secret, between you and me."

She found Dodie in the little kitchen, endeavouring, in a half-hearted sort of way, to organize the promised snack. She had started to lay the table and was on the point of opening a tin of soup.

Carrie said, "Don't open it."

Dodie, startled, turned to face her younger daughter. "Why not?" She looked out of place in a kitchen, dressed as she was in her neat, formal clothes, and without a hair out of place. She hadn't even tied on an apron, and held the soup tin at arm's length, as though the opener might bite her.

"Because we're all going out to lunch. My treat. Lucy and I have decided a little self-indulgence is in order. She suggested someplace called Rosetti's. Is that all right by you?"

"Well. Yes." But Dodie still sounded doubtful. "I thought we'd agreed on soup and pâté. Here."

"You're quite right. We did. But minds have been changed."

"It's almost one o'clock. Will we get a table?"

"Why not? Would you like to ring them up? Do you know the number?"

"I think so."

"Then do that. And keep the can of soup for your supper. Where's Nicola?"

"In the drawing-room."

"Sulking?"

"No. Delighted with herself."

"Let's make a pact. Over lunch, no word of Florida. Lucy's had enough."

"Well, I most certainly have."

Carrie found Nicola deep in an armchair, turning over the pages of the new *Harpers and Queen* that she had bought on her way home from the travel agent. "Are you planning a new wardrobe for Florida?"

Nicola closed the magazine and dropped it on the floor. "I know what you think, Carrie, and I don't give a damn."

"Why should you care? And why shouldn't you go if you want to?"

"Do you really mean that?"

"Anything's better than hanging around here, creating discord and being resentful."

"Thank you *very* much."

"Oh, Nicola . . ." Carrie sat on the arm of the sofa. "Let's call a pax. We're going out for lunch. It'll cheer us up. And we're not going to talk about Florida, or Bournemouth or Christmas, or anything."

"Is this Lucy's idea?"

"No, mine. And I must congratulate you. She's sweet-looking and sweet-natured, which is more than one can say about most fourteen-year-old girls. You've done a good job."

"Well." Nicola, with the wind thus taken out of her sails, allowed herself a wry smile. "Thank you." And then hastily added, "But it's not been easy."

"I don't suppose bringing up children ever is. I wouldn't know. Now, come on, get your skates on. Ma's ringing the restaurant to be sure there's a table for us. And Lucy and I are going to eat great mounds of carbonara."

Over their mother's fireplace was a gold-framed Venetian mirror, which reflected back all the pretty charm of the double room. Nicola stood up and went to inspect herself in this, touching her hair and drawing her little finger across her painted lips. Then, through the mirror, her eyes met those of Carrie's. She said, "There is still a problem, though, isn't there?"

"I'll try to find a solution."

"Carrie, why did you come back from Austria?"

"Oh." Carrie shrugged. "A snap decision."

"Well, whatever the reason, I'm grateful." Nicola reached for her fur jacket, and then spoilt it all by saying, "At least it takes some of the pressure off me."

The lunch out proved a good idea. Both Dodie and Nicola relished the restaurant life, and their spirits lifted visibly even as the little party walked the short distance from Farnham Court to Rosetti's. The cold of the grey December day was a good excuse for Dodie to wrap herself into her new black fur-trimmed coat, and as she led the way through the glassed doors and into the warm and delicious-smelling interior of the restaurant, various charming and smiling Italians moved forward to greet her, to relieve her of her coat, to make her feel both pretty and important. The place was not large, and there were a number of diners already ensconced, but a corner table had been reserved for them, and once they were all sitting, Carrie wasted no time and ordered a round of drinks. Gin and tonics for Dodie and Nicola, Coke for Lucy, and a Tio Pepe for herself. Then she chose a bottle of wine to drink with their meal. Relaxed by alcohol, and soothed by the pleasant atmosphere of the little restaurant, tensions gradually loosed off, and conversation became, if not sparkling, then reasonably easy.

They had, after all, not been together for some years, and there was a great deal of chat and gossip to catch up on. Old friends, old acquaintances, distant relatives. Carrie was told about Dodie's cruises in the Mediterranean and about one particular Greek island with which she had fallen in love. "My dream would be to build a little house there." And Carrie, questioned, told them a bit about Oberbeuren and the magic of the mountains in summer, when walkers came to stay at the big hotel and the white ski-slopes became green pastures where cattle grazed and cowbells rang out in the glass-clear air.

Dodie and Nicola kept their word, and no mention was made of Christmas, Florida, or Bournemouth.

By the time they had finished their coffee and Carrie was dealing with the bill, it was time for Lucy to go. One of the obliging waiters went out and stood on the cold pavement, with his long white apron flapping in the wind, until he caught the eye of a cruising taxi-cab and flagged it down. Carrie gave Lucy some money to pay the fare, and they saw her safely aboard. Perched forward on the seat, she opened the window.

"Carrie, I haven't said thank you. It was a lovely treat."

"My pleasure. Enjoy the movie. And I'll ring you."

"Don't let it take too long."

"Soon as I can. Shan't waste a moment."

Nicola was more practical. "Lucy, when will you be home?"

"About seven."

"Take care."

"I will."

The taxi rolled away and they stood and watched it go, and then turned and began to stroll back down the pavement in the direction of the river. At the corner of Farnham Road, they paused to say goodbye.

"You've cheered us up no end." Dodie, warmed by quantities of good food and drink, was prepared to be generous. "So lovely to have you home again. Keep in touch. Let us know what you plan to do."

"Yes, of course. 'Bye, Ma." She dropped a kiss on her mother's cheek. "'Bye, Nicola. Shall I see you before you fly off?"

"Oh, probably. I'll be around. Thanks for the lunch."

"If I don't see you, have a great time."

"I have every intention of doing just that."

They parted. Carrie watched them go, the two ridiculously identical women, each totally bound up in her own affairs and problems. They didn't change. She turned and went on walking, and it wasn't until she was half-way across Putney Bridge, the east wind cold and damp on her cheeks, that she remembered Sara's note on the kitchen table, and the fact that Carrie was meant to buy a vegetable for dinner, and a packet of Lapsang Souchong tea-bags. So, half-way up Putney High Street, she went into a Pakistani grocery and loaded up with cauliflower and leeks, and some tiny new potatoes. She bought the tea-bags as well, and a nutty brown loaf, and a couple of bottles of Jacobs Creek wine. The handsome young man behind the till stowed all these into a carrier-bag, and took her money.

"My God," he remarked, "this is a cold day and no mistake. You will be grateful to be getting home."

She agreed and thanked him, and went out again, and the overcast winter afternoon was already sinking into dusk. Cars drove with lights on, and shop windows spilled bright squares out onto the dank pavements. By the time she had reached the Lumleys's little terrace house, Carrie's hands felt frozen, and it was quite painful to remove her glove and struggle with the latchkey. Indoors, she turned on the hall light, dealt with the alarm, and was grateful for the warmth. She went into the kitchen and dumped the carrier-bag on the table, and then, still in her coat, filled the kettle and plugged it in. She drew the blue-and-white-checked curtains and unpacked the groceries, by which time the kettle had boiled, and she made a mug of tea. Finally, she took off her coat and draped it over the back of a chair, found her handbag with her address book, and settled down by the telephone.

Elfrida Phipps, Poulton's Row, Dibton. Carrie lifted the receiver and punched in the number. She heard the double tone of Elfrida's telephone, and waited. She waited for a long time, but there was no reply, and clearly Elfrida had never got around to investing in an answerphone. Perhaps she was out. Carrie gave up, drank her tea, and then went upstairs to hang up her coat and change her shoes. Downstairs again, she dealt with the sitting-room curtains and lit the fire. After that, she returned to the kitchen and had another shot at reaching Elfrida. Once more, no joy. After the third try, by which time Carrie had peeled the potatoes for dinner, dealt with the cauliflower, and made a marinade for some chicken breasts, she began to be a little concerned. It was, after all, a long time since they had been in touch. Elfrida had never been a great letter writer, preferring the telephone, but she had always been *there*. Perhaps, dreadful thought, she had died. This possibility hit Carrie out of the blue, but then common sense got the better of her, and she knew that if anything had happened to Elfrida, then Jeffrey would have let her know.

Jeffrey. She would ring her father. Jeffrey would surely know the whereabouts of his cousin. His number at Emblo was one that Carrie knew by heart, so she lifted the receiver once more and put through the call. This time she was successful, and he answered almost at once.

"Jeffrey Sutton."

"Jeffrey, it's Carrie."

"Darling girl. How are you?"

"I'm fine. Cold, though."

"Isn't it hellish weather? We're almost being blown off the cliff."

"How are Serena and Ben and Amy?"

"They're well. Serena's taken the car to fetch them from school. So I'm sitting in solitary state writing cheques and paying bills. What can I do for you?"

"Have you a moment to talk?"

"How long a moment?"

"Like an hour."

"For heaven's sake, what's up?"

"I'm looking for Elfrida. I've been ringing the Dibton number, but there's no reply."

"She's not there."

"Not *there*?"

"She's in Scotland."

"What is she doing in Scotland?"

"She went last month. She's been there ever since."

"Why didn't you tell me when I rang you up last week?"

"There seemed to be other, more important things to talk about. Like you."

"Yes." Carrie felt a bit shamefaced. "Well. I'm sorry."

"I didn't realize that Elfrida's whereabouts were so important to you."

"Well, it's important now. Why did she go to Scotland?"

Jeffrey said, "It's a long story," and proceeded to tell her. That, in Dibton, Elfrida had these friends. A family called Blundell. They had been enormously hospitable to Elfrida, and she was clearly very fond of them. But then disaster, tragedy, had struck, and Mrs. Blundell and her daughter had both been killed in a horrendous road accident. Mr. Blundell, devastated, had left Dibton and escaped to Scotland, where, it seemed, he owned some small property. Elfrida had gone with him.

Listening in some horror to this sorry tale, Carrie found herself becoming increasingly bewildered. She knew Elfrida very well. Knew her to be kind-hearted and impetuous, without ever much thought for the day ahead. But even so, it all sounded a bit precipitous.

She said, voicing the first thought that came into her head, "Is she in love with this man?"

"I don't know, Carrie. I don't really know what's going on. She told me about it over the telephone, and she sounded more distressed than elated."

"In that case, she isn't in love with him. She's just being caring."

"She told me that he had asked her to go with him, for company and solace, and she'd said yes."

"What sort of solace? I ask myself."

"They were leaving the next day, driving, doing the long journey in stages."

"Whereabouts in Scotland are they?"

"Sutherland. Far North. I've got the address and the telephone number somewhere. I didn't want Elfrida disappearing into the blue without any person knowing where she was."

"Has she been in touch since she got there?"

"No. I imagine she has other matters to occupy her mind."

It was all very frustrating. Carrie said, "Oh, damn."

"What's that for?"

"I really *wanted* Elfrida. I wanted to get hold of her. To talk to her."

"Is there some problem?"

"You could say so."

"With you?"

"No. Not me. Your granddaughter, Lucy Wesley."

"Explain."

So then it was Carrie's turn to talk. To try to make clear to her father, in as few words as possible, the hopeless situation that existed at Farnham Court. Nicola taking off to spend Christmas in Florida with her new American boy-friend. Lucy refusing to accompany her. Dodie refusing to be left with Lucy, and instead planning a genteel festive season at the Palace Hotel, Bournemouth. And both Nicola and Dodie refusing to compromise or give way a single inch.

"So there's an impasse," she finished.

"What about Lucy's father?"

"Going skiing. Doesn't want her. It's all so dreadfully unfair, and she's such a nice child, she deserves better. I don't mind taking her on for Christmas, but I haven't got a house or a job or anything, so I thought of Elfrida."

"You should come to *us*." Jeffrey sounded agonized with guilt and Carrie hastened to reassure him.

"Jeffrey, we can't possibly come to Emblo. I know there's no space and it's not fair on Serena."

"Then why don't you ring Elfrida in Scotland. She can only say no, and she'd love a chat. You can hear the whole saga of Mr. Blundell from her own lips, and then you'll be far more in the picture than I am."

Carrie hesitated. "Doesn't it seem a bit intrusive?"

"I don't think so."

"I haven't seen Elfrida, nor spoken to her, for so long."

"All the more reason to telephone. Look, don't ring off; I'll find that number and her address. I put it down somewhere. . . ."

Carrie hung on. Faint noises could be heard, of drawers being opened and slammed shut, the rustling of papers. *It's a stupid idea*, she told herself. *We can't possibly go so far just to spend Christmas.* And then, another voice, *Why not?*

"Carrie?" He was back. "Got a pencil and paper?" Hastily, Carrie scrabbled around and found Sara's shopping list, and a Biro stuck in a blue-and-white mug. "This is the phone number." She took it down. "And this is the address. The Estate House, Creagan, Sutherland."

"Sounds frightfully grand."

"I don't think it is."

"How do you spell Creagan?"

He spelt it out for her.

"Perhaps I should write a letter," Carrie was beginning to lose her nerve.

"That's feeble. And it'll take too long. Telephone. Right away. Speak to Elfrida. And, Carrie . . ."

"Yes."

"Send her my love."

Oscar

In mid-winter, it was an alien land. Monotone beneath a sky scoured white by the wind. The hills, sweeping down to the coast, were already topped by an icing of snow, and the snow merged with the clouds so that the summits of the hills were lost to view, veiled, blurred, as though already absorbed by the doleful heavens.

It was alien because Oscar did not remember the landscape thus. Always, as a boy, he had come in the summer to visit his grandmother at Corrydale, and in summer, so far north, the afternoons had stretched on and on until ten or eleven o'clock at night, and at bedtime the shadows of trees fell long, across golden sun-washed lawns.

He walked, with Horace. He had left the house after lunch, setting out with a stout stick to help him on his way, and insulated against the cold by a fleece-lined jacket and an ancient tweed hat pulled low over his brow. His boots were sturdy, built for walking, and once he had traversed the streets of the little town and climbed the hill to the gate above the golf links, he was able to step out at some speed; so after a bit he forgot about feeling cold and was aware of his body, warm beneath all the layers of wool, and the quickened pace of his heartbeat.

Horace bounded cheerfully ahead, and they followed a footpath high above the links, winding between thickets of gorse. After a mile or so, this path led over a stile and along the track of a disused railway, where once, coming from London, Oscar had chuntered his way into Creagan on the small branch line, with many stops for level crossings and gates to be opened.

The sea lay to his right, beyond the links and the dunes. Steel-coloured beneath the winter sky, cheerless; the tide far out. He stopped to listen and heard the breakers on the beach, driven in by the wind, and the cry of gulls. Observing the gulls, he saw, to his mild surprise, that there were a few hardy golfers out, brightly dressed figures striding down the fairways, hauling their clubs on trolleys behind them. He remembered that when his grandmother played golf, she had always employed a caddie, and always the same man, an old reprobate called Sandy, who knew every curve and hazard of fairway and green, and advised her accordingly. A good deal of the time, Sandy teetered on the verge of drunkenness, but when he caddied for Mrs. McLennan, he wore the mien of a sober judge and behaved accordingly.

The old railway track petered out into a thicket of broom, and rounding this stretch, Oscar saw that they had reached the end of the links, the turn of the course, and the ninth tee. Now, the next stretch of coastline revealed itself, another wide and shallow bay, an old pier, and a cluster of fisher cottages, huddled down, single-storied, crouched from the teeth of the wind.

It was then that he heard the voices. A man calling, a murmur of conversation. He turned his head and saw, below him, a group of four men making their way to the tee. Oscar was instantly wary, fearing that one of them might be Major Billicliffe, and he would be spied, and forced into introductions and convivial chat. He stood very still, hoping to render himself invisible, but his fears were, thankfully, ill-founded. Major Billicliffe, tall as a tree and with his skinny shanks draped in tweedy plus-fours, was not one of the group. Instead, Oscar saw the four sturdy figures bundled up in coloured jackets and waterproof trousers, wearing white golf shoes and long-peaked American caps. Billicliffe would never be so trendy.

Major Billicliffe was the main reason that Oscar had kept a low profile ever since their arrival in Creagan. From time to time, urged by Elfrida, he had nipped across the road to the supermarket, to stock up on beer or to buy a loaf of bread, and his daily outing was a trip to the newsagent to pick up *The Times* and *The Telegraph*. On these occasions he kept an eye open, just in case Billicliffe should be bearing down upon him, loud with greeting and invitations to his terrible house.

Elfrida thought Oscar was being feeble. "He's harmless, Oscar, just a stupid old man. You must be firm if you meet him. Polite but firm."

"He is a terrifying bore."

"You can't cower indoors for the rest of your life. It's ridiculous."

"I am cowering indoors because the weather is inclement, to say the least of it."

"Rubbish. You spent the whole of Saturday raking leaves in the garden. In the pouring rain."

"Billicliffe can't get into my garden."

"He could see you over the wall. He's tall enough."

"Don't even suggest it."

This walk with Horace was Oscar's first real foray into the countryside, and he had started out because all of a sudden he was restless, filled with nervous energy, and knew a physical need to stretch his legs. Even the prospect of encountering Major Billicliffe did not put him off, and, as Elfrida constantly pointed out, he could not spend the rest of his life cowering indoors, ducking behind a sofa every time the front-door bell rang.

It was all very unfortunate. Because Billicliffe, retired factor of Corrydale, was the man who had had custody of the key of the Estate House, and calling upon him, to take possession of this key, had been their first priority.

The occasion had not been propitious. At the end of a long winter drive from Hampshire, which had taken two days, both Oscar and Elfrida were exhausted. They had travelled by the A1, battling with rain, long-distance lorries, and manic car drivers speeding past in the fast lane. Crossing the border into Scotland, climbing Soutra, the rain had turned to sleet, and then snow, and conditions had become even more dicey.

Elfrida had suggested stopping once more for a restful night, but Oscar simply wanted to *get* there, and so they had pressed on, farther and farther north, and at the summit of Drumochter the snow had been six inches deep and they had crawled along, hoping with every mile that the storm would let up for just a few hours.

Darkness fell early, and the final miles were achieved in night-time conditions. As well, Oscar found that his memory failed him, and he became confused by new road systems and bypasses which had been built since his long-ago boyhood visits.

"Why does everything have to change?" he complained pettishly, struggling to read the map by the light of a torch.

"For the better," Elfrida told him firmly. "At least we're not threading our way along a single-track lane."

Finally, they were crossing the new bridge that spanned the firth.

"In the old days," Oscar remembered, "we had to drive over the hills and about five miles inland."

"You see. Things are better. Where do we go next?"

"We have to turn left, back onto the old road, heading west."

"Will the old road still be there?"

"If it isn't, we're scuppered."

But it was there, and in the dark, they turned off the fast dual-carriage way and set out into the country. By now Elfrida was getting very tired. Finding Billicliffe's house was the final, frustrating straw. "He's in old Ferguson's cottage," Hector had told Oscar when asked for instructions and directions. "Used to be head forester. You remember him. Turn into the main gates and follow your nose. I'll ring him and tell him you're coming."

But somehow, in the darkness, they lost all sense of distance, and so overshot the main gates, and too late, Oscar saw the sign as it flashed past.

☆ ☆ ☆ ☆

CORRYDALE COUNTRY HOTEL. A.A. R.A.C. XXXV

So then they had to find someplace to turn and retrace their steps. This took a long time, and there was a muddy farmyard with a ferociously barking dog. Back again, at a snail's pace, and this time they were more successful. Once through the gates, Oscar peered around him, trying to find landmarks, but ended up becoming more confused than ever.

"I don't remember any of this," he complained, sounding as though his amnesia were all Elfrida's fault.

"Things change, Oscar. Things change."

"I can't see a single bloody house anywhere."

"Well, we can't drive round in circles for the rest of the night."

Elfrida was beginning to sound a little desperate. Oscar hoped she wasn't about to lose her cool, because she had been so wonderfully calm for two days, and he didn't think he could bear it if she became as despairing as he already felt. "Are you sure we're on the right road?"

But Oscar, by now, wasn't sure. He wasn't sure about anything any longer. He said sadly, "Perhaps we are too old for wild-goose chases."

"Oh, don't be ridiculous, of course we're not. And it's not a wild-goose chase, it's a key chase. We've got to get the key. All we have to do is find the stupid cottage."

Which, in the end, of course they did. Quite by chance, turning left onto a rutted lane that seemed to lead nowhere. But instead, all at once, there was a light, shining through naked trees. They found an open gate and a short driveway leading to a single small stone house, with a single curtained window lighted from within.

"Is this it?" Elfrida asked in doubtful tones.

Recognizable. Remembered. Oscar breathed a sigh of relief. "This," he told her, "is it."

"Thank God for that."

She turned the car in through the gate and drew up in front of the small house, the tyres scrunching on pebbly gravel. Their headlights illuminated a rural wooden porchway, a closed door. Elfrida switched off the engine. At once, nearly frightening them both out of their wits, the quiet was ripped apart by a cacophony of deep-throated barking, and furious, eerie howls.

Elfrida said, "For heaven's sake."

"A dog," Oscar observed.

"A mastiff. A Rottweiler. A hound. A Baskerville hound. I'm not getting out of this car. I would prefer to keep all my limbs."

But then there came the sound of a human voice, raised in fury, and a slammed door. The barking stopped. In the back seat, poor patient Horace sat up and gazed in a timid fashion out of the window. It was clear that he didn't wish to lose a limb either. They waited.

Oscar said, "We're just going to collect the key, and get on our way. No socializing."

"Whatever you want."

The door of the cottage was opened. Within shone the dim illumination of a small lobby. A lanky, gangling figure stood there, sagging at the knees in order to peer out beneath the low lintel, and with a hand up to shade his eyes against the glare of the car lights. Elfrida, obligingly, turned them off.

"That you? Blundell? Been waiting . . ."

The sentence was not finished, simply left hanging in the air.

Oscar and Elfrida got out of the car, both stiff and aching with exhaustion. Oscar felt his knees creaking. The outside air was bitterly cold.

"I'm sorry," he apologized, although indeed they could scarcely have arrived earlier. "Difficult, driving in the dark. It's all unfamiliar. We've come for the key, and then . . ."

He had been going to say, ". . . we'll be on our way," but Major Billicliffe overrode him.

"Of course. Got it here. Come along in. Just going to have a sniffer. You'll join me."

"Well . . ."

"Splendid to see you. Been looking forward. Come in out of the cold."

He stood aside, holding the door open in an hospitable manner, and after a moment's hesitation Oscar capitulated, although all he wanted was no further delay; to complete this hideous journey, get to Creagan and take possession of his house. But it seemed that they were in for a social encounter, with drinks.

"Thank you," he said weakly, and put out a hand to steer Elfrida in front of him. "This is my friend, Elfrida Phipps. She came to share the driving with me."

"Splendid. Splendid. Hell of a long way. Charmed to meet you, ma'am." He took Elfrida's hand, and for a mad moment Oscar thought he might be about to press a kiss upon it, so courtly and old-worldly was his manner.

Elfrida said, "Hello."

"Now, let's get the door closed, and shut the damned cold away. Come along. . . ."

They followed him into a small, low-ceilinged sitting-room, where a tiny fire in a tiled grate did little to warm the air. All seemed to be in a state of sad confusion. Sagging leather chairs, a wrinkled rug, a carpet covered in dog's hairs, ashtrays brimming with pipe ash.

At the back of the room was another door, behind which the enraged dog had been shut away. Whines and heavy breathing emanated from beyond, and every now and then they heard a thump and a rattle of a latch, as, frustrated beyond measure, the imprisoned brute flung his weight against the door.

Elfrida, naturally enough, began to look a bit nervous. "What kind of dog is it?" she asked.

"Labrador," Major Billicliffe told her. "Dear old bitch. Wouldn't hurt a fly."

Over the fire was a mantelpiece crowded with an array of objects—tarnished mugs, a golf ball, a clock which had stopped at a quarter past twelve, some dog-eared postcards and invitations, and a leather box in which Major Billicliffe kept his hearing aids. Before doing anything else, he retrieved these and proceeded to fit them into his huge red ears. Oscar and Elfrida watched, fascinated, while he made a few squeaking adjustments with the tip of his finger, before he was finally satisfied. He then turned back to them, wearing an expression of satisfaction, as though a difficult job had been well done.

"That's better. Take them out most of the time. Sometimes forget where I've put 'em. Now, what can I get you?"

He made his way across the room to where stood an old trolley on wheels, laden with bottles and with one or two smeary glasses set out on the bottom shelf. "Bar's open."

Oscar longed for a cup of tea, but knew that that would take much longer to prepare. "A Scotch would be splendid. Very small. A lot of water. . . ."

"And the lady?"

Elfrida looked a bit nonplussed. She, as well, was clearly longing for a hot cup of tea. But she said bravely, "A sherry?"

"Got some somewhere. Where's the bottle?" He held it up. It contained a very small quantity of liquid. "Just enough for one."

Pouring drinks, he talked. Oscar and Elfrida stood by the miserable fire and did not interrupt. " 'Fraid the housekeeping's a bit hit-and-miss these days. Wife died, you know, couple of years ago. Miss her like hell, but what can one do? I've got a female who's meant to come and clean." Oscar watched him splashing clumsily about with bottles and jugs, spilling water on the carpet, lifting a glass with a trembling hand. To look at, Major Billicliffe was something of an old wreck, knock-kneed as a horse on its way to the knacker's yard, and with thin, stockinged legs that ended in a pair of enormous black unpolished brogues. His head was bald, sparsely covered with a few strands of grey hair, and his eyes rheumy. A tobacco-stained moustache overhung yellowed, uneven teeth. It was hard to imagine him as a dapper upright officer in any regiment of the British Army.

"Hector rang me and said you'd be coming. Delighted. About time we had a bit of new blood about the place. How is the old boy? Funny we've never met before, you and I, but then, it's years. . . . I've been here since the sixties, came straight out of the Army. Well, not quite. Did a course at Cirencester first, had to qualify. Factor. Not a job any fool can do. Good fishing. The wife found it a bit lonely. Didn't fish. Walked the dogs. The old telly saved her reason." He had achieved their drinks, and now, with a glass in either hand, came shambling over to deliver them. "The whisky looks a bit pale. Sure that's all right?"

"Perfect," Oscar lied.

Major Billicliffe returned to the trolley in order to deal with his own thirst. Which seemed to require an enormously dark whisky in a small tumbler.

"Ought to be some eats about the place. A crisp. Sit down, make yourselves comfortable."

"We mustn't be too long."

"Won't take you five minutes to get to Creagan." Without much alternative, Oscar and Elfrida perched on a sofa, side by side. The sofa stank of dog. Across the hearthrug, Major Billicliffe lowered his tremendous height into the only armchair, his bony knees knobbly beneath the worn tweed of his knickerbockers.

"I'm retired now, of course. Good of Hector to let me buy this cottage, but it was standing empty anyway. And Hughie couldn't care less. The days of farm workers and tied cottages are over. All contractors now. Damned great machinery. Liked working for Hector, but it didn't last long. Hector went, Hughie came, and fairly put the cat amongst the pigeons. Orgies, he used to have in the big house. Bloody orgies. Disgraceful. Set a rotten example. Is that drink all right? Couldn't deal with the fella at all. Parted brass rags, as they say in the Royal Navy, but by then I'd had a bellyful and was ready to go out to grass. Now, everything's different. Hughie buggered off to Barbados and sold the place up. Hotel. You probably saw the sign. All plate glass and bathrooms. And the bar prices are daylight robbery. Never go near the place. All that's left of the estate now is the Home farm, and young Thomson . . . his father used to be tenant farmer . . . bought it when the estate was sold up. Seems to be doing all right. But I never go near the hotel. Told you. Take my pleasures in the Golf Club. Do you play golf? Quite a jolly little group of us down there. You should join. Put your name up if you like. Short walk from the Estate House. Nice old pair, been living there for years. Cochrane was their name. Then he upped and died and she's gone south to live with her daughter. Lucky for you, perhaps. Then, there's Mrs. Snead . . . keeps an eye on the place. Comes and goes. Think Hector pays her a retainer. He never said."

Oscar nodded.

"Nice woman. Nice woman. . . . Met her in the butcher's. Said she'd get the boiler going. Not my responsibility any longer, or I'd have popped in for CO's inspection."

Oscar, feeling desperate, said, "The key?"

Major Billicliffe frowned in a bewildered fashion. "Sorry?"

"The key. To the Estate House. If you could let me have it, and then we'll get out of your way."

"Ah, yes. Got it somewhere." He knocked back his drink with one expert toss of his elbow, laid down the empty glass and heaved himself to his feet. Across the room once more, to an old roll-top desk, standing open and chaotically untidy. Stooping over this, he rootled hopelessly around for a moment or two, feeling into pigeon-holes, opening and shutting drawers. At last, "Eureka," he exclaimed, and held up a large old-fashioned key tied to a crumpled label. "Knew I'd put it somewhere. Get a bit forgetful these days."

Oscar and Elfrida, finished with their meagre drinks, rose firmly to their feet. Oscar took the key from Major Billicliffe's hand. "Thank you. I am sorry we disturbed you."

"Didn't disturb me at all. Splendid to have a bit of company. Remember, I'm usually in the club most days. Don't play as much as I used to. Good to have a crack with old chums, and you can get a jolly-good sandwich in the bar." They eased their way towards the door. "You must come and see me again. And perhaps I'll pop in and call at the Estate House. See how you're settling in."

Elfrida smiled. She said, "Of course. But don't come *quite* right away. Oscar's not been very well, and we'll need a little time."

"Of course, of course. But we'll certainly see each other around."

Now, in the middle of his long walk, Oscar paused to watch the golfers, safe in the knowledge that the dreaded Billicliffe was not one of the four men. They had already positioned themselves, selected clubs, and not wishing to disturb them, nor deflect their attention, he stood motionless until the last player had whacked his ball into what appeared to be orbit. The light was already dying, and it occurred to Oscar that they would have to get their skates on if they were to be back in the clubhouse before dark. The golfer stooped to retrieve his tee, and in doing so, caught sight of Oscar.

Across the rolling fairway that lay between them, their eyes, for an instant, met. The other man raised a hand in greeting, or maybe simply an acknowledgement of Oscar's consideration. Oscar returned his salute. Then the golfer stowed his driver into his bag, picked up the handle of his trolley, and set off after his friends. Oscar watched him go. A burly figure in his scarlet jacket and bright-blue trousers. He wondered if he was a visitor to Creagan—come perhaps from the United States—or a local resident. Moments later, he disappeared behind the natural hazard of a gorsy hillock, and Oscar and the dog continued on their way.

He was beginning to feel a bit weary. Below him, between the links and the dunes, he saw the stony track used by the greenskeepers' tractors, which led back to the town. Beyond curved the long sweep of the beach, and ahead, in the far distance, he could see, silhouetted against the grey clouds, the random roof-tops and the church spire of the town. The effect was sombre as an old etching. It seemed a very long way off, and he wondered if perhaps he had bitten off more than he could chew. But then he spied the small wooden shelter provided for the convenience of golfers. As he approached, Oscar saw that it was divided into four segments, giving shelter from any prevailing wind, and each furnished with a small wooden bench. He decided to sit for a moment, to get his breath; he chose the most suitable compartment, was grateful for shelter, and made himself as comfortable as he could.

He thought about the golfers, companionably playing their game deep into the dusk of a dying afternoon, and knew an envy that was almost resentment. They were together. Friends. Talking, joking, competing. They would have a drink in the clubhouse, part, return to their families. Ordinary men.

He wondered if he would ever be ordinary again.

Once, long ago, as a boy, Oscar had played golf, but never very proficiently. Perhaps he should take it up again. Should buy himself an expensive set of clubs, with a Big Bertha driver, and astonish everybody, including himself, with a startling prowess at pitch and putt. The prospect, though amusing, did not make him smile. Now, nothing much made him smile.

Grieving. He was still grieving. He had himself often used this innocuous word, writing to friends recently bereaved of wife, parent, even a child. It was a word that covered a multitude of unexperienced emotions. *Sympathy* was another. *I send my deepest sympathy and my thoughts are with you,* he would write, and sign the letter and duly post it with the knowledge of a necessary task performed to the best of his ability.

He knew now that he had not had an inkling of what he was talking about. Grief was not a state of mind, but a physical thing, a void, a deadening blanket of unbearable pain, precluding all solace. His only protection, and one that he had built himself, was a palisade of non-communication. Here, in Creagan, he was spared the encounters, the chance meetings with a casual acquaintance. Spared the insult of the vicar's churchly comfort, the pain of another's embarrassment. The clumsy but well-meant condolences, eyes that did not meet his own.

During his walk, he had, as was his custom, observed sky, clouds, hills, birds. Had felt the wind on his cheeks and listened to the thunder of breakers on the shore. He had smelt the sweet strong scent of moss and ling . . . all with no reaction, no lift of the spirit, no marvel. No inspiration. No joy. It was a bit like looking at an indifferent painting, a huge landscape painstakingly executed, but lacking all soul.

He had always despised self-pity, and now, sitting huddled in the small wooden shelter, he fought it like a lion, striving to be positive, to count present blessings. First was the Estate House. The fact that he owned a bit of it and that it stood empty, a timely sanctuary to which he had fled. Second was Elfrida. Her reappearance after her holiday in Cornwall had been of the utmost relief to Oscar. Her companionship had saved his reason, and in her own uncomplicated way she had got him through the blackest times, comforting by simply accepting his limitations. When he fell silent, she left him alone. When he felt compelled to talk, Elfrida listened.

And third was the knowledge that, even if he did not stay forever in this remote northern community where once he had been a boy and been happy, there was no need, or even the possibility, of returning to the house that had been Gloria's. Already, her two sons had taken possession of the Grange, and put it on the market. And in a way Oscar was grateful to them, because their swift and not wholly commendable actions had spared him the ordeal of existing in a space haunted by memories of Francesca, and filled only with a cold and numbing silence.

I must go on, he told himself. Move forward, a step at a time. But at sixty-seven, with most of his life behind him, it sometimes seemed impossible to summon the energy. That deadening blanket, compounded of shock and terrible loss, had not only blinded and deafened him, but imbued every bone in his body with a dreadful and pervasive fatigue.

"I must go on." This time he said the words aloud, and Horace, who had been lying at his feet, sat up and looked hopeful and even smiled. He was a very smiley dog. Oscar was grateful for his company. He got to his feet.

"Come on, old chap. Time we headed for home."

By the time he finally reached the clubhouse it was dark, and

Oscar was very tired. He trudged up the right-of-way that led between the fairways and saw the blaze of lights shining out from wide windows, behind which figures could be seen, relaxed as though in a friendly pub, sitting at tables, eating sandwiches, doubtless discussing their game. Between the clubhouse and the first tee was a paved forecourt with raised beds which, in summer, would probably sport cheerful clumps of colour, begonias and geraniums. To the side of the clubhouse was the car-park, now floodlit from above. A dozen or so vehicles were still standing there, and as Oscar wearily approached, he saw a well-worn estate car, with its tail-gate down. On this a man was perched, in the act of changing his studded golf shoes for a pair of brogues. Oscar recognized the red wind-cheater and the bright-blue weatherproof trousers, but the long-peaked American cap had been removed, and cold light shone down upon a head of thick greying hair.

The man tied the last lace and got to his feet. By now, Oscar was alongside. For an instant he hesitated, debating as to whether he should stop and exchange a friendly word. Ask, perhaps, how the game had gone. But even as he wavered, the decision was taken out of his hands.

"Hello, there. Did you have a good walk?"

Oscar paused, then turned to face him. "A bit too far, perhaps. I'm out of practice. How did you get along?"

"We gave up on the fifteenth. Chickened out. Too dark and too cold." He stooped to retrieve his golf shoes, chucked them into the back of the car, and slammed shut the tail-gate. "Not the weather for an enjoyable game." He came forward. Oscar saw a ruddy countryman's face and a pair of piercingly blue eyes. "Forgive me, but you're Oscar Blundell."

Oscar found himself disconcerted by being not only recognized, but identified. He said "Yes," and it sounded like an admission.

"I knew you'd come back to Creagan." (What else did he know?) "I've only been here for twenty years, so I never met your grandmother, Mrs. McLennan. But I did have the pleasure of a good friendship with Hector. Just for a short while, before he handed Corrydale over to Hughie and went south to live. I'm Peter Kennedy, by the way." He stuck out a hand, which Oscar took in his own gloved one. "Welcome to Creagan."

"Thank you."

"You must be exhausted. That's a long hike in the teeth of the wind. I'm just going in for a cup of tea. Would you care to join me?"

Oscar was silenced, hesitating, torn by conflicting emotions. It was true. He was bone-weary, and the thought of sitting down for a bit in the warmth, indulging in the solace of a restoring and hot cup of tea, was a very tempting one. On the other hand, he was not sure if he felt brave enough to go into that brightly lighted and convivial clubhouse. He would perhaps be introduced, have to talk to strangers, answer questions.

But there was something so warm and genuine about his new friend, so disarming and sincere, that he could not bring himself to refuse the invitation outright. Instead, he searched for some excuse.

"I have the dog."

"We'll put him in my car. He'll come to no harm for a little while."

"I . . ." It had to be said. "I would prefer not to encounter Major Billicliffe."

Peter Kennedy's cheerful face creased into an understanding smile. "Don't worry." He laid a hand on Oscar's arm. "He went home five minutes ago. I saw him drive off."

"You'll think me uncharitable."

"No. I don't think that. So you'll join me?"

"Yes. Yes, I will. I would like to. Thank you very much."

"I'm delighted."

They dealt with Horace, incarcerating him in the back of Peter Kennedy's estate car, along with the shoes and the golf bag. He gazed at them reproachfully through the back window, but Oscar hardened his heart.

"I won't be long," he told the dog.

They walked together, side by side, around the corner of the clubhouse, and up the shallow flight of steps that led to the main door.

Peter Kennedy opened this and held it for Oscar to go through into a foyer, hectically carpeted and lined with cabinets containing silver trophies and shields. Portraits of former captains glowered down at them. To the right, glassed doors fed into the main room, furnished with tables and comfortable chairs, and with a small bar in the corner. As they entered, one or two people looked up, but by and large nobody took much notice of them.

"We'll go and sit over there. There's a free table, and we'll be quiet. . . ."

But before they could do this, a swing door by the side of the bar flew open, and an elderly waitress appeared. She wore a black skirt and a white blouse, and her white hair was marvellously waved and dressed. Spying them, she was at once all smiles.

"Mr. Kennedy. I didn't think we'd be seeing you this evening."

"Hello, Jessie. Are we too late for a cup of tea?"

"Never too late. You must be frozen, out playing on a day like this." Her eyes turned to Oscar, who had removed his tweed hat and was standing there, bundled up in all his layers of coats and sweaters. "Have you been playing, too?"

"No. Just walking."

"Jessie, this is Mr. Oscar Blundell. He's come to stay at the Estate House."

"Oh, my, that's who you are. I'd heard you'd moved in, but I haven't seen you around. Are you a golfer, too?"

"I'm sorry, no."

"We'll have to rectify that. Now, Mr. Kennedy, where do you want to sit?"

But before there was time to tell her, an interruption occurred. From across the long room there came a shout, a deep voice ringing out like a clarion, startling everyone, and causing frowns from a group who were crouched around the television.

"*Peter!* Come away over, and have a word. I haven't seen you for a week or more."

Peter Kennedy swung around, and Oscar, following his gaze,

saw, in the far corner, a heavily built and aged man sitting in a wheelchair, with a tumbler of whisky ready to hand on the table in front of him.

"Peter!" He was waving a knotted stick, as though it were possible that he had neither been heard nor seen. "Come and give me all the news."

"Would you mind, Oscar, if I left you for a moment? It's old Charlie Beith, and I must go and pay my respects. . . ."

"Of course."

"I'll be just a moment. Jessie will take care of you." He went, making his way down the length of the room. "What a great surprise," he was saying. "Are you having a day out, Charlie?" And the old man in the wheelchair greeted him with such delight and affection that Oscar felt that he was in some way intruding, and turned away.

Jessie took charge. "Come and sit down and get comfortable. Take your coat off, or you'll not feel the benefit when you go out again. Would you like a scone? And do you prefer Indian or China tea?"

Oscar said, "I'm sorry, but who is that?"

"Charlie Beith? He's a real character, over ninety, though you'd never know it. Used to farm out at Toshlands, years ago. His grandson's running the place now. He was doing fine till a couple of years ago, when he had a stroke. He lives in the old people's home, and Mr. Kennedy's a regular visitor. One of his daughters brought him up here this evening, just for a bit of a change and some cheerful company. He's as bright as a button up top."

"In fact," Oscar hesitated, "I didn't mean the old man. I meant Peter Kennedy. I've only just met him in the car-park. He knew my uncle. But I don't know . . ."

"You mean you don't know what he does or who he is? You must be the only soul in Creagan who doesn't. He's our minister. The minister of the church."

The minister. The vicar. The rector. Whatever. The man whose job it was to comfort not only the physically, but the emotionally crippled as well. Peter Kennedy's spontaneous friendliness had seemed genuine, but this new knowledge rendered it depressingly suspect. Did he already know why Oscar had returned to Creagan? Had he been told about the ghastly deaths of Oscar's wife and child? And if so, who . . . ?

But I did have the pleasure of a good friendship with Hector.

Had Hector, with only the best of intentions, been in touch with Peter Kennedy? Explained the situation? Suggested, perhaps, a pastoral visit? Comforting chats; counselling; a gentle urging back to a church in which Oscar no longer believed?

Jessie said, "Are you all right?"

He looked into her concerned and motherly face and realized that his own was suffused with heat, his forehead wet with sweat. A heat kindled not by the warm room and his layers of outdoor clothes but an inner turmoil that was frighteningly akin to panic. He knew that he could not stay there, or he would suffocate.

With a huge effort, he made himself speak. "I am sorry. It's very warm. I've just remembered . . ." His voice sounded unreal, like a voice from another room. "I promised. I must get home. A telephone call . . ."

"But what about your tea?"

"I'm afraid I can't. . . ." Backing off, he tried to apologize again. "I'm sorry. Please explain to Mr. Kennedy. Another time . . ."

He turned away from her, and carefully, slowly, made for the door. The plate glass was heavy to open, and swung shut behind him. He crossed the foyer and opened the second set of doors, and stepped out into the bitter air. The cold wind was an assault, and he stopped to steady himself, to let the icy air fill his lungs. He could feel the sweat chilling on his brow and pulled on his old tweed hat. He was all right. He was surviving. All he had to do was get himself home. To be safe. Alone with Elfrida. He went down the steps and crossed over to the car-park and retrieved Horace from Peter Kennedy's car. Then he was on his way, walking at a tremendous pace, dragging the dog behind him. Escaping.

ELFRIDA

In Dibton, the Women's Institute was great on mystery tours. These usually took place on a Saturday afternoon, and entailed the ladies' being piled into a bus and whirled off to some unknown destination. Quite often, this was a Stately Home, with gardens to be viewed, and a gift shop where they could buy flowered tea-towels, bookmarks, and packets of home-made fudge. After the shopping, tea would be partaken at some local hotel. A proper tea, with fish and chips. Then they would all pile into the bus once more, and be driven home.

These outings were very popular.

Spirited away so abruptly, by circumstances outside her control, to the north of Scotland, to Creagan and the Estate House was, Elfrida decided, the mystery tour of all time. From the moment she and Oscar departed from Dibton, she had no idea of what lay in store for her, and there never came an appropriate moment to ask. So precipitant had been their departure, so swift the packing process, and so brief the time for goodbyes, that nit-picking details of their destination lost all importance. They just had to get away.

There were, of course, essential arrangements to be made. Oscar's car had to be serviced, checked, and filled with petrol. He saw to that. His stepsons, Giles and Crawford, were informed of his imminent departure, and his bank manager alerted as to his change of address.

As for Elfrida, she handed the key of Poulton's Row over to her neighbour, with as few explanations as possible, and asked her, as well, to keep an eye on the poor little Ford Fiesta, abandoned on the pavement outside her cottage.

"When will you be back, Mrs. Phipps?"

"I've truly no idea. But I'll keep in touch. Here's the car key as well. Use it if you want, it'll do it good." Rather as though it were an old dog, needing daily exercise. "I've turned the water off at the mains, and locked all the windows."

"But where are you going?"

"I think, to Scotland."

Then Oscar had to get in touch with Hector McLennan and put him in the picture, while Elfrida telephoned her cousin Jeffrey in Cornwall and tried to explain to him the circumstances of what she was about to do. She did not make a very good job of this, and it took him some time to get the hang of the situation. When he finally did, however, he only said "Good luck," and once she had given him the address and the telephone number of Oscar's house, he let her go and rang off.

Without any clear idea of what sort of clothes she would need, she packed a suitcase with an assortment of garments (warm) and shoes (stout). Then, an ancient, squashy, zipped bag, for her most precious things, the possessions that had always travelled everywhere with her. The silk shawl, wrapped around the little painting by Sir David Wilkie. The Staffordshire dogs; her clock; her current piece of tapestry. On top went a few photographs in silver frames, and half a dozen books. That was all. Oscar's luggage was scarcely more bulky. A leather hold-all, packed by Mrs. Muswell, a bulging brief-case, and his fishing gear.

"Do you intend to go fishing, Oscar?"

"No idea. But I can't travel to Scotland without my rod. It would be almost sacrilegious."

There was space for all this in the back of Oscar's Volvo, and still room for Horace, his blanket, biscuits, and water bowl. Horace, like

Elfrida, had no idea what was in store for him, but leaped happily into the car and made himself comfortable, clearly deeply relieved that he was not going to be left behind. He did not trust suitcases standing about the place.

"We are travelling light," Elfrida observed to Oscar, but he was too anxious and distracted to make any comment on her remark. Instead, he turned away to give last-minute instructions to his loyal Mrs. Muswell, who had stood by him all through the dark days, and now stood on the doorstep, clearly much distressed, as though at any moment she might burst into tears.

"Mrs. Muswell."

"Send me a postcard," she told him bravely, but her voice was not steady.

"Of course. Goodbye. And thank you for everything." And he gave her a quick peck on the cheek, which caused Mrs. Muswell to go to pieces. As they drove away from the Grange, Elfrida saw through the back window the gallant pinafored figure blowing her nose and wiping her eyes with a handy handkerchief.

"What will become of her?" Elfrida asked, feeling like a traitor.

"Giles has promised he'll see her right. She should have no difficulty in finding a job. She's a marvellous woman."

After that they stopped talking. Elfrida drove most of the way, only letting Oscar take over when she became dangerously weary. TIREDNESS CAN KILL roadside signs shouted at the cars and lorries which streamed north on the A1. TAKE A BREAK. And she would draw the car to the side of the road at the next lay-by or motorway halt, and change seats with him.

During the first day he scarcely spoke at all, and she let him be silent and did not even suggest that they listen to Classic FM on the car radio. From time to time they stopped to give Horace a run, stretch their own legs, have something to eat, or a cup of tea. The weather was cold and bleak and darkness fell early, and after that, driving became even more stressful. Because of this, they left the motorway and drove to a small Northumberland town that Oscar remembered. And there, in the main square, found an old coaching inn that he remembered as well, and it didn't seem to be too modernized or changed. Better still, the management were kindly about Horace, and allowed him in, provided he and his blanket stayed upstairs.

On the second morning, as soon as the shops were open, Elfrida walked out into the little town, found a small supermarket, and bought provisions for their eventual arrival. A can of soup, bread, butter, bacon and eggs. A packet of coffee, a carton of milk. The man in the shop packed all this into a grocery box for her, and then she spied a bottle of whisky (medicinal?) and bought that, too.

The second day's driving was a bit better. Horrible weather, but at least Oscar was more communicative. He eyed the passing fields and farms, pointed out landmarks, gazed warily at the sky, and made his own gloomy forecasts. But yet it was not the time for chatter, for the stream of questions to which she ached to know the answer. *What will it be like, Oscar? How big is the Estate House? Will anybody have left it warm, and will there be any hot water? Will it be clean, and will there be sheets? Will people be friendly to us, and will they know you? Or will they shun us?*

It was all unimaginable. But, she told herself, grinding in second gear up the slippery slope of Soutra, with the windscreen wipers going full-tilt, and all the world drowned in the whiteness of a sudden sleet storm, this is an adventure.

As a young woman, an actress, she had travelled the length and breadth of Britain with touring companies, without ever knowing what awaited her at the end of the journey. Her memories of those days were a blur of provincial towns, musty theatres, and theatrical lodgings that smelt of boiled cabbage. But she had been young, doing a job she loved, and had been very happy. Each rattling train journey was a challenge, each grimy theatre, a new discovery. A little of that old excitement warmed her now, and she had to remind herself that she was no longer that young and ardent girl, but an elderly lady of sixty-two. *At least, I am not lonely. Not bored. Nor dead.*

The encounter with Major Billicliffe had been the final hurdle. With that accomplished and the key safely in Oscar's pocket, the hard grind of the two-day journey was behind them, and the last few miles were easy, almost carefree. Oscar drove. It was cold, but the snow had ceased, and the dark road ran downhill towards the sea, between dense stands of conifers. Elfrida opened her window and heard the soughing of wind in their branches, and smelt pine and a sturdy whiff of salty air. Then the trees fell away, and all about them were duney hillocks and stunted pines, and ahead could be seen a straight silvery line that was the sea. Far away, across the water, a lighthouse blinked, a pinprick in the darkness. Then ahead, the glow of street lights, and houses with windows lighted behind drawn curtains. A street of stone houses, like a terrace, but each house a different shape and height from its neighbour. She saw the church looming, the lighted clock like a round lantern, high in its tower. The hands stood at seven o'clock. Now larger, handsome houses, set back behind tall stone walls. Creagan. It seemed deserted. No one trod the streets; no cars. No sound, not even the cry of gulls. Another turning, another street. Oscar drew up at the pavement's edge. He turned off the engine. For a moment he was still. Elfrida waited. Then he laid his hand over hers.

He said, "Dear girl. We're here."

The Estate House. So Elfrida saw it for the first time, by the light of street lamps. Square and solid, set back from the road behind a wrought-iron railing and a forecourt of sea-pebbles. The face of the house was a child's drawing, with a door and five windows. Above these, set in the slope of the slated roof, two dormers jutted. They got out of the car, and Elfrida set Horace free. He had not forgotten the growls and howls of Major Billicliffe's hound, and was, sensibly, wary. But finally reassured, he leaped down into the road, and began tentatively to sniff for unfamiliar smells.

Oscar unlatched the gate and went up the path. Elfrida and Horace followed him. With the key he opened the door. It swung inward and he felt for a light switch and found one, and turned it on.

They entered, and Elfrida instantly felt the warmth and smelt the cleanliness of a place newly scrubbed and polished. Ahead, a staircase rose to a half-landing and an uncurtained stair window. On either side, doors stood closed, but at the end of the hall a third door was open. Oscar went down the hall and through this and turned on another light.

Elfrida closed the front door behind her, sealing away the chill of the winter evening. She followed Oscar and found him in a kitchen where stood an old-fashioned painted dresser and a wooden table. Beneath the window was a clay sink, and at its side a capacious gas cooker, dating back, perhaps, forty years or more.

Oscar said, "Hardly all-singing, all-dancing." He sounded a bit apologetic.

"It's fine," Elfrida assured him, and meant it. "Someone has left us a letter." It lay in the middle of the table, a sheet of lined paper, weighted down with a jam jar. Oscar removed this, handed the letter to Elfrida, and she read it aloud.

> *"I have turned on boiler (oil). You will need to order more oil. Beds made up in 2 rooms. Bath-water hot. Coal and wood in shed. Some of the windows won't open. Milk in fridge (scullery). Will pop in tomorrow to see you are all right.*
>
> *"Yours J. Snead (Mrs.)"*

Oscar said, "Mrs. Snead?"

"Yes."

"Elfrida, are you about to cry?"

"I might be."

"Why?"

"Relief."

That had all happened three weeks ago. It was December now, a Friday, and five o'clock on a dark mid-winter afternoon. Oscar, who had set out after lunch with Horace at his heels, had still not returned.

Elfrida blotted out images of him dead of a heart attack, his body prone at the foot of a sand dune. He was simply taking his time. Hopefully enjoying his first real expedition into the country, feeling better for the exercise, and filling his lungs with restoring fresh air. The decision to go had been his alone, and she had been careful not to appear too enthusiastic, fearful of giving him the impression that she longed to be rid of him.

She stood in the kitchen, at the gas stove, boiling a kettle. She made a mug of tea and took it upstairs to the sitting-room. They called it the sitting-room, but indeed it was a drawing-room, formal and spacious, with a huge bay window looking out over the street and the church. Hours could be wasted simply sitting on the window-seat and watching the world go by. Cars coming and going, delivery vans, and grit lorries. Shoppers pausing on the pavement to chat; strings of chattering children, like sparrows, walking to and from school.

The room was furnished, as was all the house, with the bare minimum of furniture. A thick Turkey carpet. A sofa and two chairs. A table against the wall, a glass-fronted bookcase, in which a few old books leaned against each other. No pictures, no ornaments. No clue as to the interests and lives of previous occupants. In a way, Elfrida found this lack of decoration and clutter quite therapeutic. Without pictures, knick-knacks, small bits of silver, and sets of decorative porcelain to divert the eye, it was possible to appreciate the lovely proportions of the room, the ornate cornice and the plaster rose in the centre of the ceiling, from which depended a charming Victorian chandelier.

Arriving, unpacking, she had put her modest stamp upon the place. The David Wilkie now hung opposite the fireplace, above the heavy oak table, which Oscar used as a desk. The Staffordshire dogs and her clock occupied the empty marble mantelpiece. From Arthur Snead Fruit and Vegetables she had bought a bunch of chrysanthemums, found a yellow jug, and created a not very ambitious arrangement. Her half-done tapestry lay across the seat of a chair. Earlier on, she had lighted the fire. Now, she fed it with coal and logs and then went to the window, to sit and watch for Oscar. But no sooner had she settled herself, with her mug between her hands, than the telephone rang. This was startling because it had scarcely ever rung since they had taken up residence. Elfrida hoped it was not Major Billicliffe. She set the mug down on the floor and went to answer the call. The telephone stood on the first-floor landing, on a small chest, just outside the sitting-room door. She picked up the receiver.

"Hello."

"Elfrida."

"Yes."

"It's Carrie. Carrie Sutton."

"*Carrie*. Where are *you*?"

"In London. How are you?"

"All right."

"Jeffrey told me you were in Scotland. Gave me your number. Elfrida, I've got something to ask you. It's a favour. It's a huge favour."

"Ask away."

"It's about Christmas."

It was, necessarily, a very long telephone call. Finally they were finished. Elfrida replaced the receiver at the same moment she heard the front door, downstairs, open and close, and knew that Oscar and Horace were home. She leaned over the banister and called. "Are you safely back?"

"Yes. We're here."

She went downstairs. In the hall, he was shedding himself of jacket and hat, hanging them on the bentwood hat stand. Horace had already reached for the kitchen and his drinking bowl and his warm basket. "You've been ages."

"We went for miles. The other end of the links and back. I'd forgotten it was so far." He put up a hand and ran it over his hair. He looked, she thought, exhausted.

She said, "A cup of tea?"

"I think I'm ready for something stronger."

"A Scotch. Go upstairs. There's a fire. I'll bring it to you."

In the kitchen, she poured his drink and put the kettle on again and made herself another mug of tea, because she knew that the first one would by now be cold. Horace was already asleep. She left him and went upstairs with the mug in one hand and the tumbler in the other. She found Oscar standing with a hand on the mantelpiece, gazing down into the fire. He turned his head as she came in and smiled gratefully.

"How good you are. . . ."

He took the drink and lowered himself carefully into one of the armchairs, stretching out his legs before him. Elfrida went to draw the curtains, shutting away the night. "I didn't draw them before because I was sitting in the window, watching for you. Doing a Sister Anne."

"Did you think I was dead?"

"Imagination does terrible things."

"I was delayed. Outside the Golf Club, I met a man. We talked. He asked me into the club for a cup of tea, and I accepted. Then he went to speak to an old man in a wheelchair, and I asked the waitress who he was. He is called Peter Kennedy, and he is the minister."

Elfrida waited. Finally, "So, Oscar?"

"I thought of him knowing about what had happened. The crash. Gloria and Francesca both dead. It occurred to me that perhaps Hector had forewarned him. I had thought him simply a friendly chap. But I am afraid he was being kind, sorry for me. I don't want to be helped. I want to be left alone. So I didn't stay. I walked away. Came home."

"Oh, Oscar."

"I know. Rude and mannerless."

"I'm sure he'll understand."

"I hope so. I liked his face."

"There's time. Give yourself time."

He took a deep breath that sounded like a terrible sigh. He said, "I hate myself."

"Oh, my dear, never do that."

"Do you reproach me?"

"No. *I* understand." She drank some tea, scalding and comforting. She sat facing him in a little wide-lapped Victorian chair upholstered in tartan. The firelight was warm on her shins. She said, "Perhaps this isn't an opportune moment, but I have to ask you something. I have to tell you something."

"Not, I hope, that you are about to leave me."

"No, not that. I have had a telephone call. Jeffrey's daughter, Carrie Sutton. She has returned from Austria. She wants to come and spend Christmas with us."

"But we are not having Christmas."

"Oscar, I told her. A lamb chop for lunch and no tinsel. I told her that that was what you and I had agreed. She understands. It makes no difference to her. She says she's not interested in Christmas either."

"Then let her come."

Elfrida hesitated. "There is a complication."

"A man?"

"No. Jeffrey's grandchild. Carrie's niece. Lucy. If Carrie comes, then Lucy must come, too."

There was a very long silence. Oscar's eyes turned from Elfrida's face and gazed into the fire. For a moment he looked as old as his uncle had looked that dreadful day when Elfrida had come unexpectedly upon the old man and thought for a frightening instant that he was Oscar. She said, "I told Carrie I would have to ask you. I would have to tell you about the child."

"How old is she?"

"Fourteen."

"Why does she have to come?"

"Oh, I don't know." Elfrida shrugged. "Some story about her mother going to Florida for Christmas to stay with a friend, and the daughter doesn't want to go with her. And Dodie, the grandmother, doesn't want the child. The sort of selfish muddle that is always happening in my family." Oscar made no comment on this. Elfrida bit her lip. She said, "I can ring Carrie and tell her no. I can tell her that it is too soon. A little girl around the place would be more than painful for you. It could be unbearable. I understand, and I shan't think any the less of you if you say no."

He looked at her, his gentle features filled with affection.

"I love your directness, Elfrida."

"It is the only way."

"If they come . . ."

"I'll say no Christmas."

"But the child . . . ?"

"She will be with Carrie. They can do what they want. Go to church. Sing carols, give each other presents."

"It sounds a little bleak for a youngster."

"And for *you,* Oscar?"

"It can make no difference. It can change nothing. You want them here, I think. Then tell them to come."

"You're sure? You're certain?" He nodded. "You are a dear, kind, brave man."

"There's space for them?"

"The attics are empty. Perhaps we could buy a bed, and Lucy shall sleep up there."

"We'll need to buy more than a bed."

"Not very much more."

"It's what you want. That's all that matters. Tell them they're welcome. Come whenever they want. They will be company for you. I'm afraid I am not very lively company."

"Oscar, lively company was not the point of us coming here together."

He drank a bit of his whisky, seemingly deep in thought. Then he said, "Telephone Carrie now. If they take the train or come by aeroplane, we can send a taxi to meet them at Inverness. If they're driving, warn her about the snow."

She was filled with gratitude for his generosity of spirit. To have him sitting there mulling over such mundane details made her feel a great deal better. He was being hostly, almost as though it were he who had issued the invitation, and not had it dumped upon him. She finished her tea and pulled herself to her feet. "I'll ring her. Right away." She made for the door, and then turned back. "Thank you, Oscar."

LUCY

FRIDAY, DECEMBER 8TH

I've already written down all the wonderful things that happened today, about Carrie coming back, and going out for lunch, and her saying maybe she and I can go away for Christmas somewhere. The cinema was really good, too. Well, now it is ten-thirty and I'm just going to bed. Writing this in my dressing-gown. What happened was I had a bath after supper and washed my hair, and while it was drying went into the kitchen to make a hot chocolate. Then the phone rang, and Mum came to find me and to say it was Carrie wanting to talk to me. I think they'd already had a chat. I picked up the kitchen telephone and waited till I'd heard the click and knew Mum had put the other phone down so wasn't going to listen. She does sometimes.

And then Carrie told me. We are going to Scotland for Christmas. Elfrida, Grandpa's cousin, is staying there with a friend and they both want us to go. It's a place called Creagan, and they say the house is quite big. It is so exciting, I could burst. Carrie says it's too far to drive in the middle of winter, so we're going to fly to Inverness and then a taxi will meet us and drive us the rest of the way. We're going on December 15th, and she's already booked seats.

Elfrida's friend is called Oscar, but Carrie doesn't know what he's like because she's never met him.

I said, had she told Mum and Gran, and she said no. And I said would I tell them, and she said no again, because Gran never much approved of Elfrida and it would be better if Carrie told them herself, so she's coming over some time tomorrow to break the news and calm Gran down if she starts being difficult. Mum won't say a word, because all she can think about is Randall and Florida.

I asked Carrie what I should pack, and she said fur coats and snow-shoes, but of course that was just a joke.

I can't believe I am going to Scotland.

I am already counting the days.

Carrie says it probably won't be very Christmassy on account of Oscar and Elfrida being so old. But compared with going away with Carrie, Christmas doesn't matter a bit, and I never liked Christmas pudding much anyway. She says there is a beach, and the North Sea.

I simply can't wait.

ELFRIDA

Now, Saturday morning and Elfrida was the first downstairs. She had dressed in thick corduroy trousers and two sweaters and was glad of these when she opened the back door to let Horace out into the garden. During the night, there had been a deep frost. All was iced and sparkling, and her footsteps left marks on the thick, crunchy grass of the little lawn. It was not yet light, and she and the dog emerged into the glow of a street lamp which lighted the stepped lane that led up the hill. Horace hated the cold, so she stayed with him, waiting while he nosed to and fro, shot up to the top of the garden where he smelt a rabbit, and took much time in finding exactly the right spot to do his wees. Standing freezing cold and trying to be patient, she looked up at the sky, and saw it turning sapphire-blue and quite clear. In the east, over the sea, the glow of dawn was a streak of pink, although the sun had yet to edge its way over the horizon. It was, she decided, going to be a fine day, and was grateful. They had had enough of grey skies, howling winds, and rain.

Finally Horace was done, and they scurried indoors, to the warmth, and Elfrida slammed shut the door behind her. Then she put the kettle on, found the frying-pan and the bacon. She laid the table with a checked cloth, and cups and saucers. She cracked two eggs. Oscar enjoyed a cooked breakfast, and although Elfrida did not eat it with him, she relished the smell of bacon frying.

Cautiously, she made toast. Making toast in this old-fashioned kitchen was something of a hazard, because the toaster was elderly and past its best, and behaved accordingly. Sometimes it popped up two quite reasonable, nicely browned slices. Other times, it regurgitated two uncooked slices of bread. But if in a bad temper, it forgot to turn itself off, with the result that the kitchen was filled with dark smoke, and the blackened crusts on offer were so disgusting that not even the sea-gulls would eat them.

Every now and then Elfrida told herself that they should buy a new toaster. There was a small shop in the High Street, William G. Croft Electrical Goods, its windows filled with microwaves, hair dryers, steam irons, and waffle makers, along with a number of other gadgets that Elfrida could happily live without. But a toaster was essential. One day she had gone into William G. Croft's to price the cheapest, but quailed at the expense, and departed without having made a purchase.

It was all a bit difficult, because without the little income engendered by her home industry of stitching cushions, she found herself chronically short of money, and Mondays, when she could go to the post office and collect her old age pension, couldn't come around quickly enough. She supposed that the sensible thing to do would be to find a tenant for Poulton's Row, and rent this out on a quarterly basis, thus ensuring a small trickle of cash, but the logistics of achieving this, organizing from Sutherland a let in Hampshire, were too much, and so the tentative idea was abandoned. As for Oscar, she had no idea whether or not he was in the same dilemma and was not about to ask. Probably he had a little bit put by, a stock or a share, but she knew that it was Gloria who had footed the bills for the day-to-day expenses incurred by the lush and generous life-style of the Grange.

So she struggled on with the old inherited toaster, having decided that if she did find herself with a bit of spare cash, she preferred to spend it on books or flowers.

Today, it was in a good mood, and the smell of bacon mingled with the scent of fresh hot coffee. Coffee was most important. She was sitting at the table drinking her first cup when Oscar came downstairs to join her, and at once Elfrida noticed his appearance. Normally, he wore a thick shirt under a warm pullover. Very informal. No necktie. But this morning he had put on, not only one of his better shirts, but a tie, a waistcoat, and his good tweed jacket.

She eyed him in some astonishment. "You're looking very smart."

"Thank you. I'm pleased you noticed."

"What's the occasion?"

He retrieved his plate of bacon and eggs from the hot-plate, where she had left it to keep warm.

"Because it's Saturday?"

"Not good enough."

"Because I must not allow myself to become a shabby, shambling old wreck."

"Putting on a tie isn't going to make that much difference."

He sat down, and she poured his coffee. "Thank you. No, you're quite right. I have made a small effort, because I am going calling."

Elfrida was genuinely surprised, but took great pains not to show this. She was also intrigued. "Who are you going to call on?"

"Rose Miller."

"Who is Rose Miller?"

"A very old friend."

"You've never mentioned her. Should I be jealous?"

"I don't think so. She must be eighty-five if she's a day. She was my grandmother's parlourmaid. She lives on the Corrydale estate in a very small cottage with a thatched roof. I am going to go and pay my respects."

"Why have you suddenly decided to go and see your grandmother's parlourmaid? You've been keeping such a low profile, anyone might think you're an escaped fugitive."

"Do you mind?"

"Oh, dear Oscar, I'm absolutely delighted. But I don't entirely understand your change of heart."

He set down his coffee-cup. When he spoke again, his voice was different, no longer bantering. He said, "It was yesterday. Meeting that man. Peter Kennedy, the minister. Behaving so stupidly, so rudely. And there's another thing. During the last few weeks, I've thought of myself as anonymous, but of course I'm not. If Peter Kennedy knows about me, then so will many other people. They're just too polite and thoughtful to come banging on our door. This is a small place and news spreads like wildfire. By now Rose Miller is bound to have heard I've come back. And she will be intensely hurt if I don't get in touch with her. So I have decided to go. I shall buy her a bunch of flowers from Arthur Snead, and together she and I will take a trip down Memory Lane. You don't need the car, do you?"

"No. That is the best of living here. I can walk across the square to the supermarket, I can walk down the street to the butcher, and on the way home I can go into the bookshop and browse. If I felt so inclined, I could have a little foray into the antique shop, and come back with a Victorian teapot. Or even have my hair tweaked."

"Do you mean there's actually a hairdresser in Creagan?"

"Of course. Over the barber's shop. Where else?"

She leaned across the table to remove his empty plate, and to pour herself her second cup of coffee. The gingham curtains were still drawn, so she pulled them back, and saw the lightening sky.

Suddenly, she felt more cheerful than she had for a long time. Things, slowly, were looking up. The day would be fine. Icily cold, but fine. Oscar was going calling, and next week, Carrie and Lucy Wesley would be here. Thinking about it, she decided that perhaps yesterday had been the turning point, although she had not recognized it as such.

"I shall go for a walk," Oscar had announced. "Stretch my legs, and get some fresh air. I'll take Horace with me." Elfrida, clearly, was neither expected nor invited to join them. Which was just as well, because she had no wish to go out, tramping through the wind and the rain. She managed not to show her surprise, and simply told him to wrap up warmly against the bitter weather.

But, perhaps fortuitously, Oscar had met this man, this Peter Kennedy. And, for whatever reason, had been engaged in conversation, and treated with friendliness and hospitality. The fact that, like a dog biting the feeding hand, Oscar had panicked and walked out on him was probably of less consequence to Peter Kennedy than it was to Oscar, who had been, clearly, much ashamed of his behaviour. Perhaps, during the night, he had lain awake, filled with remorse. Perhaps going to visit old Rose Miller was a way of reparation, his first voluntary step back into the company of others.

"What time will you go, Oscar?" She brought her cup back to the table. "To keep your assignation with Rose?"

"It's not an assignation, because she doesn't know I'm coming."

"Yes, but *assignation* sounds so much more exciting."

"I thought about half past ten. Would you consider that a suitable time?"

"Perfect. She'll be up and about, and she will give you a cup of tea and perhaps a biscuit." She drank her coffee. "Maybe, while you're at Corrydale, you should look in on Major Billicliffe."

"I hoped you wouldn't say that."

"Oh, Oscar, you are being feeble. He's a harmless old git, and probably dreadfully lonely. It's unkind to go on living here and just pretending he doesn't exist. After all, he was all ready with the key, and a rather dim little drink." Oscar, silent, did not look enthusiastic. "You could just drop in, casually, to pass the time of day. Perhaps ask him along for a drink or something when Carrie and Lucy are here. You could say it was a party."

Cunningly, Oscar steered the discussion off at a tangent. "When are they coming?"

"Friday. I told you. They're flying to Inverness on Friday morning, and I've asked the taxi-man to go and get them."

"I didn't know we had a taxi-man."

"Alec Dobbs."

"I thought Alec Dobbs was the undertaker."

"He is, but he does taxis as well."

"Useful fellow."

Elfrida sipped her coffee. She had now forgotten about Major Billicliffe and was thinking instead about Carrie and Lucy's arrival. "There isn't much time, is there? I'll have to get around to finding some furniture for the attic. There must be a second-hand shop around somewhere. I shall make inquiries."

"Whom will you ask?"

"The butcher? Or the newsagent?"

"Or the undertaker?"

"Mrs. Snead, of course! Mrs. Snead will be bound to know. . . ."

This fascinating discussion might have gone on forever had they not been disturbed by the shrilling ring of the front-door bell, which caused Horace, startled out of his wits, to sit up in his basket and bark with agitation.

Elfrida shushed him, and went out of the kitchen and down the hall. The doorbell had been the postman, and there were two letters on the mat. Which seemed another good omen, because they had scarcely had any correspondence delivered since the day they arrived.

She stooped and picked up the letters and carried them back to Oscar.

"One is for you, typed and business-like, and probably from your bank manager. And the other is for me."

"Now it's my turn to be jealous."

"I don't think so." She felt for her spectacles in the pocket of her sweater and put them on. She eyed the envelope suspiciously. "Rather neat, spiky old writing." She picked up a knife and slit the envelope and took out the letter. She turned the page over to find the signature, and smiled.

"Oscar, it's from Hector. That dear old man, writing to us." She sat down and unfolded the thick blue paper. "And a *cheque*! A cheque for five hundred pounds."

Oscar's jaw fell. "Five hundred pounds? Are you sure?"

"See for yourself. Made out to you." She handed it over. He stared at it in some bewilderment, and then said, "Perhaps you'd better find out what it's all about."

So Elfrida read aloud.

"My dear Oscar and Elfrida,

"I have not written before, because I wanted to give you both time to settle in. I trust you had a safe journey and found the Estate House in good condition.

"I have to confess that, after you left, I felt impelled to write a letter to Peter Kennedy, the minister of the parish church in Creagan. I know your desire for privacy and anonymity, to give you the opportunity to come to terms with the tragedy which you have suffered. But I could not help worrying about you, and Peter is a good man, and a good friend, and I knew I could trust him to keep your sad circumstances to himself. He was a regular visitor to Corrydale before I handed it over to Hughie, and I much enjoyed his company and his keen mind. I expect he will be in touch, and would like you to accept his concern, and possible offer of comfort.

"I hope you are not offended by my action.

"I am also a little anxious in case the Estate House is under-furnished and under-equipped. As you know, I have not seen it for years, although, since the Cochranes departed, I have arranged for its day-to-day upkeep. As I feel responsible for persuading you to leave Hampshire and take up residence in Creagan, I would be happy to supply any extras that you feel would make life more comfortable. So I am enclosing a cheque for five hundred pounds which I hope will be sufficient for your needs.

"The weather in London is still grey and cold. I do not go out very much, but observe it from my window.

"I hope you are both well. I would appreciate a letter or a telephone call to set my mind at rest.

"I saw in The Times *that the Grange is on the market. The boys have lost no time.*

"With my best wishes to you both,
"Sincerely,
"Hector"

In silence, she folded the letter and put it back into its envelope. She said, "I shall write this morning."

"It's enormously generous. And we really don't need anything."

"Oh, yes we do," Elfrida told him firmly.

"Like what?"

"Like a new toaster that doesn't burn the toast, or blow up or electrocute me. This one is archaic. And I've got to get a bed for Lucy, and it would be nice to have curtains on the stair window."

"I never noticed any of these things," said Oscar, looking a bit ashamed.

"Men never do."

"Perhaps you could buy a dishwasher?"

"I don't want a dishwasher."

"Or a microwave?"

"I don't want a microwave either."

"Or a television set?"

"I never look at television. Did you?"

"Only the news. And 'Songs of Praise.' And the proms."

"But aren't we lucky, Oscar, to have such simple needs?"

"We are certainly fortunate." He picked up the cheque and eyed it. "In more ways than one. Before I go and see Rose, I shall call in at the Bank of Scotland and open a joint account for the two of us. And you shall go mad, buying furniture."

"But the money's not for me."

"It is for both of us."

"And will the Bank of Scotland be so obliging?"

"I have banked with them since I was a boy. I can see no difficulties."

"You are being dynamic, Oscar. And you won't forget the flowers for Rose?"

"No. I shall not forget."

The day turned into one of dazzling brightness. The red sun rose in the eggshell-blue sky, and there was not a breath of wind. Ladies, shopping, trod cautiously down the pavements, anxious not to slip or fall, and they wore thick boots and were muffled up in woollen hats and gloves. But the cold did not stop them from pausing to gossip, their breath clouding like steam as they chattered away.

The church, behind the black lacework of bare trees, glowed golden in the sunlight. Over its spire gulls wheeled, and jackdaws settled on the weather-vane at its peak. Frost iced the grass of the ancient graveyard, and cars, driven down from remote hill farms, wore blankets of snow. One of them had a Christmas tree sticking out of the open tail-gate.

Having done a little cursory housework, made beds, set the fire, and humped a basket of logs up from the outdoor shed, Elfrida sat in her bay window and observed all this seasonal activity. Oscar had departed, having spent some effort on defreezing his windscreen and getting the wipers to work. Elfrida hoped that Rose Miller would be pleased to see him, and guessed that she would.

She turned to the table, the thin sun warm on her back, and started her letter to Hector.

The Estate House
December 9th

Dear Hector,

How very good of you to write, and thank you, from Oscar and myself, for your very generous cheque. It is more than welcome for a number of reasons. We are a bit short of essentials, but have managed very well without them. But now I have a young cousin, Carrie Sutton, coming to stay for Christmas, and she is bringing her niece, Lucy, who is fourteen, so it will be good to be able to cheer the place up a bit and make it more homely. We do need a new toaster, but that's about all, though I shall buy some furniture for Lucy's room (she's going to sleep in the attic!) and your cheque will come in very useful for that reason. I shall find a second-hand shop.

Oscar is well. He has been very withdrawn ever since we got here, and I have, from time to time, become a little depressed about him, wondering if he ever would emerge from his cloud of grief and begin to go forward again. He did not want to see anybody, nor even speak to any person. Yesterday, however, he took Horace, my dog, for a long walk, and by the Golf Club was approached by Peter Kennedy. He liked him very much, and said he had a nice face. He was invited into the clubhouse for tea, and went, but then realized that Peter Kennedy was the minister, took fright, and fled.

He was terribly upset about this, but I think the incident brought him up short, and he realizes he can't hide away forever. So this morning he has gone in the car to pay a call on Rose Miller at Corrydale. It is his first voluntary step out into the world of other people, and I am filled with gratitude and hope that the Kennedys won't be far behind. But, whatever happens, Oscar mustn't be goaded, but allowed to take it all at his own pace.

We are really all right, and the days pass peacefully. This is a very tranquil part of the world, and I take my dog Horace for long walks on the beach, sometimes returning after the sun has set. We have no television, but really don't need one. Oscar brought his little radio with him, and we pass the long evenings playing canasta and listening to Classic FM.

We had a long drive up from Hampshire, and were—

So intent was she upon her letter, so unheeding of voices in the street below, that she did not hear the wrought-iron gate open and shut, nor the tread of footsteps up to the front door. When the doorbell rang, she was so startled that she dropped her pen. From downstairs Horace, as usual, filled the house with panic-stricken barking. She got up and went out of the room and ran downstairs.

"Oh, Horace, be quiet!" Down the hall to open the heavy door, swinging it wide to the sunshine, to the penetrating cold, to an unknown female figure.

"Sorry about the dog. . . ."

"No matter . . ."

Her visitor was a woman perhaps in her late thirties, tall and slender and marvellously unconventional in her appearance. She had very dark, almost raven-black hair, cut in a fringe and hanging loose and straight to her shoulders. She wore a battered Barbour over a long red woollen skirt and what looked like Doc Marten boots. A tartan muffler was wound about her neck, framing a face beautifully boned and innocent of make-up. Her cheeks were tanned, rosy this morning with cold, and her eyes deep-set and dark as black coffee. In one hand she carried a plastic shopping bag, and in the other a little rural basket containing eggs.

She smiled. "Hello. You're Elfrida Phipps? I hope I'm not disturbing you, but I'm Tabitha." Elfrida was no wiser, and puzzlement clearly showed on her face. "Tabitha Kennedy. Peter Kennedy's wife."

"Oh." Elfrida made much effort not to appear too astonished. She had never seen any person in her life less likely to be a minister's wife. "How really nice to meet you." She stepped back indoors, holding open the door. "Do come in."

But Tabitha Kennedy hesitated. "Not if you're busy. I just brought you some eggs. From my hens."

"I'm not busy and fresh eggs are a real treat. Come on, I'll give you a cup of coffee."

Tabitha stepped through the door, and Elfrida closed it behind her. "Do you mind coming into the kitchen . . . ?" She led the way. "I'll put the kettle on, and then we'll take our coffee upstairs. Or would you rather have tea?"

"I'd die for a cup of coffee, I'm frozen. Peter's got the car, so I had to walk down the hill. I thought I was going to fall flat on my back, it's so icy." She followed Elfrida into the kitchen, put the basket of eggs on the table, and hung her plastic bag over a chair.

"Oscar's got the car, too. He's gone to Corrydale to call on someone called Rose Miller."

"Goodness, there'll be a reunion. Rose always adored Oscar. Never stops talking about him. Do you know I've never been in here? If I did come to the Estate House, it was very formal, straight up the stairs and into the big room. The Cochranes were a funny old couple, very reserved. Not, you might say, into entertaining. But once a year, Peter and I were asked for tea and polite conversation. It was always a bit of an ordeal. How are you settling in?"

Elfrida, having filled the kettle and put it on to boil, began reaching for a tray, and cups and saucers. "We're fine."

Tabitha looked about her. "This kitchen reminds me of an exhibit in one of those National Heritage museums. My grandmother had one the very same. I don't suppose the Cochranes went in for gadgets, but if they did, Mrs. Cochrane has certainly removed the lot. Have you got a dishwasher?"

"No. But I've never had one, so it doesn't matter."

"How about a clothes washer?"

"There's an archaic one in the scullery. It takes hours, but it does work. And my dryer is the washing line at the top of the garden."

"A scullery! Can I look?"

"Of course."

"This door? Better and better. Tiled floors and clay sinks, and wooden draining boards. But you've got a fridge."

"I hardly need one in this weather."

Tabitha closed the scullery door and came back into the kitchen, to pull out a chair and sit at the table. "Do you use the big upstairs sitting-room?"

"All the time, though it's a lot of running up and down stairs."

"What about the ground-floor rooms?"

"One's a very gloomy Victorian dining-room. Lots of heavy, dark mahogany furniture, and plush curtains, and an upright piano with candle sconces. The other, I think, was the original estate office. I don't suppose the Cochranes ever used it. There's still an old roll-top desk, and a table with special drawers for collecting rents. I'm afraid we've kept the doors shut on both of them. We either eat in here or by the fire."

"Much simpler."

"And Oscar doesn't seem to mind."

Tabitha said, "I'm glad Oscar's not here. One of the reasons I've come is to apologize, and now I shan't have to."

"*Apologize?* For what?"

"Peter sent me. He's afraid he was rather crass and pushy yesterday afternoon. He hopes so much that he didn't upset Oscar."

"I think Oscar feels he's the one to apologize. It was rude, just running away like that, but he panicked and fled. He was filled with remorse. He knew he'd behaved dreadfully badly."

"Hector wrote and told us about his wife and his child dying in that appalling car accident. It takes a long while to move out of something like that, and get back into life again."

"It's called grieving."

"I know. It can't have been easy for you."

"As a matter of fact, it's been hellish."

Elfrida heard herself come out with this, and was amazed that the impulsive words had been spoken, because the moments of hellishness she had never acknowledged, nor admitted, even to herself. "I think frustration is the worst, because there is not a mortal thing one can do to help. And then, impatience. And then guilt for feeling impatient. More than once, I've had to bite my tongue. And another thing is, I'm quite a sociable animal. I don't mean endless parties, but I like making friends and getting to know people, but because of Oscar I've had to keep a low profile. I've probably created a very snooty impression."

"I'm sure not."

"Mrs. Snead has been my lifeline. We have long conversations over cups of tea."

"I'm glad she's working for you."

"Today . . . today I have a feeling that the hellish time might just about be behind us. For Oscar's sake, I hope it is. He's such a sweet man, he didn't deserve what happened. Perhaps going to see Rose Miller is a step forward."

"We were always there, Peter and I, but we decided you both needed a bit of time. It's sometimes difficult to gauge exactly the right moment. . . ."

"Don't think about it. Please."

"If Peter came to see Oscar, would that be a good idea? They could put things right between them."

"I think it's a marvellous idea, but tell him to telephone first."

"I'll do that."

The coffee was made, the jug set on the tray. Elfrida picked it up. "Let's go upstairs. It's more comfortable."

She led the way, and Tabitha followed. "I'm always impressed by this beautiful staircase. It gives such a grand feel to your entrance. Peter says the banisters are made of Baltic pine, brought back as ballast on the herring boats." She paused on the half-landing to gaze out at the garden. This, still frosted, and bleak with mid-winter, climbed the slope of the hill in a series of terraced lawns, with a path and small flights of steps running up its centre. At the very top was a stand of pines, filled with jackdaw nests. "I'd forgotten how much land there is. You can't see it from the lane because of the high wall. I love a walled garden. Old Cochrane was a great gardener. He kept the Manse supplied with free lettuces."

"Oscar gardens, but so far he's just swept up a few leaves."

"In spring, there are daffodils and the terraces are purple with aubrietia. And there's a lilac, too. . . ."

Elfrida, laden with the tray, went on upstairs, and behind her, Tabitha continued her running commentary.

"It hasn't just got a grand feel, it really *is* imposing. The size is unexpected, like Dr. Who's Tardis . . . it all gets bigger and bigger. . . ." Low sun streamed through the open sitting-room door. ". . . And I always thought this drawing-room one of the loveliest. . . . Oh, look, you've been allowed to keep the chandelier. That must have come from Corrydale." She looked around her at the empty walls and spied the little painting that Elfrida had brought with her from Dibton. "Heavens, what a darling." She moved to inspect it more closely. "This wasn't here, was it?"

"No. It's mine." Elfrida set the tray down on the table by the window.

"It's a David Wilkie. It has to be."

Elfrida was impressed. "Yes, it is. I've had it for years. I take it with me to every house I live in."

"How did you come by such a precious possession?"

"It was given to me."

Tabitha laughed. "Someone must have liked you very much."

"It looks a bit like a stamp on a blotting pad; too small for such an expanse of wall."

"But enchanting."

Elfrida went to put a match to the fire.

"Do we need a fire?" Tabitha asked. "Everything feels so warm."

"That's the best. An oil-fired boiler and central heating. When we came, I was so afraid it would all be piercingly cold, but we're snug as bugs. The boiler does the water, too, so scalding baths."

"And of course these old Victorian houses were so solidly built there's not a draught in the place."

The fire kindled, snapped, and crackled. Little flames leaped. Elfrida put on a chunk of coal, another log. "Shall we sit by the window?"

"Let's. The sun is so gorgeous." Tabitha unwound her muffler and unzipped her Barbour, which she took off and tossed onto a chair before coming to settle herself on the window-seat. "Do you sit here and watch all the goings-on? Already you must know enough about us locals to write a book."

"It is pretty fascinating." Elfrida pushed aside the letter she had been writing to Hector. "Have you lived here long?"

"About twenty years. We were married just before Peter came here as minister."

"How old were you?"

"Twenty." Tabitha made a face. "Some of the parishioners didn't approve at all, but at the end of the day, it all worked out. Both our children were born in the Manse."

"How old are they?"

"Rory's eighteen. Just left school. We sent both of our offspring to the local Academy. He's got his Highers and a place at Durham University, but he's not taking it up till next year. So we're into his Gap year, and goodness knows what he's going to do with himself. Peter says he doesn't care provided the boy is either earning or learning. And Clodagh's twelve, and for some reason, mad on horses. We haven't worked out why she had to choose such an expensive hobby."

"She might have gone for hang-gliding."

Suddenly, they were both laughing, and it was lovely to be gassing to a girl-friend over a cup of coffee as though they had known each other forever.

She looked at Tabitha, sitting there in her black polo-neck sweater, and with her young girl's hair, and was filled with curiosity. "Do you like being a minister's wife?"

"I adore being married to Peter. And I'm not totally a minister's wife, because I teach art at the school. I'm a qualified teacher, with all the right degrees. Five mornings a week."

"Are you an artist?"

"Yes, I paint and draw. But I teach crafts as well. Pottery and sewing. The senior girls stitched all the kneelers in the church. It was a huge project. And every mother in Creagan has a rather wobbly pot for her begonias."

Elfrida said, "I was an actress." And then felt a bit shy, and wished she hadn't said it, because it sounded as though she were capping Tabitha's talent.

But Tabitha was gratifyingly amazed. "Were you really? Actually, I'm not a bit surprised. I can just see you on the stage."

"I wasn't exactly Ibsen material. It was light stuff. Musical comedies, that sort of thing. I was in Rep for years, playing every sort of part from teenager to ragged crone."

"Were you famous?"

"No, not a bit. But I was always working, however humbly."

"That's what matters, isn't it? Doing what you like, and being paid for it. That's how I feel, too. Really good for one's self-respect. Peter understands. It's one of the reasons I like him so much. I can't wait for you to meet him. I'd ask you up to the Manse, but perhaps we'd better wait until he and Oscar have sorted themselves out. Once they've done that, I'll issue invitations. Which means a telephone call."

"I can't think of anything I'd like more."

"What are you doing for Christmas?"

"I don't think we're doing anything. It's Oscar. And I understand because it can be a dreadfully emotive time. But it *is* tricky because I've got a cousin coming to stay next Friday and she's bringing her niece with her. . . . I've told them we won't be very festive, but they're coming anyway."

"How old is she?"

"Carrie? About thirty. But the niece is fourteen. She's called Lucy, and I've never met her. I just hope she isn't too shy. Or too un-shy, for that matter. I . . . I hope she won't be bored."

"There's so much going on in Creagan at Christmas, she'll have a wonderful time. All the local children get together—"

"She won't know the local children."

"We'll introduce her to Rory and Clodagh and then she'll meet them all."

Elfrida felt a bit doubtful about this. "Won't they mind?"

"Mind? Why should they mind?"

"Well . . . a strange child. From London."

"All the more reason to take care of her," said Tabitha, and suddenly Elfrida caught a steely glimpse of the schoolteacher, keeping order. And the minister's wife, raising her children to true Christian standards. And knew that Tabitha Kennedy, for all her bohemian appearance and youthful attitudes, was a person to be reckoned with. Heightened respect made her like her even more.

A thought struck her. "I've got to buy furniture. We're fairly short of everything here, because the house has never been anything more than semi-furnished for a let. The bedroom for Carrie is all right, but I thought I'd put Lucy up in the attic. It's lovely and light, but there's . . ." She hesitated. ". . . Would you come up and look at it with me? Tell me what I have to get?"

"Of course. Nothing I'd like more." Tabitha had finished her coffee, and now pushed back the cuff of her sweater to look at her watch. "And then I must fly. Peter's got an early meeting in Buckly this afternoon, and I must feed him soup before he goes."

"If you haven't got time . . ."

"Of course I have. Come on, show me. I'm a dab hand at interior decoration."

"On a shoe-string."

"I'm a minister's wife. What else?"

They climbed the stairs to the upper floor and the attics. One, windowless, contained three old trunks, a dressmaker's dummy, and a lot of cobwebs. The other, with its huge skylight and combed ceiling, was filled only with pale winter sunlight.

Tabitha was enchanted. "What a wonderful room. Any young girl would die to have this all to herself. Are you going to put down a carpet? The floor-boards are lovely. And it's got a radiator, too, cosy as anything. You'll need a bed, of course, and perhaps a chest of drawers. Or a little dressing-table. What about a television set?"

"We haven't got a television set."

"Yes, but teenagers go all peculiar without something to goggle at! Rory's got an old one he doesn't use any more. I'll have a word with him about it. And a few lamps. And a blind for the skylight. Otherwise it might be a bit spooky."

Elfrida said, "I've got a bit of money. Hector sent it. But not much. I thought a second-hand shop. . . ."

"There's a marvellous market in Buckly."

"I've never been to Buckly."

"I'll take you. You can get everything there, off stalls."

"Beds?"

"Oh, marvellous beds. And sheets, pictures, and objets d'art. Also terrible old clothes, and wardrobes and carpets. Next week. Some afternoon . . . Tuesday? Would Tuesday be all right?"

Elfrida, whose diary had been sadly blank for nearly a month, simply nodded.

"Could we go in your car? Peter's bound to need his."

Elfrida nodded again.

"What fun we'll have. I can't wait." She looked at her watch again. "That's settled then. Now I simply must fly or Peter will fume."

When Tabitha had gone, Elfrida returned to finish her letter to Hector.

. . . here by seven o'clock on the second day. This missive is taking a long time to write because I was interrupted by the arrival of Tabitha Kennedy, come to call. I am sure, very soon, Peter and Oscar will clear up their misunderstanding. Tabitha is lovely, and is going to take me to some market in Buckly to buy things for the house.

Thank you again for your kindness and generosity. I hope you keep well, and that the weather will be kinder so that you can get out and about.

With much love from us both,
Elfrida

She read this through, put it in an envelope, wrote the address, and found a stamp. Then she went downstairs, and in the kitchen did a cursory inspection of the contents of the fridge, deciding that all that was needed were vegetables and perhaps some fruit. Horace was sleeping in his basket and clearly did not wish to be disturbed, so she left him there, bundled herself up for the outdoors, and stepped out of the front door. This, she did not lock behind her. She had learned that, in Creagan, nobody locked doors.

The cold was deep-freeze, but the low sun had melted away some of the frost and the pavements were black and wet. Even so, Elfrida trod as carefully as any of the other shopping ladies, because right now she needed a broken leg as much as she needed a hole in the head.

She posted the letter and then crossed the street to Arthur Snead Fruit and Vegetables. For once the little shop was empty: just Mr. Snead, leaning on his counter, was reading the racing results. But seeing Elfrida, he straightened up and folded the newspaper away.

"'Ullo, Mrs. Phipps. 'Ow are you this fine morning?"

Arthur Snead was the other half of Mrs. Snead, who always referred to him as Arfur. The Sneads had proved a comforting bonus when Elfrida first arrived in Creagan, not simply because Mrs. Snead cleaned the Estate House and was a mine of useful information, but because they were Cockneys, and Elfrida, having lived in London for so much of her life, relished the sound of their familiar voices, which somehow had helped her to feel a little less isolated. The Sneads had arrived in Creagan five years ago from Hackney. Elfrida had heard all about this unlikely move over several cups of tea with Mrs. Snead. About how Arfur 'ad started life with a barrow in the North End Road, and finally managed to buy a little shop of 'is own. Then the council developers 'ad come and slapped a compulsory purchase on 'im and 'e'd been so fed up, 'e'd seen this ad, in a gardening magazine—'e'd always taken that magazine because of 'is allotment . . . grew wonderful marrows—and 'e'd said to Mrs. Snead, *'Ow about it, old girl?* And Mrs. Snead, loyal to the end, had said, *Okay, Arfur,* and they'd come. Bought the shop, and the little flat over it, and never looked back. A nice class of people they were, 'is customers, and 'e'd joined the bowling club, and got 'ooked on sea-fishing. As for Mrs. Snead, she was now a member of the Church Guild, went on outings, and from time to time, sang in the choir.

Respected and accepted by the local community, they were still known, without malice, as White Settlers.

"You'll need to watch out, my darling, I've 'ad your man in this morning, buying chrysanths for another lady."

"I know. Someone called Rose Miller, and I'm managing not to be jealous. Have you got any sprouts?"

"Nice bit of broccoli. Came in this morning. The lorry 'ad a really bad time getting over the 'ill. Says there's snow six inches deep up there. And there's Cyprus potatoes."

She bought the broccoli and the potatoes and some tangerines in a net bag, and two rather sad-looking grapefruit which Arfur let her have at half price.

"Going straight 'ome, are you?"

"No." Elfrida had made up her mind. "I'm going to buy a new toaster. The one we've got is lethal."

"Well, leave your bags 'ere, and I'll 'ump them across the road for you. Put them inside the front door."

"You are kind. Why do potatoes have to be so heavy? Thank you, Arthur."

And so, unburdened, on down the street to William G. Croft Electrical Goods. The door gave a ting as she went inside, and Mr. Croft, in his khaki overall, emerged from the open door of his back room, where he spent most of his time mending vacuum cleaners or tinkering with television sets. He recognized her instantly from her previous visit.

"Good morning, Mrs. Phipps, and so you're back again."

"Yes. Toasters. But this time I'm going to buy one."

"And did the other one blow up?"

"No. But it might at any moment."

"And which was the model that you looked at?"

"The cheapest. But I think I'd like something a little more . . . modern."

"I have the very thing. . . ."

He fetched it, in its box, and on the counter unpacked it for Elfrida's inspection. It was extremely smart, streamlined and bright blue. He showed her how it worked, which wasn't very difficult, and how, if you turned a knob, you could have very pale toast or you could have very dark toast.

"And it has a year's guarantee," Mr. Croft finished, as though this made it irresistible. Which, of course, it was. Elfrida said she would have it. "The only thing is, I haven't enough money to pay for it right now. Would you keep it and I'll come back tomorrow, or another day."

"There's no need for that, Mrs. Phipps. You take it with you now, and pay for it the next time you're passing."

"Are you sure?"

"I have no fears that you'll be running away with it."

So she took the toaster home, unpacked it, and plugged it in and made herself two perfect pieces of toast, which she spread with Marmite and ate. She threw the old one in the bin, and as she did so, heard the front door open and shut and knew that Oscar had returned. Munching toast, she went out into the hall to meet him.

"You're back. How was Rose Miller?"

"In splendid form." He took off his hat and hung it on the newel-post at the foot of the banister. "We had a great crack, and a glass of elderberry wine."

"So much for cups of tea."

"Why are you eating toast?"

"I bought a new toaster. Come and look." She led him back into the kitchen. "Isn't it smart? You told me I would go mad buying things, so I did. Only thing is, I haven't paid for it yet. I said I'd go back tomorrow."

"I'll come with you." He took off his thick jacket and pulled out a chair and sat down. Elfrida eyed him. For a man who had just returned from sipping elderberry wine with an old admirer, he looked tired and preoccupied. Perhaps the elderberry wine had been a bit too strong for eleven o'clock in the morning.

"Are you all right, Oscar?"

"Yes, I'm fine. I did what you told me, Elfrida. I went to see Major Billicliffe."

"Oh, good man."

"No. Not good. I don't feel good at all."

"Why not? What happened?"

He told her.

Rose Miller's cottage at Corrydale was situated on the little road beyond the erstwhile factor's house, and he had passed it by on the way to pay his call. *Another day,* he had said to himself. *Billicliffe can wait until another day.* But then, primed with elderberry wine and on his way home, he had heard the dog howling. The sound was as arresting as a cry for help, and Oscar had been instantly rendered alert with concern. There could be no question of driving by. He had turned his car into the lane that led to the small stone house with its rural porch, and, turning off the engine, had heard the dog howling once more.

Listening, Elfrida was aghast, already dreading the end of the story.

"What did you do?"

"Got out of the car and went to ring the bell, but nothing happened except the dog stopped howling and started barking. So then, I tried the door, and it was open. I went in, and called out, but no answer."

"Perhaps he'd forgotten to put his hearing aids in."

"No one there. And the dog had been shut in that same back place, hurling itself at the door, just as it did on our first evening."

"You didn't let it loose?"

"Not then. Not then, I didn't."

"Was there nobody there?"

"Then I tried the other ground-floor room. The chaos there was even worse than that sitting-room. Drip-dry shirts hanging over the backs of chairs, old papers and boxes piled on a table, golf clubs all over the floor. But there was a staircase, so I went up and opened the door at the top, and peered in. And there was the old boy, in bed. . . ."

"He wasn't dead?"

"For a moment, I thought he was. And then I said his name, and he stirred. . . ."

"Thank heavens for that."

He had not been dead. But he looked ghastly, and was clearly very unwell. However, realizing that he had a visitor, he had tried to rally himself, pulled himself up on his pillows, put on a brave face. When Oscar drew up a chair and sat at his bedside and asked what was wrong, Major Billicliffe explained. He had been feeling pretty rotten for a month or two now. Ghastly gripes in his stomach, a disinclination to eat. Yesterday, his cleaning lady had turned up, and been so concerned by his appearance that she had telephoned the Creagan G.P., Dr. Sinclair. The long and the short of it was that Dr. Sinclair abandoned his morning surgery and drove immediately to Corrydale, where, after a fairly thorough examination, he told Major Billicliffe that he thought it best if he went over to the hospital in Inverness, just for a few days, for tests, in order to get to the root of his troubles. He had left sedatives and a pain-killer, and the district nurse would call in every day."

"When does he have to go to Inverness?"

"Monday. Dr. Sinclair's booked him in."

"And how will he get there?"

This, of course, was the problem. An ambulance would probably make the long journey from Inverness and pick the old boy up, but if the roads were impassable because of the snow, then it would probably mean a helicopter. Telling Oscar all this, saying the word *helicopter*, Major Billicliffe's weak voice had faltered, and Oscar realized that the old man, the old soldier, was very frightened. Not simply by the idea of being whisked away in a helicopter, but by the prospect of hospitals, tests, doctors, illness, pain, and a possible operation.

It was at this juncture that Oscar had begun to feel responsible.

There didn't seem to be anyone else. So he had suggested to Major Billicliffe that he, Oscar, should come in his car, and drive him, personally, to Inverness. To the hospital. Where he would stay until the old man was safely installed.

At the offer, Major Billicliffe had become quite emotional. "But why?" he had asked, fumbling for a grubby handkerchief to wipe away the weak tears of an invalid. "Why should you bother about a stupid old duffer like me?"

And Oscar had told him. "Because I should like to. Because you are part of Corrydale. Because of my grandmother and Hector." Major Billicliffe looked unconvinced. Oscar finished, "Because you are my friend."

Elfrida was much touched. "You are sweet. And that was exactly the right thing to do. He won't be nearly so afraid if you are there."

"I just hope to God we don't get stuck in a snowstorm."

"Oh, cross that bridge when you get there. What about the dog?"

"I went downstairs and let her loose in the garden. She was bursting for a pee. And not fierce at all, just a dear old Labrador needing a bit of attention. Her name, incidentally, is Brandy."

"Interesting."

"After she'd dealt with her little problem, I put her into the car and took her back to Rose Miller, and filled Rose in with all that had occurred. She was very distressed that she'd had no idea of what was going on. That he had been under the weather, and that she hadn't been round to his house to see if there was anything she could do. By the time I left, she was already girding herself up to go and do a bit of tidying up and cooking for him. At eighty-five years old, there's nothing she loves so much as a challenge. Funnily enough, she seems to be quite fond of old Billicliffe. She kept saying, 'He's mad on the whisky, but he's a dear, good chentleman, and too proud to ask for help.'"

"And what about the poor dog?"

"Rose is going to arrange for her nephew, Charlie Miller, to look after the dog until Billicliffe comes back from hospital. He works on the estate, for the hotel people, and there's a shed for the dog to sleep in, and Charlie will feed her and take her around with him."

"You seem to have arranged everything."

"I think he'll be all right. It's only two days, and then he'll be in hospital."

"Oh, Oscar, what a morning you've had."

"But I'm glad I went." He smiled. "So that's it. How about you? Besides buying a toaster, what else have you been up to?"

"I've had a lovely morning. Better than yours. I wrote to Hector, and Tabitha Kennedy came to see me. I've so much to tell you."

"Then tell me over lunch. Let's treat ourselves. I need cheering up. Let's celebrate clear consciences and Hector's generosity. Let's go to the pub, and we'll have a sandwich, or perchance a pie, and I'll stand you a gin and tonic, and we'll drink to . . ." He hesitated. "Us?"

"Lunch. Out. Do you mean that?"

"Of course."

"Oh, Oscar." For a ridiculous moment, Elfrida felt a bit weepy, but instead came around the table, put her arms about him, and hugged.

It was a good day.

Oscar

After a late breakfast on Sunday morning, Oscar, bundled up as usual against the cold, walked down the street to the newsagent's to pick up the weekly wedge of Sunday papers. The little town was empty and quiet. No cars at this early hour, and only the sound of the gulls and the jackdaws, forever hovering and wheeling and settling on the church tower. It was another brilliant day, cloudless and with no breath of wind. All was petrified by frost, and his footsteps rang on the deserted pavements. He felt as isolated as an Arctic explorer.

Returning, he met Elfrida and Horace setting out for a good long walk along the beach. Elfrida wore a thick woollen hat, like a tea-cosy, pulled down over her ears, and her blanket coat, trimmed with fringe.

She said, "Come with us," but he declined her invitation, because he wished to settle down with the Arts section and catch up with all that was happening in London. Galleries, operas, and concerts. He also enjoyed reading the gardening articles. World news, for the moment, was going by the board.

"How long will you be?" he asked her.

"No idea, but home in time to grill your chop. And I've put a rice pudding in the oven."

Oscar liked rice pudding. Elfrida had made him one before, and it had been splendid, creamy and rich, and lightly spiced with lemon zest.

"Which way are you going?" he asked her.

"Along the dunes. Why?"

"If you are not back by dark, I shall call up a posse and come searching."

"I promise you, I shall tread carefully, like Agag."

"Do that."

They parted. He went indoors, and up the stairs to their magnificent sitting-room. Elfrida had laid the fire, so he lit it, and then went downstairs again and out to the shed, to fill a second basket with logs. If the fire burnt all day, then one basket was not sufficient to last until bedtime. With the flames blazing nicely, he selected the Arts section and settled down in considerable comfort to read.

The church bells disturbed him. The tower clock told him that it was half past ten. He dropped the paper, went over to the window-seat, and perched there, half-turned so that he looked down onto the street. He found it fascinating, on Sunday mornings, how the empty town slowly but steadily began filling up.

The church was coming to life, preparing itself for the weekly influx. The main doors had been opened, and vergers, elders—whatever they called them—in dark suits or kilts strode up the path from the gate and disappeared inside. Oscar recognized Mr. W. G. Croft, who had sold Elfrida their new toaster. Presently he heard, as though from very far away, the tones of the organ. "Sheep May Safely Graze." Muffled by stone-thick walls, but recognizable, to Oscar's professional ear, as a good instrument, and competently played. So often, in country churches, an organist had to do his best with an aged and breathless piece of equipment and a creaky choir, so that he was obliged, while pedalling, to sing loudly, in order to lead the congregation and give them some idea of the tune.

At first, Oscar had found having the church so close as a neighbour a little disconcerting. A constant reminder, nudging at his shoulder, of all he had lost. He watched the cars draw up and groups of people converging, walking from street corners, stepping down the hill. He knew that he only had to cross the road and he would be swept up into the stream, and, like a swimmer caught in a current, sucked through those imposing doors and into the soaring nave.

The windows of the church were tall, arched in gothic style. But from the outside, the colours and patterns of the stained-glass were dimmed. He knew that to appreciate their jewel-like beauty one had to view them from within, the light of day streaming through the colours and throwing lozenges of ruby and sapphire and emerald onto worn flagstones.

Perhaps this was symbolic. Perhaps, isolated from the church, there were other delights, pleasures, comforts, that, because of his present state of mind, he deliberately denied himself.

It was an interesting supposition, but disturbing, too, and one on which he did not wish to dwell. He left the window and went back to the fire and his newspaper. But when the congregation in the church across the street began to sing their first hymn, he lowered the paper and listened, staring into the flames.

"Hark, a thrilling voice is sounding,
Christ is nigh, it seems to say.
Cast away the dreams of darkness
O ye children of the day."

A good old classic Advent hymn. He remembered rehearsing the choir at the school where he had taught, imploring them to sing as though they truly believed the message of hope.

He thought, I must get in touch with Peter Kennedy.

But Sunday was the busiest day of a rector's week. Perhaps tomorrow. Or the next day.

Meantime . . . he settled his spectacles and endeavoured to concentrate his mind on *The Sunday Times* and an erudite critique of Jonathan Miller's production of *Fidelio* at Covent Garden.

MONDAY, DECEMBER 11TH

Monday was one of Mrs. Snead's days, the other being Thursday. She came at nine on the dot, while Elfrida and Oscar were still drinking the last of their breakfast coffee, and her arrival was heralded by the slam of the back door when she let herself in. Then a pause while, in the scullery, she divested herself of anorak, headscarf, and boots, hanging the garments on her useful hook. She always carried a flowered plastic shopping bag in which were stowed her working clothes, an apron and a trendy pair of trainers. Oscar and Elfrida waited. Then the door was flung open, and bang, she was there.

"Morning, all."

An entrance, thought Oscar, that any actress would be proud of.

"Morning, Mrs. Snead."

"Blimey, it's parky." Rubbing her hands together to get her circulation going, Mrs. Snead kicked shut the door behind her. "There's a wind goes through you like a knife."

Elfrida put down her coffee-cup. "Have a cup of tea."

"I wouldn't mind, before I get started in. Kettle's boiled, 'as it?" She caught sight of the new toaster. "Well, just look at what we've got 'ere. Love the colour. Been shopping, 'ave you? About time, too, that other old thing was a killer. What did you do with it? Bin it, I 'ope." She clashed around, finding a mug and a tea-bag and the milk carton. Her tea made, she pulled out a handy chair and sat to join them.

"What's this I'm 'earing about Major Billicliffe?"

They both stared at her. Then Oscar said, "News travels fast."

"Charlie Miller was in Arfur's yesterday evening, buying a cabbage. 'E told 'im. Says 'e's got to look after the dog. Say 'e's going to Inverness to the 'ospital. 'Ope it's nothing serious."

"We hope so, too, Mrs. Snead. And Oscar's going to drive him over."

"Charlie said something like that to Arfur." She eyed Oscar. "You up to it, Mr. Blundell? It's a long way."

"I think I'll manage, Mrs. Snead."

"At least it's not snowing. What time do you 'ave to be off?"

"As soon as I've finished breakfast."

"Got a mobile phone, 'ave you? Ought to 'ave a mobile phone."

"No, I haven't got one. But we shall be all right."

"Well, let's 'ope so, anyway. No point in being pessimistic. Now, Mrs. Phipps, before I forget, Arfur says to ask you, do you want a Christmas tree, and if so 'e'll reserve one."

"A Christmas tree?" Elfrida looked uncertain. "Well . . . I don't know."

"You must 'ave a tree. Wouldn't be Christmas without a tree."

"Yes. Perhaps. But we thought we wouldn't bother."

"A tree's no bother. It's fun. Decorating and all that."

Elfrida appealed to Oscar. "What do you think?"

He decided it was time to put her out of her misery. "That's very thoughtful of you, Mrs. Snead, but we're getting our Christmas tree from Corrydale."

Elfrida's jaw dropped. And for once in her life, she was quite cross with him.

"We're getting one from *Corrydale*? Why didn't you say? Here I am telling Mrs. Snead we don't want a tree, and the next thing you're telling me you've already booked one. You are impossible."

"I'm sorry."

"When did you organize all this?"

"On Saturday, when I went to see Rose. I told you, Charlie works in the gardens there. They've got a whole plantation of Christmas trees, and Rose said she'd speak to him, and he'd cut us a good one."

"You should have said."

"There was so much else to tell you, I forgot. I thought it would be nice for Carrie and Lucy."

Elfrida stopped being cross. "That was a lovely idea. When is it coming?"

"We have to telephone Charlie, and go and fetch it."

By now, Mrs. Snead had pricked up her ears.

She was a small, spare lady, with tightly permed grey hair, and always wore sparkling, dangly earrings. Sitting there with her head cocked and her bright eyes not missing a trick, she reminded Oscar of a cheeky sparrow.

"'Aving visitors, are you?"

"I haven't had time to tell you yet, Mrs. Snead. But my cousin and her niece are coming for Christmas. Lucy's the niece. She's fourteen."

Mrs. Snead was highly delighted. "That's really lovely. That'll cheer you up, 'aving young people around the place. When are they coming? And where do you want them to sleep? We'll need to get the rooms cleaned up and polished."

"I thought I'd put Lucy up in the attic."

"The attic! But there's not a stick of furniture."

"There will be, after tomorrow. Tabitha Kennedy's going to take me to the market in Buckly. She says we can buy anything there."

Mrs. Snead sniffed. "It's not new stuff," she warned. "All second-'and."

"It'll be good enough, I'm sure."

"I'd 'ave thought you'd 'ave liked a nice suite." She was clearly disappointed in Elfrida's lowly taste. "Saw one in Inverness last time I was there. Lovely, it was. Walnut veneer with filigree brass 'andles. And the bed 'ad a peach satin 'eadboard and valance."

"It sounds very pretty, Mrs. Snead, but a bit grand. And I don't want to have to drive all the way to Inverness."

Mrs. Snead, pondering over this new domestic situation, sipped her tea. She said, "We're a bit short of sheets and stuff. You don't want to buy *them* second-'and. Never liked the thought of a used blanket. There's a draper in Buckly, not much good for clothes, but they run a line in soft furnishings. You could 'ave a word with Tabitha Kennedy and pop in there."

"I'll do that."

"Oh, well." Mrs. Snead finished her tea and sprang to her trainered feet, to fling the dregs of her mug into the sink. "Sitting 'ere chatting won't get the baby bathed. Where'd you want me to start, Mrs. Phipps?"

"Let's get going on the attic. Get it swept and scrubbed and the skylight cleaned, and then, when any furniture arrives, it can be carried straight upstairs and put into place."

"'Oo's going to do the carrying, I'd like to know?" Mrs. Snead could be quite protective and fierce. "Not you and Mr. Blundell, I 'ope. You'll give yourselves 'ernias."

"I shall organize a van. With removal-men."

"You can borrow Arfur if you like."

"That's very kind. . . ."

"'E's 'andy with a screwdriver. I will say that for 'im." With this parting shot, Mrs. Snead collected brooms, dusters, and her tin of polish, and set off up the stairs. A moment or two later could be heard the roaring of the ancient Hoover, accompanied by Mrs. Snead's voice. "I want to be Bobby's girl," she sang.

Elfrida stifled a giggle. Oscar said, "Not only does Mrs. Snead dust for us, but brings with her music that takes me back over the years. She is indeed a remarkable lady."

"What memory does her singing evoke for you, Oscar?"

"Schoolboys' studies, smelling of sweaty gym shoes and throbbing with pop."

"That's not very romantic."

"I was a bachelor schoolmaster. Romance did not fly my way." He looked at his watch. "Elfrida, I must be going."

"You will take care, won't you?"

"I shall endeavour to."

"It's beside the point, but I think you're a saint."

"I shall ask Mrs. Snead to polish my halo."

"Oscar . . ."

"What is it?"

"Good luck."

That night, the wind veered around to the east, and in the early hours of the morning Oscar awoke to the whining, piping sound of an imminent gale and the rattle of rain flung at window-panes. He lay awake for a long time, thinking about Godfrey Billicliffe. At last he knew his Christian name, because he had learned it in the course of helping the Ward Sister to fill in countless forms, before leaving the sick old man to her tender mercies.

The undertaking had not been as demanding as he had feared. The drive to Inverness had gone smoothly, and old Billicliffe, encouraged by caring attention, had talked non-stop the entire way over. Oscar had learned much about his life. His career in the Army, his spell in Germany with the British Army of the Rhine. How he had met his wife in Osnabrück. How they had married in Colchester. How they had never been blessed with children. Oscar, at the wheel of his car, was thankfully not expected to make much response to this stream of reminiscence. From time to time, all that was required was a casual agreement, or a nod of the head, whereupon Godfrey Billicliffe bumbled on.

It was not until they were speeding down the motorway across the Black Isle, and Inverness was in view across the water, that Major Billicliffe fell silent. For a moment Oscar wondered if he had fallen asleep, but glancing sideways saw his passenger was still awake. Perhaps simply brooding. After a bit he started talking again, but now it was not about the past that he spoke, but his present and his future.

"Been thinking, Oscar . . ."

"What have you been thinking about?"

"What's going to happen. . . . Turning my toes up . . ."

"You're not going to turn your toes up," Oscar assured him, hoping that he sounded robust.

"Never know . . . Not as young . . . Have to be prepared. Ready and prepared for all contingencies. Learned that in the Army. Prepare for the worst and hope for the best." Another long pause. "Wondered . . . up to you, of course . . . if you'd agree to be my executor. Good to know . . . Capable hands . . ."

"I'm not so sure my hands are capable."

"Rubbish. Hector McLennan's nephew. Not that his son was great shakes . . . you . . . different kettle of fish. Friends all dead. Thought you might . . . Appreciate it . . ."

His unfinished sentences Oscar found maddening. He said, as calmly as he could, "If you want. If it would set your mind at rest, I'd be happy to be your executor. But . . ."

"Splendid. All settled. . . . Tell my lawyer. Nice feller. Did all the conveyancing when I bought my house from the Corrydale Estate. Keen fisherman. Liked the cut of his jib."

"Has he got a name?"

Major Billicliffe gave a snort, which perhaps was meant to be laughter at Oscar's quirky question. "Course he's got a name. Murdo MacKenzie. Firm's MacKenzie and Stout. South Street, Inverness."

"Murdo MacKenzie."

"I must tell him you're my executor. Settled . . . ring him up." He thought about this. "Suppose I can ring up from the hospital? They'll have telephones." He finished doubtfully, "Won't they?"

"Of course. The nurse, I am sure, will bring one to your bedside."

"Bit different from the old days," said Major Billicliffe, as though he had once languished in the military hospital at Scutari. "Medical officers' rounds and bedpans. And a matron like a sergeant-major. No telephones then. . . ." Remembering, he fell silent once more, and did not speak again until they had reached their destination.

The hospital was the Royal Western. Oscar found it without too much difficulty, and once arrived, matters were taken out of his hands, and all he had to do was accompany Major Billicliffe on his way. A porter appeared with a wheelchair and took over the new arrival, while Oscar walked alongside, carrying the necessary suitcase, a heavy and battered bit of equipment fashioned from what looked like elephant hide. Upstairs in a huge lift, and then the long corridors of polished linoleum, and finally the ward. Ward 14. The Ward Sister was ready and waiting for admission, with her clipboard and her forms. All went smoothly until she came to Next of Kin.

"Next of Kin, Major Billicliffe?"

Suddenly, he looked bewildered. "Sorry?"

"Next of Kin. You know. Wife. Children. Brothers or sisters."

He shook his head. "I have none. I have no one. . . ."

"Oh, come along, there has to be someone."

Oscar could not bear it. "Me," he said firmly. "I am Major Billicliffe's next of kin. Oscar Blundell. You can write it down. The Estate House. Creagan."

Sister did so. "Have you got a telephone number?"

Oscar gave it to her.

Finally, all was written, recorded, and signed. And it was time for Oscar to leave. He said goodbye.

"You'll come again?"

"Of course. Provided we don't get snowed in."

"Thank you for bringing me. Obliged. . . ."

"Not at all."

And he walked away from the old man and his suitcase, and told himself that it wasn't his fault. There was no reason to feel as shifty as a traitor.

He could have done no more. Later, when there was news of the invalid, he and Elfrida would set out on the long drive once more, and go to visit Godfrey Billicliffe. Elfrida, if anybody, would cheer him up. She would probably take him grapes.

A clout of wind struck the house. Oscar turned into the pillows and closed his eyes, and all at once found himself thinking about Francesca. This often happened in the dark hours of a restless night, and he dreaded the inevitable aftermath, a torment of rekindled, anguished loss. Francesca. Soundless, his lips formed her name. Francesca. He slid his hand beneath his pillow to fumble for his handkerchief, knowing that he would probably weep. But instead of weeping, he became aware of a sort of quiet, as though he were more at ease with himself than he had felt for weeks. Francesca. He saw her running across the sunlit lawns of the Grange, towards him. And the image stayed, poignant, but especially sweet.

Holding it close, he slept.

TUESDAY, DECEMBER 12TH

The next morning dawned a day of dismal weather. The sparkle of the big freeze was drowned in showers of sleety rain, driven in from the sea, and the street was filled with bobbing wet umbrellas. At midday, the huge gritting lorry appeared, trundling back to its depot, with snow crusted beneath its mudguards and windscreen wipers going full-tilt.

Elfrida had bought herself a notebook, and over lunch, which was soup and some Stilton she had found in the supermarket, she made lists.

"I've got to think of everything," she told Oscar importantly. "There isn't time for forgetting. They'll be here on Friday. Do you think Lucy will want a dressing-table?"

Oscar, who was trying to do *The Times* crossword puzzle, set it nobly aside and removed his spectacles, as though the better to think.

But "I have no idea" was all he could come up with.

"And a bed, of course. . . ."

With some effort, he applied himself to the problem. "A wardrobe?"

"We'd never get a wardrobe under those combed ceilings. Some hooks on the wall would do." She wrote, in her notebook, *Hooks*. "And coat-hangers." She wrote *Coat-hangers*.

Oscar sat back in his chair and watched her with amusement. He had never seen Elfrida so focused and organized. For a moment she reminded him, in the nicest possible way, of Gloria; planning and plotting and writing lists and making things happen.

"When does Mrs. Kennedy come?"

"Half past two, she said she'd be here. I said I'd drive her in your car. You don't need it, do you?"

"No."

"If you felt frightfully energetic, you could take Horace for a walk."

Oscar, hedging, said, "I'll see," and went back to his crossword.

But when Tabitha Kennedy arrived, Elfrida was up at the top of the garden, unpegging a line of wet washing which should never have been pegged out in the first place. So, when the doorbell rang, it was Oscar who went downstairs to open the door.

She was booted and raincoated, but her head was bare, and her dark hair blew in the wind. She put up a hand to push a strand from her cheek. "Hello. I'm Tabitha."

"Of course. Come in out of the wet. Elfrida won't be a moment, she's getting a lot of wet clothes off the line. I'm Oscar Blundell."

"I know." She had a lovely smile. "How do you do." They shook hands. "I hope I'm not too early."

"Not at all. Come upstairs, it's more comfortable than standing around here."

He led the way, and she followed, chatting as though she had known him forever. "Isn't it disappointing, the rain, after all that lovely frosty weather? There've been burst pipes all over the place and the plumber's run off his feet." In the sitting-room, the fire burnt brightly, and a pot of Arthur Snead's forced hyacinths filled the air with their fragrance. "Oh, aren't they heaven. They really smell of spring, don't they? I said to Elfrida we'd have to go in *your* car, but Peter's at home today, so he let me bring *our* car. Anything rather than come shopping with me. He hates shopping more than *anything*."

"I sympathize. It's very good of you to help Elfrida out."

"I'll love it. I adore spending other people's money. We'll probably be quite late back. The market won't close till five, and by then we'll both be ready for a restoring cup of tea."

Downstairs, a door slammed, and Elfrida's footsteps came running up the stairs. She appeared at the door in her blanket coat and her tea-cosy hat. "Tabitha, I am sorry; have you been waiting? It's on days like this that I long for an electric dryer. But only on days like this. Now, I just have to get my bag, and my list, and the car keys. . . ."

"You don't need them," Tabitha told her. "I'm driving you."

They departed at last, in some excitement, reminding Oscar of a couple of young girls setting off to enjoy themselves. He stood at the window and watched them go, getting into the well-worn estate car, slamming doors, fixing seat-belts, moving away across the square and out of sight.

He was alone. Horace slept by the fire. Aware of his own procrastination, Oscar made another attempt to finish the crossword, but was defeated and laid the newspaper aside. There were other things, he knew, that he had to do. He pulled himself out of his chair and went across the room to the heavy oak table which stood against the wall opposite the fireplace, and which he used as a desk. He made space, pushing aside a file or two and his brief-case, and settled down to write two long-overdue letters. One was to Hector McLennan, thanking him for his generosity, and doing his best to sound positive and reassuring. The second was to Mrs. Muswell, who had looked after Oscar during the worst time, and whom he had abandoned so abruptly. The memory of her standing, weeping, at the door of the Grange as he and Elfrida drove away had been pricking his conscience ever since. Now, he assured her that he was well, thanked her for her loyalty, and said that he hoped she had found other congenial employment. He sent his best wishes. He signed his name.

He folded the letters, addressed envelopes, found stamps. They were ready for posting.

Peter's at home today.

Now.

He went out of the room, where, on the landing, stood the telephone. He found the phone book, looked up the number, memorized it, and punched the digits. He heard the ringing tone, but only once, as though the instrument stood on a desk, at a man's elbow, ready for instant response.

"Creagan Manse." The warm, familiar voice. "Peter Kennedy."

At half past five, Oscar, bundled up and hatted, let himself out of the Estate House and set off on the stepped lane that led up the hill. Elfrida and Tabitha Kennedy had not yet returned, so he left the light burning in the hall, as a welcome for when they eventually came home. And a note for Elfrida on the kitchen table. *Gone out for a while. I shan't be late.* He left Horace as well, having done his duty and taken the dog for a walk and fed him his biscuits and lambs' hearts. Lambs' hearts, for Horace were the treat of all time, and he had guzzled the lot and then retired to his basket for a snooze.

He walked between high walls and garden trees. It was very dark, an overcast evening, but the wind had dropped and a drizzling rain fell. At the top of the lane, a steepish climb, he paused to get his breath, and then continued on his way along the footpath that leaned up against the slope of the hill. The town dropped below him. He looked down on the other gardens, roof-tops, the lines of the streets marked with lamps. In the tower of the church, the clock face shone like a full moon.

A little farther on—by now his eyes had adjusted to the darkness—and he could make out the long line of the distant coast, stretched like an arm out to sea, and holding in its fingers the intermittent pinprick signal of the lighthouse. There were no stars.

A gate led out into a wide road, lined on the right-hand side by large stone-built Victorian houses set in spacious gardens. The first house was the Manse. Oscar remembered its location from sixty years ago, when he was sometimes brought for tea by his grandmother, and to play with the then-incumbent's children. He remembered the house and the family who lived there, but had forgotten all their names.

A light burnt over the door. He went up the path, sea-pebbles crunching beneath the soles of his boots. The front door had been painted bright blue. He pressed the bell.

Suddenly he shivered. He told himself that it was because of the cold and the damp.

He heard the inner door open, and then the blue door was flung wide, and he was dazzled by light. Peter Kennedy stood there, warm with welcome. He wore a thick polo-neck sweater and a pair of worn corduroys and looked comfortingly unchurchly.

"Oscar! Come away in." He looked over Oscar's shoulder. "Did you not bring your car?"

"No. I walked."

"Good man."

He went indoors, into the hall. Saw the Turkish carpet, the fumed-oak hall-stand, the antique cist on which stood a neat stack of parish magazines. A riding hat had been dumped on the newel-post of the banister, and on the bottom stair stood a pair of football boots and a stack of clean and folded laundry. All left there, Oscar guessed, until the next obliging person would collect them and bear them upstairs.

". . . take your coat off. The children are both out, so we've got the place to ourselves. I've a fire on in my study. I've had an afternoon of it, catching up on paperwork and writing a long-overdue article for *The Sutherland Times*." Oscar divested himself of gloves, jacket, and hat, and Peter Kennedy took them from him and laid them on an impressive oak chair, which looked as though it might, at one time, have seated a bishop. "Now, come along in. . . ."

He led the way into his study, a bow-windowed front room which had probably been intended as the dining-room of the original house. It was thickly curtained against the dreich evening, and softly lit by three lamps—one on the huge littered desk, and two more burning on either side of the fire, where stood two ancient leather armchairs. Walls were lined with shelves of books, and after the airy emptiness of the Estate House, all felt safe and dark and warm. A bit like going back to the womb.

As well, there was a marvellous smell, which Oscar finally traced to the chunks of carefully stacked peat smouldering in the fire basket.

He said, "A peat-fire. I'd forgotten about peat. Sometimes when I put the dog out at night, I can smell the smoke from chimneys. I must try and get hold of some, just for that smell."

"I'm very fortunate; one of my parishioners has his own peat-patch, and he keeps me supplied. Now come and sit down and make yourself comfortable. Would you like a cup of coffee?" Oscar did not immediately reply, and Peter looked at his watch. "A quarter to six. We could jump the gun, and enjoy a glass of Laphroaig. I keep it, but only for special occasions."

Malt whisky. Laphroaig. Irresistible. "I think I'd like that more than anything."

"I thought you might, so I am prepared." And Oscar saw on the desk—along with a word processor, a stack of books, papers in some disarray, and a telephone—a small tray, neatly set with the bottle of Laphroaig, two small tumblers, and a jug of water. So much for the coffee. He was touched. "The girls aren't back yet?"

"No." Oscar lowered himself into one of the chairs, which was surprisingly soft and comfortable. Above him, in the centre of the mantelpiece, stood a clock, the sort that is presented to retiring ministers or schoolmasters after forty years of loyal service. It had a soft, solid tick, smooth and sweet as a carefully set metronome. "I think they planned on treating themselves to a tea-party once they'd finished their shopping."

"I'm sure. I hope they were successful." Carrying the two glasses, Peter handed Oscar his drink, and then settled down in the other armchair, facing his visitor. He raised his glass.

"Slàinte."

"Good health."

The Laphroaig was like nectar. Clean, delicious, slipping down his throat. Warming.

Peter went on. "Buckly's rather a depressing town at the moment. Most of the people are unemployed. The woollen mill went to the wall, and for skilled weavers and spinners, there is little alternative work."

Oscar frowned. "The woollen mill? Not McTaggarts?"

"Yes. McTaggarts."

"Gone bust? I had no idea. Astonishing. It's like being told the Rock of Gibraltar has crumbled. What happened?"

Peter told him. "The old man died, the sons weren't interested. The work-force got a bit of financial help, a grant, and took it over themselves. They were doing all right, and then we had a spell of dreadful weather, the river burst its banks, and the place was flooded. Everything lost, destroyed."

Oscar was appalled. "Is that the end of it, then?"

"There's some word of a take-over. One of those big textile conglomerates. Sturrock and Swinfield. From London. But so far, nothing very much seems to have happened, and the people in Buckly are beginning to fear the worst. Which is, that nothing is *ever* going to happen."

"What a tragedy." Oscar frowned. "I can't think why I haven't heard about this before. I suppose . . . just now . . . I don't read the newspapers properly, and certainly not the City pages. And here, I only take *The Times* and *The Telegraph,* so I don't get the local news. As well, I haven't talked to many people. Except Mrs. Snead. That, of course, is why I am here. To apologize to you. I should have come before, but I didn't."

"Please. Don't feel bad. I realized that I had taken you unawares, and I should have waited for a more suitable occasion to make myself known to you. I hope you weren't too upset."

"I don't know what came over me. It was ridiculous."

"Please, think no more of it. No harm has been done. Another time, you must join me there, for tea, or for a drink, or whatever you want. The best would be if you felt like joining the club, and then, when the good weather starts again, we could have a game. You do play?"

"I used to play with my grandmother when I was a boy, but I was never much good, even then."

"I'd be delighted to give you a game."

"I have no clubs."

"We'll borrow some from the pro. It's such a splendid course, it would be sad to live here and not experience at least one round. Your grandmother was a good golfer. When I came here, I heard a lot about her prowess. She was Lady Champion two years running. One way or another she must, by all accounts, have been an exceptional lady."

"Yes, she was."

"And musical, too."

"Yes. And an inspired gardener. She was extremely accomplished." Oscar took another sip of the Laphroaig, and then set the glass down on the table beside him, where it glowed like a jewel in the soft light of the lamp. He said, "Godfrey Billicliffe also invited me to join the Golf Club. But I'm afraid, at that particular moment, we were in the throes of a rather traumatic encounter. Both Elfrida and I were exhausted after our long journey. All we wanted was to get the key of our house and escape. I'm afraid we were very offhand."

"He can be daunting. I understand. I understand, as well, that you drove him to hospital yesterday morning."

"How did you know that?"

Peter Kennedy smiled. "There are few secrets in this small community. No, don't worry; it wasn't idle gossip. Dr. Sinclair rang me to put me in the picture. It was very good of you."

"Did you know he was ill?"

"No. I don't think anybody knew. He's been something of a problem ever since his wife died—gone downhill at a frightening pace. Lonely, I think, but too proud to admit it, and none of us had the nerve to suggest that he sell up and move into the Old People's Home."

"My stepsons exhorted me to go into a retirement home in Hampshire, but that was because they had inherited their mother's house and wanted me out of the way so that they could put it up for sale. I found the notion dire. Like the beginning of the end."

"How did *you* guess there was something amiss?"

"I went to see Rose Miller. On the way home, I heard Billicliffe's dog howling. So I called in. To set my mind at rest, I suppose. Both Elfrida and I had been feeling rather bad about the old boy. And I found him upstairs in bed, obviously very poorly. He was frightened, too. Frightened of the prospect of ambulances or helicopters. He seemed so dreadfully alone. Saying I'd drive him to Inverness in my car was the least I could do."

"I have to go to Inverness on Friday for a meeting with the

moderator. I'll pop into the hospital and pay a visit. See how he's getting on. . . ."

"I said I would stand as his next of kin. So my name and telephone number are on all the countless forms we had to fill in, and I imagine that if there is any news, then I shall be informed."

"Well. Keep me in touch."

"Of course."

"Now. Tell me about your uncle. Hector. How is Hector?"

"Growing older. Living in London. He came down to see me after . . . after the funeral. He didn't come to the funeral, because he'd had flu and his doctor, very rightly, forbade him. It was Hector who suggested that I leave Hampshire and come back here. . . ."

"I know, Oscar. He wrote me a long letter. I was so dreadfully sorry. I wanted to come right away, to talk with you, and to let you know that if there was anything I could do . . . could say. But my instinct told me that for the time being you needed to be on your own. I hope you didn't get the impression that I was either uncaring or inattentive."

"No. I didn't think that."

"Sometimes . . . just to talk. To a stranger. A person disassociated . . . is very often easier."

"Like confiding in a man met on a train journey. A man you know you will never see again."

"Not entirely." Peter smiled. "Because I hope you will see me again."

"It's difficult to know where to start. It all seems to go a long way back."

"Life tends to."

"I never thought I should be married. I thought, always, that I would remain a bachelor all my life. I had my work, as a schoolmaster, teaching piano and training the choir. For company, other masters and their wives. My passion was music. The school was Glastonbury, a lesser-known public school, but excellent for all that. I was very happy there. And then I grew older, and the headmaster retired, and a new, younger man came to take his place. The head had always been a close friend, and although his replacement was perfectly competent, pleasant, and traditional, I decided, after a year, that the time had come for a change. As well, I had been offered the post as organist and choirmaster at Saint Biddulph's in London. I thought about it for a bit, but not very long. The music at Saint Biddulph's had always been renowned for its excellence, and the choir was secure, funded by a generous endowment that had been made by a grateful parishioner some years before. So I changed direction and moved to London. I lived in a comfortable, spacious flat on the second floor of an old terraced house, only five minutes or so from the church, and the ladies of the parish made certain that I had a competent housekeeper and was well cared for.

"They were halcyon days. I suppose, the peak of my fairly modest career. Two of the choristers were professional concert singers, there was enthusiasm from the public, and we were able to enlarge our repertoire and perform, on special occasions, some ambitious chorales. Palestrina's *Salvete Flores Martyrum,* Schubert's setting of the Twenty-Third Psalm, Fauré's *Requiem*. Glorious stuff.

"I met the Bellamys soon after my arrival at Saint Biddulph's. They lived in some style in a house in Elm Park Gardens, and from the first were enormously hospitable and kind to me. When George Bellamy became ill, I used to go to their house to keep him company, play backgammon with him. When he died, I arranged the music for his considerably important funeral.

"After the funeral, I thought that Gloria would no longer want me coming and going. That the reason for my visits was now over. But she continued to invite me to various small social affairs. A drinks party or a dinner or a Sunday luncheon. Sometimes we went to the cinema together, or spent a day at Kew. I thought little of it, but much enjoyed her company. And then, one day, in a quite matter-of-fact fashion, she said that she thought it would be a good idea if we married. She explained that she did not enjoy living without a man, and she felt that I, in my advancing years, would be glad of a wife to take care of me. It all sounds, I know, a little cold-blooded, but the truth is that I was extremely fond of her, and she, I think, of me. We were neither of us in our first flush of youth, and so old enough to make a success of what others saw simply as a marriage of convenience.

"She was a wonderful wife. Warm, generous, and kind-hearted. I had never, since I was a boy coming to Corrydale, known such material comforts, such ease of living. She and George had sons, Giles and Crawford, but now they were adult, had fled the nest, and set up establishments of their own. And Gloria was still a comparatively young woman and brimming with physical vitality. When she told me she was pregnant, I was quite ridiculously incredulous. I had never, in all my life, imagined that I would become a father. And when Francesca was born, that tiny child, I was filled with a wonder which I don't suppose I shall ever experience again. It was as though a miracle had occurred. And she never stopped being a miracle.

"Sometimes, as she grew older, and was running about and talking nineteen-to-the-dozen, and generally making the usual din that all children make, I would watch her, and still find it unbelievable that she was actually mine, that I had helped to create this beguiling, beautiful, miniature human being.

"Then Gloria was left this house in the country, in Hampshire, and we moved from London and started our new life in Dibton. I have to admit that I missed Saint Biddulph's, but music was still part of my life. I taught a little, and from time to time played the organ for Morning Service in the village church."

Here, Oscar paused, to reach for his glass and to take another sip of the Laphroaig. A glowing lump of peat slipped, with a whisper, into the bed of the fire. The clock gently ticked on.

Peter spoke. "Your friend. Elfrida. Have you known her for always?"

"No. We didn't meet until she came to live in our village. She was alone, and Gloria made friends with her, and generally took Elfrida under her wing. She was amusing, full of life, and we all enjoyed her company. Francesca was forever bicycling off to visit her in her little cottage. She made Francesca laugh. She was in Cornwall, staying with a cousin, at the time of the accident. She returned after the funeral, with no idea at all of what had happened. When Hector suggested I leave Hampshire and return to Creagan, I knew I couldn't do it on my own. The journey seemed too arduous, and I dreaded being alone. So I asked Elfrida to come with me. It is a measure of her generous heart that she agreed. She is company for me, and in the blackest moments has always been able to make me smile. When I first met Elfrida, I remember she asked me if I was religious. I told her that it is hard *not* to believe when you have been steeped in the liturgies and traditions of the Anglican Church for most of your life. And that I felt I needed some being to thank.

"Because I was fortunate. I was content. The marriage was working well, and because of Francesca, I could have no regrets. But Gloria was a very strong, forceful character. And her considerable wealth was her own. She had to be handled, at times, with enormous tact. She loved company, people, parties, and sometimes she drank too much. I don't mean that she was an alcoholic . . . well, not exactly . . . simply a serious social drinker. Often, after an evening out, I would drive us home, in her car, and she resented that, and would be sullen-faced the next morning. I feel disloyal to her even talking about this. But I knew her weakness, just as I knew her many strengths.

"The day of the bonfire and the Guy Fawkes party, she said she was taking Francesca, and it occurred to me that I should go, too. But I had a man coming to see me about building a new fence for the paddock. It was a job I had been wanting to see done and finished, and I didn't feel inclined to put him off. Besides, it was simply a children's party. A big tea, and fireworks. They would be home by seven at the latest.

"And, of course, it *was* a children's party. But there were adults there, too, most of them Gloria's friends. And after the fireworks were over, and the children were still running about in the dark, in the garden, waving sparklers and working off their excitement, the adults went indoors for a drink.

"I don't know how much she had. There wasn't, thank God, an

autopsy. Driving conditions were appalling, sudden heavy rain, the roads running with water. As well, there had been some repair on the roundabout and lights had been left flashing to warn of this. Perhaps they confused her. We'll never know. The lorry driver said that her car had driven out, at some speed, straight into his path, as he swung around from the right. It was, of course, his right-of-way. There was not a mortal thing he could do. A split second. And Gloria's car was destroyed, unrecognizable, and Gloria and Francesca were both dead.

"The news was broken to me by the police. A nice young sergeant. Poor boy. I cannot describe my reaction, because I felt nothing. Numb. Empty. Devoid of any emotion. And then, gradually, the void filled with a bitter rage and resentment, against whoever, or whatever, had allowed this thing to happen to me. The world, I know, is filled with horror, and one becomes hardened. Horrified, but hardened. Watching television images of destroyed villages, starving children, monumental natural disasters. But this was *me*. This was *my* life, my being. My wife. My *child*! If a God was there . . . and I had never been totally certain that he was . . . I didn't want to have any part of him.

"Our cleric in Dibton called to comfort. He told me that God sends people only what they are strong enough to bear. And I rounded on him, and said that I wished I were as weak as water, and still had my child. And then I sent him away. We never got around to the guilt. I knew Gloria's weakness. I should have been with them. I should have been behind the wheel of the car. If only. If only is my nightmare."

"*If only* is like hindsight. A useless exercise. The accident seemed to me to have been one composed of several tragic circumstances. Who knows? Perhaps you would have died, too, Oscar, and then an even larger hole would have been left in the lives of those who knew and loved you all. . . . As for God, I frankly admit that I find it easier to live with the age-old questions about suffering than with many of the easy or pious explanations offered from time to time. Some of which seem to verge on blasphemy. I hope so much that no one has sought to try and comfort you by saying that God must have needed

Francesca more than you. I would find it impossible to worship a God who deliberately stole my child from me. Such a God would be a moral monster."

Oscar was astounded. "Is that," he asked at last, "what you really believe?"

Peter nodded. "It is what I truly believe. Thirty years in the ministry has taught me that the one thing we should never say when a young person dies is 'It is the will of God.' We simply don't know enough to say that. I am in fact convinced that when Francesca died in that terrible accident, God's was the first heart to break."

"I want to move on, to go on living, to be able to accept; to be able to give again. I don't like taking all the time. I've never been that sort of person."

"Oh, Oscar. It will be all right. Because of your profession, the Church has been so much part of your life for so many years that you will be as familiar as I am with the great biblical promises about life and death. The problem is that traumatic grief can often render them unreal. For a while, what you are probably going to need most is not people who will quote the Bible to you, but close friends who will continue to hold your hand, and lend you a listening ear when you want to speak about Francesca."

Oscar thought about Elfrida, and Peter paused for a moment, as though to give him time to argue this new conception. But Oscar did not say anything.

"Life is sweet," Peter went on. "Beyond the pain, life continues to be sweet. The basics are still there. Beauty, food, and friendship, reservoirs of love and understanding. Later, possibly not yet, you are going to need others who will encourage you to make new beginnings. Welcome them. They will help you move on, to cherish happy memories and confront the painful ones with more than bitterness and anger."

Oscar remembered the dark night, and the image of Francesca, and how, for the first time, it had not reduced him to the painful tears of loss, but had filled his being with a peaceful comfort. Perhaps that had been the start of his recovery. Perhaps this conversation, this interview, whatever one called it, was the continuance.

He did not know. He only knew that he felt better, stronger, not so useless. Perhaps, after all, he hadn't done so badly.

He said, "Thank you."

"Oh, my friend, I wish I could give you so much more."

"No. Don't wish that. You have given me enough."

LUCY

Lucy had flown only twice in her life. Once was to France, where she had been invited for a summer holiday with the family of a schoolfriend. The second trip was to the Channel Islands with her mother and her grandmother. That was during Easter, and they had stayed in the sort of hotel where you had to change for dinner.

Both times she had found it tremendously exciting, but today she made an effort to be consciously casual about the whole business, so that any person who happened to look her way would get the impression that she was a seasoned, vastly experienced traveller.

Her clothes helped. Because her mother, perhaps to assuage unadmitted stirrings of guilt, had taken Lucy to the Gap, and there bought her daughter a number of delectable things. So she was wearing the new jeans, warm ones, lined in red brushed cotton. Her boots were pale suede with thick rubber soles, and her jacket scarlet, quilted and padded, a bit like being bundled up in an eiderdown. As well, they had bought two thick polo-neck sweaters, one navy and one white; a black miniskirt; and two pairs of thick black tights. The final item was her rucksack, navy-blue canvas piped in red, in which Lucy had packed her diary, her purse, a brush and comb, and a bar of chocolate. Last night she had washed her hair, and this morning brushed it back into a long ponytail, secured with a cotton scrunchie. She felt sleek and neat. A credit to Carrie.

Carrie looked, as always, immensely elegant, in long boots, her loden coat, and a black fox fur hat. Lucy was very aware of heads turning to watch as Carrie walked by, pushing their trolley with the luggage. The only thing was, poor Carrie had a bit of a cold. It wasn't the sort of cold that made her look ugly, simply a bit frail. She said she had started feeling rough a day or so ago—there was a lot of flu going about—but it was only a cold, and she had dosed herself with medicaments and would be fine once she started breathing the clean, cold Scottish air.

They checked in, went through Security, and waiting for their flight to be called, Lucy began to feel safe. Ever since the plans had been laid for Christmas, she had not only been counting the days, but at the same time been prey to a number of nervous forebodings. Something, she was sure, was bound to happen to put a stop to her going with Carrie. Somebody would fall ill, or Gran would decide all at once that Lucy should not stay with Elfrida Phipps, of whom she did not approve, and whom Lucy was longing to meet. Perhaps, in America, Randall Fischer would have a heart attack, or die, and the phone would ring in London to tell Lucy that she was not to come.

But, miraculously, disaster did not strike, and at last they were in the plane, and unless the aircraft actually fell out of the sky, Lucy knew that nothing now could stop them. She sat with her forehead pressed against the little window, staring down at an England spread like a greenish-grey quilt and patterned with slow-moving cloud shadows.

For, extraordinarily enough, it was a lovely, peaceful morning. Cold, but not raining, and with no wind-chill to freeze the bones. Above the clouds, the sky was a pure, pale blue, the horizon hazy. Lucy thought about people on the ground looking up, and seeing their jet stream, and perhaps wondering where the plane was heading. Just as she looked down on what appeared to be stretches of uninhabited country, the only clue to any sort of industry being a tiny puff of smoke from a group of cooling towers. She wondered which was the real life. Who were the real people.

The stewardess came around with little trays of food. Rolls and butter, marmalade, a sliver of bacon, a tiny bunch of green grapes. There was coffee or tea, and both Carrie and Lucy had coffee. Everything was teeny, doll-sized, all fitted neatly onto a little plastic tray. Lucy was hungry and ate everything, and when Carrie didn't want her roll, Lucy ate hers as well. After the trays had been taken away, Carrie read the paper and Lucy turned back to gaze out of the window, because she didn't want to miss a single inch of Scotland.

She thought perhaps when they got there, it would be raining, or even snowing, but the skies remained wonderfully clear. When the plane began to lose height, the terrain below them slowly took shape, and she saw snow on the tops of mountains and a lot of dark fur which turned into plantations of conifer. Then the blue gleam of the sea, boats, and a bridge over a wide firth. The plane banked and turned before coming in to land, and to the west stood bastions of snow-covered mountains, all glittering in the pale sunshine. Lucy knew that they could not have looked more beautiful and told herself that this had to be a good omen.

Carrie folded her paper and stowed it away. They smiled at each other. "All right?" Carrie asked. Lucy nodded.

They landed, huge tyres thumping on tarmac. She saw the terminal building . . . it looked a bit like a large golf clubhouse . . . and there were flags flying in a brisk breeze.

"We are going to be met," Carrie had told her.

"Whom by?"

"A taxi from Creagan. The driver's called Alec Dobbs."

"How shall we know him?"

"He'll be holding a board with 'Sutton' written on it."

And once they had reclaimed their suitcases from the carousel, he was there, in the Arrivals Hall. A solid-looking man in a padded windcheater, with a faded tweed cap pulled down over his brow. As well, a number of other fascinating individuals stood about. A lanky old man in a deerstalker hat. A trousered lady with wild white hair and weather-beaten cheeks and . . . best of all . . . a man in a faded and tattered kilt. Lucy could not help staring because his blue knees looked so cold.

". . . Well, and it is good to see you," Alec Dobbs was saying. "And did you have a good flight?" Not a bit like the usual run of taxi drivers, more like an old friend. He shook hands with both of them before gathering up their suitcases as though they weighed nothing, and leading the way out. The sun, low in the sky, was palely shining, but it felt considerably colder than London, and there was still an edging of old snow around the border of the car-park. The air smelt of pine, and when Lucy breathed it in, the inside of her nose felt so cold that she sneezed. She had never been to Switzerland, but decided that this was probably how Switzerland felt, with the sunshine and the snow and the pine trees, all arched by a pristine, cloudless sky.

His car was a four-wheel-drive Subaru. Loading their luggage in the back, he explained, "I have another car, a big Rover, which would be more comfortable for you, but we have high ground to cross on the Black Isle, and the snow is still lying."

Carrie got into the back of the Subaru, and Lucy sat beside Alec.

"Have you a lot of snow?" she asked him, because she had never experienced a white Christmas, and longed to do so. A white Christmas truly would be the icing on the cake.

"Not a great deal, but it stays, which means there is more to come." He had a soft voice, precise and gentle. It was the first time Lucy was to hear the voice of Sutherland.

"How long a drive is it to Creagan?"

"An hour and a quarter, perhaps. No more." Lucy looked at her watch. It was eleven-fifteen. They would be there, probably, about half past twelve. In time for lunch. She hoped it would be something hot and robust. Despite the two rolls, she was beginning to be hungry again. "Is this the first time you have come to Creagan?"

"I've never been to Scotland before."

"Well, well, you have treats in store. And you will be staying in a fine house. It stood empty for too long. It is good to have people living there again."

Carrie leaned forward. "How is Elfrida?" she asked. "Mrs. Phipps?"

"She is fine, I see her about the place, doing her shopping, walking the dog. It was she who came in to order the car for you. She telephoned this morning to be certain that I had not forgotten you."

"Do you live in Creagan?" Lucy asked him.

"All my life. I was born there, and my father before me. When he retired, I took over his business."

"Driving taxis?"

"It is not only taxis I drive."

Lucy frowned. "What else?"

"Hearses," he told her, and there was an edge of laughter in his voice. "I'm the undertaker."

Lucy was, momentarily, silenced.

It was a spectacular drive. The road led through farmlands and over bridges, and on the high ground the tyres of the Subaru scrunched over snow. It followed the shores of a long tidal sea loch, and ran through small villages with grey stone cottages flush on the pavement, along with pubs and shops and sturdy no-nonsense churches surrounded by old graveyards filled with lichened, leaning headstones. Then the last bridge, over another firth, stretching like a long arm of blue water up into the folds of the western hills.

Alec spoke. "Only another ten minutes now," he told them, "and we'll be there."

All at once some of the excitement died, and Lucy began to feel a bit nervous. It wasn't just arriving in an unknown place, and to a strange house, but the prospect of finally meeting her hosts, Elfrida and Oscar. Elfrida she wasn't so worried about, because Carrie had spoken so much about her, and she sounded as though she was ageless and tremendous fun. But Oscar Blundell, Elfrida's friend, was a different prospect altogether. To start with, he was a man, and Lucy was not used to the company of men.

But that was not all. Because Carrie had told her all about Oscar, and why Elfrida had come with him, to this little northern town, to keep him company. His wife and his daughter, who was twelve and called Francesca, had both been killed in a terrible motor smash. Carrie had not enlarged on this catastrophe, and had turned away Lucy's horrified questioning. Simply said that it had been an accident, nobody was to blame, but Oscar was still in the throes of coming to terms with what had happened.

Francesca was twelve. Lucy was fourteen. "Will he want me?" she had asked. "Won't it be awful for him, having a person of my age around the place? Do you think he will hate me?"

Carrie had smiled and given her a hug. "I said that to Elfrida, on the telephone. And she spoke to Oscar about it, and he was quite adamant that we have to go for Christmas. And it's his house we're going to stay in, so he is our host, and he has invited us. And nobody could *ever* hate you."

But still, it was all a bit complicated and daunting. Right now, Lucy could do without complications. She had enough of them in London.

Now, quite suddenly, there was a feeling of the seaside. Duney hillocks on either side of the road where grew stunted pines and clumps of heather, and a certain light that reflected off the sea. She rolled down the window and caught the smell of salt. The road ran downhill, and ahead of them was the little town, and they were in the main street almost before she realized it. And it wasn't grey and sombre like the other villages they had come through, but built of golden sandstone that seemed to reflect the glow of the thin winter sunshine. Houses on either side stood back behind walled gardens, and there were handsome buildings, and trees, and an unexpected impression of prosperity and space.

Carrie hadn't said much during the course of the drive, but now she spoke. "How extraordinary. It's like the Cotswolds. Like a Cotswold town."

Alec smiled. "A lot of visitors make that observation. But I have never been to the Cotswolds."

"Golden stone. Wide streets. And the gardens . . ."

"What many people do not realize is that we have, because of the Gulf Stream, a climate similar to Eastbourne. There can be rain storms boiling in the hills, and we play golf or walk on the beach in the sunshine."

Lucy said, "A sort of mini-climate."

"Exactly so."

The street widened out into a square, in the middle of which stood a large and lovely church and an old graveyard, all enclosed by a stone wall. The church had a tower crested by a golden weathercock, and gulls and jackdaws wheeled about overhead. The gulls made a noise like summer holidays. The tower clock pointed to twenty-five minutes past twelve.

"We have made good time," Alec observed. He drove, at stately pace, right around the churchyard wall, and drew up at the pavement's edge.

"Is this it?" Lucy asked.

He switched off his engine. "This is it."

They got out of the Subaru, but before Alec could even unlatch the gate, there came the sound of frantic barking, and the next moment the front door of the house was flung open, and down the path came Elfrida Phipps and her vociferous dog.

"Carrie! Oh, my darling girl." She flung her arms around Carrie. "You're here, you're here. I've been so looking forward . . . so excited . . . could hardly wait . . ."

Lucy, standing aside, watched. Elfrida was very tall and very thin, and she had a lot of rather wild hair the colour of marmalade. She wore trousers of some particularly garish tartan and a huge, thick grey sweater. Her eyelids were very blue and she wore a lot of lipstick. Lucy could understand instantly why Gran didn't approve. Kissing, she had left lipstick on Carrie's cheek.

Carrie said, "Elfrida, you look wonderful. Scotland clearly agrees with you."

"Darling, it's bliss. Bitterly cold, but bliss."

"You have to meet Lucy."

"But of course." She laughed. "Isn't this ridiculous, Lucy? We're relations, and we've never set eyes on each other. But your grandfather was my most favourite cousin and we used to have wonderful, wild times together." She put her hands on Lucy's shoulders. "Let me look at you. Yes, I thought so. Pretty as paint. This is my dog, Horace, who, I am pleased to say, has stopped barking. He's been looking forward to meeting you because he hopes you'll take him on long walks on the beach. Oh, Alec, you've got the suitcases. Is that all? Would you be a saint and carry them upstairs for us? Come along, everybody, and we'll go into the house out of the cold, and you can meet Oscar. . . ."

They all streamed up the path and into the house in single file, Elfrida leading the way, then the dog, then Carrie, Lucy, and finally Alec, laden with luggage. He kicked the front door shut behind them, and they went down a long hall and up a wide staircase. Lucy liked the feeling of the house. Solid and secure, with sturdy banisters and a thick stair carpet. And the smell of old polished wood and well-worn furniture, and the faint suggestion of something delicious cooking in the kitchen.

Elfrida was still talking. "How was the flight? Not too bumpy? Thank goodness there isn't a howling gale."

They had reached the first-floor landing. The pleasing staircase rose on, to the upper floor. On the far side of the landing a door stood open through which streamed a shaft of sunlight.

Elfrida raised her voice to call. "Oscar! Here they are!" And then, in her ordinary voice again. "He's in the sitting-room. You two go and say hello, and I'll show Alec where to put the suitcases. Carrie's in here, Alec, and then Lucy's upstairs. Can you deal with another climb . . . ?"

Carrie looked at Lucy, and smiled reassuringly. She took Lucy's hand in her own, which was comforting, and, hand in hand, they went through the open, sunlit door into a beautiful sitting-room, white-walled, not over-furnished, but filled with light. A little fire was burning in the grate, and a tall bow-window faced out across the street, and the church was so close, you felt you could reach out a hand and touch it.

He was waiting for them, standing with his back to the fireplace.

He was as tall as Elfrida, but not so thin as she, and he had a fine head of silvery hair, and a quiet and kindly face, not rugged, but strangely unlined. His eyes were hooded, and drooped at the corners. He wore a checked shirt and a woollen tie, and over these, a blue Shetland sweater.

Carrie said, "Oscar. How do you do? I'm Carrie Sutton."

"My dear. . . ." He came forward to greet them, and Lucy thought he must find himself a little astonished to be welcoming a guest as sensationally glamorous as Carrie. But pleased, as well. "How good to see you. Have you had a peaceful journey?" They shook hands.

"Perfect," Carrie told him. "No problems."

"And Alec found you all right? Elfrida's been mad with excitement all morning, rushing to the window to see if you had come."

"It's so good of you to have us." Carrie looked about her. "And what a marvellous house you have."

"I own only half. I am part-owner."

"That doesn't make it any less special." She let go of Lucy's hand, and put an arm around her shoulder. "This is my niece, Lucy Wesley."

Lucy swallowed her nervousness. She said, "How do you do?" He looked down at her, and she willed herself to meet his eyes. For what seemed a long time, he said nothing. She knew that he must be thinking of his own daughter, twelve years old, and now dead. She knew that he must be comparing her with Francesca, and was probably swamped by mixed emotions, including pain. She hoped that she compared favourably. There wasn't much else she could do. And then he smiled at her, and took her hand between his own, and his clasp was warm and friendly, and after that she wasn't nervous any longer.

"So you are Lucy?"

"Yes."

"And you are going to have to sleep in the attic."

Carrie laughed. "Oscar, you don't make it sound very tempting."

"Attics never do sound tempting. Old trunks and the heads of defunct moose. Don't worry, Lucy. Elfrida has made it entrancing for you.

"Now." He let go of Lucy's hand and looked out of the window, at the clock on the church tower. "It's half past twelve. Why don't you both go and find your rooms and get settled, and then we'll have a drink, and then lunch? Elfrida has spent much of the morning concocting a shepherd's pie. She thought you would need something heartening to eat after your long journey."

Lucy's spirits rose. The worst, the initial encounters, were over. Elfrida was funny, and Oscar was kind. And Elfrida had said she was as pretty as paint. And they were going to eat shepherd's pie for lunch.

They ate in the kitchen. "We've got a dining-room," Elfrida explained, "but it's so dark and gloomy, we never eat there. And there isn't a hatch through from the kitchen or I would spend my time scuttling to and fro with dishes."

"Much nicer in here," said Carrie, and Lucy agreed with her. A long table, a gingham cloth, unmatched wooden chairs . . . all comfortably informal. It wasn't a smart kitchen. Dodie, Lucy knew, would die if she were asked to do anything under such old-fashioned conditions. For one thing, it was rather dark and lightless, facing out onto the wall of the neighbouring garden. And there were bars on the windows, to keep out intruders, or possibly to stop overworked cooks and kitchenmaids from escaping. And yet, like the rest of the house, it had a pleasant, settled feel about it, and there was a big sideboard, painted dark green, with an assortment of china displayed, and hooks for jugs, mugs, and cups.

They ate the shepherd's pie, which was delicious, and then a pudding made of stewed apples and meringue, and there was a jug of cream, and after that Carrie and Elfrida had coffee. But Oscar did not want coffee. Instead, he looked at his watch and said, "If Horace and I do not set out for a walk *now,* then we won't be home before darkness falls." He looked down the length of the table at Lucy. "Would you like to come with us?"

"For a walk?"

"We could go on the beach. And then you will know the way."

She felt very gratified to be invited. "Yes, I'd love to."

"Perhaps, Oscar," said Elfrida, "you could wheel her round the town first and show her where the shops are. It won't take more than five minutes, and then you can head for the dunes."

"Certainly, if that's what she'd like. Have you got a warm coat, Lucy?"

"I've got my new jacket."

"And a warm hat. The sea-wind can freeze your ears off."

"Yes, I've got that, too."

"Then go and get ready, and we'll set off together."

"Shall I help to clear the table?" Lucy asked.

Elfrida laughed. "How well brought up you are. Of course not. Carrie and I will do that when we've finished our coffee. Off you go with Oscar before it gets too cold."

Five minutes later, they set off together, the elderly man, the girl, and the dog. Horace wore his lead, and Lucy held its other end in her gloved hand. She had pulled a thick woollen hat down over her ears, and zipped herself into her new jacket. Oscar wore a heavy wind-proof with a checked lining, and a tweed hat which she thought suited him, and made him look distinguished and handsome.

As they went through the gate, "We'll do the town first," he told her, and so they did. Down the street, all around the church wall. The gift shop, the chemist, the bookstore, the butcher, the newsagent.

"This is where I come to pick up the morning papers. If I want to be lazy and lie in my bed, then you can do it for me."

The petrol pumps, a shop displaying knitted sweaters, a small hotel, a window full of beach toys, the supermarket. Beneath a leafless tree, Lucy paused to look through a wrought-iron gate, up a flagged path, to where a side door of the church stood open.

For some reason, she longed to go inside. She could see a porch, stoutly doormatted, and then an inner, closed door.

"Is the church open?" she asked.

"Always. Just this side door. For visitors, I suppose."

"What's it like inside?"

"I don't know, Lucy. I have never been."

"Can we go now? Just for a moment. . . ."

He hesitated. "I . . ."

"Oh, do, let's. Churches are so nice when they're empty. Like empty streets. You can see their shape. Just for a moment."

He took a deep breath, and for a moment she thought he was going to refuse, to say, *There's not time.* Or, *Another day.* But he let it all out in what sounded like a deep sigh. "All right," he said.

Lucy opened the gate, which squeaked on its hinges, and they went up the path. Inside the porch, they found a notice.

VISITORS WELCOME, BUT PLEASE, NO DOGS.

So they tied the end of the lead to the handle of the outer door, and left Horace sitting on the doormat. He did not look pleased.

Inside, the church was empty. Their footsteps rang on the flagged floor and echoed up into the roof. Sunlight poured through the stained-glass windows, and three of the arms of the cruciform shape were lined with pews, all facing the central aisle, so that it was a little like three churches. The walls were stone, and the arched ceiling soared upwards, high above them, the plaster between the curved beams painted the blue of a summer sky.

Lucy wandered off to investigate. She read the words on old memorial slabs, people from another age who had been true servants of God and regular worshippers. There were a lot of noble and titled names, as well as ordinary people. It was all much larger than she thought it would be, and by the time she had inspected everything, from the ornate font to the kneelers, each handsomely upholstered in hand-stitched needlepoint, Oscar had tired of standing, and was settled comfortably in the front pew, waiting for her.

She felt a bit guilty and went to sit beside him. "I'm sorry."

"Why?"

"For being so long."

"I am pleased that you are interested in such things."

"Carrie told me that you were an organist. That you taught music."

"That's true. I was choirmaster as well." He looked down at her. "Do you play the piano?"

"No. I've never started to learn. Mummy said it would take too much time out of lessons and games and homework and things. Anyway, there isn't a piano in my grandmother's flat."

"Would you like to play?"

"Yes, I think I would."

"It's never too late to start. Do you listen to music?"

Lucy shrugged. "Only pop and such." She thought about this. "Except sometimes, at school, we get taken to concerts. We went to an open-air concert in Regents Park this summer. There was a huge stage and a proper orchestra."

Oscar smiled. "Did it rain?"

"No, it was a fine evening. And at the end of the concert they played the *Music for the Royal Fireworks,* and there was a fireworks display at the same time. I really loved that. The music and the bangs and the lights and the rockets all went along together, and made everything doubly exciting. Now, if I hear the music again, I can see fireworks as well, and the night sky, all filled with every sort of star."

"An experience."

"Yes. It was lovely." She sank her chin into her new jacket and gazed up at the tall stained-glass window which faced them. She said, "I wouldn't want a birthday in the middle of winter. I wouldn't want to be born on Christmas Day."

"Why not?"

"Well, for one thing, you'd probably only get one present. And for another, it's usually rather dark and gloomy weather."

"When is your birthday?"

"July. Much better. Only thing is, I'm usually at school."

"Still, it's summer."

"Yes."

Oscar thought for a moment, and then he said, "Actually, I don't think Christ was born in wintertime. I think he was probably born in the spring."

"Really? Why do you say that?"

"Well, the shepherds were guarding their flocks, which probably meant that it was lambing time. And they were watching out for wolves, in case they came and ate the babies. And for another, scientific evidence tells us that there was a strangely bright star at that time, two thousand years ago, and in that place."

"Then why don't we have Christmas in the spring?"

"I think the early Christians were a cunning lot. They simply adapted what was left to them by the pagan inhabitants of the countries which they converted. There had always been the celebration of the Winter Solstice, the shortest day of the year. I suppose to cheer themselves up, those pre-Christians had something of a party, lit fires, caroused, burnt candles, plucked mistletoe, baked cakes." Oscar smiled. "Got drunk; indulged in lustful practices."

"So the early Christians just used the same party?"

"Something like that."

"But added other bits as well."

"Their belief in the Son of God."

"I see." Considered, it seemed a very practical arrangement. "What about Christmas trees?"

"They came from Germany. Brought by Albert, Victoria's Prince Consort."

"And turkeys?"

"Turkeys came from America. Before that, goose was the traditional bird."

"And carols?"

"Some old, some new."

"And wassailing? What does wassailing mean? I've never known."

"Just boozing. A wassail was a drink of spiced ale."

"And stockings?"

"I don't think I know where stockings are from."

Lucy was silent for a moment. Then she said, "Do you like Christmas?"

"Parts of it," Oscar told her, sounding cautious.

"I don't really like it much. There's such a build-up and then it's sort of . . . disappointing."

"Which proves that we should never expect too much." High above them, the church clock struck half past two. The chimes were distant, melodious, muffled. Oscar said, "Perhaps we have lingered long enough."

Lucy fell silent. The church was very quiet. From what seemed like far away, other sounds impinged. A passing car, a man's voice calling out. The long cry of a wheeling sea-gull high above the clock tower. She looked upwards, and there noticed, for the first time, the discreet uplighters, high above, fitted within the lip of the carved stone cornice. They were not lighted now, which was why she had not seen them before, but . . .

She said, "It must be lovely in here when all those lights are on. Like floodlights, like sunshine, shining on the blue ceiling. . . ."

"I expect they turn them on on Sundays for Morning Service."

"I'd like to see that."

He said quietly, "If you want to, you can." And then he got to his feet. "Come along. We're meant to be having a walk. We have to get as far as the beach, and before very long it will be dark."

CARRIE

Oscar, Lucy, and Horace were gone, off for their walk. The heavy front door of the Estate House slammed shut behind them, and Carrie and Elfrida were left alone, still sitting at the kitchen table, with the remains of lunch, and their coffee. They smiled at each other. Two women of different generations, but old friends, who had not been together, alone, for too long, and now relished their peaceful privacy.

Carrie said, "What a perfectly sweet man."

Elfrida, she thought, for all her sixty-two years, looked as vital and energetic as a young girl. Her slenderness became her, the uncompromising blaze of suspect hair, the eccentric clothes, the slash of lipstick, all declaimed a healthy denial of advancing years. Her very presence was like a shot in the arm.

"Isn't he?" she said, with satisfaction.

"I'm so pleased they've made friends. Lucy was apprehensive. I told her, of course, about his wife and his daughter, and she was afraid that Oscar mightn't want her about the place, reminding him of Francesca. She thought he might find her presence distressing. Even, that he might hate her."

Elfrida was sympathetic. "Poor little thing. But perceptive, too. And I don't think Oscar *knows* how to hate any person. And if he did, he would never say so, nor ever show it. We had a slight hiccup when we arrived here, in the shape of a rather sad old bore from whom we had to collect the key of the house. I must say, he was rather disquieting. Kept telling Oscar that he'd put him up for the Golf Club, and they would meet over a drink. Oscar was terrified. He spent the first couple of weeks cowering indoors, or scuttling across the road to the supermarket with his hat pulled over his eyes like a criminal, in mortal fear of meeting Major Billicliffe and having to ask him back for a gin. But then he discovered the old chap was actually quite ill. He found him languishing in his bed, under the doctor, as they say. And the next thing was that he'd offered to drive him over to the hospital in Inverness, because he felt so sorry for him. Major Billicliffe's a widower, and all alone. So you see, Oscar's not very good at hating. You could never call him one of your consistent, paid-up, professional haters."

"I think he's a darling. I just hope it's not going to be too much for you both. Having us here."

"It's brilliant, just what we need."

"It doesn't have to be an all-singing, all-dancing Christmas. Lucy and I both have a fairly low expectation of what is known as the Festive Season."

"Us, too. Though, once he knew you were coming, Oscar did, privately, order a Christmas tree."

"Lucy will love that. She can decorate it. Poor child, my mother was never much good at creating a magic atmosphere, and Nicola's too idle. But I truly think Dodie's grateful to you. Because now she can go and spend her giddy holiday in Bournemouth with a clear conscience."

"How is she?"

"Just the same." No more needed to be said.

"And Nicola?"

"Ditto. Unlike wine, they do not improve with age."

"And your father?"

"Haven't seen him. But we spoke on the telephone."

"I had such a wonderful month with them all, at Emblo, in October. And then I got home to hear this terrible thing that had happened to Oscar. It was like moving out of one world and into another. Life can change with such shocking abruptness."

"I know." Carrie thought about Andreas, and then didn't think about him. She said again, "I know."

A silence fell. Carrie finished her coffee and set down the little cup. She knew what was coming next, which it did.

"And *you,* Carrie?"

"Me? I'm fine."

"I don't think you are. For one thing, you look tired and pale. And dreadfully thin."

"Look who's talking. Admit, Elfrida, we'd neither of us have ever won a prize for the most voluptuous."

"Why did you suddenly come back from Austria?"

Carrie shrugged. "Oh, reasons. Whims."

"I don't believe that."

"Sometime, I'll tell you. I promise. But not just at this moment."

"You're not ill?"

"No. I'm fighting a cold and I am a bit tired, but I am not ill."

"Did you chuck up your job?"

"Yes."

"Will you get another?"

"I think so. In fact, the travel company I worked for overseas telephoned the other evening, and the next day I went along and saw them. I've been offered a job . . . a good job . . . in the London office. I haven't accepted yet, but I probably will when I go back after Christmas."

"And your house?"

"Let till February. Until then, I can camp with friends or rent."

"I feel you're unhappy. I wish I could help."

"You are helping. By having us here."

"Not very exciting."

"I don't want excitement."

Elfrida was silenced. She finished her coffee, and then sighed, and ran a hand through her unruly, fiery hair. "In that case, I will say no more. Now. . . ." Her manner changed, she became cheerful, in charge once more. "What would you like to do this afternoon? Perhaps a nap. I'll find a hot-water bottle. . . ."

Bed and a hot-water bottle. Carrie could not remember how long it was since some other person had cherished her. Had said, *You look tired.* And, *How about a little rest?* She had spent too many years being strong, looking after others and their problems. Cancelled reservations; faulty ski-tows; unsuitable bedrooms; trains and buses that ran, through no fault of their own, late. The lack of snow, or the fact that there was too much of it. A band playing too loudly into the early hours of the morning; lost passports, money, hair dryers. . . . And then returning to London to be faced with another set of family problems which needed to be surmounted.

She realized that she was tired of being strong. Tired of being the sturdy pillar against which everybody leaned. Upstairs was her bedroom. Her suitcase already in possession. She had gone there to shed her coat and comb her hair before lunch, and had seen, with some satisfaction, the enormous double bed, downy and soft, with its white cover, and great brass bedstead like the polished rails of some well-kept ship. She had longed, right then and there, to climb beneath the blankets and sleep.

Perhaps a nap. She was filled with grateful love for Elfrida. She said, "I don't think there's anything I'd like more. But first, can I be shown your house? So that I know my way around. It seems so enormous, I might get lost. I'd imagined the two of you domiciled in some little cottage, and here you are in a veritable mansion."

"Of course." Elfrida got to her feet.

"What about the washing-up?"

"I'll do it later. We haven't got a dishwasher, but I've never had one, so it doesn't matter. And I rather like splashing around in time-honoured fashion with lots of suds. Come along. . . ."

She led the way out of the kitchen, and Carrie followed her down the hall to the two ground-floor rooms. "It all used to belong to the Corrydale Estate," Elfrida explained, sounding a bit like a tour guide. "The factor and his family lived here, so that's why it's so huge.

We inherited only the most essential bits of furniture, and there's no point cluttering ourselves up with possessions." She opened a door. "This was the estate office, and as you can see, it's totally uninhabitable. Like a junk-shop. And *this* is our dining-room. Utter gloom."

It was indeed daunting, redolent of long, dull meals and boiled cabbage.

"But I love the table," said Carrie. "And a sideboard built for massive haunches of venison. And a piano! Shall we have concerts?"

"I should think so. God knows when it was last tuned."

"But Oscar plays."

"Not just now. These days, he listens to music, he doesn't make it."

They went upstairs. "Lucy's in the attic. I did it all up for her, but I'm sure she'll want to show you herself. And you've seen the sitting-room, and the bathrooms, and this"—she opened another door—"is the second spare bedroom. I could have put her in here, but it's very small and a bit dreary. The attic seemed to me a much more attractive space for her, and I had all the fun of putting it together."

Carrie peered into the small and undistinguished room, almost totally taken up with another enormous bed. It was, clearly, unoccupied, and for the first time she began to feel a bit uncomfortable, not knowing, but suspecting, what was going to happen next. Her interest in seeing over the house had been just that. Interest. Not curiosity. But her innocent request felt now a bit like taking the lid off Pandora's box.

"Elfrida . . . ?" Elfrida either didn't hear, or took no notice. Instead, she opened the final door with a flourish that had a touch of defiance about it.

"And this," she said, "is us."

It was a spacious and important room, the master bedroom of the original house, with tall windows facing out over the light of the dying afternoon, the street, and the church. In it stood a looming Victorian wardrobe, a pretty Victorian dressing-table, and a chest of drawers. And an enormously high and wide bed. Over this was spread Elfrida's scarlet silk shawl, the embroidery faded, the fringe beginning to fray, but still marvellously opulent and recognizable from the old days and Elfrida's house in Putney, where Carrie had stayed with her for six weeks or more, nursing Elfrida back to health after an operation.

And other possessions. A man's ivory brushes on the chest of drawers, a pair of brogues neatly placed beneath a chair, dark-blue pyjamas folded on a pillow. And a pleasant masculine smell, compounded of polished leather and Bay Rum.

There fell a small silence. Then Carrie looked at Elfrida and caught on her face a faintly abashed expression, and was amused, because Elfrida had never betrayed the smallest sense of shame about her many and varied sexual encounters.

Now, she said, "You're not shocked?"

"Elfrida, I'm me. I'm not Dodie."

"I know you're not."

"You're sleeping together?"

Elfrida nodded.

"You're lovers?"

"We are."

Carrie thought of that charming, distinguished man, with his thick white hair and gentle face. She said, "I'm glad."

"I'm glad you're glad. But I have to tell you. Explain."

"You don't have to explain to me."

"No, but I want to."

"We drove together from Dibton to Scotland. I drove most of the way, and the conditions were horrible and the A1 heavy with traffic. It had been a traumatic few days before we left, saying goodbyes and making arrangements, and I think we were both exhausted. Oscar scarcely spoke at all. By the time it was dark we'd had enough of the motorway and we got off it at some junction and drove down into Northumberland. Oscar said there was some little town he remembered with an old hotel in the main street, and by some miracle we found the town and the hotel was still there. So I sat in the car with Horace, and Oscar went in to see if they had rooms for us, and if they minded the dog as well.

"After a bit, he came out and said that they didn't mind about the dog, but they only had one room with a double bed. By then I was so tired, I'd have slept in a cupboard, so I told Oscar to go in and book it, and we wrote Mr. and Mrs. Oscar Blundell in the register, and I felt like a giddy girl sneaking off for the weekend with her boy-friend.

"We had baths, and a drink, and dinner; then, because we had an early start the next morning, we went upstairs. There then took place a ridiculous conversation, with Oscar saying he would curl up on the sofa, and me saying I would sleep on the floor with Horace. And then, suddenly, we were too tired to argue, and we just got into bed together and fell fast asleep.

"But what I didn't know was that Oscar was having these terrible nightmares. He told me later that he'd been having them ever since the crash, that he put off going to bed at night because he was so filled with dread, so afraid. That night, he woke me with his screams, and for a moment I was terrified, and then I knew I had to wake him. So I did, and he was weeping . . . it was so awful for him . . . and I gave him a drink of water and calmed him down, and I put my arms around him and held him close and after a bit he went back to sleep again. After that, I would never let him be alone during the night. When we came here, he was a bit worried at first about what people would *think*, what they would *say*. We have a sweet woman who comes and cleans for us, Mrs. Snead. . . . He was afraid she would gossip, and there would be disapproval and bad feeling. And I said I didn't care if there was, I wasn't going to leave him.

"I think, Carrie darling, that all this might sound a little suspect. Opportunist. As though, the moment Gloria was dead, I crashed into Oscar's life and leaped into bed with him. But truly, it wasn't like that. I'd always liked him immensely, but he was Gloria's husband, and I liked her, too, though perhaps not quite as much as I liked Oscar. It's rather difficult to explain. But everything I have done, every choice I have made was only with the best of intentions in mind. He asked me to come to Scotland with him, and because he was a man on the verge of desperation, I agreed.

"It could have been a disaster, but instead we have a relationship which I think is a comfort to both of us. We first made love about a week after we got here. It was, of course, inevitable. He is a very attractive man, and for some reason he seems to find battered old me attractive, too. Since then, the terrible dreams have begun to fade, and sometimes he sleeps through till morning. There are still nightmares, but not nearly so frequent. And if you do hear shouts in the middle of the night, don't be alarmed, because I am with Oscar.

"I've kept nothing secret, told no lies. I confided in Mrs. Snead, privately, at the first opportunity, the circumstances of our design for living. Mrs. Snead is a Londoner and quite unshockable, as well as being a good friend and a mine of useful information. When I had finished explaining, all she said was 'I think, Mrs. Phipps, it would be a cruel thing to let that man suffer, if you can give 'im a spot of comfort in 'is hour of need.' So that was that. And now *you* know."

For a moment neither of them said anything. Then Carrie sighed. "Poor Oscar. But how much poorer he would be without you."

"And Lucy? What shall we do about Lucy? She doesn't look a stupid child. Ought you to tell her?"

"Let's not make an issue. If she asks questions, I shall tell her the truth."

"We're so old, she'll be astonished."

"I don't think so. Her own grandfather has a very young wife and a couple of little children. Nothing new to Lucy. She's clearly taken a shine to Oscar and she'll be thrilled, as I am." Carrie put her arms around Elfrida's skinny shoulders and hugged. "It's all so sweet. Needing each other and finding each other."

"Oscar's not out of the woods yet by any means. He still has a long way to go. Some days he's been so depressed that he scarcely speaks. But I've learned to leave him alone. He has to deal with his grief in his own way."

"It can't have been easy."

"Oh, darling Carrie, nothing is. And now we must waste no more time, otherwise the day will have died. I shall find you a hot-water bottle, and you shall go to sleep."

LUCY

FRIDAY, DECEMBER 15TH

We are here, and it is now ten o'clock at night and it has been a long day. Carrie came to Gran's flat about half past eight in the morning, and she had a taxi waiting, and then we drove on to Heathrow. Mummy and Gran were still at the flat. Mummy doesn't fly to Florida till Tuesday. They were still in their dressing-gowns and being very kind. I think they both felt a bit guilty about all the discussions and crossness. They gave me Christmas presents, all wrapped, and I put them in my suitcase. Mummy gave me one hundred fifty pounds and Gran gave me fifty more pounds for spending money. I have never felt so rich and am frightened of losing my purse, but it's all right, quite safe in my new haversack.

The flight was all right and not bumpy and we had a sort of breakfast on the plane. At Inverness a nice man called Alec was there to meet us and drove us here. There was snow on a hill and it took about an hour and a quarter.

Creagan is very old, pretty, and full of quite large houses and a huge church. This is an amazing house, it is much bigger than it looks and is on three storeys. It was rented out, and a lot of the furniture, Oscar told me, came from Corrydale, the big house he used to stay in when he was a boy and had a grandmother there. I say a lot of furniture, but in fact there isn't much, and no pictures or anything. The sitting-room and bedrooms are on the first floor, but I am up again, and in an attic, which Elfrida has done up especially for me. She didn't have to paint it, as it's all white and quite fresh, but she has had to buy furniture, which was very kind of her.

So. My room. It has a sloping ceiling and a skylight (no window) and a striped blind on the skylight, but I don't suppose I shall ever pull it down, as I am able to lie in bed and look up at the sky. Like being out of doors.

The bed is dark wood, and there is a blue-and-white-striped duvet and a tartan rug in case I feel cold. There is a white dressing-table, with a swing mirror and little drawers, and a chest of drawers as well. Then, a bedside table, a lamp, and a very useful table against one of the non-sloping walls. I think it must once have been a kitchen table, as it's a bit battered, but just right for writing up diary or writing letters, et cetera. Then there are two chairs and some hooks on the wall for me to hang my clothes. I haven't brought very many. The floor is scrubbed floorboards and in the middle is a wonderful thick rug with lots of bright colours, and by my bedside there is a sheepskin for stepping out onto on cold mornings. I find it all so different and romantic.

Elfrida and Oscar are really nice. I thought they would be terribly old. They are old, but don't look it, or talk like it. Elfrida is very tall and thin with orangey hair, and Oscar is also tall, but not quite so thin. And he has a lot of white hair, a very soft voice, gentle eyes. Before we left London, Carrie told me about his wife and his daughter Francesca being killed in a terrible car smash. And their dogs as well. I was rather dreading meeting him, because it is difficult sometimes to know what to say to someone who has suffered something so awful. But he is really nice and didn't seem at all upset when he saw me and Carrie. We had lunch, and then he asked me to go out for a walk with him and Horace. Horace is Elfrida's dog. So we went, and it wasn't too cold, and we looked at shops and sat in the church for a bit, and then we went out again, and crossed the golf links and went to the beach. The beach is lovely, long and clean, with no plastic bottles or rubbish. Lots of shells. I picked up two scallops. I shall go again, and take Horace with me.

I am really happy. I've never lived in such a big house, but it has a nice feel, as though well-to-do and cheerful people had always lived here. It has a big garden, too, at the back, but not much growing there at this time of year. Tomorrow I shall explore.

OSCAR

Oscar, rather to his surprise, was having a bonfire.

At Dibton, at the Grange, he had become an enthusiastic gardener, mostly because he was retired, and a little piano teaching and the occasional Sunday-morning duty in the village church still left him with time on his hands. To begin with, he was totally inexperienced. Had never even watered a window-box. But, starting up, he realized that long-forgotten wisdoms came floating up from his subconscious, wisdoms left over from the holidays he had spent at Corrydale with his grandmother, a natural gardener so experienced and accomplished that others came to view the glories of Corrydale and seek her advice.

The practical aspects he taught himself—by trial and error, and by intensive study of huge gardening tomes. As well, he had the help of the two local men who came in to cut grass, do a bit of forestry, and deal with the heavy digging. Before long, his new hobby had absorbed him, and he enjoyed the physical exercise, the pleasures of planning and planting, and the simple satisfaction of being out of doors.

Coming to Creagan in the middle of winter, there wasn't much he could do about the steep terraced garden that climbed the slope behind the Estate House. He had swept up a number of dead leaves and cleared blocked drains, and that was all. But this morning, at breakfast, Elfrida had complained about an overgrown lilac bush that spilt out over the path and got in her way when she went up to the washing-line with her basket of wet laundry.

Oscar said that he would deal with the wayward lilac.

After breakfast, he took down the key of the potting-shed from its hook on the dresser, and went out to investigate. It was a strange sort of day, overcast, and with only a slight movement of chill air. From time to time the clouds parted to reveal a scrap of blue sky, but looking, he could still see the snow lying on the hills, which meant there was more to come.

He managed to turn the rusty key and tug the warped wooden door open, revealing a dark and musty interior scarcely lit by a small cobwebby window. There was a potting-table, on which lay a lot of earth, some broken flowerpots, a stack of yellowed newspapers, and a few archaic tools, like dibbers and billhooks. There was no mower or trimmer, nor any piece of modern equipment, but around the walls, on huge masonry nails, hung heavy old forks and spades. A rake, a hoe, a rusted saw, a formidable scythe. All were in dire need of care and attention, and he thought he would clean and oil them all, but could find no oilcan amongst the chaos and decided that that particular job must wait.

In a box filled with nuts, bolts, and rusted spanners, he found a pair of secateurs, ancient but more or less workable. Using these, he went out and dealt with the lilac, which left him with a pile of branches in need of disposal. There was no wheelbarrow, and indeed a wheelbarrow would be useless in this precipitous plot, so he found a ragged potato sack, stuffed the branches into this, and lugged it up to the top of the garden where, behind an old plum tree, there were the blackened remains of some previous bonfire.

He decided, then, to clear out the potting-shed and burn all the rubbish while it was a dry, still day, and while he was in the mood.

There was a great deal of it, and it took several journeys up and down the path to get it all collected. He made spills out of the newspaper, chopped up some rotted wooden seed-boxes, and got his fire started. Soon it was blazing nicely, and he was raking up leaves and getting quite warm. He took off his jacket, hung it on the plum tree, and worked in his sweater. The thick smoke rose and billowed and made everything smell of autumn. Then he started in on some smothering ivy, cutting and tearing it back off the old stone wall, and so intent was he on this labour that he did not hear the back gate open and shut, and he did not see the man who walked up the path behind him.

"Oscar."

Startled, Oscar swung around, to face Peter Kennedy. Peter was dressed for golf, in his red jacket and with his long-peaked baseball cap pulled down over his brow.

"Heavens, I never heard you."

"I didn't mean to sneak up on you. But I'm on my way to the Golf Club, I'm playing at half past ten. I saw the smoke from the fire, and guessed I'd find you here."

"What can I do for you?"

"Nothing, really. But I wanted to tell you that I was in Inverness yesterday, and I dropped in at the hospital to see Godfrey Billicliffe."

"That was good of you. How is he?"

Peter shook his head. "Not good news, I'm afraid. He's very ill. He has cancer. . . ."

Cancer. Oscar said, "Oh, God."

". . . I think, he already had his own private suspicions, fears. But never said a word to anybody. He told me he'd been feeling unwell for a long time, but had never gone to see the doctor. Just dosed himself with pain-killers and whisky. He didn't want to be told . . . he was frightened of the truth."

"He was frightened that day I found him in his bed."

"I know."

Oscar thought about the sick old man, remembered the weak tears that had brimmed his rheumy eyes. "Does he know?" he asked.

"Yes. He persuaded the young consultant to tell him."

"How long has he got?"

"A little time. He's dying. But he's comfortable and quite peaceful, I think, rather enjoying all the attention and the nurses taking care of him. It will be a relief."

"I must go and see him."

"No. He asked me to tell you no. He's doped and frail, and already has the look of a man on his way out of this world. But he asked me to send you his regards and to say how grateful he was for your kindness."

"I didn't do anything."

"You did. And you were there when he most needed a friend."

Oscar kicked, with the toe of his boot, a smouldering twig into the heart of his fire. For a moment, remembering his reluctance even to speak to old Billicliffe, dodging around street corners in mortal dread of meeting him, he hated himself.

He said, "Did you speak to the doctor in the hospital?"

"Yes. When I'd said goodbye, I tracked the consultant down, and he confirmed what I already knew."

"What can I do?"

"Little, really. Perhaps write him a note. Send him a card. He'd like that."

"It seems a bit tame."

"He really is quite peaceful. Not struggling, not distressed. Sleeps most of the time, but when he did open his eyes, he recognized me, and we spoke and he was perfectly lucid. I think, accepting."

Oscar sighed hugely. "Well, I suppose that's it, then." He thought of practicalities. "I'm down as his next of kin."

"They'll let you know. Or myself. We'll keep in touch."

"Thank you for telling me."

"I knew that you would want to know. Now I must be off, and leave you to your bonfire."

Oscar laid down his rake. "I'll come with you to the gate."

They walked down the path in single file. At the gate, Peter paused.

"There's something else. It occurred to me that perhaps you might be missing your music." He felt in the pocket of his red golf jacket and produced a small brass key. "The church is always open, but the organ locked. I have discussed it with Alistair Heggie, our organist, and he is happy for you to use it any time you feel so inclined. Here. . . ." Before Oscar could protest, Peter had taken his wrist and pressed the key into his outstretched palm, closing his fingers about it.

Oscar said, "Oh, no. . . ."

"You don't have to. You might not even want to. But I'd like to think that you can, if the impulse takes you, and if you feel it would help."

"You are too kind."

"Just put it somewhere safe." Peter grinned. "It's our only spare." He turned as if to go, and then turned back again. "I think my brain is going soft. I very nearly forgot. Another of the reasons I came in search of you. Tabitha says would you all like to come up to the Manse for a drink and a mince pie on Tuesday evening at six. Everybody's welcome. Nothing formal. Don't dress up. Our children will probably be around. . . ."

"Tuesday." Oscar, still holding the key, made a mental note. He must not forget to tell Elfrida. "Tuesday at six. I think we'd like that very much."

"Splendid." Peter went through the gate and latched it behind him. "We'll see you then."

"Have a good round. And thank you for coming."

LUCY

On Monday morning, when Lucy descended from her private eyrie in the attic, she saw, on the first-floor landing, that Carrie's bedroom door was closed. Her first thought was that perhaps Carrie had overslept, and wondered if she should wake her up, and then, fortuitously, decided against it.

Downstairs, she found only Oscar and Elfrida in the midst of breakfast. This morning Oscar was eating sausages, and Lucy hoped there would be some for her. Sausages for breakfast was one of her ideas of heaven.

"Lucy." As she appeared through the door, he laid down his coffee-cup, and smiled. "How are you this morning?"

"I'm fine, but where's Carrie?"

"Carrie's really not well." Elfrida got up from the table to collect Lucy's sausages from the hotplate. "I don't think she's got flu, but she certainly isn't throwing this horrible cold off. Two sausages, or three?"

"Three, please, if there's enough. Is she still in bed?"

"Yes, I looked in to see her, and she said she'd coughed all night, and hadn't been able to sleep, and was feeling thoroughly fed up with herself. I took her up a cup of tea, but she doesn't want anything to eat. When the Health Centre opens at nine, I'm going to ring Dr. Sinclair and ask if he'll come around and have a look at her."

"Does he make house calls?"

"The Health Centre's only across the road."

Lucy sat down to her sausages. "In London, doctors never do house calls. You have to go and sit in the waiting room with all the other sick people. Gran always says you come out with more things wrong with you than when you went in. Do you think she's going to be all right? Carrie, I mean. She must be all right for Christmas."

"We'll see what Dr. Sinclair says."

"Can I go and see her?"

"I shouldn't, until we know what's wrong. It might be frightfully contagious and then you'd come out in spots. Or running sores. Like poor Job."

Lucy ate her sausages, which were delicious, and Elfrida poured her a cup of coffee. She said, "It's really disappointing, because we'd planned a long walk on the beach this morning, with Horace."

"No reason why you shouldn't go."

"Will *you* come, Oscar?"

"I can't, this morning. I've got a lot of letters to write, and then I'm going to get my hair cut. After that I'm going to the bookshop to order two books, and then I am going to pick up the meat from the butcher."

"Oh, I see." It was hard not to sound downcast.

He smiled. "You can go on your own. Take Horace. He will guard you. You can be a lone explorer."

Lucy brightened. "Can I?"

"Of course."

She mulled over this new prospect of freedom while she ate her sausages, and found that she was rather taken with the idea of setting out, with the dog, all by herself. For obvious reasons she was not allowed to go for long, solitary walks in London, and if she did have some arrangement made with Emma, her mother always had to know where she was going, and when she would be back. But here, in Creagan, it was obvious that such precautions were not necessary. Elfrida and Oscar didn't even lock their front door. In the town, cars and lorries drove very slowly, and shoppers quite often walked in the middle of the road, stopping from time to time to chat, and on the streets and pavements there always seemed to be unaccompanied children skateboarding or otherwise flocking around in gangs. The day that Oscar had taken her as far as the beach, she had seen youngsters climbing rocks, riding bicycles, and not an adult in view. As for sinister men in raincoats, drunks, or drug addicts, they simply didn't seem to exist in this wholesome climate. Perhaps, like germs and mildew, they did not flourish in the cold.

The back door opened and slammed shut.

"Mrs. Snead," said Oscar, and in a moment she was with them, bursting into the kitchen, wearing a pink track suit and a dashing pair of trainers.

"Oh, it's 'orrible again," she told them. "Black clouds. Looks like snow to me." She saw Lucy. "'Ullo, what are you doing 'ere? Come to stay? Where's your auntie?"

She had a head of tight grey curls and wore pink glass earrings to match her track suit.

"She's in bed. She's not well."

"Oh, that's too bad. Seen the doctor, 'as she?"

"Elfrida's going to ring him up and ask him to come."

"Well." Mrs. Snead gazed at Elfrida. "What a turn-up for the books. I mean, 'aving an invalid. And only just got 'ere. That's bad luck. You're Lucy, aren't you? Mrs. Phipps told me about you. What do you think of your room? We 'ad a lovely time doing it all up for you. It was just an empty old attic before."

"Have a cup of tea, Mrs. Snead," said Elfrida, and Mrs. Snead said that would be very nice, and proceeded to make herself a mug, with a tea-bag, and then settled down at the table to drink it.

Lucy knew that Gran would disapprove violently of such familiar carryings-on, and, perversely, liked Mrs. Snead all the more.

The morning progressed. Mrs. Snead Hoovered, Lucy and Oscar washed up the breakfast dishes, and Elfrida went off to telephone the doctor. At ten o'clock, the doorbell rang, and Lucy ran downstairs to let him in, but he had already done so, and she found him wiping his boots on the front-door mat.

"Hello, there," he said when he saw her. He had a very Highland voice, but he was quite young, with a wind-burnt face and gingery eyebrows, like caterpillars. "Who are you?"

"I'm Lucy Wesley. I'm staying here."

"That's nice. Now, where's the invalid?"

"She's upstairs. . . ."

Elfrida was hanging over the banister. "Dr. Sinclair. You are a saint to come." He climbed the stair, but Lucy did not follow him. Instead, she went back into the kitchen, where Mrs. Snead was sorting laundry for the clothes washer. "That the doctor come? I 'ope it's not serious."

"I thought it was just a cold. She felt rotten flying up, I know. It's so miserable for her."

"Oh, cheer up, she'll be all right. Now, would you like to do something for me? 'Op upstairs and bring down the towels in Mrs. Phipps's bathroom. And then I'll give you the clean ones to put in their place."

Dr. Sinclair did not take long. He and Elfrida went into Carrie's room, and Lucy, collecting towels, heard their voices behind the closed door. It was reassuring to have him here, but she hoped that he would not diagnose some sinister bug, an illness that would demand antibiotics and two weeks in bed. When he had finished with Carrie, he and Elfrida did not at once come downstairs, but went into the drawing-room, to talk to Oscar.

Lucy, having finished her laundry duties, hung about for a bit in the hall, and then could wait no longer, and went to join them. The three of them were sitting on the window-seat, talking about somebody called Major Billicliffe. Major Billicliffe, it seemed, was in hospital in Inverness and very ill. They all wore rather long faces. And then Elfrida turned and saw her standing in the open door, and smiled.

"Don't look so worried, Lucy."

The doctor got to his feet. "Is Carrie all right?" Lucy asked him.

"Yes, she'll be all right. All she needs is a bit of rest. Sleep and lots of drinks, and I've left a prescription for that cough. Leave her in peace, and she'll be up and about in a couple of days."

Lucy was much relieved. "Can I go and see her?"

"I'd leave her for a moment."

Elfrida said, "Why don't you take Horace for his exploring walk?"

"Where are you going, Lucy?" the doctor asked.

"I thought along the beach."

"Are you interested in birds?"

"I don't know their names."

"There are beautiful birds on the beach. I'm calling in tomorrow to see your aunt, so I'll bring my bird book with me, and then you can look them up."

"Thank you."

"Not at all. Not at all. Well, I must be off. We'll be in touch, Mr. Blundell. Goodbye, Mrs. Phipps."

And he was away, running downstairs, letting himself out, slamming the front door shut behind him. Lucy, looking from the window, saw him get into his car and drive off to his next call. There was a dog on the passenger seat, gazing from the window. A big springer spaniel with floppy ears. And she decided it must be nice, being a country GP and having a dog in your car.

Mrs. Snead was right. It was a daunting sort of day, though not actually raining. Which was odd, because the weekend had been so soft and still, and Oscar had been able to have his bonfire. With Horace on his lead, Lucy let herself out of the Estate House, went through the gate, and set off across the square, and then turned up the road that led to the Golf Club. There were not very many golfers around, and only a few cars in the park. The right-of-way led across the links, curving up and over the natural undulations of the land, and when she reached a shallow summit she saw the whole horizon, cold and still as steel, and a great arc of sky, grey with low cloud. It was half-tide, and small waves washed up onto the shining wet sand. Far away, she could see the lighthouse, and when she reached the little car-park, flocks of kittiwakes were pecking over the rubbish bins, as though expecting crusts or stale sandwiches. Horace saw them and, of course, barked, and they all fluttered off, pretending to be frightened, flew around for a moment, and then settled down again to their scavenging.

Lucy unclipped Horace's lead and he ran ahead of her, down the ramp and onto the sands. In the shelter of the dunes the sand was deep and soft and difficult for walking, so she went out onto the wet hard sand, and looking back, saw her own footsteps, with Horace's footpads circling them, like a line of stitching.

There were rocks, and small rock-pools at the point, and then the big beach, curving northwards. Ahead, a long way off, the hills folded in on each other, grey and forbidding, and dusted with snow. The sky beyond them was dark as a purple bruise, and she felt the light wind on her face, so cold it was like opening a deep freeze.

She was alone. Not another soul, not another dog on the beach. Only birds skimming over the shallow breakers.

In this enormous, empty, airy world, she saw herself tiny as an ant, reduced to total unimportance by the sweep and size of nature. A nonentity. She rather liked the feeling of being without identity, of knowing that nobody knew *exactly* where she was, and that if she met somebody, they wouldn't know *who* she was. So, she belonged to nobody but herself. She walked hard, keeping warm, pausing only every now and then to pick up a scallop shell or a particularly eye-catching pebble or shard of glass worn smooth by the sea. She put these treasures in her pocket. Then Horace found a long piece of seaweed, which he carried in his mouth like a trophy. Lucy tried to get it from him, and it turned into a game, with Horace running and Lucy chasing. She found a stick and flung it into the waves, and Horace forgot about the seaweed and dropped it, and went galloping into the water, only to discover that it was too cold and wet for comfort before beating a startled retreat.

The beach ended at another outcrop of rocks, with pools and crannies of pebbles, and there was a strong reek of seaweed. Lucy paused to get her bearings. Hillocky dunes separated the beach from the golf links, and as she hesitated, trying to decide which way to go next, Lucy heard the sound of a motor and saw, above the rocks, a tractor come trundling towards her, over a rise. The tractor pulled a bogie, so it wasn't moving very fast. But clearly, there had to be a sort of road. She decided that she would walk home that way, and with some difficulty hauled her way up a sandy cliff and into the dunes. Horace bounded ahead of her, and out of sight. The dunes made a little hill, thick with rough grass and rushes, and reaching the summit, she saw the track.

Horace was already down there, waiting for her. But not looking Lucy's way. He had, it was obvious, sensed strangers. He stood, ears pricked, with his plumy tail up like a flag. Watching. Lucy looked, and saw, coming up the slope from the direction of the town, another dog walker, striding out in purposeful manner. She was dressed in boots, thick trousers, and a sheepskin coat, and wore a tam-o'-shanter slanted at a cocky angle over cropped grey hair. Her dog, running free, spied Horace and stopped dead. The two animals eyed each other for a long moment, and Lucy was all at once petrified with dread, because the other dog was a Rottweiler.

"Horace." She had meant to call him, but her mouth was dry, and his name came out in an agonized whisper.

Horace either didn't hear her, or pretended not to. And then, stupid mutt that he was, began to bark. The Rottweiler slowly moved forward, his shining body tense, muscles flexed. A snarling sound came from deep in his throat, and his dark lips rolled back from his teeth. Horace, holding his ground, gave another timid bark, and with that, the Rottweiler pounced.

Lucy screamed. Horace screamed as well, a dog-scream that sounded like a howl for help. He was being flattened, bitten, and bruised, and however he struggled, could not escape.

The dog's owner was of no use at all. She had a chain leash in her hand, but it was obvious that she was too wary to start manhandling her pet while he was in this frame of mind. Instead she produced a pea whistle, which she blew sharply, and proceeded to shout orders, like a sergeant-major.

"Brutus! Brutus! Down, boy! Down! To heel! . . ."

The Rottweiler took absolutely no notice whatsoever.

"Brutus!"

"Get *hold* of him," Lucy wailed, hysterical with horror. Horace, Elfrida's darling dog, was about to be murdered. "Do *something. Stop* him!"

She had forgotten about the approaching tractor. Now, like the cavalry in some old Western, it trundled into view, in the nick of time; the door was flung open, the driver jumped down and, sprinting the last few yards and without showing the slightest fear or hesitation, went straight into action, landing his heavy boot into the muscled backside of the Rottweiler. "Get off, you bloody brute!" The startled Rottweiler abandoned Horace and turned to attack this new enemy, but the young man grabbed his studded collar and, with some strength, hauled him away from his prey.

Lucy, in a thousand years, could never have imagined any person being so level-headed, strong, and brave.

"What the bloody hell do you think you're doing?" he demanded of the dog's owner, grabbing the chain leash from her hand and somehow clipping it to the collar of the snarling, struggling beast. He then dragged the animal towards her, and she took the leather loop in both her hands.

There then followed the most stupendous row.

"Don't you swear at me—"

"Why didn't you keep the dog on its chain?"

"He was *attacked.*" Now that danger was over, she became belligerent. Her voice was not the voice of Sutherland. In fact, she sounded as though she came from Liverpool or Manchester.

"He was no such thing. I saw it all—"

"There's no harm in Brutus unless he's *attacked. . . .*" She was having a terrible time trying to control her dog and became quite red in the face with effort.

"He's a monster—"

"Roobish!"

"Where do you live?"

"And what's that got to do with *you*, young man?"

"Because if you lived here, you'd know better than to walk a savage dog on a public footpath."

"I do *not* live here," said the woman, as though this were something to be proud of. "I'm a *visitor*. Staying with my sister in her caravan."

"Well, go back to her caravan, and take your dog and shut him up."

"Don't speak to me in that tone of voice."

"I'll speak to you any way I like. I work for the Golf Club; I'm one of the staff."

"Oh, hoity-toity, are you. . . ."

"Take that dog and go. Just go. If I see him running free again, I'll report you to the police."

"And I shall complain of impudence—"

But at this point, Brutus took charge. He had spied two innocent golfers striding down the fairway, and with his blood up, and a desperate need to sink his teeth into some other throat, set off on the hunt. His owner, willy-nilly, went too, trailed in his wake, her short, trousered legs going like pistons.

"Never been so insulted," she threw back over her shoulder. Clearly a woman who liked to have the last word. "I'm not forgetting this. . . ." They heard no more. She was out of earshot, and her voice blown away by the wind.

She was gone.

Lucy, by now, was sitting on the wet, prickly grass with Horace gathered up in her arms, his head pressed against the front of her new red jacket. The young man came to kneel beside her. She saw that he was very young, his face wind-burnt, his eyes blue. He had short yellow hair which looked as though he had dyed it, and there was a gold ring in his left ear.

He said, "Are you all right?" And Lucy, to her eternal shame, burst into tears.

"Yes . . . but Horace . . ."

"Here." Gently he touched and examined poor Horace, stroked the long hair off his face, making comforting, murmuring noises as he did so. "I think he'll be all right. Just superficial cuts and bruises."

"He only *barked*," Lucy sobbed. "He *always* barks. He's so stupid. I thought he was going to be *dead*."

"Lucky he isn't."

Lucy sniffed. She couldn't find a handkerchief. She wiped her nose with the back of her hand. "He's not even *my* dog. He's Elfrida's. We just came for a walk."

"Where from?"

"Creagan."

"I'll take you back in the tractor. I can take you as far as the clubhouse. Can you walk from there?"

"Yes, I think so."

"Well done. Come along then."

He helped her to her feet, stopped to lift Horace up, and, carrying him, led the way back to the tractor. This he had abandoned with doors open and the engine throbbing. Lucy clambered up into the cab. There was only one seat, but she perched herself on the very edge of this, and Horace was placed at her feet, where he sat and leaned heavily against her knee. Then the young man jumped up beside her, slammed the door shut, and put the tractor in gear. Lurching over the bumps and with the bogie rattling away behind them, they moved forward.

Lucy had stopped crying. Tentatively, she asked, "Do you think Horace will be all right?"

"When you get home, give him a bath, with disinfectant; you'll be able to gauge the damage then. If there are any really bad bites, he might need stitches. Might need to go to the vet. He'll be bruised, that's for sure. And stiff for a couple of days."

"I feel so guilty. I should have looked after him better."

"Not a thing you could do. I think that female must be barmy. If I see her hellish animal again, I'll shoot it."

"He's called Brutus."

"Brutus the Brute."

Despite everything, Lucy found herself smiling. She said, "Thank you so much. For helping."

"You're staying at the Estate House, aren't you? With Oscar Blundell?"

"Do you know him?"

"No, but my father does. My father's Peter Kennedy, the minister. I'm Rory Kennedy."

"I'm Lucy Wesley."

"That's a pretty name."

"I think it's horrible." It was rather snug, sitting high up in the cabin of the tractor, sharing a single seat with this brave and kind young man. She liked the feel of his sturdy body pressed against her own, the oily smell of his thick jacket, the warmth of unaccustomed physical contact. "It sounds like a missionary."

"Well, there are worse things. I've got a small sister called Clodagh. She doesn't like her name either. She wants to be called Tracey Charlene."

This time Lucy laughed.

"Didn't I see you in church yesterday?" he asked.

"Yes, but I didn't see you. I suppose because there were so many people. I wanted to see the lights turned on, shining on the ceiling. It's beautiful. Elfrida came with me. Carrie would have come, too. She's my aunt. But she's had this cold and she stayed indoors. This morning the doctor came, and she's got to stay in bed. There's nothing awful wrong with her. She just has to rest. Otherwise, she'd have been with me, and probably that dogfight would never have happened."

"Nothing worse than a dogfight. But not a thing you could have done to stop it."

This was comforting. "Do you work on the golf course?"

"Yes, for the time being. This is the start of my Gap year. I finished Highers in July, and next year I go to Durham University. I caddied for Americans all summer. That was really lucrative, but they've all gone home, so I'm helping out for the head greenkeeper."

"What are you going to do then?"

"I want to go to Nepal. I can get a job there, teaching in a school."

Lucy was impressed. "What will you teach?"

"Reading and writing, I suppose. Just little kids. And sums. And football."

She thought about this. She said, "I'm rather dreading my Gap year."

"How old are you?"

"Fourteen."

"You've time enough to make plans."

"The thing is, I don't want to go somewhere strange and *scary*. All by myself."

"Scary?"

"You know. Crocodiles and revolutions."

He grinned. He said, "You've been watching too much television."

"Perhaps I'll just stay at home."

"Where do you live?"

"London."

"Do you go to school there?"

"Yes. A day-school."

"Up here for Christmas?"

"I came with Carrie. I live with my mother and my grandmother. My mother is going to America for Christmas. In fact, she's flying out tomorrow. And my grandmother is going to Bournemouth. So Carrie and I came here."

"What about your father?"

"They're divorced. I don't see him much."

"That's rough."

Lucy shrugged. "It's all right."

"My mother told me I have to lend you my old TV. Do you want it?"

"Have you got one?"

"Sure."

"Well, it would be kind of you, but I'm managing very well without one."

"I'll look it out." For a bit they thumped along in silence, up and over the bumpy track. Then he said, "I believe you're all coming up to the Manse for a drink tomorrow evening. There's a hooley in the school hall, at seven o'clock. Clodagh and I are going. Do you want to come with us?"

"What's a hooley?"

"A dance."

Lucy was at once filled with anxiety. She hated dancing, could never remember which was right and which was left. She had been to *parties,* but never a dance. And at parties she was usually consumed and silenced by shyness.

She said, "I don't know."

"What don't you know?"

"If I want to come to a dance."

"Why not? It's just the school-kids, practising reels for the hogmanay parties. Good fun."

Reels. "I don't know how to do reels. I don't know the steps."

"So it's high time you learned." Still she hesitated, but then he turned his head to smile down at her, in a friendly and encouraging manner, and rather to her own surprise she found herself saying, "All right. Yes. Thank you. Do . . . do I have to dress up?"

"Heaven forbid. Jeans and trainers."

All the time they had been talking, it had been growing threateningly dark. It was now that the first large white flakes of snow began to fall. They drifted from the leaden sky and lay on the front of the tractor, and gathered against the windscreen. Rory turned on the wipers. He said, "I wondered when that would start. You could see the snow-clouds, coming down from the north. I heard the weather forecast this morning, and they said we're in for some heavy falls."

"Is it going to be a white Christmas?"

"Would you like that?"

"I've never had a white Christmas."

"Good for sledging. Hard work for the roadmen and the snowploughs."

By now they were near the end of their journey, grinding up the slope that led to the clubhouse. Rory turned the tractor into the car-park, killed the engine, opened the door, and climbed down.

"Will you be all right now?"

Snow settled on his hair and the shoulders of his thick donkey jacket. Lucy clambered down behind him, and he reached into the cab and lifted Horace down and set him on his feet. Horace gave himself a shake, and even wagged his plumy tail. The snow drifted and swirled all about them, and the ground beneath their feet was already iced with crunchy flakes. Lucy felt one settle on her nose and brushed it away. She took the lead from her pocket and Rory clipped it onto Horace's collar.

"That's it, then." He grinned down at her. "You get home now."

"Thank you so much."

"See you tomorrow evening."

"Yes."

She walked away from him, down the hill, into the falling snow. Bravely, Horace limped along beside her. A disinfectant bath, Rory had told her, and then, perhaps, a visit to the vet. She hoped Elfrida would not be too upset, but was pretty sure that she wouldn't. She would be sympathetic and would understand that none of it had been Lucy's fault. Behind her, she heard the tractor start up, and turned back to wave, but there was too much falling snow in the way for Rory to see.

She trudged on, feeling quite shattered by emotion and excitement. It had been a momentous outing. A long walk, a dogfight, a tractor ride, a snowstorm, and an invitation to a dance. She could scarcely wait to get home and tell Oscar and Elfrida all about it.

ELFRIDA

It was an enormous relief to Elfrida when she heard the front door open and Lucy's voice calling out. It was now nearly midday, but dark as evening, and the world beyond the kitchen window blanketed with falling snow. Ever since the snow started, drifting down from a granite sky, she had been worrying about Lucy, blaming herself for being irresponsible and letting the child go off on her own, imagining every sort of horror. Oscar, upstairs by the fire, was not nearly so concerned. He read his newspaper and assured Elfrida, each time she rushed to gaze from the window, that the girl was sensible, she had the dog with her, she couldn't be mollycoddled for the rest of her life.

All of which Elfrida knew was true; so she returned to the kitchen to do something about lunch, peeling potatoes, but keeping her ear cocked, like a dog. When she heard Lucy in the hall, calling her name, she abandoned the potatoes and rushed out to meet her, wiping her hands on her cook's apron. Lucy and Horace stood on the doormat, both encrusted in snow, and with a terrible story to tell.

It was told in the warm kitchen, while Lucy shed her coat and hat and pulled off her boots. ". . . This horrible dog, a Rottweiler . . . and it didn't have a lead . . . and it went for Horace and bit him, and then there was a tractor . . . Rory Kennedy . . . and he was frightfully brave . . . and had a dreadful row with the Rottweiler lady . . . shouting at each other . . . she stumped off . . . and Rory Kennedy brought us back to the Golf Club in his tractor and then it snowed. And, oh, Elfrida, I am sorry, but I *couldn't* stop it. And poor Horace has got bites and bruises. Rory said we have to give him a disinfectant bath, and maybe take him to the vet. Have we got any disinfectant? Because if not, I can go down to the chemist and get some. . . . It was *so* frightening. . . . I think he might have killed Horace. . . ."

She was clearly much upset by the whole incident, but, in an extraordinary way, excited as well, having come through the entire adventure and brought Horace home alive. Her cheeks were pink, and her eyes bright. She was a sweet child, of course, but serious-minded, and docility did not suit a fourteen-year-old. This metamorphosis was hopeful, and Elfrida forgot about all her anxieties, and knew that by sending Lucy off on her own she had done exactly the right thing.

As for Horace, he sat on the floor and looked sorry for himself.

"What happened, Horace?" Elfrida asked him. "Were you attacked by a savage hound?"

"He did bark," Lucy had to admit. "But not very much."

"Only stupid dogs bark at Rottweilers."

Elfrida went upstairs for a bottle of Dettol, and Lucy filled the big clay sink in the scullery with warm water and then they lifted Horace into this, and all the snow that was stuck to his paws and his chest melted away. There wasn't a shower, but Elfrida found an old jug and used this to pour the hospital-smelling water over his back and his legs and his neck.

He sat in sodden, suffering silence, but by the end of his bath Elfrida had discovered no serious wounds, simply a series of nips and punctures which would in time heal themselves. His stomach was badly bruised and one of his ears a bit torn, but by and large he appeared to have emerged from his battering with little lasting harm.

Lucy sighed with relief. "So we won't have to take him to the vet?"

"I don't think so. Just as well. I don't actually know where the nearest vet is, but in this snow, we couldn't drive anywhere." She let the water out, lifted Horace out of the sink, and carried him into the kitchen, wrapped like a Bedouin in a thick clean bath towel. Gently, she patted him dry. "Now we've got two invalids. Perhaps we should put up a notice saying ESTATE HOUSE NURSING HOME."

Lucy was struck by guilt. "How awful. I actually forgot about Carrie. Is she still asleep?"

"I expect so. I haven't heard a sound."

"Where's Oscar?"

"In the sitting-room."

"I must go and tell him everything that's happened."

"He'll be enthralled. But, darling, your jeans are soaked. I think first you should go and get some dry clothes on. Bring the wet things down and we'll string them up on the pulley."

"All right." Lucy started to go, but at the open door turned back.

"Elfrida."

"What is it, duck?"

"Rory Kennedy's terribly nice. And he's got dyed hair."

"Dyed hair?" Elfrida put on an expression of horror. "What *would* your grandmother say?"

Lucy told her, in Dodie's voice. " 'Dis-gusting!' " And she grinned and was gone, and Elfrida heard her running, two at a time, up all the stairs to her attic bedroom.

It was three o'clock that afternoon before Elfrida went to check on Carrie. The snow had stopped, but the dark day was already dropping into evening, and she had had to turn on lights and draw curtains.

She gently tapped on Carrie's door, and opened it. "Carrie?"

"I'm awake."

In the half-light, Elfrida saw her head turn on the white pillow. She moved forward to switch on the little bedside light. Carrie stretched, and then smiled at her. "What time is it?"

"Three o'clock."

"It's like night."

"I know. It's been snowing. We've had about four inches. But it's stopped for the moment." She went to close the window and draw the thick curtains, and the small bedroom at once became enclosed and cosy, with the single light burning and corners thick with shadow. Elfrida perched herself on the edge of the huge bed. "How do you feel?"

"Stunned. How could I sleep so long?"

"You were tired out. Would you like something to eat? Or a cup of tea?"

Carrie thought about this. "I'd adore a cup of tea. And I've got to go to the loo."

She climbed out of bed; long thin arms and legs and a long nightdress. She reached for her dressing-gown and wrapped herself in it, tying the sash tightly about her narrow waist. Elfrida left her and went downstairs to boil a kettle. She set a tray for the two of them, and found some very delicious and expensive biscuits which Oscar, on one of his shopping expeditions, had been impelled to buy. She carried the tray upstairs and found Carrie back in bed, having washed her face and cleaned her teeth and combed her dark hair. She had put scent on, too, her own special perfume, and clearly felt much more presentable.

"Elfrida, you are an angel. I am sorry. So much trouble."

"No trouble at all. I'm just so happy you were able to have a rest."

"It's so quiet. Where is everybody?"

"Once the snow stopped, Oscar and Lucy decided to go shopping. Just in the town. They've gone to look for decorations for the Christmas tree."

"Where will they find them?"

"No idea. Probably the ironmonger. Lucy took Horace for his walk and had a tremendous adventure. . . ." She told Carrie the long saga of Horace and the Rottweiler, and Carrie was suitably horrified, but impressed, too, by Lucy's composure, the manner in which she had conducted herself.

"What an adventure! Quite frightening, but probably just what she needs. She leads such a dull, unexciting life in London with Dodie and Nicola. They are both of them such selfish brutes, and neither has a scrap of imagination. I can't imagine what my life at Lucy's age would have been like if it hadn't been for Jeffrey. And of course, she hasn't got a Jeffrey, and she hasn't got a proper father. Dodie and Nicola have such terribly limited horizons, there can be no stimulation at all. All they talk about is other people—mostly bitching—or clothes."

"What does the poor child do all day?"

"Most of the time, she's at school. She's got a nice little room of her own in the flat, and a friend called Emma. . . ."

"I suppose she never sees a man. Or a boy."

"The school is all-girls, and if she does visit her father, the dreaded Marilyn is always much in evidence. Jealous, probably, stupid cow."

"I think she was rather taken by Rory Kennedy. Quite apart from being immensely brave and rescuing Horace, he has dyed hair. And an earring."

"Too exciting."

"We've all been asked up to the Manse tomorrow evening for a drink with the Kennedys. I'd love you to be able to come, because I want you to meet Tabitha Kennedy, but perhaps you aren't feeling up to such wild sociality."

"I'll see."

"And then, apparently, there's some shindig on in the school hall, all the children are going to dance reels. Rory asked Lucy if she'd go with him and his sister, and she's all bright-eyed and bushy-tailed about this, and says she's going to wash her hair tonight."

Carrie drank her tea, which was scalding-hot and smoky-tasting because Elfrida had made it with Lapsang Souchong tea-bags. She said rather sadly, "I have an awful feeling that when the time comes to go back to London, we're going to have terrible sadness and tears."

"Don't say it. I can't bear to think about it."

"I've been thinking about this job with the travel company. In London. I've decided I'll take it. Maybe just for a year. Then I can be around for Lucy, try to brighten things up for her a bit. I'll bludgeon Dodie into submission, force her to let me take Lucy to Cornwall to stay with Jeffrey and Serena. You know, she's never seen Jeffrey. She was just a baby when they divorced, and Dodie's resentment and grudges show no signs of abating."

"Poor woman."

"Why do you say that?"

"Because she has nothing else to think about. More tea?" Carrie held out her empty cup and Elfrida refilled it.

"Did Nicola ring today?"

"Nicola? Were you expecting a call?"

"No. But tomorrow she's flying to Florida. I thought she might have called to say goodbye to Lucy. But she obviously hasn't."

"Lucy never spoke about it. To be truthful, I think she's too preoccupied with doggy adventures, Rory Kennedy, and buying Christmas tree decorations with Oscar."

"Good for Lucy."

They fell silent, sipping tea, companionable. The house was very quiet. Elfrida said, as casually as she could, "Is this a good time to talk?"

Carrie raised her head, and her beautiful dark eyes gazed into Elfrida's face.

"Talk?"

"You said you would tell me. Some time. Later. Why you left Austria. Why you came home so precipitantly. Why you are taking this job in London. Perhaps now, with no person to interrupt, is as good as any. I'm not prying, I just want to know. Not so much about Austria, as why you are so worn out and sad-looking."

"Is that how I look?"

"But no less beautiful."

"Oh, Elfrida, what a star you are. I don't feel beautiful. I feel old and finished. I'm nearly thirty now. It's like a watershed. And I don't know what's waiting for me on the other side of the hill. Since I last saw you, the years have gone so fast. Thirty once seemed an age away. Now, before I know it, I shall be forty and then fifty and I have to make something of my life. But the simple prospect of decisions and meeting new people and finding old friends drains me of all energy."

"That's probably why you caught this horrible cold. Why a small virus has laid you so low."

"Psychosomatic, you mean?"

"No, I don't mean that. I mean physically vulnerable."

"Vulnerable. I never thought any person would use that word about me."

"Everybody is vulnerable."

"I thought I was strong." Carrie had finished her tea, and Elfrida took the empty cup, and got off the bed to put the tray down on the floor. Then, she went back to the bed and made herself comfortable, leaning her back against the brass footrail.

"What happened, Carrie?"

"I'd been in Oberbeuren for about a year, done a winter season and a summer season. The pay was substantial and I'd found an apartment of my own, and I was doing what I liked doing better than anything else in the world. It was a good time. And then I met Andreas. He arrived with the first of the snow, he came with a party of men friends. . . . It was a yearly date they'd kept, a sort of stag-party that had started when they were all at University. They stayed in the big hotel, and I met him then. He was a banker from Frankfurt. A prestigious family business, and his father was head of it. He was married with two children. I knew from the very beginning that he was married, but I wasn't a young innocent any longer, and I told myself that I could handle it. I didn't mean to fall in love with him, and I don't think he intended to fall in love either, but it happened. It just happened.

"He was the most attractive man I had ever met; and the most generous and amusing of companions, a brilliant skier, blissful in bed. He wasn't Germanic-looking at all, not fair nor blue-eyed. In fact, he was very dark, and tall and thin, rather intellectual in appearance. He could have been a writer or a professor. But he wasn't. He was a banker.

"He came to Oberbeuren quite often that first winter. He flew into Munich in the company plane, and drove from there up into the mountains. Then he didn't stay in the hotel, but with me. And it was like a private world that nobody else could enter. I thought, when the snow melted, that he would go, too, but he loved the mountains in summer just as much as wintertime, and we walked, whole days on end, and swam in icy lakes, and slept in remote inns. And we'd wake in some goose-feather bed, and hear the cowbells as the herds came in for the morning milking.

"He travelled all over Europe on business and sometimes I would join him, in Vienna, or Luxembourg, or Munich. In Vienna it was winter, and we walked to the Christmas Market, and bought gingerbread biscuits, and sparkly stars and little painted wooden decorations. And we went to the opera that night and listened to *Rosenkavalier*, and afterwards had dinner at the Three Hussars.

"Then, about six months ago, he came again to Oberbeuren. He looked tired and a bit preoccupied. When I asked him if anything was wrong, he told me that he had asked his wife if she would divorce him. Because he wanted to marry me. I felt torn in all directions. I remembered Jeffrey and Serena; I told myself how happy they were together. But I remembered, too, the acrimony and bitterness of that particular divorce. I didn't know his wife, except that she was called Inga. I could not imagine any woman not being totally in love with a man like Andreas. So I felt guilty and ecstatic at the same time. But I didn't look ahead, because there was no point. I'd lived with Andreas, from day to day, for so long. I could scarcely remember the time when he had not been there or been the most important thing in my life.

"He didn't talk about the divorce again. He came to the mountains and we were together, and sometimes he would say things like, 'When we are married, we shall build a house here, and come every weekend, and I shall bring my children. You shall meet my children!'

"But I never made any sort of reply because I was afraid; it seemed like tempting providence.

"Then he said he had seen a lawyer. Later, that he had told his parents. Told them his marriage was over, and he was going to get a divorce.

"I think there must have been a monumental row. Andreas's family were important in Frankfurt; rich, well-connected, influential. As well, they were Catholic. I can imagine how it must have been for him. And yet I can't. I only knew that I didn't have the strength to be the one to say goodbye. So what happened to me was up to him. Andreas. It was his decision.

"He held out for about three months, and he was so strong and so sure, and so reassuring that I truly believed he would see it through, stick to his guns, and tear himself loose. But I think in the end the pressure was too much. He was obviously deeply fond of his wife and adored his children. He respected his parents and relished his lifestyle. I think he had probably been told that if he tore the family apart, then he was finished. Out on his ear.

"It's all so banal, isn't it? One has heard it all before. A story out of an old melodrama or a Victorian opera. By the time Andreas told me that it had to end, our love, and that he was going back to Frankfurt and Inga and the children, I had steeled myself to accept his decision. But when the time came to say goodbye, and I knew I would never see him again, I felt as though all life was draining from my body; it was like bleeding to death, or something ghastly like that.

"I thought I could stay in Oberbeuren and try to get on with my work, but I couldn't. I couldn't keep my mind on anything, and the job was too demanding and important to be done at half-cock. So I went to my boss and told him I was lighting out. Going back to London. I stayed long enough for them to pick a replacement . . . an efficient girl who'd worked under me . . . and then I flew home.

"I have dreams about Andreas still. Sometimes they're frightening, other times, he's there to tell me it was all a mistake, and that Inga didn't want him any more, and we could be together again. Those times I wake up feeling so happy. . . ."

There was a long silence, and then Carrie stirred, and smiled. She said, "So that's it."

"My darling girl. Thank you for telling."

"Boring, really. Like I said, banal."

"Not a bit."

"I'll recover. I'll recover from Andreas and I'll recover from my little cold in the head. Life goes on. I'm here with you. I shall pull myself together and do my best to be cheerful."

"You don't have to pretend anything."

"Will you tell Oscar?"

"If you want me to."

"Just a quick précis. I'd like him to know. It will make things easier for both of us."

"All right." Elfrida sighed deeply. "Carrie, you mustn't think this is the end of laughter and loving. Life is so extraordinary. Wonderful surprises are just around the most unexpected corners. From where you're standing, it may seem a bit bleak and empty, but look at me! I thought I was alone for the rest of my life, in my little geriatric bolt-hole in Hampshire. And the next thing, I'm in the north of Scotland living with Oscar Blundell."

"Oscar's not married."

"No." Elfrida thought of Jimbo and sighed again, confused by the twists and turns of fate. She said, "The world is full of married men."

"Not for me, Elfrida. Never again."

From downstairs there came the sound of the heavy front door being opened and shut, and the cheerful voices of Oscar and Lucy, returning from their shopping.

Elfrida pulled herself together and climbed off the high bed. "I must go and make fresh tea for Oscar. Shall I tell Lucy to come and see you?"

"Yes, do. I want to hear the adventure of the dogfight from her own lips. And to be told about her new friend."

"You won't tease?"

"Oh, Elfrida. As if I would. I still can remember exactly how it feels to be fourteen."

SAM

They stood at the bar of the Duke's Arms in Buckly, an austere little pub that had made no concessions to either the tourist trade or trendy décor. The walls were pitch-pine tongue-and-groove, the lighting bleak, the floor worn dark-brown linoleum. The owner stood behind the bar, and did not appear to be enjoying his job. Around the place were small round tables and uninviting chairs, and in a tiny fireplace a peat-fire smouldered. Over the fireplace an enormous stuffed fish, with cold eyes, hovered in its glass case, and all smelt of old beer and whisky.

Fergus Skinner said, "What'll it be?"

"A half of lager, please."

"Will you not take a dram?"

"I'm driving."

Fergus had brought Sam here, crossing the snowy road from the church hall after the meeting. It was, he told Sam, his customary haunt, unfrequented by stray women, and a place where a man could sit and enjoy a peaceful dram without some person approaching and engaging him in conversation.

"Yes, yes," he said now, acknowledging Sam's situation. "Well, that is a pity, but it cannot be helped." And he ordered a large Bells for himself. "I'm walking." But if this was meant to be funny, there was not a gleam of humour in his eye.

He was a tall man, in his early forties, but looking older, with the dark hair and pale skin of a true Highlander. His features were strong—deep-set eyes, a beak of a nose, a long lantern jaw—and his expression sombre.

But his appearance belied him. Fergus Skinner had been foreman at the mill in the old days, and when the McTaggart family broke up, it was he who had rallied the work-force, approached the Local Enterprise Company, and organized the management buy-out. Almost unanimously, he had been voted in as manager of the new enterprise, and the demise of the business, destroyed by the natural disaster of flood, had been harder on Fergus Skinner than anyone else.

But he remained undefeated, because probably the only alternative was to go under, and he was too strong a man for that. When Sam rang him from London, from the offices of Sturrock and Swinfield, asking him to set up some sort of a meeting with the work-force, Fergus Skinner had done his stuff. Put up notices alerting the public and inserted various announcements in the local papers. Because of this, the meeting had been well attended, so much so that latecomers found standing room only.

Now, they carried their drinks to a wobbly table by the fireside. The only other customer was a very old man, who sat in a corner brooding over his glass and a drooping cigarette. He seemed uninterested in either of them. On the wall a round clock, standing at half past five, ticked solidly. The barman, polishing a glass, gazed at a small black-and-white television set, but had turned the sound so low it was scarcely audible.

A lump of glowing peat slipped with a whisper into the embers of the fire. Fergus raised his glass. "Your good health."

"And the future." The lager, un-iced, tasted warm.

"The future."

It had been a good meeting, held in the Buckly Church Hall because the mill was still in a state of desolation and disrepair; damp and chillingly cold. Sam and Fergus had sat upon the raised platform, and Sam had seen not only men, but women as well, and here and there the odd child, too small to be left alone at home.

To begin with, the atmosphere had been cautious, and not exactly friendly. These people, out of work for too long, were not going to take any rosy promises for granted. Sam, getting to his feet, had started by introducing himself as the new general manager of McTaggarts, who would be taking overall charge of the reconstruction of the ruined mill and the restart of the business. The response to this was silence, and he knew they probably regarded him as simply a money man, sent from London by Sturrock and Swinfield. So he told them a bit about his background. A Yorkshire boy, born and bred to the woollen industry, and a family mill very like that of the McTaggarts of Buckly. How they, too, had been faced with financial difficulties, and been rescued by Sturrock and Swinfield, which was why he, Sam, was there today.

The atmosphere relaxed a little. People shifted, settled down in their chairs.

He carried on.

It took a long time. He went through the whole process. The feasibility study and the restructuring. A business built on traditions and good will but moving forward. So, new products. New markets. New machinery.

At the start of the meeting, he had asked for questions. Now hands were held up. "Will that mean retraining?"

He told them yes. Other questions came thick and fast. "Would there be redundancies?"

He said yes, there would be. To begin with. But once the new mill was up and going, there would come gradual expansion, and so, new job creation.

A woman rose to her feet and asked if there would be work for her, a hand finisher, or would it all be done with this new sophisticated machinery? Sam told her that with the luxury goods they intended manufacturing there would always be work for hand finishers.

The most vital question was, When? How soon would they get back to work?

At the soonest, nine months. At the latest, a year.

Why so long?

There was a great deal to be done. If any person wanted proof of this, plans were already drawn up and the blueprints on display boards at the back of the hall.

The outward appearance of the old mill would remain the same. Inside, it would be gutted and totally rebuilt. There would be a shop to attract tourists, and the architect had, in his plans, made provision for a small tea-shop and refreshment bar, both of which would offer increased employment.

And who would get the building contracts?

Sam explained that Sir David Swinfield was anxious that all tradesmen should come from thereabouts, and that all local builders, plumbers, electricians, and joiners should be approached. So, after the New Year, tenders would be sent out, and subsequent estimates considered.

Finally, it all became something of a general discussion, which was exactly the way Sam wanted it to be. Before the meeting wound up, he came down off the platform, to be amongst them all; to clarify the blueprints, to listen to problems, and to try to reassure. By the end, he felt that he hadn't exactly made a lot of friends, but that he had won some trust, and hopefully, co-operation.

It was a better start than he had expected, and no worse than he had feared.

Fergus stooped to place another lump of peat onto the dying fire. "And when," he asked, "will you be coming up to Buckly to live?"

"I'm here now, Fergus."

"But you will be going back to London?"

"Yes, of course. I'll probably be up and down like a yo-yo, but I'm based here now."

"And where are you staying?"

"At the moment, in Inverness, in a hotel."

"But you will be going home for Christmas?"

Sam hesitated. He was going to be working closely with Fergus, and decided that it was best to be brutally frank with the man and put all his personal cards on the table. That way, nothing would be muddled or misconstrued. "You know, at the moment, I don't have a home. My home was in New York. I don't even have a family. My wife and I are separated. She's still in the United States."

Fergus said, "That is a terrible thing. To have no home."

Sam grinned. "It's not so bad. Anyway, with the mill I've so much to occupy my time and my mind that I haven't even thought about Christmas. I could go back to London and be with friends, but at the moment I'd rather just concentrate on the job."

"You can hardly drive to and from Inverness every day. Even with the new bridges, it's a long journey."

"I'll find something here. I'll rent or lodge. I'll be fine."

"You would be very welcome in my house. My wife would be delighted and we have space."

"You're more than kind, but I'm better on my own." He had finished his modest drink. He glanced up at the clock. "I think I should be off. Like you said, it's a long drive."

"But you have a good car. A Land Rover Discovery. And a new one, too, it looks to me."

"Yes, it's new. I bought it in London when I knew I would be living up here. I drove it north three days ago. It's a great vehicle."

"Yes, yes, indeed. My son has a Land Rover."

"What is your son's job?"

"He is a gamekeeper. He was not interested in the woollen trade, preferred to be out of doors. He was always mad on the nature. As a boy he brought home wounded birds and sick squirrels, kept them in cages and nursed them back to health. There was always some poor wild animal in the corner of our kitchen. My wife once remarked to me that it was a good thing we didn't live in Kenya."

And he said this in such a serious manner that it took an instant for Sam to realize he was making a joke.

They went outside, and it was snowing again. Across the road, outside the church hall, Sam's dark-green Discovery stood coated in an inch of white.

Fergus said, "I think, before you set off for Inverness, you should telephone the AA. Get a check on conditions. The Black Isle can be a hazard on such a night as this."

"Maybe. I'll see how I go."

"Will I be seeing you before the New Year?"

"Bound to. I'll call you. Keep in touch."

"It has been a pleasure to meet you."

"The pleasure's mine, Fergus."

They said goodbye, shaking hands. Fergus walked away, down the long narrow street blanketed in heavy snowflakes, and leaving a line of fresh footprints behind him. Sam saw him go, and then climbed up into the big car, slammed shut the door behind him. He reached into his coat pocket for the ignition key, and brought out two keys. The one for his car and the big, old-fashioned key to Hughie McLennan's Estate House, attached to its label with a knot of string.

For a moment, Sam debated. The meeting had been something of an ordeal, taking much of his energy, but it was safely over, and he felt elated rather than tired. It would be good to get back to base, to a bath and a drink in the bar, and dinner. But on the other hand, surely, while he was so close to Creagan, it would be worthwhile taking the short detour to the town and casting his eye over the place; orienting himself, locating Hughie's house. No need to go inside. Just discover how it looked, assess its possibilities, decide if it would be worth returning, to inspect, with an eye to buying.

For a bit he sat and vacillated, and then decided to toss a coin. Heads, he would head straight for Inverness. Tails, and he would call in at Creagan. He found a ten-pence bit and tossed it, then took his hand away—it was tails. He stowed the ten-pence bit and the Estate House key in the cubby-hole on the dashboard, started up the engine, and switched on the lights.

The strong, long beams danced with falling snowflakes.

He felt adventurous.

Creagan, here I come.

There was, oddly enough, quite a lot of traffic on the road. Heavy transport driving north, churning along through the snow with windscreen wipers going full-tilt. Huge lorries stacked with timber; oil tankers and cattle floats. Cars returning home from work at the end of the day; a tractor, its warning light blinking like a star. Sam got stuck behind this for half a mile or more, and then it turned into a farmyard and he was able to pick up a bit of speed again.

The snowfall abruptly ceased. The shower blown away. There showed a scrap of clear sky, the curve of a crescent moon. He crossed a long bridge over a firth, and a couple of miles after that, his headlights touched the luminous road sign.

TOURIST ROUTE CREAGAN. 2 MILES.

He took the turning, and the single-track road wound alongside the shores of the sea loch. It was half-tide, and he saw the black gleam of water, and the mud-flats were white with snow, and the impression was surreal, dreamlike. Far away, a prick of light showed from a small house on the farther shore. After a bit, the road swung right, and he topped a hill of conifers, and then there was open country beyond, and in the distance the lights of a little town.

The sky darkened and it snowed again. He came into the town by way of a tree-lined road, and in the light of street lamps saw the church and the square and the old walled graveyard. He thought of Christmas cards. All that was missing was a crinolined lady carrying festive packages. He drove very slowly around the church, trying to get his bearings, wondering which was the empty, untenanted house that belonged to Hughie McLennan. Having accomplished a complete circuit without any satisfaction, he decided to ask for directions and drew in at the pavement edge. A couple were walking towards him arm in arm, clutching a number of carrier-bags and baskets. He rolled down the window.

"Excuse me."

They stopped. "Yes?" the man asked obligingly.

"I'm looking for the Estate House. . . ."

"You're there." The man, amused, grinned. "You're here." He jerked his head, indicating the house behind him.

"Oh. I see. Thank you."

"You're welcome." They set off on their way.

"Good night," Sam called.

"Cheerio."

They had gone, and he sat, still in his car, and stared at the house, which he had noticed but passed by, because he knew it could not possibly be Hughie's house. Hughie had said his house was empty, untenanted. And this house had windows which, behind carefully drawn curtains, were filled with light.

Sam told himself that he should simply drive on. Leave it. A busted duck. But he did not like mysteries, and knew that this one would niggle at him unless he found out what was going on. He reached into the cubby-hole for the key, turned off his lights, and climbed down from the Discovery into the falling snow. He crossed the pavement and opened the heavy wrought-iron gate and walked up to the front door. There was a bell, and when he pressed it, he heard a buzzing from somewhere inside the house.

He waited for a bit, with snow seeping down the back of his collar, and then pressed it again. All at once an outside light came on, and he stood there as though caught in a searchlight. Then there were footsteps, and the door was opened.

He was not quite sure who or what he had expected. An elderly pinafored lady, perhaps? Or a man in a V-necked pullover and bedroom slippers, resentful because some caller was disturbing his favourite television programme? What he didn't expect was a tall, dark girl in jeans and a thick pullover. A sensationally good-looking girl, one who would have turned heads on Fifth Avenue.

They stared at each other. Then she said, without much enthusiasm, "Yes?"

"I'm sorry. But is this the Estate House?"

"Yes."

"Hughie McLennan's Estate House?"

"No. Oscar Blundell's Estate House."

Spotlighted, drowned in snowflakes, wet and cold, Sam held up the big labelled key. He said, "Perhaps I have made a mistake."

She stared at the key. Then she stepped back, opening the door. "I think," she said, "you had better come in."

CARRIE

That morning, the doctor, as he had promised, had popped into the Estate House, his face red with cold and his thick Harris tweed overcoat damp with freshly fallen snow and smelling of peat. He brought the bird book for Lucy, delivered it to her, and then was upstairs, two at a time—a man with not a moment to waste—to check on the invalid. Carrie told him, from her pillows, that she was much better, had had a good night's sleep and felt a different person. But, with native caution, he suggested that she stay in bed for another day. Carrie knew that if she refused it would mean an argument with Elfrida, so she gave, gracefully, in.

When the doctor had gone, in as abrupt a manner as he had arrived, Elfrida came upstairs and put her head around the door.

"What did he say?"

"I'm all right, but I have to stay here for another day. I'm sorry."

"Why sorry?"

"Such a nuisance."

"Don't be so silly. Not a nuisance. Do you want a hot-water bottle?"

"No. Warm as toast."

"Rather a shame, you'll miss our little party tonight. With the Kennedy family. But you can meet them another time. I'm rather excited about it. Too stupid, but you know this is the first time Oscar and I have been out anywhere. We did have lunch in the pub one day, but that's the sum of it."

"I shall stay here and oversee your supper."

"It doesn't need much overseeing. I made a kedgeree which I shall put in the oven. And if we don't eat it tonight we can eat it tomorrow for lunch. Kedgeree is an accommodating dish."

"Elfrida, you've been reading too many cookbooks."

"Heaven forbid."

The day progressed, and through her window Carrie watched the weather and was glad she did not have to be out in it. Snow showers came and went; the sky was grey. From time to time she heard the faint keening of wind, whining around the old house. It was all rather cosy. She remembered as a child being ill, and in bed, and the awareness of others getting on with the business of day-to-day life without herself having to participate in any sort of way. Telephones rang, and some-one else hurried to answer the call. Footsteps came and went; from behind the closed door, voices called and answered. Doors opened and shut. She heard Oscar stumping upstairs and down again, and knew that he was filling fireside baskets with logs. Towards noon, there came smells of cooking. Onions frying, or perhaps a pot of soup on the boil. The luxuries of self-indulgence, idleness, and total irresponsibility were all things that Carrie had long forgotten.

Lucy was a frequent visitor.

"Carrie, do look. Isn't Dr. Sinclair kind? He's lent me his bird book, so that I'll know the names next time I'm on the beach."

"How thoughtful of him."

"I wouldn't mind having a doctor like him in London. Ours is dreadfully unfriendly, and we have to wait for ages." She put the book aside. "Carrie, I don't know what to wear tonight. For this dance thing." At the moment she was obviously more preoccupied with what was going to happen this evening than with the names of sea-birds.

"What are the choices?"

"Well, I've got my new jeans, but they might be a bit hot for dancing around. I've got my old ones and they're clean and Elfrida ironed them for me. Or do you think I should wear my new miniskirt and the black tights?"

"Did Rory say anything about what to wear?"

"He said jeans and trainers."

"Then wear jeans and trainers. Your old clean ones and that red-and-white-striped cotton sweater. I love you in that. It's so French. And it's always better to be underdressed rather than overdressed. I'd keep your miniskirt for Christmas."

"Christmas. It's so queer. I haven't thought much about Christmas and it's only six days away, and nobody seems in the least bit worried, or preparing. By this stage, Gran usually gets a migraine, she says there's so much to see to."

"Well, Oscar's ordered a tree, and you've bought the decorations."

"I know, but I *must* go and get some presents. For him and Elfrida. I don't know what to get. And there's other things. Food. Do you think we're even going to *have* a Christmas dinner?"

"Your guess is as good as mine, but I think, yes. Probably. It's just that Elfrida's always been very laid-back. It'll all be accomplished at the very last moment."

"What about stockings?"

"I think we'll probably give stockings a miss. Would you mind? It's not as though you still believed in Father Christmas, and coming down the chimney, and all that."

"No, of course I don't. And anyway, I think stockings are a bit silly. Except the tangerine and the bag of golden chocolate pennies."

"I'll hang those on the tree for you."

"Will you, Carrie? You know, it's rather nice, isn't it, having a different Christmas. Not knowing what it's going to be like."

"I hope it will be fun for you . . . with three old grown-ups."

"I shall be grown up, too. That's what's so special."

Oscar, Elfrida, and Lucy finally departed at a quarter to six, for the little party at the Manse. The snow showers had not stopped all day, and by now the roads were thick with the stuff and quite hazardous.

As neither Oscar nor Elfrida relished the prospect of driving up to the Manse by way of the road, fearful of skids or drifts, they decided to walk up the hill by way of the lane. All hugely muffled, hatted, and booted, they came, one by one, to say goodbye, and Carrie told them to have a wonderful time and she would hear all about it when they returned.

"I don't suppose we'll have an awful lot to tell," Elfrida admitted, "unless they've asked other guests, and one of them gets drunk."

"You can always hope."

Lucy was the last. Carrie thought she looked extremely pretty, with her bright eyes and her excited smile. She wore her new red padded jacket and her boots and her big woollen hat, and had her little haversack slung over her shoulder.

"What's in your haversack?"

"My trainers and a comb. And a bar of chocolate."

"You'll have such fun."

"I don't know when I'll be home."

"It doesn't matter. Nothing matters. Rory will probably deliver you. If you want, you can ask him in. For a beer or something. Whatever you want. Someone will be around."

"Can I really? Well . . ." She debated this. "I'll see."

"You do that. Now, off you go."

"'Bye, Carrie."

"Goodbye, darling." They hugged and Lucy kissed her. "Have a great time."

They went at last, and Carrie heard the back door slam behind them. She waited five minutes or so, just in case something had been forgotten and they all trooped back again, but this didn't happen, so she got out of bed and ran a wonderful scalding bath, soaked for ages, then put on jeans and her thickest sweater, did her hair, splashed on some scent, and at once felt a great deal better. *I am recovered,* she told her reflection in the mirror.

She went out of her room and downstairs to check on the kedgeree and Horace. Both seemed in good health, although Horace was very quiet, and suffering from his bruises. To make up for his injuries he was being fed like a prince, on lambs' hearts and gravy, and was not required to venture forth farther than just outside the back door.

Carrie stopped to fondle his head. "Do you want to come upstairs by the fire?" she asked him, but Horace did not. He closed his eyes and went back to sleep again, warm in his basket and with his tartan rug.

She found a bottle of wine, poured herself a glass, and went back to the sitting-room. Here, the curtains were drawn, the fire blazing, and a single lamp left burning by one of the fireside chairs. She put another log on the pyre and settled down with Oscar's morning newspaper.

Outside, in the street, a few cars swished slowly to and fro, but the snow deadened all sound, and most people by now were safely at home. She was in the middle of a feature article about a well-known, if elderly actress who had done a television series in London; it had become enormously popular and she had found herself basking in global fame. Carrie had just got to the Hollywood bit when, causing her almost to jump out of her skin, the fearsome buzz of the doorbell drilled through the house.

Under normal circumstances, this would have been followed up by Horace's manic barking. But he had not forgotten yesterday's salutary experience with the Rottweiler, and this did not happen.

Carrie said, "Damn." She lowered the paper and waited. Perhaps it was some person whose car had broken down and now wanted to borrow a telephone. Or a local tradesman delivering a bill or a Christmas card. Or three small children in a row, all set to sing "Away in a Manger."

Perhaps, if she did nothing, they would all go away.

The bell shrilled again. No use, she'd have to go. In some exasperation she tossed the paper down, sprang to her feet, and ran downstairs, turning on switches as she went, so that the hall was a blaze of light. The big door was unlocked, and she flung it open to the snow and the cold and the solitary man who stood there, with the beam of the outside light streaming down upon him. He had dark, very short hair, and wore a thick navy-blue overcoat, the collar turned up around his ears. His hair, his coat, his ears were all liberally sprinkled in snowflakes, as though somebody had dusted him with icing sugar, like a cake.

She glanced over his shoulder and saw the large and prestigious vehicle parked in the road. So this was neither a man seeking help nor a tradesman nor a carol singer.

She said, "Yes?"

"I'm sorry. But is this the Estate House?"

His voice was pleasant, his accent . . . more of an intonation than an accent . . . was familiar. American?

"Yes."

"Hughie McLennan's Estate House?"

Carrie frowned. She had never heard of anyone called Hughie McLennan. "No. Oscar Blundell's Estate House."

It was his turn to hesitate. And then he held up in his gloved hand a large key, with a label knotted to it with string. On the label was written, in large black capitals with a waterproof pen, ESTATE HOUSE. As unsubtle as a clue in an old-fashioned mystery film. But how had he . . . ? He said, "Perhaps I have made a mistake."

There must be, of course, explanations, but it was too cold to stand there on the doorstep and listen to them. Carrie stepped back, opening wide the door. "I think," she said, "you had better come in."

But he hesitated. "Are you sure?"

"Of course. Come on."

He went past her, into the house, and she closed the door against the cold and turned to face him.

He looked a bit embarrassed. "I'm really sorry. I hope I didn't disturb you."

"Not at all. Hadn't you better take your coat off? We'll hang it here, there's a radiator and it'll dry."

He had put the key back into his pocket and now pulled off his leather gloves and unbuttoned his overcoat and shucked it off. She saw that he was conventionally, even formally, dressed, in a dark-grey flannel suit and a tie. She took the heavy coat from him and hung it on the old bentwood hat stand.

"Perhaps," he said, "I should introduce myself. Sam Howard."

"Carrie Sutton." They did not shake hands. "Come up to the sitting-room. There's a fire on there."

She led the way, and he followed behind her; up the stairs, across the landing, and into the huge sitting-room. Entering, he observed, as newcomers invariably did, "What an amazing room."

"It's unexpected, isn't it?" She went to pick up the abandoned newspaper. "And lovely during the daytime, because it's always full of light." She laid the paper on the table by her chair. "Would . . . would you like a drink or something?"

"You're more than kind. I'd love to, but I'm driving."

"Where are you driving to?"

"Inverness."

"*Inverness.* In this weather?"

"I'll be okay."

Carrie doubted this, but gave a mental shrug. It was no business of hers. She said, "Then why don't we both sit down, and you can tell me why you have the key to Oscar's house."

His expression was rueful. "To be honest, I'm not quite sure." But he came and settled himself in Oscar's chair, and at once looked quite relaxed and at home, and not at all as though he had just walked in out of the snow, unexpected and unasked. She thought that he had an interesting face, neither handsome nor homely. Unremarkable, but interesting. His eyes, deeply set, were unusual. He leaned back in the chair, his long legs crossed at the ankles. "But I am sure we can clear up the confusion. Tell me, did Mr. Blundell once live in Hampshire?"

"Yes, he did."

"And does he have an elderly uncle living in London?"

"I've no idea."

"And a cousin called Hughie McLennan?"

"I'm afraid you're asking the wrong person. I'm just a guest. I don't really know anything about Oscar's family. This is the first time I've met him, and I've had flu and I have been in bed, so there hasn't been much opportunity for finding things out about each other."

"I see."

"And Oscar and Elfrida . . . she's a sort of cousin of mine, and Oscar's friend . . . they're out. They've gone out for drinks. They won't be back till about eight o'clock." She glanced at the little clock in the middle of the mantelpiece. "It's nearly seven now. If you wanted to wait—"

"No, I can't wait. I must be on my way."

"But I still don't know why you have a key to this house."

"I was given it by Hughie. He wants to put the property on the market. Put it up for sale."

Carrie stared at him. "For *sale*?" She could feel her jaw drop. "But it's *Oscar's* house."

"I think they are joint owners."

"I know they're joint owners. Oscar told me. But even so, Hughie McLennan, whoever he is, has no right to put a house up for sale when he doesn't even own it."

"Yes." He agreed with her. "It does seem a bit suspect."

"And why would you want to come and look at it anyway? Do you want to buy it?"

He said cautiously, "I thought I might."

"What for?"

"To live in. I have a new job, in Buckly. Getting McTaggarts, the woollen mill, back on its feet again. I shall be based here, and I'll need somewhere to live."

"Where's Buckly?"

"About twelve miles south. I've just come from there. Spent the afternoon having a meeting with the work-force."

"Wouldn't it be better to live in Buckly?"

"The mill accommodation has all been sold off. It probably would be more convenient, but I was told about this place, given the key, and thought I'd come and, just quickly, drive around, have a look at the town. To be truthful, I thought the house would be empty. But then I saw the lights on, and decided to ring the bell and solve the mystery."

"But we haven't solved it."

"No. Not really. And we won't until I speak to Mr. Blundell. And I'm afraid there's not time for that. Maybe, another day. . . . Right now, I think I should make tracks."

"And *I* think it's important that you see Oscar. It's only fair on him that he should know what has happened . . . what is happening."

"I really must. . . ." He was on his feet. Carrie stood, too, and went to the big bay window and drew back the heavy curtain. Outside lay a wintry scene. Snow fell heavily, steadily, and his Discovery, parked at the pavement's edge, was already blanketed. No cars moved, and no person trod the streets. She thought of the road to Inverness, the long miles, the hill that climbed the Black Isle from the bridge over the Cromarty firth.

She, unlike Elfrida and Oscar, was not nervous of driving in snow. She had spent three winters in the mountains of Austria, and after that, nothing much fazed her. But this, obscurely, was different. There was a relentlessness to this weather. This snow was not going to stop, nor be blown away. The storm was here for the night.

She turned. He had stayed by the fireside. She said, "I don't think you should go."

"You don't?"

"Come and look."

He joined her, and together they gazed out at the clearly deteriorating conditions. First he didn't say anything, and Carrie felt a bit sorry for him.

"It really is bad."

"Yeah. Fergus Skinner, the manager at the mill, said I should phone the AA and get a report. I didn't think it was necessary at the time, but perhaps I was mistaken."

"I would say that would be a good idea."

"I have my mobile, but no number."

"I'll find it for you."

She went out onto the landing and came back with the phone book and looked up the emergency number. "Here it is. Do you want to write it down?"

He produced a pen, she read it out, and he wrote it on the margin of the phone book, and then took his mobile from his pocket.

She left him sitting by the window, with the opened curtain and a backdrop like a stage setting. She put another log on the fire and stood, watching the fresh flames.

He got through almost at once. Inquired about road conditions, the A9 to Inverness. Then, a long silence as he listened. Then, "How about tomorrow?" Another pause. "Okay. I get the picture. Thank you. Goodbye."

Across the room, they looked at each other. She didn't say anything, but knew that the news was the worst. He confirmed this. "You were quite right. The road is impassable. To be honest, I had no idea it would be so bad."

"I'm sorry."

"I . . ." He was stowing away his mobile. "I think I'd better be off. Get out of your way."

"Where?"

"Sorry?"

"Where will you be off to?"

"There'll be some guest-house, hotel . . . I'll check in there."

"There is no hotel or guest-house open in Creagan at this time of year. Everything closes down for the winter. You'll find nothing."

"But surely . . ."

She said, "You'll have to stay here. With us."

"*Here?* But I can't do that!"

"Why not?"

"You don't know me. I'm a stranger. I can't just come and—"

"Of course you can. Anyway, there doesn't seem to be an alternative. There's an empty bedroom, I know. An empty bed. It would be ridiculous not to use it."

"But . . ."

Carrie smiled. Now that matters were settled, and she had won her point, she was rather enjoying his discomfiture. "What do they say? Any port in a storm."

"But . . . Mr. Blundell . . ."

"I expect he will be delighted to have another guest. And most interested in what you have to tell him. And his companion Elfrida will be pleased, I'm sure. There's nothing she likes better than unexpected arrivals and impromptu house parties. You don't even have to worry about dinner. There is a kedgeree in the oven, and plenty of hot bath-water. All mod cons. What more could any man want?"

He shook his head, defeated by her insistence. "Nothing, I guess."

"A toothbrush?"

"I have one in the car. And my electric razor. But if it's all right by you, I should make another call."

"Feel free." (He obviously needed to ring home, wherever that was; explain to his wife what had happened.) "You don't want anybody worrying."

He took out his mobile once more and punched the numbers. Carrie wondered if she should make some excuse and go from the room, not wishing to overhear a private and personal conversation: loving words, messages for the children. But before she could do this he had got through and was speaking to the receptionist at some hotel in Inverness. "Just to let you know I shan't be back tonight. I'm stuck here, in Creagan, in a snowstorm. I'm all right. Staying with friends. Maybe back tomorrow. Just keep the room. Thanks. 'Bye."

Call finished.

"Is that all?" Carrie asked.

"That's it."

"No more calls?"

He slipped his mobile back into his jacket pocket and shook his head. "Nope."

"Right. Well. In that case, why don't you have that drink?"

"Well, that would be very kind."

"I shall have to go down to the kitchen and bring something up for you. We don't keep a drinks tray up here, because there isn't a drinks table. Oscar's wine-cellar is a slate shelf in the scullery."

"Let me come and help."

"No, you stay here and make yourself comfortable. What would you like? There's everything."

"Scotch?"

"Soda, water, or ice?"

"On the rocks?"

"Fine. I shan't be a moment."

She ran downstairs, and in the scullery found a tray on which she loaded the whisky bottle, the filled ice bucket, a glass, and then the bottle of wine. She carried the tray upstairs and found her visitor, not by the fire, but on the other side of the room, gazing intently at Elfrida's little picture. In order to do this, he had put on a pair of horn-rimmed spectacles which made him look rather scholarly.

When Carrie appeared, he took these off. "What a fine little painting."

"Yes. It belongs to Elfrida. She brought it with her from Hampshire. She's had it for years. It's a David Wilkie. She says it's her insurance policy, against the day when she runs out of money and doesn't want to become a bag lady. As you can see, there are no other pictures in this room, so it looks a bit lost."

"It's certainly a treasure . . . here, let me have that." He took the tray and held it while Carrie made space on Oscar's table, shunting aside a few files and papers. She said, "I'll let you do your own drink."

"How about you?"

"I'm onto the wine."

"Can I refill your glass?"

"Certainly, if you'd like to."

She went back to her chair by the fire and watched him, liking the neat movements of his hands. Intrigued, in an objective sort of way, because his appearance at the Estate House, his reason for being there, and his reason for staying on (bad weather) all seemed like a sort of contrivance. The plot of a play, perhaps. The start of a film which could turn out to be disturbing, even terrifying.

He came across the room, with her wine and his whisky, handed her her glass, and then sat again where he had sat before.

He said, "Good health."

"And to you, too."

"You said you'd just had flu?"

"Not very badly. I slept it off."

"And you're visiting?"

"I live in London. I have a young niece; I brought her with me. We're staying for Christmas and the New Year."

"Has she gone to the drinks party, too?"

"Yes, and then on to some sort of reel party with all the other children of the town. Goodness knows when she'll be home. Do you know this part of the world well?"

"No. I don't know it at all. I come from Yorkshire. Then I was based in London for a bit, and then New York for six years."

Carrie smiled to herself because she had been right about the accent.

"Hence the Scotch on the rocks."

"Exactly so."

"What is your job?"

"I'm basically a wool-broker. . . . I work for Sturrock and Swinfield."

She was impressed. "Goodness."

"They bought out my father's woollen mill in Yorkshire some years ago, and I've been with them ever since."

"New York and all?"

"New York and all."

"This is going to be a bit of a culture change, isn't it? Working up here."

"Yes," he agreed with her. "A bit."

"What did you say the mill was called?"

"McTaggarts of Buckly."

"Is it a going concern?"

He said bluntly, "No," and then briefly enlarged on this. Explained the chain of events that had brought it down.

"And is this what you are expected to take on?"

"Not entirely on my own."

"You mean you have Sturrock and Swinfield behind you?"

"That's right. And capital, expertise, architects, and designers."

"And when it's all up and going, what will you produce?"

"Everything. A very wide scope. Traditional tweeds and tartans, but as well we'll head for new markets. The fashion trade. Luxury woollens."

"When will you be in production?"

"The mill has to be gutted and rebuilt. So, maybe nine months. A year."

"Why don't you just bulldoze it away and start afresh?"

"Because it's a particularly beautiful old building. Stone, with steep gables and long arched windows. It's over a hundred and fifty years old. Part of the little town. It would be vandalism to destroy it."

"And *you* have to have someplace to live?"

"Yes." He smiled. "But I can't sort that one out until I've spoken to your host."

"Did Hughie McLennan, whoever he is . . . did he mention a price?"

"Yes."

"Am I allowed to be told?"

"A hundred and fifty thousand. Between the two cousins. The two owners."

"So if Oscar gave Hughie seventy-five thousand, he could buy him out."

"He could."

"It's not that much money, is it?"

"By today's standards, no."

"But Oscar mightn't have seventy-five thousand. In fact, I'm pretty sure he hasn't. And he's so unworldly, he wouldn't know where to lay his hands on such a sum. Anyway"—she shrugged—"it's absolutely none of my business and nothing to do with me. I just think it would be nice if he could stay here."

"I promise you, I'm not going to throw him out."

"You couldn't. It's his house."

"Half house."

"Sitter's rights. The security of his own bricks and mortar."

Suddenly, defusing a small tension, he laughed. "You're so right about that. I bought my first flat, freehold, when I went to work in London. It was a great feeling. That's some years ago now."

"Where was your flat?"

"Eel Park Common."

"How funny."

"Why funny?"

"I've got a little house in Ranfurly Road. That's only about half a mile away."

"Is that where you live?"

"I will, in February, when I get the tenants out." Sam looked a bit confused, and Carrie suddenly felt sorry for him, because, perhaps, she had not been particularly forthcoming. The thing was, she didn't really want to talk about herself. "I've been in Austria for three years, in Oberbeuren, working for a travel firm called Oversees. That's why I let my house. But now I'm back, based in London again. I'm still with the firm, but I've been offered a job in their head office, in Bruton Street."

"Are you going to take it?"

"Yes. Why not?"

"You'll miss Austria and the mountains."

Carrie said, "Yes." For a moment, neither of them spoke, and the silence was fraught with unsaid words. Then she moved in her chair and looked across at him. "Your glass is empty. Would you like another drink?"

Elfrida

Oscar and Elfrida, arm in arm, and making their way with tremendous caution, walked home together. It was nearly eight o'clock, very dark, with thickly falling snow, but there were street lamps all the way and so no need for the torch which Oscar, with some forethought, had tucked in his pocket. As they proceeded along the footpath that led along the top of the hill, the town was spread below them, and they could see, beyond the topmost leafless branches of other people's trees, the round lighted face of the clock tower. All looked so transformed, so magical that Elfrida was compelled to stop and gaze.

She said, "Oscar, I do wish I could paint."

As she had a firm hold of his arm, he had to stop, too. "Is this an appropriate moment to dwell on the might-have-been?" he asked.

"Why not?"

"I have snow trickling down the back of my neck."

"But wouldn't it be lovely to be able to capture such a scene? To pin it down forever? The snow, falling into the light of street lamps and bright windows. And the clock, like a constant moon. The only thing one couldn't paint would be the smell of peat-smoke."

"It would, I agree, be a satisfying exercise. But please, let us go home."

The lane sloped steeply down alongside the wall of Oscar's garden.

There was a handrail there, and they descended in single file, holding on to this like passengers leaving an aircraft. At the bottom was their back gate, and the bright light suspended over their own back door.

Safely home.

In the scullery, emulating Mrs. Snead, they shed wet coats, snow-encrusted boots, and sodden hats, and hung them about the place to dry. Elfrida said something about supper, but Oscar wanted to wait for a bit. He was full of smoked-salmon sandwiches and mince pies. As well, he had been prudently abstemious, because of the walk home, and wanted a large whisky before settling down to yet more food.

Elfrida went ahead of him, and in the kitchen greeted her dog with loving words, and was opening the oven door to peer at the good-tempered kedgeree when she heard him say, "My whisky has gone. My bottle of whisky is not here."

"Are you sure?"

He joined her as she closed the oven door, looking a bit put out, which, because he was Oscar, wasn't very much. "It's walked."

"Perhaps Carrie felt like a tot."

"I thought she was meant to be still in bed."

"You can still be in bed and feel like a tot. Haven't you got another bottle?"

"Yes, but *that* one was open."

"Let's investigate."

They went out of the kitchen and upstairs, but on the landing, Elfrida paused. For, from behind the closed door of the sitting-room, she heard the low murmur of voices. Oscar heard them, too. They looked at each other in some mystification. Oscar said, "I think I know where my bottle is."

"Shh." Silently, Elfrida tiptoed to Carrie's half-open bedroom door. She peered in, and then returned to Oscar's side.

"Not there," she told him in a dramatic whisper. "Empty bed."

Oscar, gamely joining in, also dropped his voice. "And she has a visitor."

"Who can it be?"

"A mystery. Why don't we go and find out?"

Which they did.

Opening the sitting-room door, they came upon a peaceful and companionable scene. The lovely room, curtained and softly lighted. The fire blazing, the two most comfortable chairs drawn up to its warmth. And in them, looking as though they had known each other forever, Carrie and a complete stranger. Possibilities instantly flashed through Elfrida's mind. An old acquaintance of Carrie's, perhaps, come in search of her. A long-time admirer, staunchly constant. . . .

Carrie turned her head and saw them, and at once rose to her feet. "Elfrida. You're back. We didn't hear you. Did you have a good party?"

"Yes, it was splendid. But you're not meant to be out of bed."

"I got bored."

By now the unknown man was also on his feet, standing in front of the fire, and waiting to be introduced. Elfrida's first impression of this stranger was one of business-like formality, in his beautifully cut dark-grey suit, his neat tie, and his closely barbered head of hair. He was tall and long-legged, with a tanned complexion that accentuated his light hazel eyes. And despite her sixty-two years, she knew a frisson of physical attraction that dimmed in no way her affection for Oscar. It was just a sort of recognition, an ardent memory of how things, once, had been for her.

"Elfrida, this is Sam Howard. Elfrida Phipps. And my host, Oscar Blundell."

"How do you do?" They all shook hands.

Sam Howard said, "I'm really sorry about this intrusion."

"Why is it an intrusion?"

"Because I'm in your house, unasked. . . ."

At this juncture, Oscar spied his whisky bottle. "There it is! I wondered where it had gone."

Carrie laughed. "Did you think I was secretly boozing? I am sorry. I brought it up to give Sam a drink. Do you want one?"

"Badly. I purposely had an abstemious evening, so that I would be fit to walk Elfrida home through the snow."

"In that case," said Carrie, "I shall give you one. But I'll need to get down and get some more glasses. What about you, Elfrida? I'm having a glass of wine. . . ."

"I'll join you." Elfrida suddenly felt tired. She sat, with some relief, in the middle of the sofa, with her long legs stretched out in front of her. "I've been standing for two hours, eating sandwiches and mince pies."

"Anyone else there?"

"Oh, yes, a proper party. Three other couples; all so chatty and welcoming."

"How about Lucy?"

"She disappeared with the Kennedy children to some other room, and hasn't been seen since. They'd gone to the reeling by the time we left. Just the way it should be."

"That's good. I'll get those glasses and another bottle of wine. And soda for Oscar. . . ."

She left them, and Elfrida heard her running downstairs. Oscar by now had sat himself down in his own armchair and they were left with the strange man. Oscar, Elfrida knew, had no idea what he was going to say to him, and so she came to his rescue. She did this by smiling in her most friendly fashion, and saying, "Now tell us exactly who you are, and why you're here. You must be an old friend of Carrie's."

"Actually, I'm not."

He reached for a chair and pulled it up to sit near Elfrida, leaning forward to speak to her, with his hands clasped between his knees. "I never met her before this evening."

"Goodness," said Elfrida faintly.

He began to explain, and they listened. He was Sam Howard. He worked for Sturrock and Swinfield, the textile conglomerate that had taken over the defunct woollen mill in Buckly. McTaggarts. He was coming here to work as managing director.

Elfrida was none the wiser, but Oscar picked it up at once.

"Peter Kennedy told me about McTaggarts' being taken over, but I didn't realize that things were already moving."

"They aren't exactly moving yet, but we're on our way."

"That's splendid news."

"I hope so."

"When does it all get going again?"

"We have to rebuild the place first."

Elfrida interrupted. "What happened?"

"There was a long series of misadventures," Oscar told her. "And then a flood which destroyed everything." He turned back to Sam. "Have you been in this business for a long time?"

"All my life, really. My father owned a small mill in Yorkshire."

"Well, bless my soul. Where are you based? In London?"

"I have been. But I've been working in New York for the last six years. Then, in November, I got called back to London, to take this project over."

"Does this mean you're going to be living up here?"

Now Carrie reappeared, with a second tray bearing bottles and glasses. Sam sprang to his feet and went to relieve her of this, and they spent a moment or two juggling for space on Oscar's table, shifting the ice bucket and setting out the glasses. The wine bottle was still frosted from the fridge, and Sam drew the cork neatly, poured wine for Elfrida, and brought it over to her.

"How about you, sir?"

"Oh. . . ." Oscar looked gratified. It was pleasant to sit by the fire and have some other man deal with hostly duties. "A whisky and soda would be splendid. And no ice."

Sam poured the drink for him. "Does that look about right?"

"Perfect."

He topped up Carrie's glass. "What about you?" Elfrida asked him, but he said he was all right, he hadn't finished his second drink, and then he rescued it from the little table by the fire and returned to his chair at her side.

Carrie said, "How far have you got?"

"Sorry?"

"Explanations."

"We've heard all about the woollen mill," Elfrida told her. "Surely there's not more excitement to come?"

"You'd be surprised, Elfrida." She was back in her chair, curled up like a cat.

Elfrida waited. "Surprise me, then."

Sam Howard took over again. "This is all rather personal and very complicated. Just say that before I came up here, after I got back from New York, I was staying in London with old friends—Janey and Neil Philip. They have a house in Wandsworth. One evening, an old acquaintance of Janey's parents came for dinner. He was called Hughie McLennan."

He paused, perhaps deliberately, giving time for this bombshell to sink in. Which seemed, to Elfrida, forever. Then Oscar spoke. "*Hughie!* You wouldn't be talking about my cousin Hughie?"

"Yes, I think I probably am."

"But Hughie's in Barbados."

"No. He was back in London. To see friends and deal with various business matters, I guess. Then he was going off to spend Christmas and the New Year with somebody called Maudie Peabody in the south of France."

"What an extraordinary coincidence."

"We talked for a bit, and then he learned . . . I think Janey told him . . . that I was coming up here, to Buckly, to take over at McTaggarts. And he asked me where I was going to live. And I said I didn't have any place, but that I'd have to find somewhere. And from his pocket he produced the key to this house. He said he owned half of it, and his cousin the other half. But that he wanted to sell."

Oscar said, "Well, I'll be buggered," and Elfrida decided that his bad language, under the circumstances, was really very mild. "What a little shyster he is. Always was. Why the hell didn't he get in touch with me?"

"To give him his due, I think he did try to telephone. You lived in Hampshire, I believe. He rang Hampshire, but got no reply."

"His father . . . Hector. Hector knew where I was, that I'd come here, back to Creagan. Why didn't Hector tell him?"

"I think he hadn't seen his father. And didn't plan to get in touch until he came back from France, before he returned to Barbados."

"Well, what a turn-up for the books." Oscar, shattered at the perfidy of his cousin, took an enormous slug of his whisky, and brooded a bit over the whole monstrousness of the situation. "Why did he suddenly decide to sell this place? We've boxed along for so many years, sharing the trickle of rent, I never imagined he'd want to put it on the market. And certainly not without discussing it with me."

"My guess is that he needs a bit of ready cash."

"Not surprised. Alimony for three ex-wives must cost a bomb. But then he always went through money like a hot knife through butter." He thought of something else. "Did you come to this arrangement through an agent?"

"No. He intended going to Hurst and Fieldmore the day after I met him. But decided that a private sale would be more satisfactory on all sides."

"You knew I shared the ownership?"

"Yes, he told me."

"And what did you say?"

"I said nothing could possibly be arranged until you, his cousin, had been consulted."

"So why are you here?"

"He had the key with him. He said, as I was coming north, why not have a look at the house. He told me it was empty. That an old couple had been living here, renting it out, but that the husband had died, and the wife gone elsewhere to live. With that, he simply took the key out of his pocket and handed it over to me."

"Wasn't that rather trusting?"

"Very. But under the circumstances, I suppose he reckoned I was as good a bet as any."

"And a straight sale would save agents' fees?"

"Precisely."

"Did he mention a sum?"

All the time they were talking, Sam had not moved in his rather inadequate and upright chair. His stillness was remarkable, and across the space that lay between them, his eyes stayed on Oscar, his regard intent. Now, down to the nitty-gritty, he did not blink, showed no sign of discomfiture. He said, "A hundred and fifty thousand."

"Would you be prepared to pay that?"

"I haven't seen over the house yet."

"But if you wanted to buy it . . . ?"

"Of course."

"Split down the middle, seventy-five thousand?"

"That's right."

"Suppose I wanted more?"

"It's negotiable. I'm simply quoting your cousin."

"I see." Oscar finished his drink, and without saying anything, Sam Howard got to his feet, went to get the empty glass, and took it over to refill it. He brought it back and handed it to Oscar. He said, "Now that you know how it all came about, I really have to apologize to you both. I'll give you Hughie's key, and we'll forget the entire business. It's just that I had to tell how it all came about. So that you understand."

"Of course." Oscar looked at the fresh drink in his hand. "Thank you," he said, and set it on the table beside him.

Elfrida, who had managed, with some difficulty, to keep silent and not butt into the conversation, now felt that the time had come to get her word in.

"You've made everything extremely clear, Mr. Howard. . . ."

"Sam."

"All right. You've made everything extremely clear, Sam, but I still haven't worked out how you got here?"

"I drove north a couple of days ago."

"Is this your first visit to the mill?" Oscar asked.

"Yes."

"You said you were called back from New York in November. And now it's nearly Christmas. Sounds as though Sturrock and Swinfield have been dragging their feet a bit."

Sam grinned, acknowledging this. "I expect it does. But I went with the Chairman to Switzerland to cost the new machinery we're going to buy. We were there for a good week."

Elfrida asked, "Are you staying in Buckly?"

"No. At an hotel in Inverness. This afternoon was my first meeting with the work-force. There was a good deal to be thrashed out. When it was over, and I'd had a beer with Fergus Skinner . . . he's the local representative, who'd organized it all . . . I started back to Inverness, and then had this idea that I'd make the diversion to Creagan, and come and case the joint, as it were. A passer-by told me that this was the Estate House, and it was so obviously lived in and tenanted that my curiosity was aroused; so I got out of the car and rang the bell. I was never much good at mysteries."

"I see." Elfrida decided it was all very exciting. She could picture it. The handsome stranger, the ring of the doorbell, and . . . Carrie. Going downstairs to open the door and let him in.

She looked at Carrie, curled up in the other armchair. All this time, she had not said a single word. Sometimes it was impossible to guess what Carrie was thinking, and this was one of them.

She said, "Carrie, I hope you have asked Sam to stay for dinner."

Carrie began to laugh. She turned her head, and a glance passed between her and Sam that Elfrida decided was almost conspiratorial. As though, already, they had an amusing secret to share. And then he smiled, and all at once looked much younger, less mature. Less serious and responsible.

He said, "More confessions."

What on earth had they been up to? "More confusion," Elfrida remarked, quite sharply, and Carrie took pity on her. "Elfrida, Sam is staying the night with us. I've asked him and he has to. All the roads to Inverness are blocked with snow. We rang the AA and they told us. And there is not an hotel or a guest-house open, as you know, so we have another guest for the night. Do you mind? I'm sorry. Do you mind very much?"

Elfrida said, "I can't think of anything I would like more." And it was almost impossible to keep the pleasure out of her voice.

It was nearly midnight. Elfrida lay in bed, and beside her, Oscar read his book, *Love in the Time of Cholera*. The lamp on his side of the bed was the only illumination, and the rest of the room was shadowed. The thick curtains had been opened a little, no more than a chink, allowing a shaft of light to penetrate from the street below, and a draught of icy air from their slightly opened window. Fortunately, both Oscar and Elfrida agreed on such small matters, as neither could sleep in stuffy darkness.

The shaft of light fell across the brass rail at the foot of the bed, making it gleam like gold. The vast mahogany wardrobe, polished weekly by Mrs. Snead, loomed against the wall, and on the old-fashioned dressing-table stood Elfrida's silver-framed photographs, her ivory-backed hand mirror, her bottle of scent. It was her room. Their room. Oscar's house.

She thought back over the many events of the evening, most of them unexpected. She, Oscar, Sam, and Carrie had finally sat down to their supper in the kitchen at nine o'clock, by which time the kedgeree was a bit dried out, but nobody seemed to mind too much, and certainly nobody complained. With the kedgeree they had eaten peas (frozen, from the top of the old fridge), and then peaches and cream, and Oscar had opened a bottle of white wine, and, when that was done, another bottle. They were on to coffee when Lucy and Rory Kennedy returned from their dancing, both looking red-cheeked from leaping about, or perhaps the cold walk home from the school hall.

Lucy looked a bit surprised to see another person at the table, but was introduced to Sam, and the circumstances of his presence explained to her. She was much impressed.

"Do you mean you're *snowed in*?" she asked incredulously.

"Seems so," said Sam.

"It's too exciting. Like an Agatha Christie. By tomorrow, one of us may be murdered."

"Not by me."

"Oscar, then. Oscar, you'll have to be the villain. You creep around at night with a knife, or a rope to strangle people with. And in the morning, nobody will know it's you, and the police will come, and a frightfully clever detective."

"Why do I have to be the villain?" Oscar protested.

"Because you're the nicest of all of us, and it's always the most unlikely person. It's got to be you."

Oscar then asked about the reel party in the school hall, and it seemed that Lucy had had the most marvellous time, and done all the dances except a terribly difficult one called The Duke and Duchess of Edinburgh, which you had to learn. And there had been a proper band, and lemonade to drink when you got really hot and thirsty.

Carrie was amused. "Rory, who organized all this?"

"The headmaster, and one or two of the senior boys. It was good. Everybody came. Even the little kids."

Oscar offered Rory a beer, but he said he'd rather have hot chocolate, and Lucy said she wanted hot chocolate, too, and that she would make it for both of them. Space was made at the table, and they pulled up chairs and joined the party, drinking hot chocolate and eating biscuits out of Elfrida's tin.

Finally, Rory said it was time he went home. He got to his feet, and Sam asked him, "What's the weather doing?"

"Well, it's stopped snowing, but that's about all you can say for it. I'll tell my dad that I met you. And about McTaggarts and things starting up again. He'll be delighted."

"Don't let him be too delighted. It's going to take a bit of time."

"Well," said Rory philosophically, "you've got to start somewhere. Lucy, I'll try to get that television set down tomorrow afternoon; it all depends on what's going on at the golf course. Not much, I should think. There might be a bit of sledging, but if there is, I'll let you know. Give you a buzz."

He departed by way of the back door, because it was handier for home, and Lucy saw him off. She came back into the kitchen smiling, and then the smile was almost at once lost in an enormous yawn.

Carrie put out an arm and drew her close. "You're tired. Go to bed."

"Can I have a hot bath first?"

"Of course. You had fun?"

Lucy kissed her. "It was the best."

While Oscar and Sam sat over their coffee, and the brandy which Oscar, surprisingly, produced from his slate-shelf wine-cellar, Carrie and Elfrida washed up the dishes and then went upstairs to raid Mrs. Snead's linen cupboard and make up the last spare bed for Sam. They found sheets and pillowcases, a bath towel, and an extra blanket in case he felt cold. Carrie inspected the wardrobe, which was empty save for two coathangers, and from which emanated a strong smell of moth-balls. Elfrida went back to the cupboard and returned with a duster and a lace-trimmed linen runner, and after she had done a swift clean-up, placed the runner on the top of the chest of drawers. Carrie set and wound the bedside clock.

"What more," asked Elfrida, "could any man need?"

"Fresh flowers? Face tissues? A mini-bar?"

"By the time Oscar's finished with him, the last thing he'll need is a mini-bar. I haven't even got a spare toothbrush."

"He's got one. He told me. And a razor. He'll be fine."

"Jimmy-jams?"

"He probably sleeps in the buff anyway."

"And how do you know?"

"Instinct, Elfrida. Feminine instinct."

Suddenly, they were both laughing. Carrie said, "You're a saint. I had to ask him to stay, but the best was knowing you wouldn't mind."

"I think it's lovely. I've always loved a full house. And this is a house for parties and people. Oscar and I have been rattling around in it for too long. Now it's full." She said this in tones of greatest satisfaction. "Stretched to its limits. A family house. Just the way it should be."

A family house. Elfrida lay in bed and felt the house around her, like a shield, a carapace, a refuge. It was a house that she had liked from the very start, and had come to love. Filled with friends, it had become a home. Oscar's home. But Hughie wanted to sell it, and somehow the very thought of Oscar's having to go along with Hughie's plans, and leave the only place that had ever belonged to him, was almost more than Elfrida could bear.

Oscar had come to the end of his chapter. He marked his book and closed it, and laid it down on the bedside table.

"Are you still awake?" he asked.

"Yes."

"I'm sorry."

"I'm just awake."

He turned off the light, but it was not dark because of the chink in the curtains.

She said, "Oscar."

"What is it?"

"If Hughie wants to sell his half of this house, couldn't you buy him out, and then it would all be yours? For always."

"Seventy-five thousand."

"You . . . you don't have seventy-five thousand?"

"If I sold everything I owned, I might scrape up twenty."

"You could get a mortgage."

"Not for that amount. Not at my age. And I've always had a horror of mortgages. People say, 'Get a mortgage,' but what they really mean is, 'Borrow money.' It frightens me. I've never had much, but I've never been in debt. I couldn't start now."

"If I had seventy-five thousand, would that help?"

"If you had seventy-five thousand, it would belong to you. It wouldn't be to bail me out."

"I love this house so much."

"Do you, dear girl?"

"It is so strong, so unpretentious, so . . . adaptable. Can't you feel it, like a heartbeat, keeping us all going, sheltering; taking care of us all?"

"I think I am not as fanciful as you."

"You can't lose it, Oscar."

"Hughie can't sell it without my consent."

"But he needs the money." She lay silent, carefully framing in her mind what she was going to say. "Oscar. Listen to me. If I sold my little picture, my David Wilkie, how much do you think that would fetch?"

"That is your treasure."

"No, it is my insurance. And perhaps now is the time to release it."

"It is your insurance. Not mine."

"Oscar, we are together. We are too old to prevaricate about such small details."

"Seventy-five thousand is not a small detail. It is a lot of money."

"If it is worth what I think it is, then we should sell it. If we don't get the seventy-five thousand for it, then we can fill in the gap with a mortgage. It's sense. Why keep a little picture if you can buy security? If you could buy this house? If you could live here for the rest of your days? You'd like that, wouldn't you? You'd like to be here, for always? I can't bear to think of this darling place going to other people. I want you to have it. I want you to be here."

For a long time, Oscar did not say anything. Then he reached for her hand and took it in his own. His hand felt warm and she was close to him.

He said, "You are the dearest person."

"Go to sleep."

"You are the most generous."

"We'll talk about it," she told him. "In the morning."

Lucy

Wednesday, December 20th

It is half past eight in the morning, and I am writing my diary. I should have written it last night, but I was so tired I just had a bath and went to bed, so got up early this morning to write it down before I forget.

It was fabulous.

We walked up to the Kennedys' house, because Oscar didn't want to drive the car in the thick snow. I have never seen such snow except in photographs. It didn't take very long because we took a short cut. The Kennedys' house is called the Manse, because Peter Kennedy is the minister. It is a big old place, not unlike this one, but very furnished and with things everywhere.

Carrie didn't come with us because of her cold.

When we got there, other people were there as well. We were all introduced. Mrs. Kennedy is called Tabitha, and is very pretty and young-looking, and unusual. Rory told me she teaches art in the school. Then we left all the grown-ups in the sitting-room and went into the kitchen, and there were three other boys there, friends of Rory's from school, and his sister Clodagh, who is twelve, and very skinny and sharp with bright-blue eyes and fair pigtails. We all sat around and drank Coke, and Clodagh was very flirty. The table was already laid, and we had a sort of high tea there, an enormous macaroni and cheese and salads, and then a very rich chocolate cake and ice-cream. When that was finished, we all got ready again and walked down the hill and along the road to the school. About half a mile. The school is old, but has lots of new buildings around it, and the gym was one of them. They call it the hall, but it's a gym as well.

There were lots and lots of children of all ages, from about seven to grown-up. The headmaster is called Mr. McIntosh, but they all call him Waterproof behind his back, but I bet he knows about this. He was quite young and very nice. There was a platform at one end of the hall and a proper band. An accordionist, a drummer, and a fiddler. There was a terrible din, and everybody was larking around, and then Mr. McIntosh told everybody to be quiet, in quite a soft voice, and they were. He said it was time to get started and we were going to do a Strip the Willow because it wasn't too difficult for little ones and learners (me).

Rory and the others who had been with us helped get everyone into line, with partners and things. It didn't seem to matter who your partner was. Boys danced with boys, and girls with girls, if they wanted, which seems to me a very sensible arrangement. Two boys wanted to dance with Clodagh, but Rory said he would do it with me.

We stood about half-way up the line so I could see roughly what it was all about. The music was very lively and jiggy and made you feel you couldn't stand still, with a tremendous beat from the drum. It wasn't a very difficult dance, just spinning round and round with your partner, or some other person in the line, and then coming all the way back again. Sometimes you were armed by a huge boy who pulled you just about off your feet, and then the next one would be tiny, and you'd have to be careful not to spin him off his feet.

By the end we were all hot and breathless, but there was lemonade and then we started again.

We did an eightsome reel, but with sixteen people, which makes it all the more complicated. And then something called Hamilton House, which was fun because you set out with one boy and then spin with another. And then the Dashing White Sergeant, when you go all round the room in threes, the lines in opposite directions, so by the end you have met absolutely everybody. Then the Gay Gordons, but Rory said that was a silly dance, so we didn't do it but drank lemonade. I didn't dance with him all the time, but with lots of other people who were friendly, even though I didn't know their names, and came and asked me. Most people were in jeans and old clothes, but some boys wore their kilts, with Rugby shirts, or old tweed waistcoats.

The time absolutely flew, and it was so strange because however breathless and hot you felt, as soon as the music struck up again, you simply didn't want to stay off the floor.

It all ended at about ten o'clock, and nobody wanted to go home, but once the band had gone, there wasn't much point, so we all went out to the cloakroom and found our things again, and put them on. Clodagh and the others went back to the Manse. One of the boys had a sledge and they took turns dragging each other along the road and up the hill. But Rory walked back to Oscar's house with me. It was such a beautiful night, with the snow still falling softly, and everything smothered in it.

Carrie had said to ask him in for a beer, so I did, and he came in. And then, more surprises. They were all in the kitchen, finishing supper. And Carrie was up and about, and a strange man was there, too. He is called Sam Howard, and is going to live up here, and run some old woollen mill in Buckly. Very nice-looking and I should say just about the right age for Carrie. I thought perhaps he was an old friend, but it seemed he'd been snowed in, couldn't get back to Inverness, and was staying the night. We'd seen a rather handsome Range Rover thing outside in the street, but hadn't put two and two together.

Anyway, we had hot chocolate and some biscuits with them, and then Rory went home. But he says he is coming today with the television set for my room. Not that I need one, because so many things are happening here all the time that I don't think I shall have time to look at it.

The best is knowing that things are going to go on happening. I've never felt like this before. In London, a treat is over and there aren't any more, but being here there are unexpected treats every single day.

Now I suppose I had better get dressed and go down and eat breakfast. There is a smell of bacon drifting up which is very appetizing.

ELFRIDA

Elfrida was, as usual, the first downstairs in the morning. On the turn of the stairs, she drew back the curtains (a marvellously grand and threadbare pair that she had bought at the market in Buckly), and gazed out at the day. Actually, it was the night, because it was still dark, but it had stopped snowing, and by the light of the street lamp she could see the garden, all shape and form obliterated. Bushes and trees drooped beneath the weight of the snow, and shrubs, pillowed, had lost all identity. It was very still and quiet.

She went on downstairs and into the kitchen. Horace, it seemed, was beginning to recover. As she opened the door, he clambered out of his basket and came to greet her, plumy tail waving. She stroked and patted him, and they held a small conversation, and then she opened the back door and he stepped out. When he came indoors again, his face wore an expression of indignation. He had not expected such inconvenience, especially in his present delicate state of health.

He returned to his basket and sulked.

Elfrida dealt with breakfast. Laid the table, made coffee, found bacon. It was the last of the bacon and they would have to buy more. In fact, she was really going to have to start thinking about Christmas food; she had been putting this off from day to day, but now there was so little time left that probably all the shops would be denuded and she wouldn't be able to buy so much as a mince pie. She found an old envelope and a pencil, and as she fried the bacon, started in on a tentative list. She wrote *bacon.* And then *tangerines.* And then decided not to write anything else until she had her first cup of coffee.

She was drinking this when the kitchen door opened, and Sam Howard appeared. Elfrida was wearing her tartan trousers and a dark-blue sweater with knitted sheep grazing about all over it, but Sam was still in his sharply cut and formal suit because, of course, he had nothing else to wear. He looked a bit out of place, and Elfrida's first thought was for his comfort.

She said, "I shall lend you a sweater."

"I clearly look as peculiar as I feel. Overdressed."

"Not at all. You look very nice. But a bit like a chairman about to make a speech. How did you sleep?"

"In great comfort. I remember beds like that in my mother's house."

"I have cooked you bacon for breakfast."

"I smelt it, wafting up the stair."

"I'll fry you an egg."

"I can do that. I'm extremely handy."

"Not in your best jacket. It will smell of cooking. I shall go now and find you something a little less formal."

She went upstairs. Oscar was in the bathroom shaving, so she raided his chest of drawers and unearthed a pleasing blue Shetland jersey with a polo-neck. Back in the kitchen, she found Sam in his shirt-sleeves, neatly frying himself his egg. She tossed him the sweater. "Too cold for shirt-sleeves." And he caught it and pulled it on, his head emerging from the ribbed collar like the head of a swimmer rising from the deep.

"That's much better," Elfrida told him. "Now you can relax."

He fried the egg and flipped it onto the plate, and added a couple of rashers of bacon. Elfrida put more bread into her new toaster, and then filled his coffee-cup. They sat at the table together, and it felt companionable.

"The snow has stopped. . . ."

"I feel so bad about last night. . . ."

They both spoke at the same instant, and then stopped, waiting for the other to carry on.

Elfrida said, "Why do you feel bad? It was no trouble at all. All we did was feed you on some rather dried-up kedgeree and put a pair of sheets on a bed."

"I didn't actually mean that, although it was very kind of you. I meant barging in, clutching the key of your house, and saying I'd come to buy it. I lay awake last night and went quite cold with embarrassment at the thought. I just hope I didn't offend Oscar, or upset him."

"Oscar's not that sort of a man. For a moment he was a bit cross, but with Hughie, not with you. And I must agree, I think Hughie has behaved in a shabby fashion. But according to Oscar, he's never done anything else. However, I can't pronounce, because I've never met him. Did *you* like him? Hughie, I mean."

"Not really. Very smooth. Rather passé. Kept fondling his tie."

Elfrida recognized the tiresome habit at once. "Oh, I hate men who do that. I can just *see* him."

"The key's still in my coat pocket. I'll give it to Oscar."

"He's not that worried."

"I . . ." Sam set down his knife and fork and reached for his coffee-cup. "I . . . suppose Oscar wouldn't think of buying Hughie out?"

"We talked about it last night. You have to understand Oscar and I haven't known each other for all that long. But, at the beginning of November, his wife and child were killed in a terrible car crash, and he had to leave Hampshire, and I came with him. We share a bedroom and a bed, but we have no foreseeable future together. I am not, as yet, permanently a part of his life, simply a sort of spare wheel, to keep the car going until he's sorted himself out. So it is difficult for me, either to press him into some sort of action, or even to make suggestions."

"Will he go back to Hampshire?"

"No. The house he lived in, with Gloria, is already on the market."

"So this is his only property?"

"Yes. And it's half a property."

"But wouldn't it be sensible for him to buy Hughie out?"

"Yes. Sensible, but not financially possible. I have only just found this out."

"You mean he doesn't have the wherewithal?"

"Exactly that."

"A mortgage?"

"Won't think about it."

"I see." Sam returned to his bacon and eggs, but his presence was so strong and sympathetic that Elfrida went on. Confiding in him, as she felt she could confide in no other person.

"I said, we talked about it last night. He told me that if he sold everything he owned, he couldn't raise more than twenty thousand. And I said, 'Oscar, I have my little picture.'"

He looked up, and across the breakfast table, their eyes met and held. And Elfrida guessed that this possibility had already occurred to him.

"You are talking about your David Wilkie?"

"Exactly. It was given to me, years ago. I've never had it valued, because I've never insured it. But like any old woman living on her own, I have always allowed myself to believe it is worth a lot of money. My backup, in possible times of penury and trouble."

"Would you sell it?"

"For Oscar, I would do anything. Short of leaping off a cliff or shooting myself. And after all, what is a little picture? It's given me pleasure for many years, but we have to keep some sense of proportion. Surely, to be able to own such a lovely house as this is of more importance."

"I agree with you," said Sam. "You've no idea how much it's worth?"

"Not really. And this is scarcely the time and the place to start getting it appraised. I am a stranger in this part of the world. I have no connections of any sort, and wouldn't know where to start. There's an antique shop across the road, but that's about as far as I can go."

Sam was silent for a bit. And then he said, "Janey Philip . . . she's married to my oldest friend. I was staying with them in London when

I met Hughie. . . . Janey used to work for Boothby's, the fine art dealers; I could ring her. I'm sure she'd have some bright suggestions."

"It's a bit close to Christmas to start trying to sell pictures."

"We don't have to do it right away."

"And the snow. The snow precludes everything. Are you still snowed in with us, Sam? I hope so." He put down his coffee-cup and started laughing. She frowned. "What's so funny?"

"You. Most people would be desperate to get rid of the stranger."

"I don't feel you're a stranger. But I suppose it was a stupid thing to say. You obviously want to get on. Get back to Inverness." She finished, "Get home."

"Elfrida, I am going no farther than Inverness."

"But . . . home . . . ?"

"At this precise moment I haven't got one. Except an apartment in New York. That's where I lived for six years, but my wife and I separated, and then I had to come back to the UK to do this job in Buckly."

"Oh, Sam, I'm sorry."

"Why sorry?"

"Your wife . . . I didn't know."

"Just one of those things."

Separated. "So you're still married?"

"Yes."

"Children?"

"No."

"Parents?" Elfrida persisted, beginning, even to herself, to sound a bit desperate.

"My parents are both dead. Our old Yorkshire home sold up."

"So what will you do for Christmas?"

"I haven't thought about it. Christmas, at the moment, is a nonstarter. I'll probably just stay in Inverness until the orgies of hogmanay are over, and then get back to Buckly and start getting the show on the road. At the moment, to be truthful, that's all-important. I'm giving family and celebrations a miss this year."

"You must spend Christmas with us."

"Elfrida . . ."

"No. I mean it. I couldn't bear you to be sitting in an hotel lounge in Inverness, wearing a paper hat and being all alone. It's ludicrous. Oscar and I didn't mean to have Christmas either. We thought we'd go pagan and celebrate the Winter Solstice with a lamb chop. But then Carrie and Lucy asked themselves, and Oscar went out and ordered a Christmas tree, and he and Lucy bought some decorations. And I'm just sitting here, thinking about food. I'm useless at this sort of thing, and all I've written down is bacon and tangerines. But we could gather a bit of holly and go and shoot a turkey, or whatever one does. And anyway, it's the people who count, isn't it? The friends you spend Christmas with? Don't go. It would be such fun for all of us to be together."

She finished, and he was silent, and she wondered if, as usual, she had overdone it and made a fool of herself. "Oh, Sam, you do what you want to do. That's all that's important."

He said, "You're the most hospitable, generous person I think I've ever met. But I tell you what I'll do. I'll ring the AA and see what's happening on the roads. If they're clear, then I'll go back to Inverness and get out of your hair. I really have a hell of a lot of work to do. If they're still impassable, then I'll accept, with much gratitude, your invitation."

"Oh, good. I'll pray for blizzards. Do my snow dance."

"What will Oscar say?"

"He'll say, 'Splendid,' and go and read his newspaper."

Sam pushed back the cuff of Oscar's sweater and looked at his beautiful Rolex watch. He said, "It's nearly nine o'clock. If you don't mind, I shall go now, to incarcerate myself in my bedroom with my mobile phone, and start making calls."

"Why don't you do that? But first have another cup of coffee."

Carrie was the next to appear. "Where is everyone? I thought I heard voices."

"You did. It was Sam. But he's gone back to his room to do telephoning."

"There's still the most dreadful lot of snow." Carrie poured coffee and put another bit of bread in the toaster. She took a rasher of bacon and ate it with her fingers. Then she sat down and saw the old envelope, with the start of Elfrida's shopping list. "What's this? Bacon and tangerines. We *are* going to have an orgy."

"I was trying to start in on Christmas. I simply must pull myself together and try to make a plan or two. I've been procrastinating, and now we've only got four days."

"Why don't you let me take over? I'm a professional organizer, and there's nothing I like more than making lists. Where can I go and do a mammoth shop?"

"There's a supermarket across the bridge, at Kingsferry. You'd have passed it on your way here from the airport. It's called PriceRite. The only thing is, I'm not sure if you'll get there in this snow. It depends whether the road's been cleared. But when Sam's spoken to the AA, we'll know."

"PriceRite. Sounds hopeful."

"You can buy everything, from dog biscuits to rose manure. I've only been there once, because, just being the two of us, we didn't seem to need an enormous amount of food. But we do now."

"Is Sam going back to Inverness?"

"Depends: If he's marooned, then I've asked him to stay. Over the festive season, as they say."

Carrie's face showed no expression. She simply said, "In that case we'll be five in the house . . ." and drew the envelope towards her, picked up the pencil, and started in. "Now. Are we going to have a Christmas feast?"

"Yes. I suppose. Christmas-day lunch? Or dinner?"

"Oh, dinner, much more festive."

"We'll never get a turkey into that little oven."

"Then we'll have chickens. Two chickens."

Carrie wrote furiously. Chickens. Brussels sprouts. Potatoes. Cloves for bread sauce. Frozen peas. Carrots. Masses of fruit. Butter. French bread. Cranberry sauce. Cinnamon sticks . . .

"And the wine?"

"Oscar will want to deal with the wine."

"Smoked salmon?"

"My favorite."

"And nuts and stuff. Mince pies?"

"Could you buy them? I'm useless at pastry. We can cheat, and soak them in brandy. Christmas cake. I'll make the cake. Christmas pudding."

"Should we have a cold ham? Terribly useful for Boxing Day and sandwiches."

"Brilliant. And a big pot of soup. I'll make it." For once, Elfrida felt competent and efficient. Soup was her speciality, chicken stock and any handy vegetable. She called it garbage broth. "And perhaps crisps and dips in case we decide to have a party."

"A party?"

"Shouldn't we?"

"Who would we ask?"

"Well . . ." Elfrida considered the options, which were not many. "The Kennedy family. And the doctor and his wife. And the nice bookshop man and his wife. They were at the Manse yesterday, and he and Oscar got on like a house on fire. . . ."

Oscar, on cue, came through the door.

"With whom did I get on like a house on fire?"

"The bookshop man."

"He's called Rutley. Stephen Rutley. And his wife is Anne."

"How clever you are to remember. Oscar, we are going to have a little party. So we shall ask them."

"When shall we have a little party?"

Carrie and Elfrida looked at each other, because this had not been decided. Then Carrie said, "Saturday. Saturday night is party night."

"The day before Christmas Eve."

Oscar said, "I shall have to buy some drink."

"If the bridge is open, Carrie's going to PriceRite in Kingsferry to do all the shopping. Perhaps you could go with her."

"Yes, perhaps I could. Elfrida, somebody seems to have finished the bacon."

"Oh, Oscar, I'm sorry. That was me," Carrie admitted. "I ate the last bit. I'll fry you some more."

"There isn't any more," Elfrida told her.

But it didn't matter, because there were sausages in the fridge and Carrie cooked those instead, and then Lucy appeared and Elfrida left them at it and went upstairs, feeling much happier now that a few plans had already been made and she was spared the ordeal of an hour or more spent in PriceRite, pushing a trolley down the crowded Christmas aisles and searching hopelessly for the ground coffee.

In her bedroom, she did a little desultory tidying up, making the bed and spreading upon it her red silk shawl. She folded clothes and put them away and then sorted out the contents of the linen basket in the hope of doing a wash and hanging it out on the line to dry. Which, perhaps, she could, because out of doors the sun was creeping up into a clear sky, and all the snow sparkled where the light touched it, and shadows were a wonderful smoky-blue. Below, in the street, the morning was on its way. The first of the shopping ladies; slow-moving cars; a man at the wheel of a van, sitting, parked, and eating a restorative ham roll. A girl came out of the bakery with a broom and started brushing the pavement. She wore her overall and a stout pair of rubber boots. Overhead, the sea-gulls wheeled, and perched on the weather-vane of the church, preening their feathers in the fine morning.

She tore herself away from the lovely sight, gathered up the laundry, and dumped it on the bathroom floor. Later, she would take it downstairs. She went into the sitting-room, still dim and shrouded from last night, drew back the curtains, and the low sun flooded in and filled all with light. The detritus of the previous evening stood about. Empty glasses, Oscar's whisky bottle; cushions squashed, chairs in disarray. She collected glasses and tidied up a bit, and then knelt to deal with the remains of last night's fire. Her most unfavourite task, but one which had to be done each morning. Oscar always said to leave it for him to do, but *his* job was humping logs and it seemed a bit unfair to let him cope with a bucketful of ashes as well.

She was brushing the hearth when, from behind her, she heard Sam speak. "Elfrida. I'll do that."

"Oh." She turned and he was standing in the open doorway. He closed the door behind him, and she abandoned the hearth-brush and stood up, dusting her hands on the seat of her tartan trousers. "Don't worry. I do it every morning. I'll finish it later. . . . What's the news?"

He looked rueful. "I'm afraid you've got me for Christmas."

"Wonderful." She made no attempt to keep the satisfaction out of her voice. And then thought it might be tactful to be a bit sorry for him. "Poor Sam. You're stuck. You have no choice. Come and tell me."

She went to the window-seat, and he came and sat beside her. Through the glass the thin sun felt almost warm.

"The roads are passable until the Cromarty Bridge, but the Black Isle is a no-go area, and Inverness is totally snowed up. No traffic in, no traffic out."

"They must have had much more snow than us."

"Yes. It seems they did."

"Carrie and Oscar are planning a huge shopping expedition to PriceRite. That's across our bridge. Do you think they'll be able to make it?"

"They'll make it that far, no problem. The snow-ploughs have been out. It's just farther south that the trouble starts."

"Have you telephoned your hotel?"

"Yes, I've done that. And to my chairman, David Swinfield, in London. And I've spoken to Janey as well. . . ."

"Janey . . . ?" Elfrida frowned, having already forgotten who Janey was.

"Janey Philip. I told you. Neil's wife."

"Oh, yes, of course. Sorry. The one who used to work for Boothby's."

"That's right. She was most helpful. She went off and found one of the current Boothby catalogues and did a bit of research. And there's a Boothby's local representative for this part of the world. He lives at Kingsferry House, and he's called Sir James Erskine-Earle."

"Heavens." Elfrida was much impressed. "How frightfully grand."

"She gave me his phone number as well, but I haven't rung him yet. I thought I'd better have a word with you first. Just be sure that you really *do* want to sell your picture . . . or at least have it appraised."

"I've barely mentioned it to Oscar."

"Do you want to talk it over with Oscar?"

Elfrida thought about this, and then said, "No, because he might try to persuade me not to."

"An appraisal doesn't mean you have to sell. And, whatever, you really should insure it."

"I don't suppose I'd be able to afford the premiums."

"So what do you say? Shall I give him a ring?"

"Yes. Do that. See what he says."

He left her, and Elfrida stayed where she was, gazing across the room to where her little treasure hung, lonely in the middle of a large empty expanse of wall. It had been part of her life for so long . . . the old couple sitting at the table with their family Bible; he so sombrely attired, she proud in her red dress and her daffodil-yellow silk shawl. Their faces watchful, wise, and kind. Their stillness emanating a certain dignity, a repose. They had been comforting companions for a number of years and seen her through a number of distraught and desolate days. She was very fond of them.

But they were not as important as Oscar.

Five minutes later, Sam was back, looking pleased with himself. "All fixed." He settled himself beside her once more.

"You spoke to him? Sir James Erskine-Earle?"

"Yes. No trouble. He answered the phone himself. And he's coming over to Creagan this afternoon. It's to do with the War Memorial; he's on some committee or other. He's going to drop in about four o'clock and cast his eye over your painting. He sounded rather interested."

"Oh, Sam." All at once, Elfrida felt a bit nervous. "I'm not sure if I can wait that long."

"You'll have to."

"We'll give him a cup of tea. I'll buy some scones. Did he sound nice?"

"Perfectly amenable."

"It . . . it's rather exciting, isn't it?"

"It could be."

"Shall I tell Oscar?"

"I would, if I were you. You don't want to start feeling underhanded."

"No. You're quite right. Thank you, Sam, for your trouble."

"My pleasure. The least I can do. Now, you said Carrie and Oscar were going over to Kingsferry to shop. Instead, why don't I take her, and then I can help loading trolleys and carting everything home?"

Elfrida thought this a marvellous idea, and for more reasons than one.

"Brilliant. How kind you are. Oscar will be delighted. He loathes shopping."

"I have ulterior motives." (Better and better.) "Because I must buy clothes. I can't go round looking like a tailor's dummy for the next five days. Do you think Kingsferry would rise to a Gent's Outfitters? And a chemist, because I haven't got any toothpaste."

Elfrida said brightly, "Of course," but felt slightly let down because she had hoped his ulterior motive was getting Carrie to himself.

"And I should like to buy some wine for Oscar . . . perhaps I should have a word with him before I go."

"That would be a good idea. About wine, Oscar has strong opinions."

"And rightly so."

Outside, in the brightening morning, the sea-gulls clamoured, perched on the ridge of the high roof, floating and circling around the tower, relishing the clear air. Elfrida turned her head to watch them. She said, "In one way, I should like you to have this house. It has such dignity and solidity, just right for the important head of a company." She looked at him sitting there in Oscar's blue sweater, and it already felt as though he had been with them all forever. "It's strange, isn't it, the way things happen? You with your key, and then the snow tumbling down. And here we all are. And it is very satisfactory having young and competent people around us again. Carrie organizing everything, and you making decisions that I never could. I've always been useless at decisions. I've always worked on impulse, and some have been disastrous. Oscar and I have been two old things for too long. Mrs. Snead said visitors would cheer us up, but it's more than that. And I know that without actually talking about it we've both been dreading Christmas. Under the circumstances, I felt it could be nothing but a bitter and sad time. But now, with you and Lucy and Carrie with us, it *can't* be as emotive as we had feared." She thought about this, and then smiled. "Whatever, there's nothing we can do to stop it happening. So we might as well make it fun. Perhaps it will be like one of those parties one longs not to have to go to; and then it turns out to be one of the most memorable and the best. Do you know what I mean?"

Sam said he knew exactly what she meant.

LUCY

Half past ten in the morning, and everyone was occupied.

Sam and Carrie had departed in Sam's impressive Discovery for Kingsferry and PriceRite. Before they could go, however, a certain amount of physical labour had been necessary, and Sam had found a shovel in Oscar's shed and cleared the snow from the path that led from front door to gate, and then a broom, with which he had brushed piled snow from his car. And had squirted anti-freeze on his windscreen. Finally Carrie joined him, and they set off on their expedition together, armed with a list that went on forever, and which had taken a great deal of time and communal thought to compose. Carrie wore her loden coat and her black fur hat, and Sam was buttoned up into a handsome navy-blue overcoat that made him look very successful, which he probably was. Driving away, they left an opulent impression.

Elfrida, having hung her washing out in the still, cold air, had taken Horace for a small walk. Just up the hill to the closed and shuttered hotel, and home by the station. Otherwise, she said, his muscles would atrophy and he would never move from his basket again. Oscar was by the fire in the sitting-room, reading his newspaper. He had clearly been much relieved when told he didn't have to go shopping.

So Lucy sat at the table in her bedroom, and made her own plans.

This morning she would shop for her Christmas presents. She had given Mummy and Gran theirs before she left London, but there were still a lot more to go. Having her holiday money made everything much easier, because it meant she wouldn't have to penny-pinch.

Elfrida, Oscar, Carrie. Now she added Sam. And Mrs. Snead. And Rory. And perhaps Clodagh, too; otherwise it might look a bit odd.

She couldn't think of anybody else.

She found her haversack and put the list into it and checked on her purse, which bulged in satisfactory fashion. She put on her padded jacket and her boots and went downstairs. On the way, she looked around the open sitting-room door.

"Oscar."

"Yes, my duck."

"Oscar, I'm going out to do some shopping."

"Right."

"When Elfrida gets back, will you tell her?"

"I shall do that."

She left him and went on downstairs. Christmas, all at once, was becoming real. Over breakfast, plans had been laid, and Lucy was told that they were going to have Christmas dinner in the evening, a proper grown-up party. In London, where Christmas was usually a fairly tame affair, the great feast always took place at lunch-time, which meant there was an awful lot of day left over. But a party in the evening meant that there would be something to look forward to all day, and Lucy could wear her new black miniskirt and her white sweater. Going down the long hall thinking about this, she paused, and then, on an impulse, opened the door of the desolate and disused dining-room. It was dark and gloomy and in dire need of a good dust and polish, but in her imagination she saw it lit by firelight and candles and groaning with delicious foods. Things like crystallized fruits and a pudding aflame with brandy. And goblets of wine, and the glow of china and gleaming silver dishes filled with nuts and chocolates.

An idea took shape, but there wasn't time, right now, to think it through, so she closed the door and then let herself out of doors, into the cold sweet morning and the dazzle of snow. Across the street stood a big council lorry, with an extending ladder, and two burly men were occupied in draping strings of fairy lights around and over the branches of the bare trees which stood within the churchyard wall.

She started off down the pavement to do the rounds of the modest shops. By now, they too were in the festive spirit, with mock snow sprayed on windows and displays arranged with red satin bows and plastic holly. In the ironmonger's window a chain-saw wore a tinsel ribbon and a card saying SUITABLE FOR CHRISTMAS GIFTING.

Lucy wondered who would fall for that one.

She came to the jersey shop, went inside, and found every sort of pullover, cardigan, tam-o'-shanter, sock, and glove. Knitted thistles on the front of sweaters, ethnic patterns that looked as though they had been designed by some mad Peruvian. In the end she unearthed a red cashmere scarf, very fine and very long, which she knew would look quite perfect wound around Carrie's elegant neck.

And it would keep her cosy as well.

Next was the bookshop. And there, to serve her, was Mr. Rutley, who ran the place, and whom she had already met at the Manse. He greeted Lucy like an old friend, and was immensely helpful. After a bit of browsing, discussion, and changing minds, she chose a book for Oscar, a coffee-table book filled with full-page colour photographs of old Scottish country houses, castles, and gardens. She was sure that he would love it. Mr. Rutley said that if he didn't, he could change it, but Lucy knew that even if he didn't like the book, Oscar wouldn't dream of changing it, because he was that sort of person, and would rather fall down dead than hurt someone's feelings.

For Sam, at Mr. Rutley's suggestion, she got an ordnance survey map of Creagan and the surrounding district, which included Buckly. It seemed a bit dull, but on the other hand was probably the most useful thing he could own, coming as he was to live and work in the neighbourhood. As well, it was quite expensive. So Lucy bought it, and some cards, and wrapping paper with holly, and some glittery string. Mr. Rutley put it all into a carrier-bag and took her money.

"I hope we'll see you all again over Christmas, Lucy."

"Yes. I do, too. Thank you."

"Have fun."

The chemist was next. That was much quicker. Some lavender soap for Mrs. Snead, and for Clodagh, little hair ornaments that she could clip to the end of her pigtails. Rory was a bit difficult because Lucy hadn't the faintest idea what he would really like. It would be easier to choose if she had a brother of her own, or even a friend who was a boy. Then she saw a big bottle of Badedas. Her father had always used Badedas, in the safe old days when she was a little girl, before the divorce. He would soak in his bath, and the scented steam, smelling of chestnut oil, would fill the upstairs half of their house. Perhaps Rory would like to soak in Badedas after a long day's stint on the golf course. She wavered for a moment or two, and then, unable to come up with a better idea, bought it.

Elfrida was the most difficult. What could one give to Elfrida that would begin to pay back for all the laughs and the spontaneous affection that she had given Lucy? There was no inspiration in the chemist's shop, so she went out and walked on down the street, past Arthur Snead Fruit and Vegetables.

Then, struck by a brilliant idea, she retraced her steps and went through the door, which went *ping* when she shut it.

"Mr. Snead?"

"'Ullo, there."

"I'm Lucy Wesley. I'm staying at the Estate House. Mrs. Snead is a friend of mine."

"Oh, yes. She told me about you."

"If I ordered some special flowers for Elfrida, would you be able to deliver them on Christmas Eve?"

He looked a bit doubtful, pursing up his lips. "Christmas Eve's a Sunday, darling."

"Well, Saturday, then. Saturday would be better, actually, because they're going to have a little party."

"The truth is, darling, it's dicey just now, with the snow. Nothing's getting through from Inverness, and that's where all my regular stuff comes from. What were you thinking of? Chrysanths? Carnations?"

Lucy screwed up her nose. "Not really."

"I've got Stargazer lilies in the back. Delivered yesterday, when the roads were still open. But they're pricey."

"Stargazers?"

"Lovely tight buds, and in the cool. Should just be starting to open in a day or two."

"Could I see one?"

"Course you can."

He disappeared through a door at the back of his shop and reappeared holding a single stem of creamy, elliptical, tightly closed buds. They looked just the same as the ones Gran bought from the flower-seller on the street corner in Fulham, and they sometimes lasted as long as two weeks.

"How many have you got there?"

"I've got a dozen in there, but like I said, they're pricey. Three pounds a stem."

Three by six was eighteen. Eighteen pounds. But they would look so beautiful in Elfrida's sitting-room. They would open slowly, spreading out into pale-pink petals, and fill the whole house with their heady fragrance. She said, "I'll have six and pay you now, but would you keep them here until Saturday and then bring them over?"

"Course I will. And tell you what, I'll wrap them in special paper and put a big pink bow on."

"I've got a card. I bought it in the bookshop. If I write the card, you can put it in with the flowers."

"I'll do that very thing."

He lent her a pen and she wrote the card.

Elfrida—
Happy Christmas and lots of love from Lucy

She put it into its envelope and wrote ELFRIDA PHIPPS, licked it down, and gave it to Mr. Snead, and then handed over the eighteen pounds. A terrible lot to spend on flowers, but worth it.

Mr. Snead rang up his till. "If you're wanting mistletoe, let me know. I've got a branch or two, but it sells like hot cakes."

Mistletoe was synonymous with kissing.

"I'll see," said Lucy cautiously.

She said goodbye and set off for home, laden with purchases and feeling tremendously Christmassy. Once back, she would go straight upstairs to her bedroom, close the door, and settle down to wrapping all her presents in holly paper, tying them up in glittery string, and then hiding them in her bottom drawer. As she crossed the square, she saw the car parked outside Oscar's house, an old estate car with its tail-gate open, but thought nothing of it, because in Creagan people parked their cars all over the place, wherever they could find space. However, as she pushed the front door open, she heard voices from the kitchen and, investigating, there found Elfrida, stirring a pot on the cooker, and Rory Kennedy. On the kitchen table stood the television set, and a small black plastic trolley with wheels.

When she appeared in the open doorway, laden with shopping bags, they stopped talking, and turned to smile. Rory said, "Hi," and he was wearing a grey fleecy jacket and rubber boots, and looked hugely masculine. Because his presence was so unexpected, Lucy was all at once lost for words, and yet delighted all at the same time.

"Hello. I . . . I thought you were coming later on. Like tea-time. I thought you'd be working."

"Not much to do on the golf course in weather like this. The greenkeeper sent us all home. So I borrowed Dad's car and brought the set down for you."

Lucy looked at it. It seemed much more sophisticated than the one she had in London. "I thought it would be old. It doesn't look old at all."

"It's colour. Just that I got myself a bigger one. I brought the stand as well, in case you didn't have anywhere to put it."

Elfrida lifted her pot off the cooker and put it down on an iron trivet. She said, "I think it's amazing. We'll all be coming up to the attic to sit and goggle. Lucy, perhaps you'd better show Rory where it's got to go in your bedroom."

"It's four flights of stairs," Lucy told Rory.

He grinned. "I think I could just about manage."

She led the way, her carrier-bags bumping against her legs. "You been shopping?" Rory asked, from behind her. She thought that only he would be able to carry something very heavy up so many stairs and still have breath left over for conversation.

"Yes. Christmas presents. I didn't have time in London."

The top landing and the door that led into her room. She went through and dumped the carrier-bags on her bed, and Rory followed her and put the television set carefully down on the floor. Straightening, he looked appreciatively about him. "Hey, this is a cool room. And lots of space. Do you always keep it as tidy as this?"

"Sort of," Lucy told him casually, not wanting him to think her pernickety.

"Clodagh's room's a perpetual tip. Ma's always getting at her to put her things away. I'll nip down and get the table and then we'll get it set up."

When he had gone, pounding down the stairs again, she quickly bundled all the carrier-bags in the empty bottom drawer and shut it firmly. It would be a shame if he guessed about the Badedas.

In a moment he was back with the little trolley. They found a suitable power socket, and Rory put the set on the table and plugged it in. There was no aerial point, but the set had its own aerial, and Rory switched it on and then fiddled with the aerial until the picture stopped being fuzzy and became quite clear.

"It's really good," Lucy marvelled.

"I can get it better." He was sitting cross-legged on the rug, intent on what he was doing. He punched knobs, switched channels. "Superman" was on for children, and then an old black-and-white film. Then a lady showing them how to make Christmas cards decorated with cut-outs from a seed catalogue. Rory checked the sound, gave the internal aerial another tweak. Lucy settled herself on the floor beside him.

"... and then you finish it off with a little bow of pretty ribbon. Like this. I think you'll agree any person would be delighted to receive such a personal card...."

Rory said, "Not me," and punched another button. A broadly Scottish announcer was telling them about the weather, which, in the foreseeable future, was not conducive to hill-walking or climbing.

"Do you want me to leave it on?" Rory asked.

"No. I know how to work it now."

He switched it off. "Just don't touch the aerial. I think I've got it as good as it gets...."

"It's really kind of you to let me borrow it, and to bring it."

"No problem. Finishes everything off." He looked about him once more in admiring fashion. "Is this all the stuff my mother helped buy? It's great. She loves going to the Buckly market more than anything; she always comes back with some bargain. A tatty old linen pillowcase, or a china fairing, or something useless. Our house is full of junk, but there always seems to be room for more. At home, in London, do you have a room like this?"

"No. It's not nearly so big. And it hasn't any sort of look-out from the window. But it's pretty. And at least I don't have to share it with anybody. I've got my books there, and my computer. My things."

"What's it like, living in a city?"

"It's all right."

"Must be great, all those museums and exhibitions and concerts and plays. I've only been once. My dad took me when he had to attend some conference, and we stayed in an hotel, and went to a theatre every night. It was hot weather, and we used to have our meals in pubs, sitting out on the pavement, and watching all the weirdos wandering past. It was good. More exciting than Creagan."

"It's different if you live there all the time."

"Suppose so."

"It can be quite nice if you've got a proper house with a garden. When I was little we had a house in Kensington with a proper garden, and that didn't feel like living in a city because there was always a bit of green grass, trees, flowers, and things. But then my parents divorced and now we live in a flat, me and my mother and my grandmother. It's near the river and it's got a balcony and a nice view, but there's nowhere to *be*. To go and lie on a bit of lawn and read a book. My friend Emma . . . she's at school with me . . . she lives in a proper house and sometimes we have a barbecue in the garden."

She couldn't think of anything else to tell him, and was painfully aware that it all sounded very dull.

After a bit he asked, "Are you homesick?"

She looked at him in astonishment. *"Homesick?"*

"Well, you know . . . missing your mother. Your things. Everything. Clodagh's hopeless. She won't even go away for a night, bawls like a baby."

"No," Lucy heard her own voice, all at once surprisingly sharp and strong. "No, I'm *not* homesick. I'm not even thinking about going back to London. I'm simply putting it out of my mind."

"But . . ."

"You don't understand. It's not like here. It's not like this house. Like your house. Full of people and friends your own age coming and going. It's my grandmother's flat, and she doesn't want my friends around the place. She gets headaches, she says. Sometimes Emma comes, but Gran doesn't really like her much, and so it's always a bit tense, and we spend most of the time in my room. Once she came, and both Mummy and Gran were out, so we spent the whole afternoon in the bath, washing our hair and putting on scent and painting our toenails with silver polish. When I'm in Emma's house, it doesn't seem to matter what we do. Her mother's out most of the time, working. She edits a magazine. And the au pair is usually quite fun and lets us cook and make disgusting puddings."

She stopped, giving Rory an opportunity to comment in some

way on this flood of confidence, but he said nothing. After a bit, Lucy went on.

"It's so different here. You can do anything, and if there's nothing to do, you can go out and shop and walk about, or go to the beach, or exploring, or out at night and nobody stops you. And here, they all call me duck, or darling, but at the same time they treat me like a grown-up. As though I were a person, not a child. Gran and Mummy call me Lucy. Just that. But I never feel I'm a proper person. I'm fourteen now, and sometimes I feel I've done nothing except go to school. It wouldn't be so bad if I had a brother or a sister. 'Specially a brother. Because just being with women all the time can be dreadfully lowering. They talk about such unimportant things. Like clothes, or restaurants, or other people. . . ."

"Where do you go to school?"

"It's called Stanbrook. Quite near where we live. I get the tube, two stops. I really like it, and the teachers, the head; and I met Emma there. We do things like go to concerts and art exhibitions, and we go swimming and do games in the park. But it's all-girls, and sometimes I think it would be really fun to go to a comprehensive. You'd meet so many different people."

Rory said, "How about your father?"

"I don't see him much, because Mummy doesn't like me seeing him; and anyway he's got a new wife, and she doesn't want me around much either. I've got a grandfather, called Jeffrey Sutton. He's Carrie's father. But he lives in Cornwall with a new young wife and two little new children."

"Can't you go and stay there?"

"Yes, I could, but Gran's bitter about him, and unforgiving, and his name is scarcely ever mentioned. One day I'll really be brave and strong and say I want to go and stay. But I suppose I'll have to wait until I'm a bit older to do that."

"You don't have to wait. You have to do it *now*."

"I think," said Lucy sadly, "I haven't the nerve. I simply hate rows and asserting myself. I did have one row with Mummy and Gran about having my ears pierced. Everyone at school has got pierced ears, but they wouldn't let me. It's such a little thing, but the row went on for days, and I couldn't bear it, so I just caved in. I'm dreadfully feeble about things like that."

Rory said, "I think you'd look good with pierced ears. You could have gold rings." He grinned. "Like me."

"I wouldn't just have one. I'd have two."

"Get them done here. There's a jeweller in Kingsferry."

"My mother would die."

"Your mother's in America?"

"How did you know that?"

"Elfrida told Ma and she told me."

"She's got a boy-friend, Randall Fischer. She's in Florida with him. She went for Christmas. That's why I came here with Carrie. I was asked, too, but I didn't want to go. I'd just have been in the way. Besides," she added, "I don't really like him much."

He said nothing to this, and it occurred to Lucy that he was very good at listening. She wondered if this gift came naturally to him, or whether his father had taught him the importance of silence at the appropriate time. And she remembered that day in London when Carrie had suddenly appeared, just when Lucy was yearning for a confidante. She had thought that she could talk to Carrie, could open her heart to her, but Carrie, returning from Austria, was obscurely different, and clearly in no mood for confidences. Withdrawn, perhaps, was the word, as though some part of her had stayed in another place. But Rory Kennedy was different. Rory had time to listen, and was clearly sympathetic. Lucy found herself filled with grateful affection.

She said, "I'm sorry. I didn't mean to say all this. It's just that it's all been so much fun. Being with Elfrida and Oscar, and learning to do reels, and all the other people of my own age. And thinking that Christmas this year is going to be a real one, and not just eating roast pheasant with Mummy and Gran, or even going out to some boring restaurant because they can't be bothered to cook. And the snow and everything. And the church. And the fairy lights going up. . . ."

Her voice trailed away. She was finished. There was nothing more to say. She thought of the flat and London, and then stuffed the image away at the back of her mind and slammed down an imaginary lid. There was no point remembering. No point thinking about having to return. No point in spoiling this moment, this hour, this day. Now.

He was watching her. She met his eyes, and smiled. He said, "Do you want to come sledging this afternoon?"

"Are you going?"

"Why not? I'll ring up some of the others. We'll go to the golf course . . . there are some really good slopes." He glanced at his watch. "It's nearly twelve. We'll need to get off early, before it gets dark. How about you come back home with me now and we'll get my ma to give us some food, and get hold of the others?"

Lucy said, "I haven't got a sledge."

"We've got three or four in the garage. You can borrow one of those." He pulled himself to his feet. "Come on."

"But won't your mother . . . ?"

"*No,* she won't mind. She won't complain, and there'll be enough food to feed an army. There always is." He reached down and took her arm and hauled Lucy to her feet. "Stop being so worried," he told her. "Stop putting difficulties in your own way."

"Is that what I'm doing?"

"Not any more."

ELFRIDA

The Kingsferry shopping expedition had been highly successful. Not only had Sam and Carrie brought back with them a load of cardboard boxes stuffed with food, vegetables, cereals, fruit, and Christmas goodies, but boxes of wine, crates of beer, mixers, Coke, and six bottles of Grouse whisky. Moreover, they had managed to run down the whereabouts of the Gent's Outfitters, where Sam had kitted himself out with a wardrobe of country clothes—corduroy trousers, warm shirts, a thick ribbed sweater, a pair of Timberland boots, and a Barbour jacket.

Sam put his new clothes on for lunch, and they all admired his suave and casual appearance. After lunch, he shrugged himself into his Barbour, and he and Oscar set off to walk to the Golf Club, where Sam had made an appointment with the secretary, because he wished to talk about the possibility of becoming a member. Elfrida, watching them go as they strode side by side down the snowy pavement, thought that they looked companionable. It was good for Oscar to have a bit of masculine company.

So she and Carrie were left to prepare for the arrival, at four o'clock, of Sir James Erskine-Earle. The first thing to decide was where they should give him his tea. Elfrida thought the kitchen . . . no point in standing on ceremony. But Carrie said that was all right for someone you *knew,* but perhaps Sir James would be a bit put out if asked to put his knees under the kitchen table and drink his tea from a mug.

Elfrida saw her point. "Then we'll have it in the sitting-room."

"What, all perched around the fireside?"

"Why not?"

"Men hate perching. Unless they're trained to it, like vicars. They can't manage cups, saucers, and fairy cakes all at the same time. Let's have it on the table in the bay window . . . all laid out and proper, like Mother used to do."

"I shall have to find a dainty tea-cloth."

"Bet there's one lurking in Mrs. Snead's cupboard. Shall I make some scones?"

Elfrida was impressed. "*Can* you?"

"Of course. And you can go and buy iced fancies from the baker."

Elfrida put on her blanket coat and went. The baker didn't sell iced fancies, but had gingerbreads instead, so she bought one, and a jar of home-made bramble jelly.

"Are you having a party, Mrs. Phipps?" asked the girl, giving Elfrida her change. And Elfrida said, no, not exactly, just somebody coming for afternoon tea.

Back at the Estate House, Carrie's scones were already in the oven and smelling delicious. Elfrida produced the gingerbread and the jam, found a tray, and stacked it with the best, if mismatched, plates, cups, and saucers. She found a sugar-bowl and a butter dish, and even a butter-knife.

"We are going to be very genteel," she said. She found teaspoons, and gave the inside of the teapot a good scour.

Upstairs, she unearthed a tea-cloth from Mrs. Snead's linen cupboard. Starched and ironed, it looked quite festive spread upon the old table. She laid out five plates and small knives, the cups and saucers, the butter dish, and the jam jar. There weren't any flowers, but perhaps Sir James Erskine-Earle wouldn't mind too much about that.

She turned from the table with the empty tray in her hand and looked across the room at her little picture, which, perhaps, after today, would be gone forever. It was hanging very slightly crooked, so she went over to set it straight, giving it a loving pat, as though it were a child encouraged to be on its best behaviour.

"*If* I may not have time to say goodbye," she told it, "I will now. It's been lovely having you."

Oscar and Sam returned from the Golf Club in good time, and good heart. The interview with the club secretary had been satisfactory. Sam had been told that there was a waiting list for members, but as he was going to be a resident of Buckly, it would probably be possible to jump the queue. They had been introduced to the captain and a few other members, admired portraits and trophies, and then walked home.

Oscar had, clearly, enjoyed his small outing. Recalling his only other visit to the Golf Club, which had ended so disastrously with a panic-stricken escape, Elfrida gave silent thanks and wanted to hug him. But instead she went upstairs to comb her flaming hair and put on another layer of lipstick.

When he came, on the dot of four o'clock, Sir James Erskine-Earle was something of a surprise. The front-door bell shrilled and Elfrida ran down to let him in, and was a little taken aback to be faced by a man so young. And although he had come straight from some meeting about the War Memorial, he was attired as though for gardening, in elderly tweed knickerbockers and a jacket that seemed to have lost most of its buttons. His shirt collar was frayed and his V-necked pullover had a small hole in it. When she opened the door he removed his tweed cap, and she saw his mousy hair, cut like a schoolboy's.

"Mrs. Phipps?"

"Yes. Sir James . . ." They shook hands. "Please come in." Leading him upstairs, "It is so good of you to come at such short notice," she said.

"Not at all." He had a charming voice and an ingenuous smile. "I always enjoy such occasions, when I am asked to cast my eye over something special."

She led him into the sitting-room and introduced him to the

others, who were all standing about looking a bit ill at ease, as though it were they whom Sir James Erskine-Earle had come to appraise. "Oscar Blundell. And Carrie, my niece. And Sam Howard, who is coming to run the old woollen mill in Buckly."

"We spoke on the phone, I think. How splendid to meet you. You're with Sturrock and Swinfield? I was at Eton with one of the Swinfields, but I think not your chairman." He looked about him. "This is a most surprising house. From the outside one has no idea of its splendour. It was part of Corrydale, I understand."

"Yes, but hasn't been for some years," Oscar told him. "Perhaps you knew my uncle, Hector McLennan?"

"No, not well. I was working in London for some years. I didn't come north until my father died and we all came to live at Kingsferry. Bit of a culture shock for my family, but they seem to have taken it in their stride." He moved, inevitably, over to the window, as newcomers always did. It was dark, but Elfrida had not drawn the curtains, and across the street the twinkling Christmas fairy lights shone like jewels against the old stone face of the church. "What an outlook. And so close to the church. You must be able to hear the organ from here. Marvellous instrument. We're so fortunate. . . ." He turned back to face them all. "But I mustn't waste your time rubber-necking. Where is this picture you want me to see?"

"It's . . ." Elfrida cleared her throat. "It's here."

"I see. In solitary state."

"We have no other pictures."

"May I take it down?"

"But of course."

He crossed the room, gently took the frame in his hands and lifted it down, holding it as delicately as if it were a piece of the finest porcelain. "What a lovely thing." He tilted it beneath the light of the lamp that stood on Oscar's table. "Sir David Wilkie."

"Yes. I've always believed so."

"A portrait of his parents. Did you know that? Painted, I suppose, about 1835."

"I didn't know it was his parents. I thought just a sweet elderly couple."

A silence fell. All faintly unnerved, they waited for his verdict. Sir James Erskine-Earle took his time, first reaching into the pocket of his reprehensible jacket to bring out a pair of rimless spectacles. Putting these on, he now resembled a young and penniless student. Perhaps a medical student, for his hands were as sensitive as a surgeon's. Peering, he examined. Touched with his fingertips, turned the painting over, and closely inspected the back.

Finally, he laid the picture carefully down on Oscar's table. "How did you come by it, Mrs. Phipps?"

"It was a present. A long time ago. Thirty years. From a friend."

"And do you know where he bought it?"

"I think in a junk-shop. In Chichester."

"Yes." He nodded. "That figures."

"I've . . . I've always believed . . . been led to believe . . . that it's an original. But I've never had it appraised, nor insured."

He looked at her, the reflected light from the lamp flashing from his spectacles, and he smiled. That engaging, youthful smile. He turned to lean against the table and took his spectacles off. He said, "I am really sorry, but it's not the original. It's a copy."

The stunned silence that followed was because nobody could think of anything to say.

"It is a most charming and beautifully executed work, but it isn't the original."

Oscar found his voice. "How can you know?"

"For one thing, it's not signed. The style, the subject, I agree, is unmistakably Wilkie's, but there is no signature. The other reason I know that it is a copy is that, oddly enough, the original passed through Boothby's sale-room in Bond Street only about a year ago. It went to a dealer from the United States who was bidding for some museum or other. It was larger than your little painting, Mrs. Phipps, which leads me to believe that this copy was never intended as a forgery, but more as a work of respect and admiration. A student, perhaps, wishing to emulate the master's style. It is certainly an extraordinary simulation . . . the brushwork, the colour, the light. A beautiful piece of art. If imitation is the sincerest form of flattery, one wonders who it was who set himself to embark upon such a painstaking task."

Again, silence fell upon the room. Finally, Elfrida made herself ask the dreaded question.

"What is it worth, Sir James?"

"Please. Jamie."

"Well . . . Jamie . . . what do you think it is worth?"

"If it had been the original, I should have said in the region of eighty-five thousand pounds. I can't remember the *exact* sum it went for, but something like that."

"And as it isn't the original, but only a copy?"

"A thousand? Maybe more, maybe less. It would depend on the market. Nothing is worth anything unless somebody wants it."

A thousand. A copy, and worth only a thousand. Elfrida's little nest-egg, her insurance against an impoverished and lonely future. A thousand. In a funny way, for herself, she didn't particularly mind. There was no point in selling it, and so she could go on enjoying it for the rest of her life. But for Oscar she knew an agonizing disappointment. All her plans for buying Hughie out and ensuring Oscar's security were to come for nothing. All her dreams reduced to dust, to rubbish. She saw them as though being swept away, out of reach, so much flotsam in a swift-flowing river. Gone.

For a dreadful moment she thought she might be about to burst into tears. In some despair she turned to Carrie, and Carrie's beautiful dark eyes were upon her, warm with sympathy and understanding. Elfrida opened her mouth to say something, but there were no words, and Carrie came to her rescue.

"I think," said Carrie, "that I shall go downstairs and boil a kettle, and we'll all have a restoring cup of tea."

And then Sam spoke, for the first time since he had been introduced to Jamie Erskine-Earle. "I'll come with you, lend you a hand."

Elfrida knew perfectly well that it didn't take two people to boil a kettle, but she was grateful to Sam for his tact, and for removing his presence from a difficult situation. She found herself wishing that Sir James Erskine-Earle would remove himself, too. Asked, he had come to appraise her little painting, and she knew that it wasn't his fault that it was a fake, but his knowledge and expertise had spoilt so much, and now Oscar would have no alternative but to sell his half of the house. She didn't mind so much about Sam having it. But she minded dreadfully about Oscar *not* having it.

When the others had gone and closed the door behind them, there was a pregnant silence. Perhaps Jamie Erskine-Earle sensed Elfrida's resentment, for he said, again, "I am so sorry."

She knew impatience; with herself and with him. "Oh, for goodness' sake. It's not your fault."

Carefully, precisely, he rehung the little picture. The old lady in her yellow shawl gazed benevolently down at him, as Elfrida found herself incapable of doing. He said, "At least . . . it will continue to give you joy."

"It will never be quite the same as before."

Oscar, sensing tension, moved into the conversation. "It is very precious to Elfrida, nevertheless. I am relieved that she has no reason to let it go."

"Oh, Oscar, I have *every* reason. It's simply a *picture*. But not for a thousand. That sort of money is laughable."

"Elfrida. It will be all right."

She turned her back on both of them and went to the fire, in need of something to do that might assuage her disappointment; she took a log from the basket and hurled it onto the flames. She stood watching it catch, and flame.

And then, behind her, Jamie spoke again. "I'm sorry, I do hope you don't think I'm being curious, but who is the owner of that interesting little clock?"

For an instant, Elfrida thought that she had misheard. She turned to frown at him in puzzlement. "The *clock*?"

"It caught my eye. So unusual . . ."

Oscar told him, "It is Elfrida's."

"I wonder . . . may I look?"

Elfrida nodded. She moved aside, and Jamie Erskine-Earle put his spectacles on again and came to her side and took the little clock down from its place in the middle of the mantelshelf. For the second time she and Oscar watched in silence while he examined it with minute care. Waiting, Elfrida decided that if he told her it was a worthless bibelot, no more, she would brain him with the coal shovel.

He said, "A travelling chronometer. Marvellous. How did you come by this little treasure?"

"Do you mean treasure as sentimental, or treasure as in trove?"

He answered politely. "I'm not sure."

Brusquely, she told him. "It was left to me by an elderly godfather. An old sea-faring man." And then, knowing that she sounded thoroughly cross, relented a little. "You can see, one dial is for hours, one for minutes, and one for seconds. I have to wind it every day. I suppose I could get it fitted with a battery, but it seems . . ."

"Heaven forbid. It's far too rare."

"Rare? Surely it's just an old-fashioned sea-going clock?"

"Practical. But handsome, too."

She looked at it, in his hands, and all at once the clock took on a new lustre, as everyday and familiar objects sometimes do when admired by another. The outside leather was worn, but inside still rich and dark; and the lid, which folded across like the cover of a book, was lined with a bruised pad of velvet the colour of coral. Around the circular face, which contained the dials, the leather was decorated with a wreath of miniature golden leaves, and this pattern was repeated around the edge of the frame. The key, the hinges, the tiny locks were brass.

She said, "I don't even know how old it is. . . . Perhaps you can tell me."

"Alas, I am not a clock expert. But," he added, "I have a colleague who *is*. If you want . . . if you will let me . . . I can show it to him."

"Why?"

"Because I think it is special."

"How special?"

"We used the word 'treasure.' "

"You mean, you think it's worth something?"

"I would rather not say. I'm not sufficiently specialized."

"It wouldn't be worth seventy-five thousand pounds, would it?" She asked the question bluntly, expecting a rueful shake of the head, or even derisive laughter.

But Jamie Erskine-Earle did not laugh. He said, "I really don't know. Mrs. Phipps, would you . . . would you let me take it away with me? If I can't get hold of my colleague I can speak to him on the telephone, or send him a photograph of the clock. I shall, of course, give you a receipt for it, and will keep it under lock and key."

Suddenly it was ludicrous. "In Hampshire," she told him, "in my little cottage in Dibton, it sat on the mantelpiece in my downstairs sitting-room, and I never even locked the door."

"Then may I congratulate you on your good luck. It's not insured," he added, and he was stating a fact, not asking a question.

"No, of course it's not. It's just a little thing I've had for years and take everywhere with me."

"If I may reiterate, a very special little thing. May I take it with me?"

"Of course."

"If I could have . . . a box . . . or something to wrap it in. My handkerchief is not exactly suitable."

Oscar went to his table and pulled out a drawer and unearthed a sheet of bubble wrap which he had salvaged from a parcel of new books.

"Will this do?"

"Perfect. And a sheet of writing-paper for a receipt? I usually carry a pad of official forms, but of course, today I have left them at home."

He gave Oscar the clock and Oscar wrapped it into a bulbous bundle, and Jamie Erskine-Earle sat at his desk and wrote out his receipt. "I had better keep that," Oscar told him. "Elfrida is inclined to lose things." And he stowed it away in the top pocket of his jacket.

"There's just one thing," said Elfrida.

"Yes, Mrs. Phipps?"

"Don't let's talk much about the clock when Sam and Carrie come back. We all got too worked up about the David Wilkie, and I couldn't bear raised and dashed hopes again. Can we just say that you think I should insure it, and you're going to give me a valuation?"

"Of course. A splendid explanation. And one, moreover, that happens to be true. . . ."

That evening, trying to do something about supper, Elfrida felt that she had spent the entire afternoon on a roller-coaster. And because of all the excitement, disappointment, and then re-kindled expectations, she had clean forgot all about Lucy. She was stirring a bolognese sauce in a fairly distracted and unconcentrated fashion when Lucy turned up, coming into the kitchen by way of the back door.

Elfrida glanced at the old kitchen clock. It was nearly seven. She stared at Lucy, trying to remember what the child had been doing all day.

Lucy said, "Yes, it's me."

"Oh, darling, I'm sorry."

"You look as though I was the *very* last person you expected to see."

"I'm doing my preoccupied act. So much has been happening here, and you just floated out of my mind. But now you've floated in again, which is very delightful."

"What's been happening?" Lucy pulled off her woollen hat and then began to undo the fastenings of her jacket. "Have I missed something?"

"Not really. Just a nice man came for tea. Carrie made scones. I think he ate most of them."

"Who was the nice man?"

"He's called Sir James Erskine-Earle. He lives at Kingsferry House."

Lucy said, "I've just been to Kingsferry. With Rory."

"I thought you'd gone sledging."

"Yes, we did, but then it got dark, so we went back to the Manse for tea, and then Rory and I went to Kingsferry."

"Have you been shopping again?"

"No. Not exactly."

Elfrida, her attention caught, became intrigued. Lucy's expression was secret, teasing. As though she couldn't stop smiling.

"You look like the Cheshire cat. What have you been up to?"

Lucy put up a hand and tossed her long hair back from her neck, and Elfrida saw the gleam of gold.

"I've had my ears pierced. The jeweller in Kingsferry did it for me. Rory took me. And he bought me the sleepers for Christmas. Real jewellery. Earrings."

"Oh, darling . . ."

"I've been wanting them for ages. . . ."

"Let me look."

"But Mummy wouldn't let me. . . ."

"They're wonderful. So grown up. They make you look so grown up. What a generous present."

"I don't think," said Lucy, "I've ever been given anything I wanted more."

LUCY

WEDNESDAY, DECEMBER 20TH

I think this has been one of the best days of my life. Lots and lots of snow everywhere and it all looks so pretty. This morning I did Christmas shopping, and then when I got back, Rory was here, talking to Elfrida, with the television set he is going to lend me. He carried it up to my room and made it work and then we sat and talked, and somehow he was so easy to talk to that I just told him everything; about boring London and having to live in the flat, and Mummy and Gran and Randall Fischer. And about Dad and Marilyn, and about the family in Cornwall. It was so wonderful having someone listen and not interrupt and keep trying to cheer me up or jolly me along, or even to say I was talking a lot of rubbish. Or didn't know what I was talking about.

He just listened.

When I'd run out of things to say, we drove back to the Manse and Mrs. Kennedy made us beefburgers. Rory rang some friends and we all went sledging on the golf course, which was tremendous fun and totally exhausting. We sledged till it got dark and then went back to the Manse for tea, and then Rory asked his father if we could borrow the car again, and Mr. Kennedy said yes, so Rory took me to

Kingsferry. It is a very old and unexpected sort of town, with lots of shops. We parked the car and went to the jeweller, and the man there pierced my ears, in a moment, and it didn't hurt a bit. He fixed in little gold rings called sleepers.

I had told Rory that I wasn't allowed to have them at home, and he said I wasn't at home now, I was with him; and he paid for the piercing and the rings, and said it is his Christmas present for me.

On the way back in the car, we talked some more, and I feel as though I have reached a turning point, or a watershed. Rory says I have to remember a number of things. These are the things.

I get good marks at school, so I am not stupid.

If I don't assert myself a bit, nobody else is going to.

I have to assert myself by reasoned conversation, not sulks.

If I want to go to Cornwall to see my grandfather and Serena and Amy and Ben, then I should go. There is absolutely nothing to stop me. I can make my own arrangements, get my grandfather to invite me, and simply go.

I must be more enterprising. I can take care of myself. I know about things like Ecstasy tablets at parties; and about drunks and druggies and flashers and sex maniacs and homely old men who come and talk to you at bus stations.

Perhaps I should think about going to a co-educational boarding-school to do my A levels. Last two years of school. I'd never thought of that. I shall put the idea into Mummy's head, and make her talk it through. I shall get Miss Maxwell-Brown on my side. And that would only be two years away.

Just having something new to plan and look forward to makes me feel much more determined.

I wish I had a brother like Rory.

No, I don't. Because if he was my brother it wouldn't be the same.

My earrings don't hurt. When Gran and Mummy see them, they will know that I have changed. That I am doing what I want. That I can make my own decisions. I'm not a little child any more.

They had someone for tea here called Sir James Erskine-Earle. He has taken Elfrida's clock to value it for insurance. Carrie said he ate six scones.

Tomorrow is the first day of the rest of my life.

SAM

Sam opened his eyes to darkness and bitter cold. It was the cold that had woken him, and he realized that his eiderdown quilt had slipped off the bed and he was shivering beneath the inadequate comfort of two blankets and an icy, monogrammed linen sheet. The curtains at his window were, as always, drawn back, and the window open—though not very wide—and a blast of air assailed him, chill as the sensation on opening a deep freeze. During the night, it was obvious the temperature had dropped to an uncomfortable low.

He heaved himself over, reached down for the quilt and dragged it back into place. He was still cold, but its soft, downy weight was a comfort. Waiting for warmth, he reached out a hand, turned on his bedside light, and looked at his watch. Half past seven in the morning.

His room, by now familiar, lay about him, the corners deep in shadow. There was not much furniture. A huge wardrobe, which contained all he at the moment possessed, and a Victorian wash-stand doing duty as a dressing-table. It had a liver-coloured marble top, and on it stood a large flowered bowl and a ewer for water. The only mirror was inside the wardrobe door, and there was one small, ornate chair. Not a room for working in, nor a room for sitting in, but perfectly adequate for the business of sleeping.

And making business-like calls on his mobile phone.

He lay, slowly unfreezing, and wondered why it all rendered him such satisfaction. He decided that the proportions of the room were exactly right; the empty walls undemanding, the threadbare curtains of faded cretonne, long enough to lie in festoons upon the worn carpet, reminiscent of his mother's curtains in the old house at Radley Hill. They were hung by brass rings, upon a brass pole with pineapple filials, and when drawn made a satisfactory clatter.

This sound brought back the sound of his mother's voice. "Darling, wake up. It's nearly time for breakfast."

Nostalgia, perhaps, but at its best.

The whole house was the same. The spaciousness, the handsome half-empty rooms, with their elaborate cornices and tall panelled doors. The shallow-stepped staircase, rising in flights to the attics, with its banister of polished Baltic pine, the old-fashioned but perfectly recognizable kitchen; the bathrooms panelled in white-painted tongue-and-groove, complete with original Victorian fittings, and lavatory cisterns with chains and handles with PULL written on them.

It had all felt, from that very first embarrassing evening, a bit like coming home.

From the first moment, the house had appealed to Sam. Spoken to him, welcomed him. He thought back over the extraordinarily coincidental chain of events that had brought him here, at this particular time, and then left him marooned, so that he had no choice but to stay. With hindsight, it seemed as though it had all been carefully mapped out by fate. Some—hopefully benign—being; the influence of his star sign, perhaps, or the incomprehensible magnetism of ancient lay lines.

Meeting Hughie McLennan in London had been the first link in the chain. Being handed the key of Hughie's house in Creagan. Tossing a coin as he had sat in his car outside the church hall in Buckly. If it had come up heads, he would have driven straight back to Inverness, and in all likelihood would have been able to traverse the road across the Black Isle before the snow rendered it impassable. But instead it had come up tails, and he had diverted, in order to drive to Creagan.

If Sam had found the house shuttered and unoccupied, as he

expected it to be, he would not have dallied. Simply locating the place was all he had had in mind, and its position, size, and air of solid Victorian dignity would have been enough to ensure that he return for a more detailed viewing. But it hadn't been empty. Lights had blazed from upstairs windows, and, with curiosity aroused, he had left his car by the pavement's edge, walked up the path, and rung the bell.

After that, he had been caught, and there was no going back.

Now he had lived here for two days, in the company of four other vaguely connected people, and would be staying until after Christmas was a thing of the past. He had intended spending this time sorting out his own private priorities for the mill, working with laptop and calculator. But idleness had been forced upon him, on account of laptop, calculator, files, essential telephone numbers, and papers all having been left behind in his hotel room in Inverness. All he had brought to the meeting in Buckly were his mobile phone, a slim briefcase, and the key to the Estate House.

Because work was impossible, he had found it extraordinarily easy to switch off and slow down into a state of mind that he had not experienced for years. Horizons shrank. Priorities were altered. It felt a little like being on board a ship, isolated from the rest of the world but intensely involved with the other passengers. Strangers who were slowly becoming as close as the family he no longer possessed. The house, like that ship, contained them all, and did so with a certain grace, as though content to have the spacious rooms filled once more—doors standing open, fires lighted, voices calling, footsteps on the stairs.

A good house, and Sam wanted it. That was the problem. He wished to buy it from Hughie and Oscar, and have it for his own. Its location was perfect. . . . It would take him only twenty minutes, no more, to drive the empty roads to the mill each morning, and home again at the end of the day's work. He could step out of the front door and walk to the Golf Club. Short of a can of beer or a loaf of bread or a pint of milk, he only had to cross the square to the little supermarket.

As well, it would be a house with a future. His future. Owning it,

Sam would never have to leave. Unlike a tiny terrace house, or a picturesque, rose-smothered cottage, it was capable of accommodating anything he chose to throw at it. It was this awareness of longevity that most attracted him. He would soon be forty. He didn't want to go on moving; buying and selling, starting anew. He wanted this to be the last start. He wanted to stay. Here.

But half of it belonged to Oscar Blundell, and this was where he and Elfrida lived. It, and each other, seemed to be all they had. A dull fellow, Hughie had told Sam. My cousin is a dull fellow. But Sam didn't think Oscar was dull in the least. He liked him enormously and this made nothing easier.

If Sam had been Hughie, he would have kept his mouth shut about Elfrida's little picture. He would never have taken the trouble to telephone Janey in London and find out the whereabouts of the local Boothby's representative, Sir James Erskine-Earle. The thought of selling the painting had occurred to Elfrida, but she was so vaguely unworldly about practical matters that she would never have got around to doing anything dynamic on her own. At the end of the day, the visit from James Erskine-Earle had solved nothing, because the painting was a fake. So they were all back where they had started. In a way Sam wished the David Wilkie had been rare, authentic, and worth a million, so that he could put his own pipe-dreams away and go off and look for somewhere else to live.

And yet . . . he couldn't get rid of the feeling that here, in this square, unadorned, solid Victorian town house, he was destined to settle and spend the rest of his days.

Useless reflections. With some effort he put them out of his mind and got out of bed to close the window. His room was at the back of the Estate House, and in the light of the street lamp which stood by the wooden gate he saw the terraced garden, climbing up to the stand of pines, all petrified with cold, glittering with frost. There was not a breath of wind. No sound.

As a boy in Yorkshire, he had from time to time risen very early and gone out for a long hike, up into the moors to some elevated crag from which he could watch the sun rise. No dawn was quite the same as another, and the filling of the sky with light had always seemed a miracle. He remembered returning home after these early expeditions, running down grassy paths and leaping streams, bursting with high spirits and energy, aware that much of his happiness came of knowing that a huge breakfast would be waiting for him when he finally got home.

It was a long time since he had watched a sunrise. Today, the shortest day of the year, was perhaps as good a morning as any to repeat the experience. He dressed, laced his boots, pulled on his Barbour, felt in the pockets for his thick leather driving gloves. He went quietly out of his room, closing the door behind him with elaborate care, and then downstairs. In the empty kitchen, he found Horace snoozing in his basket.

"Want a walk?"

Horace, recovered from his encounter with the Rottweiler, did. Sam found Elfrida's shopping list and scribbled a note to her, and then went down the hall and took from the coat-stand his tweed cap and a muffler which did not belong to him but felt comforting knotted around his neck. He turned the key of the front door and opened it, and stepped out into the still, dark, paralysing cold of the morning. Iced snow crunched beneath his boots. As he opened the gate, he heard the sound of an engine and saw the great gritting lorry, headlights beaming, snow-plough secured, lumber across the square and down the street towards the main road.

Sam and the dog set off in the other direction.

They went by way of the Golf Club and the beach, leaving the street lamps of the town behind them. The sky was clear, and a single star hung in the dark heavens, but a mist lay along the distant margins of the sea. The tide was far out, the sand frozen, and shallow rock-pools hard as iron. The wind, stirring from the north, had an edge to it like a knife, and he pulled the soft folds of his muffler up and around his chin. He thought of other lands on this latitude, only a bit south of sixty degrees. To the west, beyond the Atlantic, Labrador, the Hudson Bay. To the east, Scandinavia and the wastes of Siberia. There, a man stepping out of doors for five minutes in mid-winter would probably freeze to death. And yet, here he was, striding like any holiday-maker down a beach with a dog at his heels, and not unduly perturbed by the cold.

The Gulf Stream was, indeed, a marvellous invention.

At a brisk pace, he covered the length of the beach, and then turned inland. He climbed over the dunes, crossed the track, the two fairways of the golf course, and then strode up the steep slope that lay beyond, a winding path which led uphill between thick clumps of gorse. By the time he reached the top he was warm with exertion, and Horace panting furiously. He came to a fence and a stile. By now the dark of the sky had paled to grey, and the star was gone. He leaned against the stile, sheltered from the north by the thick wind-break of the gorse, and turned to face the sea. He saw the long line of the horizon, the bay sweeping out to the point where the lighthouse still blinked. Beyond it, to the south-east, the sky was stained with pink, the coming light diffused by mist. It was as good a viewpoint as any. He looked at his watch and saw that it was eight-forty. He sat on the wooden step of the stile and waited.

The dog sat at his knee. Sam pulled off his glove and laid his hand on the dog's head and touched the soft, silky fur, the velvety ears. The world, the empty universe belonged, at that moment, to just the two of them. From this small elevation, it seemed limitless, new-minted, pristine, as though only yesterday had been the day of the Creation.

He remembered, for no particular reason, that afternoon in London when he had walked down the King's Road in the wet dusk, the streets clogged with shoppers and traffic, and told himself that there was no person in the world who would expect a Christmas present from him. So he had arrived in Creagan totally unprepared. But now he must, sometime, get busy, so that on Christmas morning he would have packages to hand out. Four of them. There were four. Or maybe five, including the mysterious Mrs. Snead, whom he had not yet encountered. Oscar, Elfrida, Lucy, Carrie.

Carrie.

Losing Deborah, closing up the apartment, leaving New York and returning to London and his new job, the last thing on his mind had been the possibility of another woman coming into his life. Right now, he needed an emotional involvement as he needed a hole in the head. But Carrie had been waiting for him, the last link on that extraordinary chain of coincidences, compounding the sensation that he was a helpless pawn in fate's game. He had walked, in the snow, through the gate of the Estate House, up the path, and pressed the bell. And it was Carrie who, eventually, had opened the door to him.

Carrie, with her smooth cap of chestnut hair, her dark and expressive eyes, her slenderness, her long neck. Her slanting eyebrows, the fascinating mole at one end of her mouth. Her voice, deep-toned, with an underlying suggestion of laughter, so that he could never be sure when she teased or when she was serious. Her wrists were narrow, her hands long-fingered and capable, with unpainted nails, and she wore on her right hand an antique sapphire-and-diamond ring which looked as though it might have once been pressed upon her by some besotted man, mad to marry her. Or perhaps left, as a bequest, by an adoring elderly relation.

She was totally without artifice. If she had nothing to say, she said nothing. If she spoke, or aired an opinion, it was deliberate, considered, intelligent. She did not seem to know the meaning of small talk, and while others chatted, over meals or an evening drink, she was always attentive, but often silent. Her relationship with Elfrida and Lucy was, however, deeply affectionate and caring. With the young girl, Carrie was quite protective, but not in a smothering way. Lucy came and went, but always there were endearments for her, casual hugs, a listening ear. Laughter.

As for Sam, he found it impossible to guess what Carrie thought of him. She was totally at ease, in charge of the situation, but at the same time reserved to the point of withdrawal. The one time he had got her to himself for more than five minutes—which was when they had driven to Kingsferry to do the huge supermarket shopping—he had thought that he could break through this barrier, but every time the conversation veered around to Carrie and her private life, she had fallen silent, and then, speaking, turned the conversation into a totally different direction. When Sam, with some difficulty, had run to earth the Gent's Outfitters in Kingsferry, he had expected that she would come into the shop with him; make suggestions, choices; even joke about his choice of boxer shorts and pyjamas (which the Gent's Outfitters called Intimate Apparel); or insist on choosing Sam some dreadful and unsuitable tie. But she did none of these things. Instead, she crossed the road to the ironmonger, where she bought Elfrida a new baking dish and a pudding bowl. So Sam did his intimate shopping on his own, and when he got back to the car she was waiting for him, reading *The Times,* and not overly interested in his purchases.

He found himself wondering if she had once been married, but knew that he could never pluck up the nerve to ask such a question. It was, after all, nothing to do with him. That first evening, while they sat and waited for Oscar and Elfrida to return from their party, she had imparted a little casual information about herself.

That was all. She enlarged on nothing, volunteered no gratuitous information, and he was left with the sense of a strong door firmly shut between them, and nothing was going to persuade Carrie to open it.

About Lucy, she was more open. She spoke, as well, about her own father, and when she did this, her voice warmed, her lovely eyes shone, and she became quite animated and informative. Her father was called Jeffrey, and lived, with his second and much younger wife, in Cornwall. "He's an amazing man," Carrie had said. "The most giving of men. He stayed with my mother, in some unhappiness, until Nicola and I were both adult and on our own, and only then did he light out and leave us all, and go off with Serena. If Lucy had had a father like Jeffrey, things would be so different for her. He wasn't just my father, he was my best friend. He opened every door, never stopped praising and encouraging. With a man like that behind me, I always believed I could do anything."

Anything. But sometime, somewhere along the line, something had gone wrong. And Carrie was not about to confide in Sam.

The less she spoke, the less she gave away, the more he longed to know. He wondered if this obsession was the beginning of falling in love with her. Otherwise, why should it matter so much? And what was the point of falling in love with a woman already deeply committed to her career and her ill-assorted family, who would never, in a thousand years, jettison the lot and come to live in the north of Scotland with Sam Howard?

All this quite apart from the fact that he was still married to Deborah.

The dog shifted and whined. Horace was growing cold. Sam was cold, too, but did not move. For, when he looked again, he saw that the faint shell-pink had exploded into an aureole of red and yellow, with vaporous streaks like flames. And over the shallow hills of the distant headland inched the first sliver of an orange sun. The curved rim of dazzling light touched the shifting sea, smudged shadows on the undulations of the sand, and drained darkness from the sky, so that gradually it was no longer sapphire-blue, but faded to aquamarine.

He watched, and lost all sense of time as the orange orb sailed up, out from behind the far side of the world. And it was the same fresh miracle that it had always been, and he forgot about being cold. The pinprick blink from the lighthouse, all at once, ceased. The new day had begun, and after today, the days would start to grow longer, and then it would be another year, and Sam, thinking about it, found himself unable to imagine what it might hold in store for him.

He walked back to Creagan at a brisk pace, following the narrow path that led along the top of the snow-covered links. The mist was dissolving, and the sky was a pale, pure blue, quite cloudless. By the time he reached the first of the houses, he saw that the morning was already on its way: cars came and went, shops were open; the first of the shoppers were out, with their baskets and plastic bags. The butcher was sweeping snow from his front step, and a young mother pulled her bundled baby along in a little wooden sledge.

He was ravenously hungry.

Letting himself into the house, he realized that it, too, was a hive of busy activity. From upstairs came the drone of a Hoover, and a female voice singing an old Beatles song.

"I love you, yeah yeah yeah. . . ."

The redoubtable Mrs. Snead, no doubt, come to muck them all out.

From the open kitchen door flooded light, and mouth-watering smells of bacon and coffee. He unclipped Horace's lead, took off his outer clothes, and went through the open door. There he found only Carrie, sitting surrounded by the detritus of other people's breakfasts. She was drinking coffee and reading *The Times,* but looked up, saw him, and said, "Good morning."

That first evening, a mere two days ago, when he had so gracelessly barged in, out of the dark and the snow, clutching Hughie McLennan's key, he had been knocked sideways by the unexpected glamour of the girl who had opened the door to him. She had, he later learned, been struck down by a bout of flu, or some unknown bug, and had only just risen from a bed of sickness, and because of this had looked pale, frail, and intensely vulnerable. He had still thought her sensational. But now the flu was a thing of the past, cast off by the resilience of youth, and this morning she wore a red cashmere sweater and the bright colour rendered her vital, radiant, and more attractive than ever. In his present mood of well-being he knew a physical urge to touch her, to sweep her up into his arms, embrace her, break down imagined barriers, and start to talk.

"Did you have a good walk?"

Mad impulses, prudently, retreated.

"Too far, perhaps. Horace is exhausted." Horace, slopping the water on the floor, was treating himself to a noisy drink.

"You must be frozen."

"No. I am warm from exertion. But starving."

"There's bacon." She laid the newspaper down and got to her feet.

"I guessed."

"I'll make fresh coffee."

"Carrie, I can do that."

"No." A plate sat on the warmer, covered by another plate. With oven-gloved hands she lifted it, set it down on the table, and with a certain flourish removed the top plate. He saw not only bacon, but eggs, a sausage, and a fried tomato. Everything sizzled. "I can. You start eating."

He looked at the feast in some amazement. "Who cooked all this?"

"I did. I reckoned you'd be hungry."

He felt much touched. "You are sweet."

"No problem."

He sat, and buttered a slice of toast. "Where is everybody?"

Carrie filled the kettle and plugged it in.

"Oh, around and about. They've all finished breakfast. Mrs. Snead has come, and I think Elfrida's making beds. Oscar's telephoning. We have to go and fetch the Christmas tree this morning. He wondered if you would do that, in your car. Easier to load trees in, and Oscar's a bit nervous of driving in snow."

"Where do I have to go for it?"

"Corrydale Estate. That's who he's phoning now. Some man called Charlie Miller. It's all ordered and everything, but he just wanted to be sure that Charlie was around when we went."

"We? Are you coming with me?"

"Oscar's drawn a map. I shall have to come, to be your navigator. Besides, I want to go to Corrydale. Oscar's told me all about it. How his grandmother used to live there, and then his uncle, and then Hughie. And Oscar used to spend holidays there when he was a little boy. He says the grounds and the garden used to be amazing, but of course it's different now, because it's an hotel. Anyway, I'd like to see it. The hotel's empty, so if Charlie Miller says we can, we could have a nose-around."

Sam, eating bacon, was filled with a silent satisfaction. He could think of no better way of spending this fine morning than driving Carrie to Corrydale, collecting the Christmas tree, and having a nose-around. It would be interesting to see what Hughie McLennan had once owned and then squandered. But he only said, "Right," and went on eating, because he didn't want Carrie to sense his pleasure, and then start backing off.

She spooned the ground coffee into the jug and poured on the boiling water. "Shall I make more toast?"

"That would be kind."

She made toast, and then poured coffee for him, refilled her own cup, and returned to her chair. Sam wondered if they were about to spend a few companionable moments together, but inevitably they were interrupted by Lucy, running downstairs and bursting in upon them.

"Carrie, Mrs. Snead says she's going to do a white wash and do you want anything done? Hello, Sam. Did you and Horace have a lovely walk?"

"We certainly did."

"When did you go?"

"About eight. It was still dark. We saw the sun rise."

"Oh, how lovely. I wish you'd taken me. I've never seen a proper sunrise. It must have been pretty, with all the snow on the golf course. Like Switzerland, or somewhere."

Carrie said, "Sam and I are going to Corrydale to fetch the Christmas tree. Do you want to come with us?"

"Oh . . ." Lucy made an agonized face. "Oh, I would *love* to, but . . . well . . . I've promised Mrs. Snead I'd help her. Do something. So I can't. And I really *want* to go and look at Corrydale."

Sam, loving Lucy for not coming, said, "I'll take you another time."

"Will you? Is that a promise? Oscar says it's the most wonderful place in the world, and that his grandmother used to have the most beautiful azaleas, in every single colour. And the grounds go down to the water, too, and he used to have a boat."

From upstairs, Mrs. Snead screeched. "*Lucy!* What about that laundry? I want to get it all collected. . . ."

Carrie made a comic face. "We'd better do what we're told, otherwise we'll be in trouble. Come on, Lucy. . . ."

And Sam, left on his own, drank hot fresh coffee and felt as contented as a well-fed schoolboy with a treat in the offing.

Oscar's little map of directions to Corrydale proved to be a meticulous plan of all that lay within the protection of the boundary wall. Which appeared to be a small maze of roads and drives, stands of woodland, and a long shoreline. Each estate worker's house had been drawn, in some detail, and named. Billicliffe's house; Rose Miller's house; the gamekeeper's house; Home Farm (Mains of Corrydale). The last was the gardener's house (Charlie Miller), alongside the walled garden, and the tractor shed. A little way off, along another winding driveway that ran parallel to the water, and standing, in some grandeur, all on its own, he had drawn Corrydale House, surrounded by formal gardens and with stepped terraces leading down to the meadows on the fringe of the firth.

It reminded Sam of the endpapers of a Pooh Bear book, but Carrie said it was a work of art and should be framed.

The road they followed took Sam and Carrie into new territory, where neither had ventured before. Instead of crossing the bridge over to Kingsferry, they forked right before reaching this and went by way of the old road, which headed west, winding through farmland, dipping and climbing, tunnelling down tall avenues of skeletal beech trees. All was thick with snow, but the morning had kept its promise and the sky was cloudless, the air sparkling with cold. There was little traffic, and few people about. A tractor, chuntering across a field with a load of hay for a huddle of sheep; a woman, hanging washing out in the still, freezing air; a red post-van, making its way up a rutted farm-lane.

On their left lay the great sea loch, penetrating inland for fifteen miles or more. The tide was at half-flood, and the water as blue as in summer. On the far shore, massive hills reared up into the sky, all blindingly white, save where dark rock stood sheer, or corries of scree tumbled, like waterfalls of stone.

Carrie said, "It's all huge, isn't it? Even the sky seems twice as big as it does anywhere else." She wore a black padded parka and her fur hat, and had put on dark glasses against the glare.

"No fog or pollution, I suppose. A clarity of air. Did you know that five of the finest salmon rivers in Scotland flow into this loch?"

"Who told you that?"

"Oscar."

"I supposed he fished them as a boy."

"Lucky boy."

Carrie scrutinized Oscar's map. "I think quite soon we'll be there. We come to the wall first, and then the main gate's about a quarter of a mile—"

The boundary wall appeared, almost at once, on the left-hand side of the road. Beyond this could be seen handsome trees, carefully positioned, suggesting parkland. The main gate, when they came to it, was flanked by two towering wellingtonias. A small lodge blew a plume of smoke into the air, and there was a line of washing out in the little garden, and a child's plastic tractor abandoned on the front-door step.

They saw the notice.

☆ ☆ ☆ ☆

CORRYDALE COUNTRY HOTEL. A.A. R.A.C. XXXX

Carrie said, "Here we go."

Sam turned in through the gates, and the formal drive led downhill between an avenue of huge oak trees. It was ridged with the tracks of other vehicles, recently come this way, and the snow barred with the blue shadows of the trees. After about a quarter of a mile, the road forked, and here stood a wooden signpost. To the right, HOTEL VISITORS. This track, unused, was white with virgin snow. Ahead, HOME

FARM AND SAWMILL, so they continued on their way. Carrie scanned Oscar's map.

"Next, we come to another fork and we go left again and we see Billicliffe's house."

"And who is Billicliffe?"

"He used to be the factor here. Elfrida and Oscar had to go and call on him to get *their* key. Elfrida told me he was a bit of an old bore, and the house was a tip, and they were both a little unkind about him. And then he confounded everybody by becoming extremely ill, and Oscar had to drive him to hospital. Where he is now . . . here's the fork in the road. So we go left. . . ."

The tyre tracks continued. Clearly a well-used access. There then was revealed, set back from the verge, the first of the estate workers' cottages.

"Here," said Carrie, "is where Major Billicliffe lives."

Sam, curious, slowed down to take a look at it. A small, stone-built house, soundly constructed, with a rural porch and two dormer windows set in the slated roof. A short driveway led from gate to door, where stood parked, and wearing at least ten inches of snow, an elderly Vauxhall, rusted, sad, and abandoned. The windows of the house were tightly closed, no light showed, and no smoke rose from the chimney.

"What a gloomy little place," Carrie remarked.

"Nothing's at its best when it's desolate."

They moved on, slowly, tyres crunching in icy ruts; exploring. The road twisted and turned in charmingly random fashion. Another corner, and now Rose Miller's cottage was there, a different kettle of fish altogether; snug and trim, with lace curtains at the windows, and a few cheerful hens clucking around the small garden. She had lighted her fire, and peat-smoke filled the air with its delicious smell.

They meandered on. Past the farmhouse, and a farmyard reeking with the good smell of manure, was a field of sheep, and then another little cottage, the gamekeeper's, with kennels, and a run at the back of the house from which two spaniels appeared, barking their heads off.

"Good thing," said Carrie, "we didn't bring Horace with us. He'd have a heart attack and die."

By now the loch was in view again, with fields running down to the water. More trees, another cottage, and then the north wall of the enclosed garden, a handsome stone edifice with double wrought-iron gates set in the middle. The big wooden tractor shed stood at the back of this, with wide doors standing open, and alongside it stood parked a venerable and mud-spattered Land Rover. Sam drew up alongside and they climbed out of the car. As they did so, a young man appeared from the shed with an old yellow Labrador at his heels. The young man wore a boiler suit and rubber boots, and on his head a deerstalker, the peak tipped forwards, over his nose.

"Charlie Miller?"

"Yes, that is me. Now, stay down, Brandy, and don't jump up on the lady. You're a stupid old bitch with no manners."

"I don't mind," Carrie smiled.

"You would if she covered you with paw marks." He turned to Sam. "You'll be Sam Howard."

"That's right. And this is Carrie Sutton."

Charlie Miller said, "Pleased to meet you," and he and Carrie shook hands. "Oscar phoned me. You've come for the tree. . . . It's in the shed, if you'd like to come away in."

He led the way, and they followed into the dim interior of the shed, which clearly accommodated a number of functions. Sam saw a pile of potato pallets, a stack of sawn logs, a number of old fruit boxes, turnips bagged in netted sacks. There was a good smell of earth, sawdust, and engine oil. Leaning against an aged Ferguson tractor was their cut tree.

". . . Oscar said six-foot would be tall enough, so I picked this one out. It's a good shape, and no broken branches."

"Looks fine to me."

"Two pounds a foot. Twelve pounds. Have you got a stand for it?"

"I really wouldn't know. Oscar didn't say."

"I've this." Charlie produced, from some corner, a rough wooden contraption knocked together with masonry nails. "The farmer's boy made them, selling at two-fifty each."

Sam eyed it doubtfully. "Is it going to work?"

"Oh, yes, it'll work all right."

"Right." Charlie set it down by the tree. "So that's fourteen-fifty you owe me." He was obviously not a man to beat about the bush.

Sam dug out his wallet and handed over fifteen pounds. "Tell the farmer's son to keep the change. He deserves it, if only for enterprise."

"I'll tell him," said Charlie, and the notes disappeared into the pocket of the boiler suit. "Will I load the tree for you?"

"If you would. I've put the back seats down; there should be enough space. . . ."

"No problem."

Carrie now spoke. "Charlie, do you think it would be all right if we went for a walk? We've never been to Corrydale before, and we wanted to look around, see the house. But if it's private, or we're not allowed. . . ."

"You're allowed, all right. Go anywhere you please. The hotel is closed anyway. And there's not much to look at in the gardens."

"We don't mind. Which is the best way to go?"

"Back the road you came, and then, at Major Billicliffe's house, take the left fork, and that will bring you to the gardens and the house. There's a path from there down through the trees to the water, and a track leads back to here, along the shore. While you're walking I'll net the tree and load it, and if I'm not here when you're back, I'll be away for my dinner."

"Thank you."

"No trouble. Have a good walk, now."

They set off, footsteps scrunching on frozen ruts, the air sweet as chilled wine, the thin sunshine warming their backs and causing flurries of melted snow to drift down from the upper branches of trees. These, leafless, made patterns like black lace against the brilliant blue of the sky. They went by the farm, the gamekeeper's house, and by the garden gate of Rose Miller's delectable dwelling.

"It's the sort of place," Carrie observed, "where you feel you could happily snug up and spend the rest of your life."

After Major Billicliffe's deserted cottage they left the road and took the path that led towards the main house. It was heavy walking, because now the snow was virgin and untouched, and quite deep.

Carrie said, "There must, once, have been a lot of money. This is a huge establishment, with all those estate cottages, the farm, and the walled garden and everything. I wonder where it all came from? The wealth, I mean."

"Industry, probably. Shipbuilding, steel, that sort of thing. Or Far Eastern connections. Shipping, tea, teak. I don't know. We'll have to ask Oscar."

"Oscar doesn't seem to have *anything*."

"No. I don't think he does have much."

"What's happened to it all? The money, I mean."

"What's happened everywhere. Old people died, and death duties claimed enormous chunks of the estate. The cost of living soared. The war changed everything. After the war, there was a gradual decline. Then chaps like Hughie McLennan took possession, squandered the last of the capital, and finally sold up. In the south of England, all this land would probably be littered with bijou bungalows and private building estates. But here, because of its remoteness, and the fact that the hotel chain took over the house, it's managed to stay looking—at least—the way it always has done."

"Why didn't Oscar inherit? He would have made a lovely laird."

"I suppose he didn't qualify. Hughie was the son of the eldest son. Primogeniture. Just bad luck on everyone he proved to be such a little shit."

"It seems unfair, doesn't it?"

"Carrie. Life is unfair."

"I'm so sorry for Oscar. He deserves better. He and Elfrida. They deserve some place to live together that they can call their own and know that they don't have to leave. I would like to be rich so that I could take care of them both . . . buy them a desirable residence and settle them for life. I wish we hadn't been there when they were told that the David Wilkie was a fake and worth so little. Elfrida was so filled with hope. And so certain that she owned a little treasure that would get them through and give them security. It was painful to see her so destroyed and downcast. Embarrassing. I was embarrassed."

"I was the same," Sam reminded her.

"But it's different for you."

"Why different?"

"Because if they have no money, Oscar will be forced to sell you his half of the Estate House, and then you will have what you came for."

"Do you think I am that sort of a monster?"

"I don't know. I don't know you well enough. I don't know how you think."

He let this pass. There was no point in precipitating a row so early on their expedition. Instead, "Will they stay together, do you think?" he asked.

"Your guess is as good as mine. I think they probably will. Neither of them has anybody else. But where will they stay?"

"Where they are. If Oscar doesn't want to sell, then Hughie can't."

"So what will you do?"

"Look for someplace else."

"In Buckly?"

"I don't know. So far, I've hardly seen the neighborhood in daylight, let alone investigated property for sale."

For a bit Carrie said nothing to this. They were walking at a brisk pace, her long legs keeping pace with his own as they trudged through the snow. To their left, the snow-fields swept down to the water of the loch; on their right a small wood of ancient beeches revealed dells and paths between the massive tree-trunks, and the snow was patterned with the tracks of rabbits and birds. Overhead, rooks cawed, and from the empty shores came the long bubbling cry of a curlew.

She said abruptly, "I would like to see your mill."

Sam had never imagined her being remotely interested, and found himself taken aback by this suggestion. "*Would* you?"

"You sound disbelieving."

"It's just that there's not much to see. Large, empty, damp spaces, some dye vats, and a few bits of salvaged machinery."

"But you told me it was a listed building. That, in itself, would be interesting. Can you get access? Have you got a key?" She was serious.

"Of course."

"Shall we go one day?"

"If you want."

"I like seeing buildings and houses stripped down. Empty places, bare walls. I like imagining how they were, and trying to visualize what they could become. You must feel rather excited about it all, longing to get your teeth into the challenge. Putting it together, and getting it going again."

"Yes." He thought about it, and the seemingly insurmountable problems which had yet to be addressed. "I am. But at the same time it's a fairly daunting prospect. Every now and then I shall doubtless become frustrated, impatient, and even violently angry, but difficulties can be stimulating, particularly if some other person believes you can solve them. And in Buckly, I have a good man, Fergus Skinner, on my side. I've a lot of faith in him."

"It's still a long stride from working in New York."

"If I were a much younger man, I probably wouldn't have taken the job on. But I'm thirty-nine now. Been there, done that. And for me this is exactly the right time to change course. For all the high finance in the world, nothing is so satisfactory as going back to the grass roots of the business."

"Downgrading."

"In a sense, yes. But, you see, I was born and bred into the woollen trade, and I secretly believe that there is nothing so good-looking, so comfortable, so exactly right, as a familiar, well-tailored tweed jacket. It'll stand up to anything the elements choose to hurl at it, and by evening be perfectly acceptable at anybody's dinner table. I love the smell and the feel of tweed. I love the sound of well-tuned cog-wheels, the clack of looms, the monstrous pistons of the carding machines. And I like the people who work them, the men and women who have spinning and weaving and dyeing in their blood, going back two or three generations. So I am in my own world."

"I think you're fortunate."

"Because of my job?"

"Not just." Carrie stopped, her head thrown back, to watch a buzzard floating high in the sky. "Because of coming to live up here. In this enormous, clean, unsullied place." She went on walking. "Just think, you can play golf, shoot grouse and pheasants, and fish in one of those salmon rivers you told me about." She thought about this. "You do fish?"

"Yes. I used to fish with my father in Yorkshire when I was a boy. But for trout, not salmon. And I'm not overkeen on shooting."

"Nor me. Darling little wild birds tumbling out of the sky. And then you eat them at the Savoy, and they look about the size of canaries."

By now, ahead, could be seen the wall of the formal garden, topped by an ornate wrought-iron fence. The path led to a wrought-iron gate flanked by gate posts bearing stone armorial lions, and entwined by thorny roses, blackened now by winter.

They reached the gate and there paused, gazing through the lattice of intricate curlicues at the garden which lay beyond; lawns climbing in stepped terraces, and drawing their eyes to the first sighting of Corrydale House. A Victorian mansion, gabled and turreted, built of red stone, some of which was smothered in Virginia creeper. It was large and perhaps a little pretentious, but attractive in a prosperous and settled sort of way. The windows were all shuttered from the inside, but facing south, glass panes flashed and shone with reflected sunshine. There was a tall white flag-pole at one side of the top terrace, but no flag flew from its masthead.

"Nice," said Carrie, after a bit. "What good times Oscar must have had."

Sam said, "Would you like to live here?"

"Do you mean in this house? In this place?"

"No. I just mean *here*. In Creagan. In Sutherland."

"I have a job. In London. I have to have a job. I have to earn my living."

"Supposing you didn't? Would you be content? Could you bury yourself in such an environment?"

"I don't know. I think I'd need notice. To weigh up all the pros and cons. And to leave London, I'd need to be free. No commitments. No responsibilities."

"Aren't you free?"

"There's Lucy."

"*Lucy?*"

"Yes, Lucy." She unlatched the gate and opened it, and beyond was a wide path, straight as a rule, leading across the garden towards a distant stand of beech trees. In the middle of this path, in line with the flights of steps which climbed the terraces to the house, stood a stone sundial and a curved wooden seat. Another flight of steps led down to a parterre garden, sheltered by shrubberies of rhododendron and azalea. Its formal structure, radiating from a stone statue of some mythical goddess, was composed of curves, circles, ellipses, all edged in box, and, buried in snow, resembled nothing so much as an artist's design drawn on thick white paper with a stump of charcoal.

". . . Lucy is the main reason for taking this London job. Somebody has to be there for her. Somebody has to winkle her out of that dull, enclosed, totally female life she's forced to lead. Through no fault of her own. She doesn't really stand a chance. I have to try to give her one."

Sam considered this. He said tentatively, "She seems to me to be quite a well-adjusted child. Happy, even."

"That's because she *is* happy. Here. With Elfrida and Oscar and people coming and going. And, of course, Rory Kennedy. Going back to London is going to be a real let-down."

Sam found himself resenting this maiden-aunt attitude. Carrie was too young, too beautiful, to start structuring her life simply for the sake of one small niece.

"She'll probably be all right," he said. "She's young enough to be resilient; in time, she'll make her own escape."

"No." Carrie was adamant. "You don't know her selfish little mother. You can't say that."

"So, what will you do with Lucy?"

"Oh, I don't know. Just be around; on the end of the telephone. *There.* Perhaps at Easter I'll take her away again. To Cornwall to stay with Jeffrey. He is, after all, her grandfather. Or maybe we could go skiing. His children are old enough. Jeffrey took me skiing for the first time when I was about ten, and I loved it so much, it started a whole new passion."

"Will you go back to Oberbeuren . . . ?"

"No." She had said the word almost before he had finished asking the question. "Not Oberbeuren. Somewhere else. Arosa, or Grindelwald, or Val d'Isère."

"You could go to the States. Colorado or Vermont. Sounds a long way to travel, but it would certainly be cheaper."

"Vermont." Carrie, with her hands in the pockets of her parka, strolled along beside him. "Have you skied in Vermont?"

"Yes. A number of times. We used to drive up for weekends from the city."

"We," Carrie repeated. "You and your wife, you mean?"

So this was it. The nub around which they had both been circling, the moment of truth, the point of no return. He said, "Yes. With my wife. We're separated."

"Elfrida told me that."

"Deborah. I was working in New York. I went out to East Hampton, for a weekend with a friend; and we got asked to this party, and I met her then. Her grandfather had a great house down there; lands, beach, horses, paddocks, swimming pool. The lot. When we got married, we were married on the lawn at East Hampton in front of her grandfather's house. There were seven hundred guests, ten bridesmaids, and ten ushers all dressed up like penguins. Deborah looked ravishing and I was happy to be swept along in a current that I couldn't control or resist. Then we bought this apartment in the Upper Seventies, and it was all done up regardless of cost, and that kept her happy for some time; but when it was finished and the interior designer had finally departed, I think that's when she started to get bored and restless. I had to travel all over the States, and sometimes she went back to East Hampton while I was away, and other times, she simply occupied herself having a good time."

"Children?"

"No. She didn't want babies. Not so soon. Someday, perhaps, she'd promise me, but not just now. Anyway, sometime last summer, she met this guy again. She'd known him when she was at college. Since those days he'd been married twice, but was on the loose again. In New York. Rich; smooth; pretty stupid. Randy as a tom-cat. They started what is politely known these days as 'a relationship.' I never guessed. I never knew until she told me she was leaving me because she wanted to be with him. And I was devastated. Not just because I was losing her. But because I knew she had fallen for a shit. And I knew, too, that he was the sort of guy who, marrying his mistress, was simply creating another job vacancy."

"But you're not divorced?"

"No. There's hardly been time. Six weeks after she departed I got a call from David Swinfield, asking me to come back to London. And since then . . . well, I've just procrastinated. Let it slide. Had other business to occupy my mind. No doubt, sooner or later, I'll be on the receiving end of a lawyer's letter, and after that the ball will roll."

"Will she be greedy and demand great wads of alimony?"

"I don't know. It depends on the lawyer. I don't think so. She was never that sort of a person. Anyway, Deborah has money of her own. Too much, maybe. Perhaps that was one of our problems. My problems."

"Are you still in love with her?"

"Oh, Carrie . . ."

"I know. But you feel responsible. You have anxieties about her future. You're afraid she's going to be hurt, to be dumped. You still feel protective."

After a bit, "Yeah," Sam admitted. "I suppose I do."

"If she wanted . . . if she beckoned, demanded . . . would you go back to her?"

He thought about this. He said, "No."

"Why not?"

"Because my life has changed direction. Because Deborah is part of the past and I've left that behind. I'm here now. And this is where I'm staying, because I have a job to do."

"She's still your wife."

"What's that supposed to mean?"

"That if you've been married to a person, they're part of you. You can never be free. You belong to them."

She spoke with such bitterness that Sam all at once knew that he only had to push a bit further and the closed door which had stood between them would finally, creakily, open.

He turned to her. "Carrie . . ."

But she strode on, and he had to catch her up and take her by the arm and jerk her around to face him. The black orbs of her sunglasses stared up at him, and he put up a hand and took them off, and saw, to his horror, that her dark eyes were shining with tears. "Carrie. Tell me."

"Why?" She was angry, blinking the tears away. "Why should I tell you?"

"Because I've been honest with you."

"I never made a deal. It's none of your business and I don't want to talk about it. It's not worth talking about. And you wouldn't understand."

"I could try. And I think I would understand. I've been through bad times myself. The worst was knowing that everybody was aware of what was going on except thickheaded me. Taking one day at a time, and each day like being on a treadmill and getting nowhere. Trying to come to terms with a total rejection."

"I wasn't rejected," Carrie shouted at him, and all at once her face creased up like a child's and she was in floods of tears. Furious with herself, she pushed at him, trying to escape from his grip, but he held her shoulders between his hands and would not let go, because if he did, he felt she might fall to pieces, and his strength was the only thing that kept her whole. "I wasn't rejected. I was loved. We were in love, and all we wanted was to be together. But the odds were too great. Stacked against us. Too many demands, responsibilities, traditions. His job, his family, his wife, his children, his religion, his money. I was simply his mistress. Living in the back streets of his life. I didn't stand a chance. Never did. And what I really hate is that I always *knew*. I hate myself for shutting my eyes, burying my head in the sand like a stupid ostrich. Pretending everything would work out. I'm thirty, for God's sake. I thought I could handle it. And finally, when Andreas walked away from me, I went to bits. So now you know, Sam, and now you can stop trying to find out. And perhaps you can accept the fact that I'm really not very interested in married men. And if you start being sympathetic or sorry for me, I shall scream."

He opened his mouth to protest, but at that moment, with a wrench of her body, she slid out of his hold and set off, at a run, away from him, stumbling in the snow, righting herself, carrying on. He went after her, and caught her once more. "Oh, Carrie . . ." and this time she did not fight him. Perhaps she was too tired, too breathless with sobs. He took her into his arms and she leaned against him, her shoulders heaving, weeping into the front of his Barbour.

Holding her, having her in his arms, was something he had been wanting to do all day. She felt slender, weightless, and he told himself that he could feel the beating of her heart through all their combined layers of winter clothing. The fur of her hat tickled his cheek, and her skin smelt sweet and cool.

"Oh, Carrie." It was shameful to feel so elated when she suffered from such desolation and wretchedness. Trying to comfort, he said, "It will be all right."

"It *won't* be all right."

So cold, so adamant was her voice, that he was suddenly wise, realizing that it was hopeless to continue mouthing pointless platitudes. Standing there, with his arms about her, Sam found himself uncharacteristically confused and disoriented. Normally, his instincts did not let him down; instead they told him how to deal with any situation, emotional or otherwise. But right now he knew all at once that he was totally at a loss. Carrie was beautiful, intelligent, and desirable, but also complicated. And perhaps because of this, she remained an enigma. To truly understand her was going to take much patience and a lot of time.

He accepted this. He said again, "It will be all right."

"You don't know."

Now he had the confidence and the good sense not to argue. After a bit, her furious weeping calmed down. She made motions as though to pull herself together. Gently, Sam put her away from him, and watched as she wiped at tear-stained cheeks with her padded glove.

He said, "I'm sorry."

"What for?"

"Sorry, because this wasn't what I had planned or anticipated. I didn't mean to upset you so. This was simply an outing, to pick up a Christmas tree and go for a walk. No ulterior motives. It just went wrong."

"Not your fault. So stupid . . ."

"I talked about Deborah because sometimes I need to. I didn't mean to wind you up."

"I know. Let's forget it. Pretend it never happened. Walk on, the way we'd planned."

"We did talk. To talk is always good. I thought we never would."

"Is talking so good? I'm not so sure."

"Clears the air. Makes things easier to understand."

"I don't know that I want to be understood. Just left alone. Perhaps right now I'm better off that way. Independent. Not belonging to any person."

Sam said, "Don't be too sure about that." But he did not say it aloud.

LUCY

THURSDAY, DECEMBER 21ST

This morning Carrie and Sam went and got the Christmas tree. And Mrs. Snead and I spring-cleaned the dining-room. It was dreadfully dusty and deserted. We put a notice on the door saying DO NOT DISTURB, *so that nobody came in. Mrs. Snead lit a bit of paper in the fireplace to be sure that the chimney wasn't full of jackdaw nests, but the smoke all went up and she said it was quite clean, so we shall be able to have a huge fire, which will make all the difference.*

And there were a couple of big cardboard crates which seemed to be filled with crumpled newspaper, but we explored and found some silver candlesticks, four of them, dreadfully tarnished but very handsome. We took all the rubbish across the hall and added them to the collection in the old office. There are very thick, sort of tapestry, curtains, which were a bit dusty, so we found a step-ladder in the scullery, took them down, and took them into the garden to shake them, and then hung them up again. I cleaned the window, while Mrs. Snead washed all the fireplace tiles. We moved the table, and Mrs. Snead Hoovered. Then we polished all the furniture, and then we spread newspaper and cleaned the candlesticks, which took ages, because they are very ornate and patterned. Finally, while I went out and bought some candles (tall and cream, a bit like church candles), Mrs. Snead went upstairs to look for table-cloths in her linen cupboard. There weren't any, but she found an old linen sheet, which is just as good, and we put a thick blanket underneath to protect the table. That's as far as we got, because she had to go home and give Arthur Snead his dinner, but with the candlesticks and everything, and the fire all laid, it really looks wonderfully festive.

I didn't want anybody to know about it, so that it would be a surprise, but just before lunch Carrie and Sam got back with the Christmas tree, and there was a great discussion as to where we should put it. We thought the sitting-room, but Elfrida's having this party on Saturday and as there will be quite a lot of people, she thought it might take up too much space. Then Oscar suggested the landing, but there's going to be a table there for drinks, and it would get in the way of people going up and down the stairs. So then I had to admit about the dining-room, and they all trooped downstairs, to inspect what we had been doing. It was lovely because everybody was thrilled, and it all smelt polishy, and Elfrida said she had no idea the dining-room could ever look so festive. And of course, that was exactly the right place for the tree. So Sam went out and brought it in and he'd bought a sort of stand for it as well, so that made everything much easier. And Elfrida fetched her red silk shawl from her bed and draped it around the stand to hide the raw wood and the nails. It looked beautiful and is a lovely shape and size. I love the smell of trees coming indoors; it's like pine essence for the bath.

In the afternoon, Oscar collected all the decorations we'd bought and we tied them on the tree. Sam fixed the lights and the star on the top branch. And Elfrida produced a whole roll of lovely tartan ribbon she'd bought for tying up her presents, but she said sticky tape would be just as good. So we cut it and made lovely bows and put them all over the tree, and with the tinsel and the lights turned on, it is the prettiest I think I've ever seen.

Carrie told me that Corrydale is lovely and that sometime I have to go to see it all. She said there was snow everywhere and blue shadows and sunlight, and that there are gardens stretching right from the house down to the water, and lots of big old trees. In a way, I wish I had gone with them to get the tree, but had to do the dining-room while Mrs. Snead was here because I promised to help.

Tomorrow we have to get started on the party. Elfrida has rung Tabitha Kennedy and is going to borrow some glasses because we haven't got enough. And Carrie is in charge of the food. This afternoon, after we'd dealt with the Christmas tree, we went to the baker's together and ordered sausage rolls and little quiches and pizzas. And then we ordered smoked salmon to put on brown bread. The party is to start at six and Mrs. Snead and Arthur are going to come and help. I hadn't realized that throwing a party was quite so much hard work. Perhaps that's why Mummy and Gran never throw parties in London.

Rory has been asked, of course, and Clodagh. I shall wear my new black miniskirt and my black tights and my new white sweater. I would like to fix my hair up into a sort of knot so that my earrings will show.

ELFRIDA

In mid-winter, waking to darkness in this cold and northern country, Elfrida would open her eyes and have no clue as to the time. After a little, she would fumble for her watch and squint at its luminous face, and if it was two in the morning would probably clamber out of bed, wrap herself in her dressing-gown, and stumble off to the bathroom. Sometimes it was 5 A.M. Or eight in the morning, and time to get up, but even then, not a glimmer of light showed in the sky, and all was black as midnight.

This morning, she reached out a hand, and found her watch, and it was half past seven. Beside her, Oscar still slept. She got quietly out of bed, so as not to disturb him, reached for her thick dressing-gown, pushed her feet into slippers, and went to close the window. Outside, she saw, it was snowing again, not heavily, but sleety flakes driven in by a wind from the sea. These swirled and blew around the church and through the black branches of the graveyard trees, the light of the street lamps turning them to gold. The effect was so spectacular that Elfrida knew she had to share it with some other person. Oscar would not appreciate being woken, so she left him, went out of the room, turned on lights, and went downstairs to the kitchen, where she boiled a kettle and made two cups of tea. Upstairs again to the sitting-room, where she drew back the curtains and set the two mugs on the table by the window. Then she went on up to the attic to wake Lucy.

She slept, looking innocent as a small child, her hand tucked under the sweet curve of her cheek, her long hair tumbled around her neck. Her bed stood beneath the sloping window set into the roof. The blind was undrawn, the glass blanketed with wet snow. Elfrida switched on the bedside light.

"Lucy."

She stirred, turned, yawned, opened her eyes.

"Lucy."

"Umm?"

"You awake?"

"I am now."

"I want you to get up. I want to show you something. I've made a cup of tea for you."

"What time is it?"

"Nearly a quarter to eight."

Sleepily, Lucy sat up, rubbing her eyes. "I thought it was the middle of the night."

"No. Morning. And so beautiful. Everyone else is still sleeping, but I wanted to show you."

Lucy, still fuddled with sleep, got out of bed and pulled on her camel-hair dressing-gown.

She said, "It's cold."

"It's the wind. It's snowing again."

They went downstairs, through the quiet house. The sitting-room was filled with light from out of doors. "Look," said Elfrida and led the way across the room and settled herself on the window-seat. "It's so amazing, I had to wake you and show you. I was afraid that the snow would have stopped, and you wouldn't see it. But it's just like it was when I woke up."

Lucy, staring, sat beside her. After a little, she said, "It's like one of those glass balls I used to have. It was full of water, and it had a little church; and when you shook it, there was a snowstorm."

"That's just what I thought. But these flakes are golden because of the lights; like flecks of gold."

Lucy said, "It's the sort of thing people draw on Christmas cards, and you think it could never be like that."

"And the streets so clean! Not a footprint, not a car track. As though there was nobody else in the world except us." She fell silent, and then thought of something. "I suppose there'll be blizzards and drifts on the main roads. I'm glad we don't have to go anywhere." Lucy shivered. "Here, have some hot tea."

Lucy took her tea and drank gratefully, her thin fingers wrapped around the mug, savouring its warmth. In silence they both stared at the scene beyond the window. Then a single car appeared, circling the church, and heading off in the direction of the main road. It drove cautiously, grinding along in second gear, and left a pair of dark tracks in its wake.

When it was gone, "What time is it in Florida?" Lucy asked.

Elfrida was taken aback. Lucy never talked about Florida; nor about her mother; nor about her mother's new friend. She said casually, "I don't know. Five hours ago, I suppose. About three in the morning. Warm and humid, I expect. It's hard to imagine. I've never been to Florida. I've never been to America." She waited for Lucy to enlarge on this, but Lucy said nothing. "Wouldn't you like to be there?" Elfrida asked gently. "Blue skies and palm trees and a swimming pool."

"No. I should hate it. That's why I didn't go."

"But lovely for your mother. Like a wonderful holiday."

"I don't like Randall Fischer much."

"Why not?"

"He's sort of smooth. Creepy."

"He's probably very nice and totally harmless."

"Mummy thinks so, anyway."

"Well. That's nice for her."

"I'd rather be here, a thousand times over, than Florida. This is *really* Christmas, isn't it? It's going to be a *real* one."

"I hope so, Lucy. I'm not sure. We'll just have to wait and see."

"Oscar."

Oscar, settled by the fire, looked up from his newspaper.

"My dear."

"I am about to leave you on your own."

"Forever?"

"No. For about half an hour. I telephoned Tabitha Kennedy, and I'm going up to the Manse to borrow some extra glasses for our party. She has spare boxes that she keeps for parish dos, and she says we can have them."

"That's very kind."

"I shall have to use the car. I shall drive at five miles an hour and take every precaution."

"Would you like me to come with you?"

"If you want."

"I should prefer to stay here, but am ready and willing to be of any service."

"Perhaps when I get back you could help me unload the boot and bring it all indoors."

"Of course, give me a shout." He thought for a moment. "It's very quiet. Where is everybody?"

"Sam and Carrie have gone to Buckly. And Lucy's incarcerated in her attic, tying up her Christmas presents. If you wanted, you could both take Horace for a little walk. It's stopped snowing."

Oscar did not look particularly delighted by this suggestion. He simply said, in a non-committal way, "Yes."

Elfrida smiled, and stooped to kiss him. "Take care," she told him, but he had already resumed his reading.

Out of doors, the wind was bitter and the snow treacherous. Elfrida, bundled up in boots and the blanket coat and woollen hat, emerged from the warmth of the house and paused to gaze up at the sky. She saw clouds wheeling in across a fitful sky, and gulls, blown hither and thither in the freezing air. Oscar's car was covered in snow. Elfrida brushed the fresh fall from the windscreen with her gloved hand, but there was ice beneath it, so she got in, got the engine started, and turned on a bit of heat. Presently the ice trickled away, and she contrived two arcs of clear glass. Cautiously, she set off, chugging along down the street, then turning up the hill that led to the Manse. The gritting lorry had already passed this way, and so, with some relief, she reached her destination without a skid or other mishap.

She parked at the Manse gate, trod up the path of the front garden, knocked the snow from her boots, rang the bell, and then stepped into the porch and opened the inner door.

"Tabitha."

"I'm here. In the kitchen."

Elfrida saw that the minister's house was already decked out for Christmas. A tree (not very large) stood at the foot of the stair, strung with tinsel and stars, and rather worn-looking paper chains had been festooned overhead. Through the open door at the back of the hall, Tabitha Kennedy appeared, bundled up in an apron and with her dark hair gathered back into a pony-tail. "What a day! So lovely to see you. I've got coffee perking. Come in quickly and shut the door. You didn't walk up?"

Elfrida unbuttoned her blanket coat and hung it on the newel-post of the banister. "No, I was intrepid and brought the car. Had to. I couldn't begin to carry two crates of glasses home. I'd have slipped on the lane, probably broken my leg, and certainly broken the glasses." She followed Tabitha back into the kitchen. "Good smells."

"I'm baking. Mince pies, sausage rolls, two cakes, and shortbread biscuits. You know, I like to cook, but Christmas is becoming beyond a joke. I've been at it all morning, and there's still stuffing to make and brandy butter. And the Christmas cake to ice, and a ham to be boiled. The thing is, so many parishioners call round at this time of the year, with cards, or presents for Peter, and they all have to be asked in and watered and fed, if only out of appreciation."

"I'm sorry. You're so busy and I'm interrupting."

Tabitha poured coffee into a mug. "Not at all, it's an excuse to sit down for five minutes. Pull out a chair, make yourself comfortable." She dumped the mug on the table. "What I'd really like is to be out of doors. We should be walking on the beach, or sledging on the golf course; shedding all responsibilities instead of being slave-driven by the demands of the Festive Season. I'm sure it was never intended to be such labour. Every year I swear I'll simplify and all I ever do is complicate."

Seduced by the fragrant smell of coffee, Elfrida did as she was told. The Manse kitchen was very nearly as old-fashioned as the one at the Estate House, but a great deal more cheerful, with Clodagh's artwork stuck up on the panels of doors, and an old desk piled with papers and family photographs. Clearly, this was Tabitha's domain, and where she not only cooked and fed her family, but organized her busy life, did her telephoning and wrote letters. Now she poured a mug of coffee for herself and settled down on the other side of the table.

"Tell me all the news. What's happening with you?"

"Nothing much. I left Oscar reading the paper, and Sam and Carrie have gone off to Buckly to look at the woollen mill."

"Sam's the mysterious stranger who walked in out of the snow? He's still with you?"

"He's staying over Christmas. The weather's so awful and he doesn't seem to have anywhere else to go."

"Goodness, how sad. Have he and Carrie made friends?"

"They seem to have," said Elfrida cautiously.

"Rather romantic."

"Tabitha, he's married."

"Then why isn't he with his wife?"

"She's in New York."

"Are they non-speaks?"

"Separated, I think. Don't know the details."

"Oh, well," said Tabitha, sounding philosophical. "It takes all sorts."

"It's so odd to think you haven't even met him. It feels as though we've all been together for months, but really it's only been a few days. Whatever, you'll meet both Sam and Carrie tomorrow evening. Drinks at the Estate House, six to eight."

"I put the boxes out in the hall. Six wineglasses and six tumblers and a couple of jugs. Are you going to need plates?"

"I don't think so. We're not actually feeding people. Just little snacky things. Carrie's doing those."

"How many guests do you expect?"

"I think we're about seventeen. You and Peter and Rory and Clodagh . . ."

"Clodagh probably won't come. She's been invited to a supper party and a sleepover with a schoolfriend. Do you mind?"

"Not a bit. Much more fun for her."

"But Rory will definitely be there. Who else?"

"Jamie Erskine-Earle and his wife."

"Jamie and Emma? I didn't know you'd met them."

"He came to appraise my David Wilkie painting. But it's a sham and not a David Wilkie at all, so that's another pipe-dream down the drain."

"Were you thinking of selling it?"

"I might have. But not now."

"Isn't he a hoot? Jamie, I mean. Looks about fifteen, but not only an expert in his field, but as well, the father of three lusty sons. Have you met Emma?"

"Only spoken to her on the phone when I invited them to come."

"She's really nice, and the most down-to-earth, outspoken creature you ever met. She breeds Shetland ponies, works dogs, and oversees everything at Kingsferry. Jamie's far more interested in chasing up antiques, identifying prick candlesticks, and unearthing forgotten portraits. Emma's the one who runs the farm and helps with the lambing, and gets the roof mended. Who else have you asked?"

"The bookshop Rutleys."

"Good."

"And Dr. Sinclair and his wife."

"Good again."

"I don't know their names."

"Geordie and Janet."

"And the Sneads."

"Mrs. Snead and Arthur?"

"Well, when she knew I was asking a few people in, Mrs. Snead offered to come help, and hand round, and wash glasses. But I couldn't bear to think of her being incarcerated in the kitchen all the time, so I told her to come and join in and bring Arthur with her. She said Arthur could have a tray and hand round drinks."

Tabitha drank her coffee. Then she set down her mug, and across the table, her eyes met Elfrida's. Tabitha said, "How is Oscar?"

"He's all right. He still likes being quiet. Left alone with his newspaper and his crossword."

"Peter gave him the spare key to the church organ. Did you know that?"

"No. Oscar never said. He never told me."

"Peter thought it might help. Oscar's music. That it would be a sort of therapy."

"He's never used it. He's only been into the church once, and that was with Lucy because she wanted to look around. To my knowledge, he's never been back."

"I don't imagine it would afford him much comfort."

"Comfort isn't what Oscar needs. He just wants to be left alone, to get through the days at his own pace. As for all our house guests, expected and unexpected . . . I think in a funny way he quite enjoys all the coming and going. He's very fond of Lucy. But, Tabitha, it still isn't right. Oscar and I are very close, and yet I know that part of him is still withdrawn, even from me. As though that part of him was still in another place. Another country. Journeying, perhaps. Or in exile. Across a sea. And I can't be with him, because I haven't got the right sort of passport."

"Peter would say it's a question of patience."

"Patience was never one of my virtues. Not that I ever had many."

Tabitha laughed. "Rubbish. They're just not the same as other people's. Have more coffee."

"No. That was delicious." Elfrida got to her feet. "Now I must get out of your way. Thank you for the glasses and for being a listening ear."

"I'll come and help you stow the boxes in your car. They're not very heavy, just awkward. And we'll all be with you tomorrow evening at six, dressed up in our Christmas bibs and tuckers. Very exciting. I can't wait."

Oscar

Elfrida had not been gone for more than ten minutes when Oscar, breaking into *The Times* crossword, was interrupted by the appearance of Lucy. She wore her red padded jacket and her boots and was apparently on her way out.

"Oscar."

"Hello, there, duck." He laid down the paper. "I thought you were wrapping Christmas presents."

"Yes, I am, but I've run out of ribbon. Oscar, where's Elfrida?"

"She's gone to the Manse to borrow things from Tabitha Kennedy. She won't be long."

"I just wondered if there was anything she wanted me to get in the shop."

"I think all she wanted was for Horace to be taken for a walk."

"Well, I'll go to the bookshop first, and then take Horace down to the beach."

"It's very snowy."

"I don't mind. I've got my boots on."

"Well, be sure not to get attacked by Rottweilers."

Lucy made a hideous face. "Don't even remind me."

"I'll tell Elfrida you'll be back for lunch."

Lucy went. In a moment, Oscar heard Horace's cheerful pre-walk barking, and then the front door opened and slammed shut, and he was alone once more. He returned to his crossword. Six across. *Period by river for one producing picture.* He brooded over this. The telephone began to ring.

His immediate instinct was to leave it, to wait for some other person to answer the tiresome instrument. But then he remembered that he was the only person in the house, and so, in some irritation, he set the paper down, stowed his pen in his pocket, and, heaving himself out of his chair, went out onto the landing.

"Estate House."

"I wonder, is Mr. Blundell there?" A female voice, very Scottish.

"Speaking."

"Oh, Mr. Blundell, this is Sister Thomson from the Royal Western in Inverness. I'm afraid it's sad news. Major Billicliffe died early this morning. I have your name as his next of kin."

Old Billicliffe. Dead. Oscar found himself struggling to think of something to say. All he could come up with was "I see."

"It was all very peaceful. He had a quiet end."

"I'm pleased. Thank you very much for letting me know."

"There are personal possessions you'll want to collect. If you could . . ."

Oscar said, "Of course."

"And any other arrangements . . ." Sister tactfully did not finish her sentence. But Oscar knew exactly what she was driving at.

He said, again, "Of course. Thank you. And for taking care of him. I'll be in touch."

"Thank you, Mr. Blundell. I'm very sorry. Goodbye."

"Goodbye, Sister."

He rang off, and because all at once he needed to sit down, went and perched on the bottom of the stairs that led up to Lucy's attic. Billicliffe was dead, and Oscar was not only his next of kin, but his executor. He found his head spinning with unworthy and pettish thoughts, and was grateful that Elfrida was not here, otherwise he might have voiced them aloud.

How typical of that old idiot to go and die *now,* of all times. A houseful of people, Christmas upon them, and the roads to Inverness impassable. If he had planned it all himself, Billicliffe could not have hit upon a more inconvenient moment to turn up his toes.

But then Oscar remembered leaving the old boy and stopped feeling resentful, and instead felt sad, because he had died alone, and Oscar and Elfrida, despite their best intentions, had been unable to get to the hospital to visit him, make amends for their unsocial behaviour, and say goodbye.

He pondered for a bit as to what he should do next. The ball, it was obvious, was in his court, and it was Oscar who had to take the initiative, but he found himself with no idea of how to start. And it occurred to him, sitting like a beached whale at the foot of the stairs, that it was less than two months since that ghastly evening when he had been told that Gloria and Francesca were dead, but he had little recollection of the stunned days that followed. There had, of course, been a funeral, the Dibton church packed, the vicar, who had never been much of a preacher, struggling for words, and Oscar in his good black overcoat standing in the front pew. But how he had got there he could not say, and had no memory at all of the considerable organization which had preceded the occasion. He only knew that, sometime, Giles, Gloria's eldest son, had turned up and taken over, while Oscar, rendered incapable by shock, had simply done what he was told. Giles, whom Oscar had never found the most engaging of young men, had nevertheless proved himself immensely efficient. All went on oiled wheels, and the entire nightmare process slipped by, and away, and so, into the past.

When it was all over, Oscar felt that nothing of any importance would ever happen to him again, and he moved through the dead days like a zombie. Then Giles turned up once more at the Grange, to inform Oscar that he would have to move out, as Gloria's house was going to be put up for sale. And Oscar felt no resentment at all. Giles was, once more, at the helm, and Oscar took the line of least resistance and simply went with the flow, agreeing to everything. It was only when some old folks' home was mentioned that he experienced the first stirrings of alarm.

But now things were different, and it was *his* turn to take over. How had he got himself into such a situation? He thought back to that cold morning, when he had driven Major Billicliffe over the Black Isle to the hospital in Inverness. And how the old boy had talked, meandering on in an incomprehensible stream of reminiscences. Then "Prepare for the worst and hope for the best," he had said, and asked Oscar to be his executor.

The lawyer. Oscar had, in his diary, made a note of the lawyer's name. He got up off the stair, went into the sitting-room, and found his diary on his makeshift desk. He turned the pages. Murdo MacKenzie. It occurred to him that only Billicliffe would have a lawyer with such an outlandish name. Murdo MacKenzie, MacKenzie and Stout, South Street, Inverness.

There was no telephone number, so he looked it up in the book, copied it into his diary, and returned to the landing. He sat on the stairs again, lifted the telephone off the table and set it handily beside him, then punched the number.

He thought, there will have to be a funeral. A church. A wake. People will have to be told. I must tell Peter Kennedy. And an announcement in the newspaper. Just a few lines. But which paper? The National press, or the local . . .

"MacKenzie and Stout."

"Oh, good morning. I wonder, could I speak to Mr. Murdo MacKenzie?"

"Whom shall I say is calling?"

"Oscar Blundell. From Creagan."

"Hold on a moment, please."

Oscar's heart sank. Others had spoken those words before, and he had been forced to wait a great deal longer than a moment, while listening to a tinkly rendering of "Greensleeves," or some other soupy tune. But his fears were unfounded. Murdo MacKenzie came on the line almost at once.

"Mr. Blundell. Good morning. Murdo MacKenzie here. What can I do for you?"

A good Scottish voice, strong and capable-sounding. Oscar felt encouraged.

"Good morning. I'm sorry to bother you, but I've just heard . . . from the hospital . . . that Major Billicliffe died this morning. Major Godfrey Billicliffe," he added, as though there could possibly be two.

"Oh, that's sad news. I am sorry." (He really sounded sorry, too.) "But not perhaps unexpected."

"They called me first because they had my name as next of kin. And as well, of course, Major Billicliffe asked me to be his executor. There didn't seem to be anyone else."

"No. He had no family. He told me about this arrangement, and said that you had agreed to take the duty on."

"That's why I'm calling. I suppose there will have to be a funeral, but where, and when and how? He has friends in Creagan, who will certainly want to be there, but as far as I know, the roads are still impassable, and there's no hope in hell of anybody getting to Inverness. To say nothing of the fact that Christmas is just about on us. And an undertaker will have to be approached, of course, and the bank notified, and the registrar . . ."

Murdo MacKenzie smoothly intervened. "Mr. Blundell, why don't you leave all this to me? The first thing is that Major Billicliffe left instructions with my office that he wished to be cremated, so that precludes a good many headaches. As for an undertaker, I can deal with that. There's an excellent firm in Inverness who have a good reputation, and I know them well. How would it be if I got in touch with Mr. Lugg and made all the necessary arrangements?"

"That's enormously kind of you . . . but . . . when?"

"I would suggest the end of next week. Before New Year. By then the weather should have eased off a bit, and you and any friends from Creagan should be able to make your way over the Black Isle and attend the ceremony."

"But shouldn't we have some sort of get-together . . . a cup of tea somewhere? I should be more than willing to foot the bill for that."

"Mr. Lugg . . . the undertaker . . . can see to that as well. Perhaps the lounge of an hotel . . . or the function room. It depends how many people will be there."

"And all the other details, probate and the bank and such. Freezing his account . . ."

"We'll deal with those details."

"And his personal possessions . . ." Oscar thought of Billicliffe's washed-out flannel pyjamas, his hearing aids, his battered leather suitcase. All too pathetic, and to his horror, he felt a ridiculous lump grow in his throat. ". . . his possessions. They will have to be collected from the hospital."

"I'll telephone and have a word with the Ward Sister. Do you remember the number of the ward?"

Rather to his surprise, Oscar did. "Fourteen."

"Fourteen." A pause while Murdo MacKenzie made a note or two. "I'll get my secretary to see to that."

"I really can't thank you enough. You've taken a great weight off my shoulders."

"I know that Major Billicliffe did not want you to be inconvenienced in any way. So I shall telephone Mr. Lugg, and get back to you when I know what arrangements he's been able to make. Have I got your telephone number?"

Oscar gave it to him.

"And you're at the Estate House in Creagan?"

"That's right."

"No problems, then. And if any should arise, I'll give you a ring."

"It really is more than good of you. If you could keep in touch. Thank you again. And now, I'll waste no more of—"

"Mr. Blundell!"

"Yes?"

"Don't ring off. I have something else to say. I shall be writing to you, of course, but the post is a little unreliable at this time of the year, and as we're talking now, perhaps I should put you in the picture."

Oscar frowned. "Sorry, I don't understand."

"Once he was settled in hospital, Major Billicliffe rang me, and said that he wanted to see me. I live out on the Nairn Road, and pass the hospital on my way into the office, so I called in early last Monday morning. He was in bed, of course, and very frail, but perfectly lucid. He was worried about his will. Since his wife died he had not got around to making a new one, and he wished to do this right away. He gave me instructions, the will was written that day, in my office, and he was able to sign it. You are his sole beneficiary, Mr. Blundell. He was not a man of property, nor great wealth, but he wants you to have his house at Corrydale, his car, and his dog. I'm afraid neither the car nor the dog are bequests you would have chosen, but those were his wishes. As for his money, he lived, very frugally, on his pensions, which of course, stop on his death. But he had, as well, a few savings, which, once all the funeral expenses have been settled, and any outstanding bills, should come to about two thousand five hundred pounds. . . ."

Oscar sat on his stair, with the telephone to his ear, and could not think of a single thing to say.

"Mr. Blundell?"

"Yes, I'm still here."

"I thought maybe the line had gone dead."

"No. I'm here."

"It's not a substantial legacy, I'm afraid, but Major Billicliffe was anxious that you should know how much he appreciated your kindness to him."

Oscar said, "I wasn't kind." But if the lawyer heard this, he ignored it.

"I don't know if you know the house?"

"I went there once. Once only. To get the key. But of course I knew it in the old days, when it was the forester's cottage, and my grandmother was living at Corrydale."

"I did the conveyancing when Major Billicliffe bought it from the estate. It is quite a modest establishment, but I would say with distinct possibilities."

"Yes. Yes, of course. I am sorry to be so uncommunicative, but I am truly lost for words."

"I understand."

"I never thought . . . expected . . ."

"I'll put it all down in writing in a letter to you, and then you can decide what you do next. And don't worry about arrangements over this side. I'll speak to Mr. Lugg, and put everything into his capable hands."

"Thank you." Oscar felt something more was expected of him. "Thank you so very much."

"A pleasure, Mr. Blundell. Goodbye. And have a good Christmas."

He rang off. Slowly Oscar replaced the receiver. At the end of the day old Billicliffe had come up trumps. Oscar ran a hand over his bewildered head. He said aloud to the empty house, "Well, I'll be buggered."

He thought for a long time about the little house on the Corrydale Estate. Not during the Billicliffe time, but years ago, when the head forester and his homely wife had lived there. Then, it had been a hive of activity, with four children underfoot, three dogs, a cage with ferrets by the back door, and strings of washing flapping on the line. But always a good peat-fire in the hearth, a vociferous welcome for a small boy, and a hot plate of drop scones dripping in butter. Oscar tried to remember the layout of the place, but in those days he had never gone farther than the living-room, with its smell of paraffin lamps and baking bread.

Now it belonged to him.

Oscar looked at his watch. It was five minutes past noon, and all at once, he longed for a drink. Usually, he never drank in the middle of the day, and if he did, only a glass of lager. But now he needed—he really needed—a sophisticated and restoring gin and tonic, to settle himself, and give him the necessary Dutch courage to deal with this new, and totally unexpected, turn of events.

He pulled himself to his feet and went downstairs, and through the kitchen to his slate-shelf wine-cellar. There he found half a bottle of Gordon's and a bottle of tonic, and he took these back into the kitchen, got a glass, and poured himself a restoring slug.

The front door opened. "Oscar!" Elfrida had returned.

"I'm here."

"Can you come and help me?"

He went out to greet her, bearing his glass. He said, "I am secretly drinking. I have become a secret drinker."

Elfrida did not look greatly disturbed. "Oh. Well done. I've got two huge boxes in the back of the car. . . ."

She had left the front door open behind her. He put a hand over her shoulder and pushed it shut. He said, "Later."

"But . . ."

"We'll bring them in later. Come. I want to talk to you. I have something to tell you."

Her eyes went wide. "Is it dire?"

"Not dire at all. Take off your coat and come into the kitchen, where we can sit and be peaceful."

"Where's Lucy?"

"She has taken Horace shopping. To buy ribbon, and then to go for a walk. And Sam and Carrie are not yet back. So, for once, we are on our own. Let us not waste a bit of peace. Do you want a gin and tonic?"

"If we've really started lunch-time boozing, I'd prefer a glass of sherry." Elfrida unbuttoned her coat, slung it on the end of the banister, and followed him into the kitchen. "Oscar, you're looking quite flushed and excited. What *has* been going on?"

"I shall tell you."

She sat at the table, and he brought her her glass of sherry, and then sat, too. "Cheers, my dear girl."

"And to you, Oscar."

The gin and tonic was pretty strong, but quite delicious and exactly what his stomach needed. He set down the glass and said, "If I tell you, quite slowly, because it's rather complicated, will you listen and not ask questions until I've got to the end? Otherwise, I shall become confused."

"I'll try."

"Right. The first is that Major Billicliffe died this morning. I had a phone call from the hospital."

Elfrida put her hand over her mouth. "Oh, *Oscar*."

"I know. We never got to see him. We never sat at his bedside and fed him grapes. But truly, with the roads the way they are, we could never have made the journey."

"It's not *that* so much. It's just so sad. To be all alone, and dying. . . ."

"He wasn't alone. He was in a ward, with kindly nurses and people around him all the time. Not nearly as alone as he's been since his wife died."

"I suppose so." Elfrida thought about this, and then sighed. "What a complication. And you were his next of kin . . . does that mean . . . ?"

He said, "Now, listen."

And so he told her. About telephoning the lawyer, Murdo MacKenzie, and having all responsibility removed from his shoulders by a man clearly experienced in such matters. He told her about the Inverness undertaker, Mr. Lugg, in whom Murdo MacKenzie had such touching faith; and how Mr. Lugg would be the right person to see to everything, from crematorium to function rooms.

"But when will the funeral *be*?" Elfrida asked.

"The end of next week, we thought. By then all the Creagan people should be able, with a bit of luck, to get there. The snow can't lie forever. Sooner or later, there must come a thaw."

"We should put an announcement in some paper. . . ."

"Mr. MacKenzie has taken that on as well."

". . . And let the local people know . . ."

"I'll ring Peter Kennedy."

"Oh, dear. What a terribly inconvenient time to die."

"Exactly what I thought, and then had to pull myself together and stop being un-Christian."

"Oh, well. I suppose that's it."

"No, Elfrida. That's not the end."

"More?"

"Billicliffe's will was out-of-date. His wife had died, and he had to write a new one. He has made me his sole beneficiary. No, don't say a word till I've finished. It means he has left me his house, his motor car, his dog, and his fortune. His fortune, all bills and expenses paid, is in the region of two thousand five hundred pounds. All his savings. He has been living on his pension."

"His house? He's left you his house? How terribly touching. Sweet. So kind. Did he really have no other family? No relation?"

"Nobody."

"Poor lonely man. Oh, Oscar, and we were so horrid about him."

"Just between ourselves."

"Hiding behind the sofa in case he called!"

"Don't remind me."

"What will you do with the house?"

"I don't know. I haven't had time to think. Sell it, I suppose. But it would have to be emptied of Billicliffe clobber first, and probably fumigated."

"What's it like?"

"You know. You saw. A tip."

"No, I mean, how many rooms? Is there a kitchen? A bathroom?"

"I suppose, in estate agent jargon, you'd say two up, two down, kitchen and bathroom probably added on, after the war, sticking out at the back."

"Which way does it face?"

Oscar had to work this one out. "North at the front door, south on the other side."

"And a garden?"

"Yes, I suppose a bit of land. I can't really remember. Mrs. Ferguson, the forester's wife, used to grow potatoes and leeks. And there was an apple tree. . . ."

Elfrida was silent for a moment, chewing this information over. And then, astonishingly, she said, "Why don't you go and live there?"

Oscar stared at her in total disbelief. "Live there? All on my own?"

"No, stupid, I'll come with you."

"But you thought the house was horrible."

"No house is impossible. There's no such thing as a place that cannot be improved, enlarged, redecorated. I'm sure when the forester lived there, it was a dear little place. It was hearing aids, dog hairs, brimming ashtrays, and smeary glasses that made it all so disgusting. Nothing to do with the bricks and mortar."

"But I have a house. I have this house."

"You only own half a share. That's not very secure. You could sell your half and then you'd have seventy-five thousand pounds and you could spend that on Major Billicliffe's house and live happily ever after."

"You mean . . . sell out here? Leave Creagan . . . ?"

"Oh, Oscar, don't sound so horrified. It's really quite a good idea. Sam Howard wants it, and Hughie McLennan is obviously agog to get rid of his half. I know you love it here, and I do, too, but admit, it is big and faintly unfurnished; and when Sam and Carrie and Lucy have gone, we're going to be alone again, rattling around like a pair of peas in a drum. And another thing, I always think of *here* as a family house. It's not meant for a couple of old dears like us. It should have young people, and children growing up. . . ."

"Sam hasn't got any children."

"No, but he's bound to get married again . . ." Elfrida did not finish her sentence. In the silence which followed, with some reluctance, she looked Oscar in the eye.

He said, "Not Carrie."

"Why not Carrie?"

"You mustn't matchmake."

"It's impossible not to. They're so perfect together."

"They're not perfect at all. He never stops being amiable and Carrie is remote and prickly as a gorse-bush."

"She's vulnerable just now. And yesterday, they were away for ages, getting the Christmas tree. Carrie said they were exploring Corrydale, but I can't believe that they paced along for two hours without some exchange of words."

"All that's happened is that they have been flung together by circumstances. . . ."

"Maybe so." Elfrida sighed. "You're probably right. But, discounting Carrie, this is exactly the right establishment for a man like Sam Howard. The business man, the manager of the resuscitated woollen mill, an important member of the community. I can just see him entertaining business colleagues from Japan and Germany. Giving his chairman a weekend of golf. Besides—and this is the most important thing—Sam really wants this house. I think he feels right here, he feels at home. And wouldn't it be better to sell it to him than to some stranger? And have seventy-five thousand pounds to put in your pocket?"

"Elfrida, I am not a man of means. If I did sell the Estate House, then that money would have to be squirrelled away for old age and senility. I couldn't be mad enough to sink the lot into Major Billicliffe's cottage and leave myself with nothing put by."

"We don't know how much we'd have to spend . . . on tidying things up, I mean."

Oscar said, "A lot."

But Elfrida would not be put off. "Then supposing I sell my house in Hampshire, and we use *that* money for—"

Oscar, quite firmly for him, said, "No."

"Why not?"

"Because that is *your* house. It's about all you own, and you must under no circumstances sell it. Rent it out if you can find someone who wants to live there, but you must never sell."

"Oh, well." She became resigned, and Oscar felt a brute. "It was a good idea while it lasted, but I suppose you're right." Then she perked up again. "Whatever, it's all terribly exciting, and no wonder you're looking flushed. One thing is certain, we must go and look around the poor little place, inspect it from attic to cellar. And rescue the car before it dies of cold in the snow. And the dog. What shall we do with the dog?" Suddenly, she was laughing. "What shall we do with our Baskerville hound, baying in the night, and flinging its weight against locked and bolted doors?"

"To be honest, I prefer Horace. Perhaps I can bribe Charlie Miller to keep the dog. I'll have a word with Rose. . . ."

Upstairs, on the landing, the telephone began to ring. Elfrida said, "Damn. Why are phones so intrusive?"

"Leave it. Pretend we're out."

"I wish I had the strength of mind. But I haven't." She pulled herself to her feet and went out of the room. Oscar heard her running upstairs, and almost at once the insistent ringing ceased. From the upper floor, faintly, floated Elfrida's voice. "Hello."

Oscar sat on, patiently waiting for her to return to him, mulling over her wild ideas, and wishing he could go along with them. But, if he did sell the Estate House to Sam, then the sum released would be his only capital, his buffer against an impoverished old age. They would certainly go and look at Billicliffe's house, that was only sensible. Perhaps, cleaned and painted up a bit, it wouldn't be so bad. But still, a poky and dark place in which to live after the spacious grandeur of the Estate House. He would miss, unbearably, the airy, sunny rooms, the sense of space, the good, solid feel of security. It would, indeed, be painful to sell out . . . even to a friend like Sam Howard . . . and leave it forever.

Upstairs, Elfrida still talked. He could hear the murmur of her voice, but not the words she spoke. Every now and then, she fell silent for some time and then spoke again. He could not imagine who could be on the other end of the line. He hoped that it was not sinister or disturbing news.

He had finished his gin and tonic. Standing up to rinse out the glass under the tap, he remembered the two boxes of borrowed glasses still incarcerated in the boot of the car. He went out of the kitchen and down the hall, and out through the front door into the piercing cold.

He trod down the snowy path and through the gate to where his old car stood parked, and opened the boot. The boxes were unwieldy and heavy, and he had to make two journeys, carrying them one at a time. He put the second one down on the kitchen table and then went back to shut the front door. As he did this, he heard the *ting* of the telephone, the noise it always made when one replaced the receiver. He stood at the foot of the stairs, his face upturned, waiting for Elfrida to appear. When she didn't, he called her name.

"Elfrida."

She did not say anything. She simply came down the stairs, with an expression on her face that he could not fathom. He only knew that he had never seen her eyes so bright, had never seen her look so young, with a radiance about her that had nothing to do with the noonday light shining through her flaming shock of hair.

"My dear . . ."

"Oscar." She reached him, standing on a stair above him, put her arms around him and pressed her cheek against his own. "Something simply utterly wonderful has happened to me."

"Do you want to tell me about it?"

"Yes, but I think we both must be sitting down."

So he took her hand and led her back into the kitchen, and they sat once more facing each other across the table.

"That was Jamie Erskine-Earle. About my little clock. You know he said he was going to show it to a colleague in Boothby's. Well, the colleague is in London, and in this weather there was no way Jamie could get it south. But he sent him a fax, with a detailed description of the clock, and faxed him some photographs as well. And the colleague . . . whoever he is . . . telephoned back from London this morning. And he said the clock was a very special item. A very rare timepiece. And it's French, and it was made by one J. F. Houriet, about 1830. Its official description is a Silver Chronometer Tourbillon. Just imagine, Oscar, all these years I've owned a Silver Tourbillon, and never had the faintest suspicion. And then he wanted to know how I had come by it, and Jamie told him that I'd inherited it from an elderly sea-faring godfather, but of course I've never had any idea of how it came into *his* possession. Anyway, Jamie said that it really is something of a treasure, and I should certainly have it well insured. So I plucked up my courage and said, 'Is it valuable?' And he said, 'Yes.' And I asked what it was worth, and he said at auction . . . possibly . . . guess, Oscar!"

"Impossible. Put me out of my misery. Tell me."

"Seventy to eighty thousand pounds," Elfrida gleefully shouted at him.

"I have misheard you. It can't be true."

"You haven't misheard me and it is true. Jamie said his colleague said that it's a very serious piece to any collector. Don't you adore the word *serious*? Get it into a Boothby's sale of Important Clocks, Watches, and Marine Chronometers, and the figure might rise even higher."

"I am left without words."

"And all this time, I told myself it was my little painting that would be my insurance and keep me out of the poor-house. But instead, my true treasure was my clock. Isn't it a lucky thing that nobody nicked it off the mantelpiece at Poulton's Row?"

"I might put it more strongly than that. Especially as you never locked your front door. It was always a lovely thing to own. You aren't thinking of selling it? You mustn't sell it."

"Oh, Oscar, for goodness' sake, of course I'm going to sell it. Don't you see, with that money we can really transform Billicliffe Villa into the most desirable of residences. Build a conservatory. Fling out a ballroom wing. . . ."

"Elfrida."

". . . And buy a microwave."

"Elfrida, listen. That money, if you sell the clock, belongs to you."

"Oscar, listen. It belongs to us. And we'll end our days in a charming little cottage filled with sunlight, just the way this house always is. And we shall grow potatoes, and leeks, if you want, and we shall have Rose Miller for a neighbour, and a four-star country hotel in the garden. Who could ask for more? It's so exciting. Isn't it tremendously, wonderfully exciting?"

"Of course it is. But, dear girl, we must be practical. We must be sensible."

"I *hate* being sensible! I want to go out and dance in the street. Shout our good news from the roof-tops."

Oscar considered this, as though it were a perfectly viable suggestion. And then he said, "No."

"No?"

"Just for the moment, what I would like is for nothing to be said about *anything* until I've had a chance to get Sam on his own and explain the situation. He must know that we are thinking of selling up here, because I am certain that he will want first refusal. Not having to start searching for another property will be a great weight off his mind. He has, at the moment, quite enough to think about without wondering where he's going to live. As well, he's not going to be with us forever, so we should put him in the picture before he leaves us and we don't see him again. He may need time to think it all through; perhaps raise the cash. We don't know. But I feel he must be our first consideration."

"Yes. You're absolutely right. When will you tell him?"

"I shall take him down to the pub this evening."

"And the others? Carrie and Lucy?"

"After I've spoken to Sam."

"What if Billicliffe's house proves to be a total disaster?"

"Then we shall have to think again."

"I can't wait to go and look at it. You and I. But we can't go this afternoon because of the snow. The roads are horribly skiddy. And we can't go tomorrow because of the party."

"Sunday?"

"Christmas Eve."

"As good a day as any. Sunday morning."

"All right. We'll go on Sunday morning. Perhaps we should ask

Sam to drive us in his car. That should preclude us ending up in a ditch." She thought about this, and then came up with an even brighter idea. "I know. We'll all go. Carrie and Lucy as well."

Oscar was wary. "That will entail five different people all coming up with their own opinions and ideas."

"All the better. I'm sure Sam will be wonderfully practical. He'll talk about things like soffits, and rap walls, and be knowledgeable about rising damp. And I've had another brilliant idea. If we went to Corrydale in the morning, and it wasn't raining or snowing, we could take a lunch picnic. A winter picnic. I shall make a pot of my garbage soup. Oscar, have we got a key for Major Billicliffe's house?"

Oscar had not thought about a key. "No."

"Then how shall we get in?"

"Rose Miller will have one. Or know some person who has. I have to ring her anyway, to let her know that the old boy has died, though she's probably heard by now. And I must call Peter Kennedy."

Carrie

They drove to Buckly by way of the narrow back road that wound along the coast. The prospects about them could not have been more wintry—white hills and grey skies running with clouds, driven on a wind that blew from the north, from the Arctic seas, and across great tracts of snow-covered moors. The car crested a shallow hill, and Carrie saw, below them the sea loch at half-tide, the dark conifer forests on the farther shore, and the huddle of white cottages above a disused and ruined pier.

She had never been this way before. "What is the loch called?" she asked.

He told her. "Loch Fhada. It's a bird sanctuary."

They turned along the shore road. The beach was rocky and inhospitable. The sea, racing in on the flood, was as grey as the skies above and flecked with spray. Far out, on a sandbank, a number of seals rested, and as she watched, a flight of ducks moved in from the east, to land on an isolated pool not yet drowned by the running tide.

At the far end of the loch, a road bridge spanned the water, and beyond this was wild country, a glen of scrub and bracken and dead water, edging up into the hills. At the main road they turned north, and the gritters had been out, and the snow was dirtied by traffic and by the mud thrown up by lorries and tractors. Between the road and the sea lay farmland; sheep huddled in the lee of drystone dikes, and small farmsteads sported bravely smoking chimney-pots reeking of peat. A tractor was crossing a field trailing a bogey laden with hay, and a woman emerged from a door to throw crusts to her flock of gobbling geese. Farther on, they came upon a man trudging along the side of the road, a solitary figure walking head-down against the weather; he held a long crook and his sheep-dog ran at his heels. As they approached, he paused to let them by and raised a mittened hand in greeting.

"He looks," said Carrie, "as though he had been painted by Breughel."

She remembered farms in the south of England, so bosky and green. And her father's smallholding in Cornwall, where the milk cows grazed out of doors all winter. She said, "I can't imagine working a farm in weather like this. It seems a question of survival rather than anything else."

"They're always prepared for bad weather. Winters have always been harsh. And they're a tough breed."

"They'd need to be."

They were on their way to view the woollen mill which was to be Sam Howard's future. Now, Carrie wished that she had never come up with that suggestion, so casually made. *I should like to see your mill*, she had said, with no idea that he would be so enthusiastic about the prospect of showing her around. And that had been before all that happened later; and this morning, of course, it was too late to back out, to make some excuse, to pretend that she wasn't particularly interested after all.

Too late. Too late to blot out that outburst of passionate honesty, the truth that she had been so careful to keep to herself, concealed and hopefully unsuspected. She told herself that she couldn't conceive how it had all come about, knowing perfectly well what had precipitated the breakdown of defenses, the opening up of her own unhappy heart.

It was Corrydale. The place. The sunlit snow, the aromatic scent of pine trees, the dark-blue skies, the mountains on the far side of the glittering firth. The warmth of the low sun seeping through the padding of her jacket; the crunch of fresh snow underfoot; the dazzle, the pleasure of breathing pure cold air down into her lungs. Austria. Oberbeuren. And Andreas. The place and the man; indivisible. Andreas, here. Now. Walking beside her, talking incessantly, his voice always with that undertone of laughter. Andreas. Making plans, making love. So strong was the illusion that she thought she could smell the cool, fresh, lemony scent of his aftershave. And even as she felt his presence so strongly, she had known that it was simply a figment of her own heightened imagination. Because Andreas was gone. Back to Inga and his children, leaving Carrie with such a devastating sense of pain and loss that all at once it was no longer possible to remain cool and rational.

Sam, talking about his wife, his broken marriage and the end of his job in New York, had simply compounded her misery, and when he had come out with that horrible word "rejected," she had turned on him in the sort of rage that she had never believed she was capable of, the furious words had broken free, and it was only tears that stemmed the outburst. A flood of tears that left her ashamed and humiliated, and when she had tried to run away from her own humiliation, Sam had pulled her back, taken her into his arms and held her close, as he might have held an inconsolable child.

She thought now, that in a book, in a film, that moment would have been the end. The final embrace, after reels of antagonism and misunderstanding. The camera after backing off into a long shot, panning up to the sky, to a skein of home-flying geese or some other meaningful symbol. Throbbing theme music, and the credits rolling, and the good sensation of a happy ending.

But life didn't stop at the end of the story. It just moved on. Sam's embrace, his arms around her, the physical contact, the closeness had comforted, but not melted her own coldness. She was not changed. She was still Carrie, thirty years old, and with the love of her life gone forever. Perhaps that was the way she wanted to be, with a heart frozen like the winter landscape all about them. Perhaps that was the way she wanted to stay.

Elfrida had said, so sadly, *The world is full of married men.* It was better not to get too close to another person. The closer you got, the more likely you were to get hurt.

McTaggarts of Buckly.

The mill stood on the outskirts of the small town, set back from the road behind a stone wall and an imposing wrought-iron double gateway. This was wide enough to allow the passage of a horse and cart, and overhead curved a decorative archway crowned by an ornate device vaguely heraldic in appearance.

The gate, this morning, stood open, and beyond was a spacious area set about with circular raised flower-beds contained by walls of cobblestones. All lay under snow, and the flower-beds were empty, but Carrie guessed that in summer-time there would be a fine show of geraniums, lobelia, aubrietia, and other municipally approved plantings.

The snow was virgin, unmarked by footprints or tyre tracks. They were, it was clear, the first and only visitors of the day. Passing beneath the gateway, Carrie had, through the windscreen, her first sighting of the mill, and could at once perfectly understand why the environmental authorities had deemed it worthy of being listed. There was an industrial chimney, of course, rearing up beyond the pitched roof, and other, more utilitarian sheds and storehouses set about, but the main building was both impressive and good-looking.

Built of local stone, its façade was long and pleasingly symmetrical. A central pediment was topped by a clock tower. Beneath this, a single window on the first floor, and then, below again, an important double door over which arched an elegant glass fanlight.

On either side of the pediment, the two wings were set with a double row of windows, all formally fenestrated. The sloping roof was slate, pierced by skylights, and here and there the stonework was softened by the dark and glossy green of climbing ivy.

Sam drew up in front of the big door, and they stepped down into the snow. Carrie stood for a moment looking around, and Sam came to stand at her side, his hands deep in the pockets of his Barbour.

After a bit, "What do you think?" he asked.

"I think it's very handsome."

"I told you. No question of bulldozing the lot and starting anew."

"I was expecting a dark, satanic mill. Or a factory. This looks more like a well-established public school. All that's missing are a few playing fields with goal-posts."

"The original mill buildings are round at the back, nearer to the river. This block was put up in 1865, so it's relatively new. It was conceived as a form of window-dressing. Offices, sale-rooms, conference rooms; that sort of thing. There was even a reading room for the employees, a good example of Victorian paternalism. On the first floor, the space was for finished goods, and, above again, in the lofts, wool stores. You have to remember that the business has been going since the middle of the eighteenth century. The river, of course, was the reason that the original mill was sited in this particular spot."

Carrie said, "It all looks in such good order. Hard to believe it's suffered a fatal flood."

"Well, brace yourself. You're in for a shock."

He produced, from his pocket, a considerable key, fitted this into the brass lock, turned it, and pushed the door open. He stood aside, and Carrie went past him and into a square, high-ceilinged reception hallway.

And devastation.

It was empty. The high-tide mark of the flood-water reached to nearly five feet. Above this, handsome flock wallpaper had survived, but, below, all colour had been soaked away, and it peeled from the wall in ruined tatters. The floor, too, bare boards, was much damaged: old planks rotted and broken; gaping holes revealing original joists and the dark cavities of deep foundations. There hung, over all, the pervading and depressing smell of mould and damp.

"... This was the reception area. For visitors, or new customers; an important first impression. I believe it was all furnished and carpeted in some style, and with portraits of various McTaggart founders glowering down from the walls. You can see that the plaster cornice survived, but the flood rendered everything else beyond repair and it all had to be jettisoned."

"How long did it take for the water to go down?"

"About a week. As soon as possible, industrial blowers were installed to try to dry things out, but too late to save anything in here."

"Has the river ever flooded before?"

"Once. About fifty years ago. After that a dam and a sluice were constructed in order to control the level of the water. But this time the rain was relentless, and to make matters worse, there was a very high tide, and the river simply burst its banks."

"It's almost impossible to imagine."

"I know. Come and see. Careful where you walk. I don't want you falling through the floor-boards."

Another door stood at the back of the hallway. Sam opened this, Carrie followed, and it was a bit like going through the green baize door of a large house with servants' quarters. For it led into a stone-floored space as big as a warehouse and glass-roofed for light. It was empty, echoing, and piercingly cold. Here and there were evidences of past industry, like the mountings set into the flags where once had stood the weaving looms, and at the far side an open-treaded wooden stair led to an upper gallery.

It felt dead, and sadly desolate.

"What went on here?" Carrie asked, and her voice rang back at her from the soaring roof and the empty, stained walls.

"This is a weaving shed. Fergus Skinner—he was the guy in charge of the mill at the time of the flood—told me some of what happened. That night, they went on working here until eleven o'clock, because even as the water trickled in, they were still hoping that the flood would abate. But it didn't, and the rest of the night they spent lifting everything they could off the floor. A desperate but hopeless task. What was possible to salvage was—the spinning frames, although they were badly damaged. Old wooden scouring machines survived, and the teasel-raising machines. Financially, the worst disaster was the ruination of all the finished goods. Orders worth thousands, packed and ready for delivery. It was that loss, really, that finally finished McTaggarts off."

"Was the office on the ground floor?"

"Unfortunately, yes. Fergus Skinner told me that he remembered wading in there, to see if he could salvage anything, but the water was waist-level by then, the computers drowned, and letters of credit floating towards him down the aisle. . . ."

"What happened the next day? The work-force . . . ?"

"All laid off. No alternative. But as soon as the waters subsided, about a hundred men turned up to salvage what they could. Half of the machinery had to be scrapped including the German electronic shuttle looms which had only recently been installed. So much for modern, and extremely expensive, technology. What did survive was some of the older, less sophisticated machinery. Looms which had been bought second-hand, and were already forty or fifty years old. The engineers stripped down the carding machine and cleaned it off before the rust set in, so that can be set up again. And there was some specialist machinery from Italy, but that's in store right now, and we plan to send it back to Milan for refurbishment and re-use."

Carrie, fascinated and attentive, was, nevertheless, starting to feel tremendously cold. Damp chill crept up through the thick soles of her boots, and all at once she shivered. Sam saw this, and was remorseful.

"Carrie, I'm sorry. Once I start expounding, I forget everything else. Do you want to go? Have you had enough?"

"No. I want to see it all. I want you to show it *all* to me, and tell me what you're going to do, about the new plans, and where everything's going to be. At the moment, I am completely bewildered by the prospect of doing anything at all. It's mind-boggling. Like being given a totally impossible task."

"Nothing is impossible."

"But still . . . being the guy in charge."

"Yes, but with the resources of a huge conglomerate behind me. That makes a hell of a difference."

"Even so. They chose *you* to take on the job. I wonder why?"

Sam grinned, and all at once looked, not simply boyish, but at the same time, bursting with eager confidence. He knew what he was talking about. He was on his home ground.

He said, "I suppose because, basically, I'm a Yorkshire boy. And where there's muck, there's brass. Now, come, before you freeze, and I'll show you the rest. . . ."

By the time the tour was finished, and they stepped once more into the outdoors, Carrie was chilled to the bone. She stood in the snow, waiting while Sam closed and locked the door behind him, and then he turned and saw her, hunched into her thick grey loden coat, with her hands dug deep into the pockets.

"You look frozen, Carrie."

"I am."

"I'm sorry. I shouldn't have kept you so long."

"I liked it. It's just that my feet are frozen."

"I hope you weren't bored."

"Not at all. Fascinated."

He looked at his watch. "It's half past eleven. Shall we go back to Creagan, or would you like a heartening drink? From the look of you, a Whisky Mac might be the best thing."

"Hot coffee would do the trick."

"Whatever. Come along, get back into the car, and we'll warm you up."

So they drove away from the deserted mill, over the cobbles, under the handsome gateway, and then turned right and went on down the road and into Buckly, making their way along narrow winding streets and across a small square where stood the War Memorial. There weren't many people about, but little shops had their lights on, and brave Christmas decorations in windows. Then over a stone bridge that spanned the ravine of a river in spate, and beyond this, Sam drew up by the pavement outside a gloomy-looking establishment with the DUKE'S ARMS in curly gold capitals above the door. Carrie eyed it without much enthusiasm.

"I am sure," Sam told her, "that in Buckly there are more lively spots, but this happens to be the only one I know. And it is, in its own way, unique."

"It doesn't look a riot of fun."

"We shall make it so."

They got out of the car and crossed the pavement as Sam led the way, pushing open the door and letting loose a warm and beery smell. Gingerly, Carrie followed. Inside, it was dark and seedy, but gloriously overheated. A coal-fire glowed and flickered in the old-fashioned hearth, and over the mantelpiece hung an enormous fish in a glass case. Small, wobbly tables held brewery beer-mats and ashtrays, and there seemed to be only two other customers, both of them silent, male, and very old. Behind the bar, the proprietor was intent on a small black-and-white television set, with the sound turned down to a murmur. A clock ticked, and a bit of coal collapsed in the fire with a whisper. The atmosphere was so dour that Carrie wondered if they should simply turn about and tiptoe away again.

But Sam had other ideas. "Come on," he said, and his voice rang around the room, in a very off-putting way. "Sit here, close to the fire." He pulled a chair away from a table. "I'm sure you'll get a cup of coffee if you really want one, but would you try a Whisky Mac? It's the most warming drink in the world."

It sounded more tempting than coffee. "All right."

She sat, pulled off her gloves and unbuttoned her coat, then spread her hands to the heat of the fire. Sam went over to the bar, and the barman dragged himself away from the television set and took his order. After that, in the way of all countrymen in pubs, they fell into conversation, their voices low, as though they spoke secrets.

Carrie pulled off her fur hat and laid it on the chair beside her; she ran her fingers through her hair. Doing this, she looked up and caught the eye of the old man who sat beneath the window. It was a rheumy eye, and blazed with disapproval, and Carrie guessed that the Duke's Arms was not an establishment frequented by women. She tried smiling at him, but he only munched on his dentures and returned his attention to his beer.

The exchange at the bar continued. Sam stood with his back to her, in the classic attitude of a man at ease in his pub, with one foot on the brass rail and an elbow on the polished counter. Very slowly, as they talked, the barman assembled Sam's order, pausing every now and then to check up on what the television set had to say.

Carrie leaned back on the hard chair-back, stretched out her legs, and watched them, and thought that this morning she had seen, for the first time, the other side of Sam, the man who had walked in out of the snow only three or four days ago and been forced by the vile weather to stay. He had become, with no apparent effort, nor forced bonhomie, an integral part of an ill-assorted little household. Absorbed as easily as an accomplished and experienced house guest.

She thought of him dealing, unasked, with a number of not very exciting day-to-day tasks. Like humping great baskets of logs, filling the coal bucket, walking the dog, carving a roast pheasant, and even gutting the salmon which Elfrida, in a mad moment, had been impelled to buy from the man who sold fresh fish from the back of his van. Uncomplaining, Sam had shovelled snow, pushed trolleys around the supermarket, stocked up Oscar's wine-cellar, and brought the Christmas tree home. Even better, he had set it up on its dicey-looking wooden stand, and then managed to unravel and get working the annual headache of the Christmas-tree lights.

For this noble effort, Oscar was particularly grateful.

On another level altogether, he had proved to be something of an asset when Elfrida decided to sell her picture, producing Sir James

Erskine-Earle out of nowhere, like a rabbit out of a hat. The fact that *that* particular project had come to nothing, and the picture was pronounced a fake, had upset Sam considerably, as though the worthlessness of the painting was somehow all his fault.

He was a man hard to dislike. He and Oscar (nobody's fool) had slipped at once into a companionable friendship that belied the years that lay between them. Left alone together, they never ran out of things to talk about, because Oscar enjoyed sharing memories of the days when he was a boy and had travelled to spend summers with his grandmother at Corrydale. Because of his knowledge, not only of the people, but the countryside, he was able to fill Sam in with much local information and a great many anecdotes about the district in which Sam was coming to live and work.

On Oscar's part, he clearly enjoyed the company of another man, a stranger, maybe, but one whom he had taken to instantly. He was fascinated by the progress of Sam's career, the boyhood in Yorkshire, the years in London and New York, and now the challenge of getting a defunct business on its feet again. Remembering the old McTaggarts, and the sturdy tweeds that had come from the looms, he was amazed by the enormously exciting plans that had already been drawn up by Sturrock and Swinfield—the expensive machinery ordered from Switzerland, the marvels of modern technology, the marketing prospects for new and luxury products, and the programme for retaining the work-force, McTaggarts' most valuable asset.

From time to time, with all the world set to rights, they had ambled off together, to visit the Golf Club, or drop into the Creagan pub for a peaceful, manly dram.

Elfrida, as well, was entranced by her visitor. But then, she had never been able to resist the charms of an attractive man, especially one who laughed at her dotty remarks and was capable of concocting a perfect dry Martini. As for Lucy, she had confided to Carrie one night, when Carrie had gone up to Lucy's attic to kiss her good night, that she thought Sam was almost as good-looking as Mel Gibson.

Amused, "You like him then?" Carrie had asked.

"Yes. He's gorgeous. And he's comfortable. I usually feel a bit shy with men. Like other girls' fathers. But Sam's like the sort of uncle one's known forever. Or somebody's very oldest friend."

And that was how it had been. And that was how, for Carrie, it might have stayed, had it not been for the traumatic events of yesterday.

And this morning.

Nothing, *really,* had happened. It was just that, treading behind him, following Sam through the cold and lofty spaces of the mill . . . the echoing passages, the deserted stores and dye sheds, Carrie was made aware, for the first time, of his alter ego. Before her eyes, he seemed to change. Grew in stature, spoke with confidence and authority. He vividly described to her the devastation of the flood and the destruction of machinery, computers, electronic looms. Explained the plans for the future, quoting figures—prices, profits, mark-ups—that made her head reel. Once or twice he had tried to make clear to her the details of some technicality of spinning or weaving, which she could scarcely understand because it was a bit as though he were talking in a foreign language. Irritated by her own stupidity, she felt diminished and also confused, because Sam, back in his own world, was strangely transformed. No longer the amiable house guest of the last few days, but a man in charge, a man to be reckoned with, and, at the end of the day, a man you would not choose to cross.

He returned to her at last, bearing their drinks and two packets of peanuts. "Sorry." He set these down on the table, and drew up a second chair. "Conversation."

"What were you talking about?"

"Football. Fishing. The weather. What else?" He had bought himself a pint of bitter. He raised the tall glass. Across the table their eyes met. "Slàinte."

"I don't speak the language."

"It's Gaelic for 'Down the hatch.' "

Carrie took a mouthful of her drink, and hastily set down the glass. "Heavens, that's strong."

"The classic warmer when you're out on a winter hill. That, or cherry brandy."

"What's the weather going to do?"

"There's a thaw on the way. That's why our friend is glued to the box. The wind is moving around to the south-west, and there are milder air streams on the way."

"No white Christmas?"

"Wet white rather than freezing white. And the road to Inverness is open again."

"Does that mean you're going to disappear instantly?"

"No." He shook his head. "I've been asked for Christmas, so I'm staying. Anyway, I've nowhere else to go. But on Boxing Day, I must come down to earth with a bang, pack my bags and leave." His smile was wry. "It's going to feel a bit like the end of the holidays and having to go back to school."

"Never mind. Lots of fun and games in the pipeline. Elfrida's party, for one."

"I have to be here for *that*. I've promised to mix a jug of Pimms."

"Don't make it too strong. We don't want any untoward behaviour. Like Lady Erskine-Earle and Arfur Snead dancing Highland Flings together."

"That would be disastrous."

"When . . . when you get to Inverness, will you stay there?"

"No. I have to be in London next week. The head office is open for a couple of days before the New Year, and David Swinfield's set up a meeting. Then, I think, Switzerland again. I shan't be back here until about the twelfth of January."

"Lucy and I go on the third. We're booked on the morning flight." She bit her lip, thinking about this. "I'm not looking forward to it. I think Lucy is going to be desolate, and I don't know what I'm going to say to cheer her up. I only know I wouldn't want to be her, leaving all the fun and the freedom behind and going back to that dull flat, and a mother who won't be particularly delighted to see her."

"It can't be as bad as that."

"Sam, it is."

"I'm sorry."

"I don't think there's very much you can do about it."

"I shall buy her a splendid Christmas present. What do you think she would like?"

Carrie was amused. "Have you still not done your shopping?"

"You must admit, I've scarcely had time. I shall go to Kingsferry tomorrow morning and get the lot."

"Tomorrow? It'll be a nightmare. Crowds on the pavements, queues in the shops."

"In Kingsferry? I think not. Besides, I'm accustomed to buying presents in Regent Street; or Fifth Avenue on Christmas Eve. I rather enjoy the buzz and the din. 'I saw Mommy Kissing Santa Claus' blaring out over the Tannoy. As well, there's not time for dithering."

Carrie laughed. "It's my idea of a bad dream, but I see your point. And after all your years of experience, Kingsferry High Street will not seem in the least alarming. You will shoulder your way, bravely, through the throng."

"You still haven't told me what to get for Lucy."

Carrie considered this. "How about little gold studs for her ears? Something pretty but not too over-the-top. For when she wants to take her sleepers out."

"Rory gave her the sleepers. I don't suppose she'll ever want to take them out."

"Still. Nice to know you've got another pair."

"I'll see."

He fell silent. The silence lay between them, and felt comfortable. Outside, in the street, a car passed by, and somewhere a herring-gull was screaming its heart out from a windy chimney-pot. Sam reached for one of the packets of peanuts and opened it with great neatness and dexterity, shook a few out into the palm of his hand and offered them to Carrie.

She said, "I don't really like peanuts."

He ate a couple and tossed the packet back onto the table. He said,

"I sympathize with Lucy. I decided the other morning that life at the Estate House is a bit like being on a cruise, with just a few other passengers . . . marvellously removed from all the stresses and strains of everyday life. I have a sinister feeling I could happily jog along, in low gear, for weeks. Achieving nothing."

"I suppose, if you think about it, it's all been a bit of a waste of time for you."

He frowned. "A waste of time?"

"Well, the whole point of your coming to Creagan was to inspect Hughie McLennan's house. Perhaps to buy it. And that all fell through. A busted flush. So now you're going to have to go and find some other place to live."

"That is the least of my problems."

"I'm not on anybody's side. Half of me relishes the idea of Mr. Howard, the director of the mill, living at the Estate House, a suitably dignified environment for an important man. On the other hand, at the moment, it seems to be Oscar and Elfrida's only home. Where they are happily settled for their twilight years."

"I don't think of Elfrida as twilight. More high noon. And it all boils down . . . as most things do . . . to the distasteful question of hard cash. A busted flush, maybe. But never a waste of time. Never think that."

Carrie reached for her glass and took another mouthful of her fiery and comforting drink. She put the glass down on the scarred wooden surface of the table and looked up into Sam's face. *Never a waste of time. . . .* And an extraordinary thing happened, because all at once it was as though she had never truly seen him before; and now all she knew for certain was that her recognition of him was too late, because he would go away, it would be all over, and she would probably never see him again.

Perhaps it was the warmth of the fire, or the effect of the Whisky Mac, because suddenly she felt dangerously emotional and quite unsure of herself. She thought of how injured victims, devastated by some dreadful accident, lay on hospital beds in comas, wired up to tubes and machines, whilst loved ones sat by them, holding hands, talking, hoping against hope, for some flicker of recognition or other sign. And then the miracle. The twitching eyelid, the nod of the head. The start of recovery.

Yesterday, at Corrydale, after her outburst of words and her angry weeping, Sam had taken her in his arms and held her until the tears ceased. And she had felt no warmth for him, no physical reaction to his closeness. Only a grudging gratitude for his comfort, and shame for herself, for behaving like a fool.

But now . . . the beginning of recovery, perhaps. The melting of the coldness that had been her only armour. To love. To be loved again . . .

"Carrie . . . Can we talk?"

"What about?"

"You and me. Us." Carrie said nothing. After a bit, perhaps encouraged by her silence, he went on. "It seems to me that we've met each other . . . got to know each other . . . at a bad time. We're both, as it were, in something of a state of limbo. Perhaps we both need a bit of space to get our various houses in order. Also, neither of us is free. You've taken on the moral responsibility for Lucy, and I'm still married to Deborah."

He watched for her reaction to all this, and his expression was both anxious and very serious. Carrie's response was clearly of great importance to him.

"What are you telling me, Sam?"

"Just that, perhaps, we should give ourselves a bit of time. You go back to London, take repossession of your own house, get on top of your new job. And I shall get in touch with New York, and Deborah's lawyer. I'm pretty certain by now she'll have started proceedings. I don't know how long it will take, but as we had no children, there should be no serious complications. Simply material matters. The apartment, the car, the money."

"Is that what you really want? Divorce?"

"No." He was bluntly honest. "I don't want it. Any more than I would choose to have a surgical amputation. But I have to sort out the past before I can embark on a new future. Get rid of a lot of emotional clobber."

"Will Deborah be all right?"

"I hope so. She has as good a chance as most people, and the backing of a loving and devoted family."

"Is it going to be painful?"

"Ending something that was once good is bound to be painful. But, done, and over, the hurting stops."

Carrie said, "I know what you mean."

He went on. "I shall be living and working here, in Buckly. You'll be in London. Hundreds of miles apart. But I know I shall be flying up and down to London like a yo-yo, for meetings and conferences and such. I thought perhaps . . . we could see each other again. Go to a concert; out to dinner. Start over. Afresh. As though none of this time had ever happened."

Start over. Afresh. The two of them. Carrie said, "*I* wouldn't want this time not to have happened."

"I'm glad. It's been extraordinary, hasn't it? Magic. Like days stolen from another life, another world. When it is over, and I am gone, I shall wallow in nostalgia." Carrie's hand lay on the table between them, and the firelight was reflected and sparked facets of light from her sapphire-and-diamond ring. Without curiosity, "Who gave you your ring?" he asked.

"Andreas."

"I hoped it might have been bequeathed to you by an elderly but devoted aunt."

"No. It was Andreas. We were in Munich together. He saw it on a velvet tray in the window of an antique shop, and he went in and bought it for me."

"You must wear it always," Sam told her. "It is so lovely on your hand. How shall I find you in London, Carrie?"

"Oversees. Bruton Street. It's in the phone book. And I'll be back in Ranfurly Road in February."

"I haven't been back to Fulham again since I sold my house in Eel

Park and left for New York. Perhaps I shall come. Take a trip down Memory Lane. And you shall show me where you live."

"Do that. I'll cook you dinner."

"No promises. No commitments."

"No promises."

"So we leave it like that."

"We leave it like that?"

Sam said, "Good." And, as though he were sealing their agreement, he covered her hand with his own, and she turned up her palm and wrapped her fingers around his wrist. Their drinks finished, it was, perhaps, time to leave, but both were reluctant to go. So they stayed while the barman, slowly polishing glasses with a tea-towel, gazed at some quiz show. And the two old men, heads sunken into the collars of their worn overcoats, sat on, ancient and silent as a pair of hibernating tortoises. They seemed unaware that, as they whiled away the last of the morning, the whole world had changed.

SAM

That evening, at six-thirty, Sam found himself once more in a pub, but now it was Creagan, and he was with Oscar.

"Let's go and have a drink," Oscar had suggested. They were alone in the sitting-room of the Estate House. Others were occupied elsewhere; Carrie and Elfrida clashing companionably about in the kitchen together, concocting dinner: food for the party tomorrow, and at the same time starting in on the long-term preparations for the Christmas feast. During the course of the afternoon, Rory Kennedy had appeared with large bunches of berried holly, and he and Lucy had set to decorating, and were still at it. They had gone up to the top of the garden and torn away from the wall long strands of dark-green ivy, and it was taking them much concentration and effort to twine this down the whole length of the banister, from attic to hall. Rory had been invited for supper, and accepted, which was just as well, because it all seemed to be taking a very long time.

The Creagan pub was a great deal more cheerful than the Duke's Arms in Buckly (although Sam guessed that he would always remember that charmless spot with much affection). Here, seasonal festivities seemed to have started, and there were unknown faces at the bar. In one corner a noisy party was already well under way; young men in elegantly battered tweeds and their trendy girl-friends with

London voices. They had doubtless driven down the glen from some remote family shooting-lodge opened up for Christmas and the New Year, and filled with house guests. They were, thought Sam—conveniently forgetting that he, once, had behaved just as boisterously—making an unnecessary and embarrassing amount of din.

But it all felt very lively. Open fires burnt, and decorations were festooned all about the place, tastefully entwined with holly, and cardboard Bambis and Father Christmases twinkling with glitter.

It took a bit of time to shoulder up to the bar, and then to catch the attention of the frantic barman, but finally Oscar did this and ordered two Famous Grouses, one for Sam, on the rocks, and one for himself, with tap-water. They then had something of a search for a place to sit, and ended up at a small, unoccupied table in a dark corner, away from the fire. It didn't matter. It was quite warm enough.

Oscar said, "Cheers," took a mouthful of his drink, set down the glass, and got straight down to business.

". . . I thought it would be easier to talk here than at home. The telephone is inclined to ring, or some person comes flying in with questions on their lips. I didn't want us to be disturbed."

"Oscar, this all sounds very sinister."

"Not sinister at all, dear boy. But slightly complicated. And I wanted to talk to you on my own."

"What's happened?"

"What has happened is that Major Billicliffe has died. You have heard, maybe . . . you know about Major Billicliffe?"

"The old factor who was in hospital."

"Exactly so."

"I'm sorry."

"We are all sorry, for different reasons. Whatever, he has died. I think he had been ill for a long time, far longer than any of us suspected. To cut a long story short, Sam, he has left me his house at Corrydale."

"But that's wonderful news."

"I am not so sure. It's in a fairly neglected state. . . ."

"Carrie and I looked at it when we went to get the Christmas tree. A bit desolate, perhaps, and completely snowed up, but I would have thought a good little property. And, of course, that marvellous view, down the fields and the trees to the water."

"As well," Oscar went on, sounding like a man determined to make a clean breast of things, "he has left me his car, *and* his Labrador, and a small amount of money."

Sam made a face. "I can't be too enthusiastic about the car. It looked to me as though it would never start up again. As for the dog, I think that's the one Charlie Miller had with him? Perhaps he can be persuaded to keep it?"

"Yes."

"Oscar, this is really good news. What will you do with the cottage? Put it on the market? Or you could turn it into a holiday let, a nice little earner, as they say."

"Yes," said Oscar. "I could. But Elfrida and I think that we might go and live there. I know it sounds a little outlandish, and it all depends on Elfrida's reaction when she actually gets to see over the place. You see, she's never been to Corrydale. Before you all came, we didn't do very much, I'm afraid. Kept a bit of a low profile. Kept ourselves to ourselves. And she knew that, in a strange way, I rather dreaded going back to a place where once, so long ago, I had been so happy."

"I understand."

"We did drop in, of course, on our first night, because we had to collect the key to the Estate House. But it was dark and cold, we were tired, and old Billicliffe was not the neatest of housekeepers. We couldn't wait to get away. When he was ill and I went to see him in bed, it looked even worse, and both our impressions of the place are so dismal that we shall have to think deeply before we make up our minds and do a total assessment of the situation."

"Would you like to live there?" Sam asked. "Is it not very remote?"

"Not really. A bit off the road, but neighbours all about. The Home Farm, the Millers, and Rose, who used to be my grandmother's parlourmaid. A little community. The house will probably need a bit spent on it, and we'll have to try to work that out, but the idea does have possibilities."

Sam said, "It did seem somewhat neglected, but the roof wasn't fallen in, nor windows broken. How much space would you have?"

"All the estate houses were the same design. Two up and two down. Originally. Little kitchens and bathrooms were added on after the war."

"Would that be big enough for you both?"

"I think so. We have, between us, few possessions."

"And the Estate House?"

"That's why I want to talk to you. If we go to Corrydale, Elfrida and I want you to have my share of the Estate House. That means that you can get in touch with Hughie, and tell him that you wish to buy us both out."

"*If* you move to Corrydale?"

"Yes."

"What if Elfrida decides against living there? What if you both have second thoughts once you've really looked at the place?"

"Then we shall all have to think again. But somehow I don't expect that will happen. It will doubtless need a certain amount of money spent on it to make it sound, and dry and warm. Painting and such, probably new window-sashes. That sort of thing. But between us, we could manage. And if I get seventy-five thousand for my share of the Estate House, then we should have no problems, financially speaking."

"Seventy-five thousand, Oscar?"

"That was the sum you mentioned."

"No. That was the sum *Hughie* mentioned. What you have just told me changes everything."

"I don't understand."

"Your cousin Hughie, I think, is strapped for cash. And he needs it quickly. That was why he was so keen to press his door key into my hand, and so anxious to avoid the added expense of an estate agent's cut. Personally, I think the Estate House is worth a great deal more than one hundred and fifty thousand. So you must be hard-headed,

Oscar. Before we talk any more, you must get a surveyor in to do an independent valuation. Willing seller, willing buyer. And after that, consult a lawyer to deal with the conveyancing of the property. You may be told . . . I think you will . . . that the house is worth a good deal more than one hundred and fifty thousand. Personally I should add another fifty thousand. Possibly more."

Oscar gaped. "Two hundred thousand?"

"At least. Another thing, Oscar. You may decide to put it on the open market. . . ."

"No. I want to sell it to *you*."

"A private deal?"

"Yes."

"In that case, by law, I should have to make an offer well over the valuation price." Sam smiled. "So it seems, Oscar, that you might do rather well."

"I am bewildered. Whose side are you on?"

"Yours. And Elfrida's. You have a wonderful property here, and I want desperately to buy it from you. But I couldn't look myself in the eye if it wasn't all accomplished in a totally business-like fashion."

"Do you have that sort of money?"

"Yes. And if I didn't, I have Sturrock and Swinfield, solid as a rock, behind me. There are some advantages in working for an enormous conglomerate."

Oscar shook his head, quite bemused by the turn of events. He said, "Well, I'll be buggered."

Sam laughed. "Don't get over-excited. Not until you've fully inspected your other piece of property."

"Billicliffe's place, you mean. Elfrida thought we might all go over on Sunday morning and take a look at it. Make a bit of an occasion. Take a picnic lunch. If it buckets with rain or snow, we'll have a picnic indoors. I must find out who has got the key. I'll ring Rose. She'll know."

"Are you sure you want all of us there? You mustn't be influenced.

You and Elfrida must make up your own minds. You owe that much to yourselves."

"Of course you must all come. Elfrida needs you, to tap walls and check out for death-watch beetle."

"That's putting temptation in my way. I might pretend not to find it."

"I don't think you'd do that." Oscar gave a crack of his head. "You're a good man, Sam."

"A saint. And to prove it, and seal the bargain, let me get you the other half. It would seem we're both men of property and deserve to toast one another."

Lucy

Friday, December 22nd

Why I love it here so much is because things that you want to happen, happen exactly on time. Today was absolutely filled with unexpected events. It's still dreadfully cold, and windy, too, which makes it even more cold, but somehow it's all part of everything that's going on. It hasn't snowed any more, but there's still snow everywhere, and the streets are half slush and half frozen stuff. Going shopping, you have to walk in the middle of the street.

Anyway, this morning, I packed up all my Christmas parcels, ran out of ribbon but got more, and took Horace for a walk at the same time. We went to the beach, and we were both jolly glad to get home and into the warm. In the afternoon, Rory turned up with lots of berried holly that he'd nicked from the hotel garden (the hotel is closed), and all afternoon he helped me decorate, and we put the holly over pictures (what pictures there are) and in a big jug on the landing. And then we got ivy, and found some green string, and we twined the ivy down the banisters from the top of the house to the bottom. There were a few little bugs in the ivy, but they disappeared after a bit, probably to make cosy little dens all over the place. The ivy smells very strongly, but it's a nice Christmassy smell. It took us a long time; so long that Elfrida asked Rory to stay for supper, so that we could finish it all. While we were doing this, Elfrida and Carrie were cooking in the kitchen, and getting everything ready for the next couple of days. For tea, there were hot scones, which Carrie had made.

About six, while they were still cooking supper, Oscar and Sam went off to the pub for a drink, and when they got back, Rory and I had finished all the ivy and holly, and Oscar said he thought it all looked very beautiful. Sam said it needed a long, long string of fairy lights, twined over the ivy, but of course we hadn't got that, so he said he's going shopping in Kingsferry tomorrow, and that he'll buy some for us, and bring them home.

I think he is a most thoughtful and generous person.

Supper was spaghetti and bolognese sauce and cheese, and then mince pies and cream. And over supper, when we were all talking away, Oscar told us to stop talking and listen. So we did.

He told us that he has got another house. Major Billicliffe, who was the factor at Corrydale, has died in hospital in Inverness, and he has made a will and left all he owns to Oscar, which includes this little cottage on the Corrydale Estate.

I've never been there, but of course Sam and Carrie have, and they saw it the day they went to get the tree. And Elfrida has been there, but only once, in the dark.

Anyway, what Oscar wants to do is to sell his share of this house to Sam, who wants it, and he and Elfrida will go and live in this other little place. I can't bear to think of them not being here, but Elfrida says it is a bit big for them, and I can understand that, because when we go it will be very empty for them. She says that between them they have got enough money to make Major Billicliffe's little house very nice, and they have got neighbours so won't be alone in time of emergency.

But nothing can be cut and dried until we have all gone to Corrydale to look it over. So we are going on Sunday morning, and Sam is going to drive us in the Range Rover, and we are going to take a picnic. I said could Rory come, too, and Elfrida said, But of course. We are going in the morning, so that we can get home before it gets dark, and with a bit of luck the sun will shine and it will be a real picnic.

Now it is ten o'clock at night, and I am really tired.

I do hope we all like the new cottage. In a way, I think it would be lovely for Oscar and Elfrida to live in the country. And it means that he will return to Corrydale, which was his grandmother's house, when he was small. Like a wheel, going full circle. He is so darling, I really want the little cottage to be perfect, so that when I am back in London, I can think of them both there, together.

My presents look really festive, all wrapped up. When I had finished them, I put them under the tree in the dining-room. And I found some parcels there already, and I had a good look. They were for all of us from Carrie. With a bit of luck, there'll be lots more.

Elfrida's Party

That morning, Sam was the first downstairs. Eight o'clock and the rest of the household still slept. In the kitchen, he put a kettle on to boil, and then opened up the back door and let Horace out into the garden. The weather was totally changed. The barman at the Duke's Arms had been right . . . or at least, his television set had been right. The dark morning air had lost its freezing bite; during the night the wind had dropped and moved around from the north to the west, and at the top of the garden, the pines soughed in this gentler breeze. By the light of the street lamp, Sam saw that in places the snow had seeped away, revealing patches of rough, tufty grass, and there was the fresh smell of moss and damp earth.

When Horace finally returned to him, he went back indoors, and there found Lucy, fully dressed and making toast.

"Hello. What are you doing?"

"I've been awake since seven. I was reading, and then I heard someone go downstairs, so I got up. Are you going to Kingsferry?"

"Yes. Do you want to come? I'm going to do Christmas shopping before all the crowds move in. You can come and help me carry parcels."

The roads were wet but the hard ice had gone, and the overcast sky gradually was lightening. Crossing the bridge over a flood-tide, they saw the deep waters of the firth, the colour of dark slate, penetrating westward into hills which still had not yet shed their snow, and probably would not until the end of winter. To the east, the sea was tossed into rough little waves by the offshore wind, and a pair of curlews flew, low, over the scrubby sea fields where the Highland cattle grazed.

"It's a bit like an old painting, isn't it?" Lucy observed. "You know, the sort people who have huge houses have hanging in their dining-rooms."

"I know exactly what you mean. Not exactly cheerful, but impressive."

"Are you looking forward to living up here, in Scotland?"

"I think so. I think I'm going to like it very much."

"I'd like to come in summer. See it then. Rory Kennedy says it's really good fun. They go windsurfing. And Tabitha told me that there are incredible wild flowers on the dunes, and all the gardens in Creagan are filled with roses."

"Hard to imagine at this time of year."

"Are you really going to live in the Estate House?"

"If Oscar wants to sell it to me."

"It's pretty big for one person."

"Perhaps I shall use all the rooms in rotation."

"Will you change it all, and make it frightfully new and convenient?"

"I don't know, Lucy." He remembered the apartment in New York, unrecognizable by the time Deborah and her interior designer had finished with it. "I rather like it just the way it is."

"My grandmother loves what she calls doing rooms over. The sitting-room in her flat is all pinks and blues and lots of little bits of china."

"Is it a big flat?"

"Yes, it is. Quite big. And it has a nice view over the river. But my room's at the back and I look out over the well, so I don't have a view."

And then, as though fearful of sounding complaining, she added, "But I *do* like it, and it's all mine."

"It's good to have your own space."

"Yes." She was quiet for a moment, and then said, "Actually, I'm not thinking about London just now. Usually I'm quite pleased to be going back to school and seeing friends again. But this time I'm not looking forward to it one little *bit*."

"I feel the same. Boxing Day and I head back to Inverness to get my nose to the grindstone again."

"But *you're* coming back. To live here forever."

"You can come back, too," he reminded her. "Stay with Elfrida and Oscar."

"But it won't be the Estate House. And the new cottage, if they do go and live there, mightn't have a spare bedroom."

"I don't think a small detail like that would faze Elfrida. She'd put you in the bath, or on the sofa, or in a tent in the garden."

"In the summer that might be rather fun."

Now, ahead of them, lay the lights of Kingsferry, the church spire, and the tower of the Town Hall.

"Do you know what you're going to give everybody?" Lucy asked.

"No idea," Sam admitted. "I hope to be inspired."

They drove into the High Street as the Town Hall clock struck nine, and saw that already the morning was well on its way. Shops had opened; cars swept slushily by; people bought morning rolls and newspapers; and a parked van was unloading crates of fruit and vegetables, bundles of holly, and tiny Christmas trees. The car-park behind the church was already half-full, but Sam found a slot and paid his ticket, and they set off together on foot.

Shopping was not one of Lucy's favourite things. Sometimes, in London, she went with her mother, and started out quite enthusiastically, but after two hours of trailing around overheated stores, waiting for Nicola to make up her mind about which pair of shoes to buy, or what colour lipstick, she became bored, complained of the heat, and demanded to be allowed to go home.

But shopping with Sam wasn't like that at all. A revelation, in fact. In and out of shops they went, like a dose of salts (as Mrs. Snead would say), making snap decisions and never asking the price of anything. Sam paid all the bills with his credit card, and Lucy began to suspect that he must be frightfully rich.

The goodies piled up, bundled into plastic carrier-bags. A sea-green cashmere cardigan for Elfrida, fur-lined gloves for Mrs. Snead. In the stationer's he chose a Mont Blanc fountain pen for Oscar, and a desk diary of the finest Italian leather.

Lucy spied some rolls of gold paper. She said, "Have you got stuff for wrapping up all your presents?"

"No."

"Shall we get some? And ribbon and cards?"

"You choose it. In New York, if you buy something, the girl says, 'Do you want it gift-wrapped?' and you say, 'Yes,' and she goes away and does it for you. I haven't wrapped a present for years, and I'm very bad at it."

"I shall do it for you," Lucy announced, "but *you'll* have to write the messages." She went off and returned with six rolls of paper, some packets of red labels with holly on them, and a ball of red-and-gold ribbon.

By now there was quite a lot to carry, but Sam was by no means finished. In an old-fashioned grocery store which smelt a bit like the ground floor of Fortnum and Mason and had ITALIAN WAREHOUSEMAN written in gold above the door, he spent much time choosing all sorts of delicious treats. Smoked salmon and quails' eggs, and a jar of caviare; huge boxes of Bendicks chocolates, and a Stilton cheese in an earthenware pot.

By now, the man behind the counter, recognizing a good customer when he saw one, had become Sam's best friend. Between the two of them, after some discussion, they decided on a dozen bottles of special claret, four of champagne, and finally one of cognac.

All of this, gathered together on the counter, made an impressive show. "How are we going to get all *this* home?" Lucy asked, but the grocer said he would deliver it in his van. So Sam gave him his name and the address of the Estate House, and produced his credit card once more. When all was accomplished, the grocer came out from behind his counter to open the door for them, which he did with something of a flourish, wishing them both a Happy Christmas.

"That," said Lucy, "was much nicer than trudging round a supermarket. Who's left now? You simply must have bought a present for everybody."

"Carrie?"

"I thought the chocolates were for her."

"I don't think chocs are a very exciting present, do you?"

"How about a precious jewel? There's a jeweller's a bit farther down the street. I know, because Rory took me there to have my ears pierced and buy my sleepers."

"Show me."

But before they had reached the jeweller's, Sam spied the little art gallery, which stood across the road. "Let's go and look," he said, so they crossed the road to stand on the pavement and gaze through the window. Lucy did not think there was all that much to gaze at. A Blue and White jug with twigs in it, and a small painting, gold-framed, on a little easel. The picture was of roses in a silver jug. Three pink roses and one white one. And there was a sort of scarf lying on the table, and a bit of curtain.

For quite a long time, Sam didn't say anything. Lucy looked at him and realized that, for some reason, his attention had been totally captured by the little still life. She said, "Do you like it?"

"Um? What? Yes, I do. It's a Peploe."

"A what?"

"Samuel Peploe. A Scottish painter. Let's go in."

He opened the door, and Lucy followed. Inside, they found themselves in a surprisingly spacious room, the walls covered with pictures, and, as well, a number of other objects stood about: rather strange sculptures and hand-thrown pots which looked as if they might leak if filled with water. In the corner of the room was a desk, behind which sat a young man of amazing thinness, wearing a huge, baggy, hand-knitted sweater. He had a lot of flowing hair, and a stubbly chin, and as they appeared he hauled himself, in a fatigued sort of way, to his feet.

"Hi."

Sam said, "Good morning. The painting in your window . . ."

"Oh, yes, the Peploe."

"An original?"

"But of course. I don't deal in prints."

Sam kept his cool. "May I see it?"

"If you want to."

He went to the window and reached in and lifted the picture off its easel, and brought it back to where Sam stood, holding it out beneath the overhead lights.

Sam set down his burden of plastic carrier-bags. "May I?" he asked, and gently took the heavy frame into his own hands. A silence fell while he inspected it, and the young man, apparently too exhausted to stand for a moment longer, leaned against the edge of the desk and folded his arms.

Nothing much happened after that. Lucy, bored with hanging around, wandered off to look at the other pictures on the walls (mostly abstracts), and bits of pottery and sculpture. There was one sculpture which was called *Rationality Two,* and consisted of two pieces of driftwood tied together with rusted wire. She saw that it cost five hundred pounds, and decided that if ever she needed to make a quick bit of cash, this would be as good a way as any.

Now, the two men were talking.

"Where did this come from?" Sam asked.

"An old house. Local. A sale. The old lady died. She had been a friend of Peploe when he was alive. I'm not sure the picture wasn't a wedding gift."

"You were astute to buy it."

"I didn't. I bought it off a dealer. You're an admirer of Peploe?"

"My mother had one. I own it now. It's in store in London."

"In that case . . ."

"This isn't for me. . . ."

Lucy, chipping in, said, "Who's it for, Sam?"

Sam had apparently forgotten about her, but now, reminded of her presence, laid the picture down on the desk. "Lucy, this is going to take a bit of time. You don't want to hang around." He felt in his back pocket for his wallet, took it out, and peeled off three ten-pound notes, which he pressed into her hand. "We still haven't bought the fairy lights for the banisters. There's an electrical store next to the grocer's. You nip along and buy as many as you think you'll need, and then come back here when you've got them. Leave all the shopping behind; you don't want to have to lug that with you. And if you see anything else you think we might need, get that, too. Okay?"

"Okay," said Lucy. She pocketed the money (thirty pounds!) dumped the carrier-bags under a chair, and went. She had a pretty good idea that Sam wanted to get rid of her for two reasons. He didn't want her to know how much the picture was going to cost, and he still hadn't bought a present for *her,* and of course couldn't do this with Lucy watching.

She set off, back down the street, the way they had come. She hoped Sam would not buy her a wobbly jug, but was pretty sure that he wouldn't. She wondered if the Samuel Peploe was to be a present for Carrie. And thirty pounds would buy *yards* of fairy lights.

After some discussion and a certain amount of haggling, Sam and the hairy young man came to an agreement, which ended up with Sam's buying the Peploe. While it was being wrapped up, and the necessary paperwork done, he went out and crossed the road and found, without much difficulty, the jeweller's shop, its window filled with silver photograph frames and small, ornate clocks. Inside, he was shown a selection of earrings, and quickly chose a pair of gold studs fashioned like daisy heads. The girl who had served him put them into a box and a gold envelope, and he paid her, stuffed the box into his pocket, and went back to the art gallery, where all had been accomplished. The only problem was that the young man didn't handle credit cards, so Sam had to write a cheque.

"Whom shall I make it out to?"

"Me."

"Do you have a name?"

"Yes." He produced a card. "Tristram Nightingale."

And Sam, writing the cheque, felt quite sorry for him. Lumbered with a handle like that, a man was allowed to be a bit charmless. As he signed his own name, Lucy reappeared, with yet another box to lug back to the car.

"Did you get them?" he asked.

"Yes. Four strings. I think that should be enough, don't you?"

"Ample. We'll get Rory to help us set them up." He handed over the cheque and picked up the strongly wrapped parcel. "Thank you very much."

Tristram Nightingale laid the cheque on his desk, and then, as they gathered up their packages, he loped to the door and opened it for them.

"Have a good Christmas," he said as they went out.

"And the same to you," said Sam, but as soon as they were out of earshot, he added, "With knobs on, Mr. Nightingale."

"Mr. *Who*?"

"He's called Tristram Nightingale. His parents must have been sadists. No wonder he hates the world."

"What a dreadful name. Except you'd have thought that by now he'd have got used to it. Sam, who's the picture for?"

"Carrie. Don't tell her."

"Of course I won't. Was it frightfully expensive?"

"Yes, it was, but when things are as expensive as that, you don't call it expensive. You say a good investment."

"I think that's a lovely present. And when she goes back to live in Ranfurly Road, she can hang it on her sitting-room wall."

"That's what I thought."

"And she'll remember Scotland and Creagan and everything."

"I thought that, too."

"Will you ever see her again?"

"I don't know." Sam smiled down at Lucy. "I hope so."

"I hope so, too," said Lucy. And after a bit, "It's been a good morning. Thank you for letting me come with you."

"Thank you for coming. You were a tremendous help."

By half past five that evening, the Estate House stood ready, dressed overall, for Elfrida's party.

The front door wore a wreath of holly, and the overhead light clearly illuminated a thumb-tacked cardboard notice which read PLEASE WALK IN. This, Elfrida hoped, would preclude the hassle of ringing the bell, Horace barking, and the repetitive running up and downstairs in order to greet the guests. Once through the door, the dining-room Christmas tree was revealed in all its glory, lit up, and standing knee-deep in packages. At the far end of the hall the staircase rose, entangled with holly and ivy, and sparkling with white fairy lights.

Above, the landing had been turned into a bar, where the big table from the sitting-room bay window (shunted to its new location by Oscar and Sam) was spread with a white cloth (one of Mrs. Snead's best linen sheets) and neatly set out with bottles, ice-bucket, and rows of the polished glasses borrowed from Tabitha Kennedy.

All of this had taken some time and effort, and when Mrs. Snead and Arthur arrived to take charge of the last-minute preparations, like heating up the tiny pizzas and spearing hot sausages with cocktail sticks, everyone had disappeared to shave, bathe, change, and generally doll themselves up for the evening ahead. From behind closed doors came sounds of running taps, the buzz of electric razors, and the steamy fragrance of bath-oil.

Horace, sneaking upstairs for a bit of company that wasn't the Sneads, found nobody around, so made his way into the sitting-room, and there settled down comfortably in front of a blazing fire.

Oscar was the first to emerge. He closed the bedroom door behind him and stood alone, for a moment, to savour the Christmas transformation of his house, prepared and ready for an influx of guests. He saw the neat arrangement of polished glasses, like so many soap-bubbles; the green-and-gold of champagne bottles jammed into a bucket of ice, the crisp white linen of napkin and table-cloth. The drawn stair curtains shut away the night, and the stairwell, all four flights of it, was entwined with dark ropes of greenery, red-berried holly, and starry lights. So much, he thought wryly, for the bleak Winter Solstice, which was all he had promised Elfrida. And he decided that the Estate House, normally so minimal and austere, but now dressed and adorned to the nines, was a bit like a strait-laced elderly but much-loved aunt who had put on her best finery and precious jewels for some special occasion, and ended up looking not bad at all.

Oscar, too, had made an effort, and wore a favourite old smoking jacket and his best silk shirt. Elfrida had chosen his tie, and insisted he wear his gold-embroidered black velvet slippers. He could scarcely remember when he had last dressed himself up, but the silk shirt felt luxurious against his skin, and he had slapped on some Bay Rum and sleeked down his thick white hair.

Elfrida, whom he had left at her mirror, still in her dressing-gown, and screwing in her earrings, had told him that he looked toothsome.

From the kitchen came Snead voices and other sounds of culinary activity. Mrs. Snead had arrived, not in her track suit, but wearing her best black dress, with sequins twinkling from the bodice. She had also had her hair done for the occasion, and decorated this new coiffure with a black satin bow.

As he had dressed, chatting the while to Elfrida, Oscar had not allowed himself to think back to his last Christmas at the Grange. The lavishness of that time, and the hospitality on a scale that beggared belief. Huge meals, too many guests, too many presents, too huge a tree. But somehow Gloria had got away with it all, the sheer size of everything tempered by her enjoyment, her generosity of spirit.

He had not allowed himself to think back, but now, in a rare moment of solitude, he did. And it all seemed so long ago . . . he could scarcely realize it was only twelve months . . . and it felt a bit like recalling a time out of another existence. He thought of Francesca. Remembered her running down the great staircase at the Grange, wearing a black velvet dress that was a present from her mother, and with her hair flying loose. She had always seemed to be running, as though time were so precious that there was not a moment of it to be wasted.

Only a short while ago, this memory would have shattered him with grief. But now, Oscar simply felt grateful, because Francesca would always be part of his life, part of his being. And because, after all that had happened, he had somehow survived. And, more, found himself surrounded and sustained by friends.

Below, he heard the kitchen door open, and Mrs. Snead's voice giving Arthur his orders. Arthur then appeared up the staircase bearing a tray of what Mrs. Snead called "canaypes." A bowl of nuts and small biscuits spread with pâté and such. Arthur wore his best grey flannel trousers and his Bowling Club blazer, emblazoned with a gold emblem on the breast pocket.

Climbing the last flight, he spied Oscar. "Well, there you are, Mr. Blundell, and don't you look dressy. Mrs. Snead said to bring these up, and put them round the sitting-room. 'Ot stuff's coming later. Only thing is, 'Orace sneaked off. Bet 'e's sitting by the fire. Don't want 'im eating all the goodies."

"We'll put them out of his reach, Arthur."

He led Arthur into the big room, which looked warm and welcoming and unnaturally neat and tidy. Every light and lamp had been turned on, and the fire blazed. Elfrida had filled jugs with holly and white chrysanthemums, but the best was the huge vase of Stargazer lilies that little Lucy had given Elfrida for Christmas. Arthur had delivered them during the course of the morning, all wrapped in cellophane and tied with a large pink bow, and Elfrida had nearly burst into tears, so touched and delighted had she been. They stood now on a small table by the sofa, their exotic petals slowly opening out in the warmth of the room, exuding their heavy, almost tropical fragrance.

They set out the nuts and crisps, well out of reach of Horace, who lay by the fire pretending to be fast asleep. Oscar wondered if he should boot the dog downstairs again, but left him where he was, because he looked so comfortable. Once they had disposed of the little dishes at a safe height, Oscar and Arthur returned to the bar, where they found Sam, looking sleek in his dark suit and an enviable blue-and-white-striped shirt.

"You know Sam Howard, don't you, Arthur?"

"Don't think I've 'ad the pleasure. Pleased to meet you."

"Arthur's going to be our barman, Sam."

Sam said, "I'm sure you know how to open a bottle of champagne, Arthur."

"Well, I can't say I've 'ad that much practice, being a beer man myself. But on the telly, like the Grand Prix, it's all a bit of shaking, and then squirting each other, like a fire 'ose. Dreadful waste of good booze, I always thinks."

Sam laughed. "Good fun, but I agree with you. A terrible waste. Actually, it's no problem. You don't want any loud pops, corks hitting the ceiling, or gallons of froth." He took a bottle from the ice bucket. "Just untwist the wire, and then the gentlest easing out of the cork . . . like this. And you don't turn the cork. You hold it, and turn the bottle. . . ." He demonstrated the subtle art, the cork slipped gently out with the softest of sounds, and the golden wine creamed into the waiting glass without a drop spilt.

"Well, that's very neat, I must say," said Arthur. "I never knew it could be done so quiet."

Elfrida, with the final eyelash tweaked into place, gazed at her reflection in the long mirror of the wardrobe. She had put on black silk trousers and a filmy little black blouse, over which she wore a loose green silk coat. Dangling earrings and long strings of beads were the same jade green as the coat, and her eyelids were blue, her mouth scarlet, and her hair a freshly twinked blaze of flame.

She hoped that all her new friends in Creagan would not think she had gone over the top.

Emerging from her bedroom, she found Arthur Snead all ready for duty by the makeshift bar.

"Arthur! You look so handsome. Where's Mrs. Snead?"

"Just finishing off the last of the mini kievs, Mrs. Phipps. She'll be up in a mo'. I 'ope you don't mind my saying so, but you look very dashing. Would hardly 'ave recognized you, meeting you in the street."

"Oh, thank you, Arthur. Is everybody present and ready?"

"All inside, by the fire. Guests ought to be 'ere any moment now."

"They're meant to walk in. But if they don't, be a saint and go down and open the door."

"I'll do that, Mrs. Phipps. And now, 'ow about a nice glass of bubbly? The others are already at it. Dutch courage, Mr. Blundell said. Not that I think 'e needs much courage on such an occasion of celebration."

He poured her a glass, and carrying it, she went to join the others. The room, and they, all looked wonderfully sophisticated and glamorous, like an illustration from some really glossy magazine. Lucy had somehow put her hair up, and with her long black legs and her elegant neck and her earrings, looked all at once about seventeen. As for Carrie, she was, this evening, ravishingly beautiful, with a glow to her skin and a shine in her dark eyes that Elfrida had not seen for years. She had put on a sleeveless black dress, simple as a T-shirt, but with a skirt that flowed softly from her slender hips to her ankles. On her feet were sandals that were no more than a couple of sparkling straps and a pair of very high heels, and her only jewellery were her sapphire ring and a pair of diamond ear-studs.

Seeing her, Elfrida could not imagine how any man could stop himself falling in love with her, but Sam was playing his cards very close to his chest, and seemed to take Carrie's sensational appearance entirely for granted. Which, perhaps, was a hopeful sign. Elfrida wanted above all else for Carrie to be happy again, but Oscar was right. This was too soon for conjecture; too early for matchmaking. One just had to be content with what had happened so far. Which was that Sam had turned up, out of nowhere, in the first place. And that he and Carrie seemed, at last, to have made friends.

They were all talking, but Oscar, standing by the fireplace, saw Elfrida as she came through the door. Their eyes met, and for an instant it was as though it were just the two of them, alone in the brilliantly lighted room. And then he set down his glass and came across to take her hand.

"You look *quite* wonderful," he told her.

"*I* thought I looked a bit like a battered old actress. Which of course I am. But a happy one." She kissed his cheek cautiously, so as not to leave a smudge of lipstick. "And you, Oscar?" They understood each other very well. "All right?"

He nodded. Downstairs, some person, mistakenly, rang the doorbell. Horace leaped to his feet, burst into a cacophony of barking, fled out of the room and down the stairs.

Elfrida began to laugh. "So much," she said, "for my carefully laid plans."

"I'll go," said Lucy instantly. (Probably hoping it was the Kennedys and longing for Rory to be astonished by her new and grown-up image.) She disappeared after Horace, and the next moment there floated upwards the sound of voices. "Are we the first? Are we too early?" And Lucy replying, "Of course not. We're waiting for you. Let me take your coats. Everybody's upstairs."

Elfrida's party, at last, was on its way.

A quarter past eight, and it was all over. Rutleys, Sinclairs, and Erskine-Earles had departed to the sound of goodbyes and thank-yous ringing down the deserted street. Only the Kennedys lingered, and that was because they had been late arriving in the first place, coming to the Estate House straight from the annual party at the Old People's Home. Peter, wearing his dog-collar, announced himself awash with tea and buns, but that didn't stop him gratefully downing a dram, and plunging enthusiastically into another roomful of slightly less geriatric friends.

Now, a certain languor prevailed. Sam had built up the fire, and all had collapsed into chairs, grateful to get the weight off their feet. Rory and Lucy were down in the kitchen, helping Mrs. Snead and Arthur with the last of the clearing up. Cheerful noises and much laughter floated up the stairs, and it was obvious that the party, below stairs, continued.

Elfrida, sunken gratefully into cushions, and with her shoes toed off, said, "I can't believe it's gone so quickly. We've all been beavering away all day, and the next thing you know, it's eight o'clock and guests start looking at their watches and saying it's time to go."

"That's the sign of a good party," said Peter. And added, "Time flies when you're enjoying yourself." He sat in the wide-lapped chair by the fireside, and his wife was on the hearthrug, leaning in comfort against his knees.

"I liked Lady Erskine-Earle," said Carrie. "She looked like a dear little Highland pony, all dressed up in cashmere and pearls."

Tabitha laughed. "Isn't she a star?"

"She and Mrs. Snead chatted for hours."

"That's because they're both on the fund-raising committee for the church. And the Women's Institute. Elfrida, asking the Sneads was a huge bonus. No fear of pregnant pauses with Mrs. Snead and Arthur on the go."

"Arthur was not a barrow boy for nothing," Oscar pointed out. "He never misses a trick. When he wasn't being either butler or guest, he found time to do a little business as well. Orders for New Year's Eve. Chrysanthemums for Emma Erskine-Earle, and six avocados for Janet Sinclair. Incidentally, I think Janet Sinclair's a charming person. We hadn't met her before. Only the doctor, when he came to see Carrie."

"And what is more," Carrie told Oscar, "she's an architect. She works three days a week in a practice in Kingsferry."

"And," Peter added, "she's extremely efficient. She designed a new wing for the Old People's Home, and did a good job. Only thing is, it makes the rest of the place look a bit gloomy." He laid down his glass, shifted slightly in his chair, as though his wife's weight against his knees might be giving him cramp, and looked at his watch. "Tabitha, my love, we should be on our way."

"Oh, don't go," Elfrida begged. "Unless you have to. This is the best bit of a party. Talking it all over with the last of the friends. Stay, and we'll have a kitchen supper. We'll finish up all the scraps, and we've got some soup, and there's more smoked salmon. Sam gave it to us. And a delicious Stilton. . . ."

"Are you sure?" Tabitha was clearly tempted. "If we go back to the Manse it's only scrambled eggs."

"Of course you must stay. . . ."

Here, Carrie took over. "In that case, *I* shall be in charge." She got up from the sofa. "I'll go and see what's happening in the kitchen, and find something for us all to eat. No, Sam, you stay and chat. You've done your part for the evening."

Elfrida was grateful. "Darling, you are sweet. If you want any help give me a shout."

"I'll do that."

She went out of the room and closed the door behind her. On the landing, all that was left of Elfrida's party was the table with the white cloth. Bottles and glasses had all been cleared away. The Sneads, Rory, and Lucy had clearly been hard at work.

The telephone began to ring. Carrie looked at it in some astonishment, because for some reason it was the last thing she expected to happen. It had only rung once when she picked up the receiver.

"Hello."

"Who's that?" The female voice was clear as a bell, but there was a tiny hiccup of hesitation on the line.

"It's Carrie."

"Carrie. It's Nicola. From Florida."

"For heaven's sake. How are you?"

"I'm great. Fine. What are you doing?"

"Just had a party. We're all sitting around recovering."

"Is Lucy there?"

"Yes, she's downstairs, helping to do all the clearing up. She's been having the time of her life. How's Florida? Is the sun shining?"

"Non-stop. Everything's wonderful."

"Hold on. I'll go and find Lucy. . . ."

Carrie laid the receiver on the table and went downstairs. In the kitchen, she saw that all the washing up and putting away had already been accomplished, and Mrs. Snead was now pulling on her mock Persian lamb coat and fastening the silver buttons. Arthur was enjoying the last of a final beer, Rory leaned against the sink, and Lucy was sitting on the kitchen table.

Mrs. Snead was still in full flow. "Well, I must say, that was a really good do . . ." she was saying. She hiccuped slightly and Carrie saw that the bow on her coiffure had slipped a bit, giving her a rakish appearance. ". . . and here's Carrie. I was just saying, Carrie, that was a really good do. Nice company, too. . . ."

"I certainly enjoyed it," Carrie told her. "Lucy, you must run upstairs quickly, your mother's on the telephone."

Lucy's head jerked around; her eyes met Carrie's and in them Carrie saw an expression of alarm.

"Mummy?"

"Yes. From Florida. Go quickly, because it costs a bomb."

Lucy slipped down from the table. She looked at Rory, and then back at Carrie, and then went out of the kitchen and up the stairs.

Discreetly, Carrie closed the door behind her.

"Fancy that," said Arthur. "All the way from Florida."

"It's still afternoon there. Five hours' difference, you know," Mrs. Snead informed them all importantly. Having buttoned her coat, she took off her suede court shoes and pulled on stout boots, in readiness for the short walk home. "Lucy's been a real help, I must say. We got through it all like a dose of salts, didn't we, Rory? And Arfur's put the empties out in the scullery, and a few scraps of sausages I put on a plate for Horace. He can 'ave them for 'is dinner tomorrow."

Carrie was grateful. "You've both been marvellous. You *made* the party."

Arthur drained his beer and set down the empty glass. "I'd like to agree with my wife. A very nice bunch of customers. And tell your friend I'm grateful to know 'ow to open a bottle of champagne. A real little art that one is. Next time we 'ave a Bowling Club party, I'll be able to demonstrate my skill."

"Oh, Arfur, you are a *one*."

"I always say, it's a good day when you learn something."

Mrs. Snead gathered up her possessions, her handbag and the plastic carrier into which she had put her good shoes. "We'll say good night, then, Carrie."

"Good night, Mrs. Snead. And have a great Christmas."

"Same to you. And tell Mrs. Phipps I'll be in Thursday as usual."

When they had gone, arm in arm, out into the night, and the back door had closed behind them, Rory said, "What's Lucy's mother ringing about?"

"I don't know, Rory." Carrie took Elfrida's apron from its hook and tied it on over her filmy black dress. "Probably just to say Happy Christmas."

"It's not Christmas yet."

"Perhaps she's just getting her word in early. Elfrida's asked you and your parents to stay for supper, so I came down to try and get something organized."

"Do you want me to help?"

"I think you've already done your share."

"I don't mind. I'd rather do that than make small talk."

"It seemed to me you managed rather well."

"It's not so bad if you *know* people. What do you want done?"

"Well, if you really mean it . . . perhaps you could lay the table. For eight of us. Knives and forks are in that drawer, and the plates are in that cupboard. And there's smoked salmon in the fridge. I think it's all sliced. You could maybe put it on a plate, and then we'll have to butter some bread."

She went into the icy scullery and returned to the kitchen bearing an enormous pot filled with Elfrida's latest brew of soup. She lit the gas ring on the cooker, turned the flame down low, and put the pot on top of this to heat through slowly.

Behind her, Rory said, "Lucy talked to me."

Carrie turned her head to look at him. "Sorry?"

"Lucy." Laying the table, he squared off a knife and fork. "She talked to me. About London and everything. Her parents divorced. Her grandmother. About not really wanting to go back."

"Oh, *Rory.*" He did not look at her, simply went on with what he was doing. "I'm sorry."

"What have you got to be sorry about?"

"Because in a way I feel responsible. Guilty, perhaps. Because I shouldn't have stayed away so long. Stayed in Austria, and somehow lost touch with my family. Everybody was all right. Except Lucy. It wasn't until I got back that I realized how impossible life must be for her. It's not that anybody's *unkind* to her . . . in a way, she has everything. But she misses her father. And she's never been encouraged to get in touch with her grandfather . . . my father. There's so much acrimony. It's not good to live with."

"Couldn't she go to boarding-school? That, at least, would be a different environment."

Carrie was surprised by such perception in a young man of only eighteen.

"Perhaps she should, Rory. But, you see, I am simply a maiden aunt. I don't dare make too many controversial suggestions in case I'm cast out into the wilderness as well." She thought about this. "And her school is *good.* She has a splendid headmistress whom she's really fond of. . . ."

"But it's all girls." Rory had now finished laying the table. He said, "Where's the smoked salmon?"

"In the fridge. In the scullery."

He went to get it. Carrie took a loaf of brown bread from the crock and then returned to the cooker to give the soup a stir. When he returned, she cleared a space for him, and found a large oval meat dish on which to arrange the delicate rosy slices. Rory slit the cellophane with a knife and began, neatly, to separate the slices of smoked salmon, and lay them out in overlapping layers. Carrie took a couple of lemons from the fruit bowl and started cutting them into wedges.

Rory worked on, intent and business-like, and Carrie watched him, and saw his unlikely bright-yellow hair, the ring in his ear, the blunt features, youthful but strong, well on his way to manhood. Helping the Sneads, probably washing up, he had rolled up the sleeves of his dark-blue cotton shirt, and his forearms were tanned and his hands strong and capable. Carrie could perfectly understand why Lucy liked him so much. She only prayed that Lucy, at fourteen, had not fallen in love. Because they were too young for love. Rory had his sights set on getting to Nepal, and a teenage infatuation at this moment in time was almost bound to result in a broken heart.

She said, "You've been so kind to her, Rory. A lot of guys your age simply wouldn't have bothered."

"I felt sorry for her. . . ."

"I wonder why."

"She seemed so lonely."

"But sweet. She's a sweet child." She could not resist a small tease. "And you bought sleepers for her ears."

He looked at her and grinned. "Oh, come on, Carrie. That was just giving the finger to her mum. Anyway, she wanted her ears pierced. So what? It's part of growing up." He stood back to survey the plate of neatly arranged slices of salmon. "There, that's it. Is that going to be enough?"

"Have to be. We're keeping the other lot for Christmas Day."

"Wonder how Lucy's getting on?"

"Perhaps I'd better go and see. . . . You come, too. You've worked hard enough."

"No, I'll stay here. Be the chef. I quite like cooking. I used to make gingerbread men with my mum. You go back to the others. I'll butter the bread, and there are still some little pizzas left over. I might put them in the oven. . . . Do you want me to open a bottle of wine or anything like that . . . ?"

Finally, Carrie unwound herself from Elfrida's apron, hung it on a hook, and left Rory to it. She went out of the kitchen and upstairs. The landing stood empty. The receiver was back on the telephone. No sign of Lucy. She hesitated for a moment, all at once experiencing a pang of unexplained disquiet. And then, just as before, the telephone rang.

Carrie picked up the receiver. "Hello?"

"Who is that speaking? Is that the Estate House? I want to speak to Carrie."

Unmistakable. Carrie's heart sank. "Yes," she said, "I'm here. Hello, Ma."

"It's you. Oh, thank heavens. My dear, has Nicola been on to you?"

"Yes. She rang from Florida. About twenty minutes ago. But she wanted to talk to Lucy."

"Did she tell you?"

"Tell me what?"

"Oh, my dear, she's married. She's married to Randall Fischer. This morning. They had a kind of whirlwind ceremony in a church called the Wee Chapel of the Angels, or something, and they're *married*. She didn't even let me know she'd got engaged, that they were planning this. I had simply no idea. Until I got this call from Florida. . . ."

Carrie told herself that she had to keep calm, or everything was going to go to bits. "She rang you before she rang Lucy?"

"Yes. She wanted to make arrangements."

"What sort of arrangements?"

"For Lucy, of course. What else, do you think? When she's getting back from Scotland, and that sort of thing. . . ."

Oh, God, thought Carrie. Here we go again.

". . . She's talking about a honeymoon, not flying back to London until the end of the month. She's going to cancel her flight back. Postpone it. And she expects *me* to be in London so that I can get Lucy back to school. But I've planned to stay here, in Bournemouth, until the end of January, and I cannot see why I should change all my arrangements. It's really too much, Carrie. I'm simply not up to it. I told her so. I said, 'I'm not up to it, Nicola.' But you know how selfish and unkind she can be if she doesn't get her own way. And now of course she's besotted with this man. And *he's* all she's thinking about."

"Is she going to spend the rest of her life in America?"

"I suppose so. If you marry an American, I suppose that's what you have to do."

"What about Lucy . . . ?"

"Oh, Lucy will just have to do what she's told for once. The immediate problem is who is going to look after her until her mother gets home?"

Carrie did not answer this question. She simply stood there, holding the receiver, aware of a great wave of impatience and fury directed at both her mother and her sister. She had felt this way before, many times, and doubtless would again, but she could not remember ever having been so angry. She thought of Randall Fischer and silently cursed him off for his tactlessness, his lack of imagination, of feeling. Surely he could have persuaded Nicola to give her family some warning before he marched her off to the Wee Chapel of the Angels and stuck a ring on her finger? He could not have caused more trouble if he had been a fox sneaking into a chicken coop, setting up a panic-stricken cackling and causing feathers to fly. She knew that if she made any remark, it would be wrong, finally precipitating a useless slanging-match that would solve nothing.

"Carrie?"

"Ma . . . I think it would be better if I rang you back."

"Have you spoken to Lucy?"

"No. Not yet. This is the first I've heard of the happy news."

"Are you being sarcastic?"

"No."

"You've got my number? Here, in Bournemouth."

"Yes, I've got it. I'll call you."

"When?"

"Sometime. Tomorrow, maybe."

"Don't leave it too long. I'm worried sick."

"I'm sure."

"Oh, and darling . . . you will have a lovely Christmas, won't you?"

"Lovely," Carrie told her.

She put the receiver down and stood for a moment, giving herself time to cool down, gather her wits, and face facts. Nicola was now Mrs. Randall Fischer. She had married him in Florida, in the Wee Chapel of the Angels. Carrie tried to picture the ceremony. Blue skies and palm trees; Randall Fischer in a white suit, and Nicola in some little concoction suitable for such an occasion. Had there been friends to witness the marriage? Had some old chum of Randall's been wheeled in to give Nicola away? Had the old chum's wife stood in as matron of honour, wearing an ankle-length gown and a corsage of orchids? And after the ceremony, had the four of them driven to the local country club, there to be fêted by anyone who happened to be around . . . ?

But it was all unimaginable. And how or when it had taken place didn't really matter because it was done, and could not be undone, and there was so much emotional debris littered around, waiting to be picked up, that Carrie felt she scarcely knew where to start.

Lucy. Lucy was the first. She had been given the joyous news over the telephone by her mother, had put down the receiver and disappeared. But where? Lucy didn't much like Randall Fischer, and had uncharacteristically rebelled at the very suggestion that she might spend the two weeks of Christmas in his company, and in Florida.

But this . . . ? If Nicola had her way, this would be permanent, for good. Lucy at fourteen uprooted, transported to another country, another culture, a whole new and probably unwelcome life.

Suddenly Carrie was filled with apprehension. Where *was* Lucy? Had she slammed down the telephone, run silently downstairs, out of the front door, and disappeared . . . headed for the sea, the beach, the dunes, the bitter cold? If there had been a cliff nearby, it would have been more easy for Carrie to imagine the child flinging herself from its edge and crashing to death on rocks far below. . . .

Trembling with anxiety, she pulled herself together, put such gruesome images out of her mind, and became sensible. She took a deep breath and climbed the stairs to Lucy's attic. The landing light was on, but the bedroom door firmly closed. Carrie knocked. No reply. Gently she opened the door. All was darkness. She reached for the light, and switched it on. "Lucy?" And her voice betrayed her anxiety.

A sulky hump under the blue-and-white duvet did not move or answer, but Carrie felt quite weak with relief, for at least she was *here*, and safe, and hadn't fled from the house, out into the darkness, to the dunes, the beach, and the lonely sea. . . .

"Lucy." She went into the room, closing the door behind her, and crossed over to the bed and sat on the edge of it.

"Go away."

"Darling, it's Carrie."

"I don't want to talk."

"Darling, I know. Gran rang from Bournemouth. She told me."

"I don't care if she told you or not. It doesn't make any difference. Everything's spoilt now. Everything. It always is. They always do."

"Oh, Lucy. . . ." Carrie laid her hand on the duvet, meaning to comfort, but Lucy jerked her shoulder and spurned the tentative comfort of touch.

"I wish you'd go away and leave me alone."

Her voice was choked. Filled with tears. She had been crying, and now she was angry and resentful. Carrie understood, but still felt loath to leave her.

"To be truthful, I think your mother shouldn't have done this, and certainly she shouldn't have sprung it on you over the telephone, expecting you to be delighted. But I suppose we have to try to see her point of view. . . ."

All at once, Lucy flung the duvet aside and turned up her face to Carrie's. It was swollen and stained with weeping, her hair, which she had put up so carefully, tangled and in strands around her cheeks. She was ugly with anger and misery; and Carrie realized, with despair, that the anger was directed, not simply against her mother, but Carrie too . . . because they were all adult, and there was not a single adult who could be trusted.

"Of *course* you take her side," Lucy shouted at Carrie. "She's *your* sister. Well, I hate her. I hate her because of all this, and because I've never mattered. I matter even less now. And I won't go and live in America, or Florida or Cleveland or anywhere. And I hate Randall Fischer, and I don't want to talk about it. I just want to be left alone. So *go away*!"

And she flung herself away from Carrie, pulled the duvet over her head, and buried her face in an already sodden pillow. She was crying again, wailing and sobbing; inconsolable.

Feebly, Carrie tried again. "The Kennedys are all staying for supper. . . ."

"I don't care if they are." Scarcely audible from beneath the folds of duvet.

"I could bring your supper up here."

"I don't want supper, I want you to *go away*. . . ."

Impossible. Carrie stayed for a moment, and then, knowing that it was hopeless to persist, got to her feet, went out of the room, and closed the door once more behind her.

She felt completely shattered, and without any idea of what to do next. She stood at the top of the stairs and heard the voices of the others in the sitting-room, still gathered around the fire. A burst of carefree laughter. She went downstairs, and for the third time that evening, as she reached the landing, the telephone rang yet again.

Nothing could get much worse. She picked up the receiver.

"Hello?"

"Carrie. Is that Carrie?"

"Nicola."

"Yes, it's me again." The voice was high-pitched, furiously indignant. "I've been trying to ring back for the last ten minutes. I couldn't get through. Lucy put the phone down on me. I was telling her—"

"I know what you were telling her."

"And she put the phone down on me. I couldn't finish what I was saying. I want to talk to her again. Go and get her. She has no right to ring off like that. . . ."

"I think she has every right. She thought you were calling to say Happy Christmas, and all you do is blurt out the fact that you've married Randall Fischer, and expect her to be delighted."

"So she should be. A lovely new father, a heavenly house, a heavenly place to live. If only she'd come with me, she'd have seen it all for herself. Why does she have to be so against anything I do? I've done everything for her, isn't it about time she started thinking about other people's happiness? Doesn't it mean anything to her that I'm so happy? At last. . . ."

"Nicola—"

". . . Mother's the same. She even resents me staying on a bit longer so that we can have a honeymoon. . . ."

"Nicola, *I* don't resent anything. I'm pleased for you. Honestly. But you have a child to consider, and she's not a baby. You can scarcely expect her to be over the moon when it seems that her whole life is going to be turned upside down. . . ."

"I don't want to listen to this. I can't imagine what all the fuss is about. Just go and get her for me."

"No, I won't. I can't. She's up in her room, bundled in her duvet, and crying her heart out. I've tried to speak to her, but she's too upset even to talk to me. And there are practicalities as well. We go back to London after the New Year, and Lucy has to go back to school. Who's going to be there for her? Mother wants to stay in Bournemouth."

"Can't you even do *that* for me?"

"I haven't got a house to live in."

"Well, you can go to Mother's flat and be with Lucy there. Get her back to school. . . ."

"Nicola, I have a new job waiting for me—"

"Oh, your *career*, I suppose. Your great *career*. That was always more important than any of us. I should have thought just for once—"

"*I* should have thought just for once you'd think about other people and not yourself all the time."

"Think about *myself* all the time! That is the most unkind thing to say. This is the first time in years, since Miles walked out and left me, that I've thought about myself. . . . At least Randall appreciates me. I have at last got someone in my life who appreciates me. . . ."

Carrie stopped trying to be nice. "Oh, don't talk such a load of codswallop."

"I'm not going to listen. . . ." Nicola's voice soared in righteous indignation, and Carrie relented.

"Nicola. Look. Sorry. This is getting us nowhere. I've got your number in Florida. I'll try and work something out, and I'll ring back."

"Tell Lucy to ring me."

"I don't think there's much chance of that in the foreseeable future. But try not to get in too much of a state. And I *will* try to work something out."

Finally, grudgingly, "All right," said Nicola.

"And have a good Christmas."

But Nicola, as always, missed the irony. She said, "Same to you," and rang off.

What Carrie wanted, above all, was for it to be yesterday, and none of this to have happened. To be in the empty, deserted woollen mill, alone with Sam Howard; walking through the chill and echoing sheds, following his tall figure, up stairways, across catwalks. She wanted to be back in the Duke's Arms, with the hot fire, the warming drink, the two old men, and the murmur of the barman's television. And no person to think about but herself and the man who sat across the table from her, talking about their tenuous and highly uncertain future.

But this was now, and everything was changed. She ran a hand through her hair, straightened her shoulders, turned, and opened the sitting-room door. Beyond it, they were all still there, in the same chairs, the same positions, as though nothing untoward could possibly have taken place. They had been joined, she saw, by Rory, who, finished with his chef's duties down in the kitchen, had come upstairs to find out what was happening, and why nobody had appeared to partake of the informal and makeshift meal. He sat now, opposite his mother, cross-legged on the hearthrug, with a glass of lager in his hand.

They were all talking peacefully amongst themselves, but when Carrie appeared, conversation drifted away, and heads were turned as she came through the door, as though her appearance was either long overdue or unexpected.

She said, "Here I am," which was banal, and closed the door behind her. "Sorry to keep you all waiting."

Elfrida said, "Darling, what's been going on? So many telephone calls. Rory said Lucy's mother had phoned from Florida. Nothing wrong, I hope?"

"No. Nothing wrong." Which was true but utterly untrue all at the same time. "Just everything. Another family crisis, but it's my family, so please don't be too concerned."

"Carrie. It sounds dire. Tell us."

Carrie said, "I don't know where to start," and Sam, who had been sitting at the far end of the room, got up from his chair and came over to her side. He said, "Would you like a drink?"

She shook her head, wondering if she appeared either deathly pale or flushed with unbearable exertion. He reached for a chair and drew it forward, next to Elfrida. Carrie sat down with a grateful thump, and felt Elfrida take her hand.

"Darling Carrie, tell us."

So she did. "Nicola's just been on the telephone. Lucy's mother," she enlarged for the benefit of the Kennedys, who could not possibly know who Nicola was. "My sister. She went out to Florida to stay with this man called Randall Fischer. And this morning they got married. It was the first we'd heard of it. She rang to speak to Lucy, and told her then. Lucy hung up on her, in mid-flow, as it were, and is now in tears in her bedroom, swearing black and blue that she never liked Randall Fischer and she will never go to live in America. Then my mother came on the telephone to tell me the news. Nicola apparently has postponed her flight home, and is determined to have a honeymoon with Randall before she finally comes back to London. My mother is in hysterics about this, because she wants to stay in Bournemouth until the end of the month, and refuses to return just so that she can be with Lucy. Then Nicola got back on the phone again, to tell me that Lucy had hung up on her, and the upshot of *that* was that we had the usual sisterly difference of opinion, and only just stopped short of a flaming row."

Elfrida said, "I can't bear it," which, Carrie decided, was the understatement of the year.

She went on. "So the crisis is immediate and also long-term. Immediate, because there is nobody in London to take care of Lucy and get her to school. Except, of course, dogsbody me. And of course, if necessary, I'll do it, and stay in my mother's flat until either she or Nicola gets back to London. But the long-term problem is a different kettle of fish altogether. The long-term problem is Lucy's future. Nicola's married an American, and quite naturally, will make her home out there. I think she relishes the prospect. Lucy, on the other hand, never wanted to go to America with her, even for a holiday. She doesn't particularly like Randall, and to be truthful, I don't think she's all that fond of her mother."

They had all listened attentively and with growing concern, but now, as Carrie fell silent, nobody said anything.

Then Tabitha spoke. "Oh, *dear*," she said, which was inadequate, but sympathetic.

"She doesn't *have* to go and live in America," Elfrida ventured hopefully. "How about going to her school as a boarder?"

"It's a day school, Elfrida. And there are still holidays."

"Your mother . . . ?"

"You know as well as I do, Ma would never cope on her own. Wouldn't even try."

"Perhaps Lucy's father . . ."

"No way. Number-two wife would never consider it."

"But . . ."

"This is all ridiculous. . . ." A new voice broke into the argument, or the discussion, or whatever it could be called. Rory Kennedy. In some surprise, Carrie turned her head to look at him, and saw that he had got to his feet, was no longer sitting comfortably on the hearthrug, but stood before them all, his back to the fire, and his blue eyes blazing with indignation. Taken entirely by surprise, nobody interrupted him or stopped him speaking.

"... It's ridiculous. You're all talking in circles, taking it for granted that Lucy will go back to London, just as though nothing had happened. But she can't go. She's miserable enough there, she told me so, and what's happened just now only makes everything more impossible for her. She has few friends, she has no proper home, and she's never felt loved. What has made her really happy has been staying here, with Elfrida and Oscar. In Creagan. She told me she'd never been so happy as she is here. She never wanted to go back to London in the first place. So don't send her back. Keep her here. She can stay with Elfrida and Oscar. Mum and Dad will be around, and Clodagh, and she's made friends with our friends. Then she can go to day school in Creagan. Dad can fix that with Mr. McIntosh. He'll squeeze her in somehow. He'll find a place for her. That is what I believe you should all do. I think if you let her go back to London, without any sort of plan for the future, it would be criminal. Unhappy teenagers do terrible stupid things. We all know that. Lucy belongs to you all far more than she belongs with her mother. So this is where she should be. I think you have a moral obligation to do the right thing for her. Which is to keep her here, in Creagan."

He stopped, red-cheeked from the warmth of the fire and the passion of his feeling. For a moment an astounded silence filled the room, as all the adults stared at Rory in speechless but respectful astonishment. Rory, perhaps feeling that he had gone too far, looked a bit sheepish, gave the hearthrug a kick, and apologized.

"Sorry," he said. "I didn't mean to speak out of turn."

Silence again. Then Peter Kennedy gently shifted Tabitha's weight from his knees and got to his feet, to stand beside his son. "You didn't speak out of turn," he told him, laying a hand on the boy's shoulder. "I think you are right. Well said, Rory."

Lucy lay and stared at the sloping ceiling of her bedroom, exhausted by weeping and beginning to feel remorseful about the way she had behaved to Carrie. She was not in the habit of having tantrums, and was not quite sure about her next move. Nothing was going to be all right again until she told Carrie she was sorry, was hugged, and forgiven, but she could not bring herself to get out of bed, comb her hair, wash her face, and go downstairs to face everybody. The Kennedys were all still here, and staying for supper, but that only made everything worse.

She felt headachy, drained, and yet tremendously hungry. She thought about the satisfaction of slamming down the telephone on her mother's voice, all the way from the United States, telling Lucy that she was now married to Randall Fischer, that Lucy had a new father, that they were all going to be happy ever after living in well-heeled style, and with the blissful warmth of Gulf Stream, Florida. Listening to her mother burbling on, lyrical with excitement and as insensitive to others' feelings as she had always been, had all at once become too much, and Lucy, unable to listen to one more word, had simply put the receiver back on the telephone.

Now, alone and desolate, she told herself that she had been a coward. She should, then and there, while they were still speaking, have unleashed upon her mother the full force of her indignation and shock. She should have let her know, at once, that she was terrified at the very thought of being uprooted, forced to move to a foreign country and accept the fact that her entire existence was about to be turned upside down.

But now it was too late.

She longed to be older. To be eighteen, and so an adult, with the weight of British law behind her. At eighteen, she could refuse to budge; could stay where she felt familiar and secure; make a life and a future for herself. But being fourteen was a hopeless age. Too old to be uncomplainingly shunted around, like a brown paper parcel. And too young for independence. Things before had been bad enough. Now, they had become—or were about to become—impossible.

Above her bed, her head, was the skylight. Beyond the glass, the darkness was rendered opaque by the reflected glow of the street lights below. But she could see a star, and imagined the skylight slowly opening to a gust of freezing, sea-smelling air, and herself being drawn, as though by some irresistible force, out of her bed, up, flying through the open hatchway, seeing the planet drop away beneath her, the stars grow larger every second. . . . Like a rocket, she would head for the moon, and there would never be any coming back.

A sound. A step on the stair. Carrie. Perhaps it was Carrie. If it was Carrie, Lucy was very much afraid that, without wishing to, she was about to start bawling again, and hated the feeling that she seemed to have lost control of her own emotions.

A tap on the door. She lay with her cheek on the sodden pillow, and said nothing. The door opened.

"Lucy?"

It wasn't Carrie. It was Oscar. And Lucy was tremendously embarrassed that he should find her thus, all rumpled and fusty and untidy and tear-stained. Why had he come up? Why had they let *him* come to fetch her? Surely Carrie could have returned to her, or Elfrida?

She said nothing.

He said, "Do you mind?" And then, when she still did not reply, he crossed the floor, leaving the door behind him ajar, and came to sit on the edge of her bed. His weight was strangely comforting, pulling the duvet tight around her body, and she shifted her position to make more space for him. She drew a long, shuddering breath, and said, "No, I don't mind."

He said, "How are you feeling?" As though he were a kindly doctor, and she had been ill for a long time.

She said, "Awful."

"Carrie told us what happened."

"I was horrible to her."

"She didn't tell us that. Just that you were upset. And who can wonder, having that bit of news sprung on you over the telephone? I always dislike being given news over the telephone. Somehow, one feels so impotent and removed, simply because one can't see the other person's face."

Lucy said, "It wouldn't be so bad if I really liked him. Randall, I mean."

"Perhaps you would get to like him."

"No. I don't think so." She looked at Oscar, saw the hooded eyes that always made him seem a bit sad, the gentle expression on his face, and thought that you liked people instantly, just as she had always liked Oscar. And that all the time in the world would never render her as close to Randall Fischer as she had instantly felt with Oscar.

She said, "I was so horrid to Carrie." Her eyes filled again with tears, but it didn't matter now, and it was important to tell him. "I shouted at her and told her to go away, and she was being so sweet. I feel dreadful about her."

She sniffed lustily, and felt her mouth trembling like a baby's; but Oscar only reached into the breast pocket of his lovely velvet jacket and produced a much-laundered linen handkerchief which smelt of Bay Rum. He gave it to her, and she took it gratefully and blew her nose.

After that she felt a bit better. She said, "I don't usually shout at people."

"I know you don't. And the wicked thing is, that when we're really upset, we always take it out on the people who are closest and whom we love the most."

"Do we?" She was amazed to be told this.

"Always."

"I can't imagine you ever shouting at anybody."

He smiled, his rare, warm smile that always seemed to change his whole demeanour. He said, "You'd be surprised."

"It was just that . . . I feel so awful, because I suppose I should be pleased. But it was . . ."

"I know. A shock."

". . . If it was someone I really *knew,* who lived in England, then it wouldn't be quite so bad. But I don't want to have to go and live in America and go to school there and everything. London's not much, but at least I know where I am. I can't stay with Gran because she always makes a fuss about everything, and wants to do her own thing, go out and see her friends, and have bridge parties. When she has bridge parties, she doesn't even like me going into the room to say hello. And she hates it when Emma comes because she says we make so much noise. I couldn't be with her, Oscar."

"No."

His hand lay on the duvet. She gave him back his handkerchief and he took it, and then took Lucy's hand in his own. It felt warm and safe over her fingers, a physical contact, a sort of lifeline, that made it easier to talk. She said, "I don't know what will happen. That's the worst. I don't know what I'm going to do. And I'm not old enough to do *anything.*"

He said, "I don't think you have to do anything. I think others have to do it for you."

"Who?"

"Like me."

"You?"

"Now just listen. Here's a suggestion. Downstairs, we've all been having a little chat, and we've come up with an idea. Supposing, after the New Year, you don't go back to London with Carrie? You stay here with Elfrida. And *I* shall go back to London with Carrie, and go and see your grandmother in Bournemouth."

Lucy was alarmed. "What are you going to say to her?"

"I am going to suggest that, until your mother's new life is sorted out somewhat, you should remain in Creagan, with Elfrida and myself. Just for the time being."

"But what about school? I have to go back to school."

"Yes, of course you do, but how about taking a term off from your school in London, and going to school in Creagan instead? Peter Kennedy is a good friend of the headmaster's, and he will have a word with him, and see that you get a place in the suitable class. It's a very good school, and I am sure there would be no objections from your present headmistress."

"Miss Maxwell-Brown?"

"Is that her name?"

"I can't simply *leave* school."

"I'm not suggesting that. Just take a term off. Plenty of children do this sort of thing if their parents are sent abroad, or other circumstances dictate. I am sure Miss Maxwell-Brown would be perfectly amenable to let you go for a single term, and keep the options open for your return, when this crisis has settled down, and we are all aware of what is expected of us."

"You mean . . ." Lucy felt that she had to get the facts right, because what Oscar was telling her sounded almost too good to be true. "You mean, I wouldn't go back to London after the New Year? Just stay on with you and Elfrida?"

"If you want to. Yours must be the decision."

She was silent for a moment or two, mulling this over. It seemed to her that the whole situation was fraught with obstacles. One of them being Elfrida.

"Gran doesn't approve of Elfrida," she told Oscar bluntly.

Oscar laughed. "So I believe. But she will, I am sure, approve of *me*: I shall present myself as a schoolmaster and a church organist, with an impeccable background and an unsullied reputation. Will she be able to resist that?"

Lucy said, with a quirk of humour, "Not if it means getting shed of me."

"And your mother?"

"She won't care either. She never did, much. She'll care even less now that she's got Randall."

"So no objections from her?"

"I wouldn't think so."

"Carrie's going to telephone them both tomorrow. She can outline our plans. It is, after all, just until Easter. After that we'll have to think again."

"I won't change, Oscar. I won't ever want to go and live in America."

"I don't see why you should have to. You should visit, of course, and it would be interesting and educational; it's always good to see another country, and learn how others live. But I believe that, basically, you should stay where you feel most happy."

"I've never been so happy, or at home, as I have here."

"Then why don't we settle for that. Stay on, for as long as you wish, with Elfrida and me, in Creagan. Go to the local school. Get your GCSEs. After that, you should spread your wings a bit. Maybe a co-educational boarding-school where you could take your A levels. I know several splendid establishments where I am sure you would enjoy every moment. With my schoolmasterly connections, I could make inquiries and get prospectuses, and we could all talk it over together. Go and inspect them. Let you make your own choice."

"That's what Rory said, when we talked about things. A co-educational boarding-school."

"He's a wise lad. He is your champion. It was he who stirred us all to action when Carrie broke the news about your mother re-marrying. '*You have to do something,*' he told us. And of course he was quite right."

"But, Oscar . . ."

"What now?"

"You and Elfrida don't want me living with you for *two years.*"

"Why not?"

"Because you're old. Like Gran. She always says she can't cope. Because she's a grandparent."

Oscar laughed. "Oh, Lucy, grandparents are wonderful inventions. All over the world, grandparents are, for one reason or another, bringing up their grandchildren, having a great time, and doing a good job. I think it would be fun."

"But I'm not your grandchild, so would you *want* me? Really *want* me?"

"More than anything."

"Wouldn't I be in the way?"

"Never."

"Supposing you move to the cottage at Corrydale, and sell this house to Sam. . . ."

"Well?"

". . . you wouldn't have space for me."

"We haven't seen the house yet. And if necessary, we shall redesign it. And there will be a special apartment, labelled 'Lucy's Room.' "

"Oscar, I don't know why you are so kind."

"Because we love you. Perhaps we need you. Perhaps I am being selfish, but I don't want to let you go. I need a young person about the place. I have got used to the sound of your voice, and footsteps on the stairs, and doors bursting open. And laughter. I shall hate it if you leave. Probably go into a decline."

Lucy said, "When I first came here . . . when Carrie and I flew up from London and came here, to Creagan, I was terribly nervous because she had told me about your daughter. . . ."

"Francesca."

"She had told me about Francesca, and I was afraid that I would distress you . . . remind you of her . . . make you dreadfully sad again."

"You remind me of her, but it didn't make me sad."

"What did she look like?"

"Long hair, and freckles on her nose. She had bands on her teeth. She was two years younger than you. She was always on the go, never still, except when she and I settled down in my armchair and read aloud to each other."

"My dad and I used to do that. When I was little and we were all still together. We read *The Borrowers.* And when he wanted to tease, he called me Arietty. And he put Badedas in his bath and made the whole house smell piny. What else did Francesca like doing?"

"Everything. She had a little pony, and an old bicycle, and a guinea pig in a hutch, and a bedroom full of books. On wet days, she used to go into the kitchen and make biscuits. They were always either burned or raw, and I used to have to eat them and swear they were delicious. And we listened to music together, and played duets on the piano. . . ."

"Was she good at the piano?"

"Not very."

"Was she good at lessons?"

"Not very."

"What was she really good at?"

"Living."

"That's important, isn't it?"

Their eyes met, and they gazed at each other, both silenced by the enormity of what Oscar had just said. It was as though he had spoken without thought, and the word hung between them like a lie. Francesca had been good at living, but now she was dead, her young life ended with the brutal finality of a fatal car crash.

Lucy did not know what to say. To her horror she saw Oscar's eyes fill with tears, his mouth tremble. Then, in an abrupt movement, he covered his eyes with his hand. He tried to speak, but words did not come; instead, a sound was torn from deep in his chest, a sob of utter despair.

She had never before seen a grown-up weep, rendered incapable by an almost overwhelming grief. She stared at him, wondering what she could do to comfort, and saw him shake his head, denying his own weakness, somehow struggling for control of his unbearable emotion. After a bit, to her huge relief, he took his hand from his face and reached into his breast pocket for his handkerchief. Then he blew his nose, made an effort to smile at her, reassuring. He said, "Sorry."

"It doesn't matter, Oscar. I don't mind. Really I understand."

"Yes, I think you do. Death is part of living. I have to remember that, but from time to time the truth eludes me."

"Living is important, isn't it? And remembering?"

"More important than anything else." He stowed his handkerchief away once more. "That first day, the day you arrived, you and I sat in the church and talked about Christmas and the Winter Solstice. It was then that I remembered Francesca, for the first time, without total desolation. I remembered having exactly the same conversation with her a year or so ago. Trying to explain about the Christmas star and the scientists' theory of time. And she listened but was not convinced. She didn't want to be convinced. She liked the story just as it was.

"In the bleak mid-winter
Frosty wind made moan,
Earth stood hard as iron,
Water like a stone.

"That was the way she wanted Christmas to be, and for Francesca it wouldn't have been magic any other way. Because the carols and the darkness and the presents were all part of a time when life took flight, and the whole world soared to the stars."

Lucy said, "That's how this Christmas is going to be."

"Stay with us."

"I do love you, Oscar."

"There's a lot of love around. Don't ever forget that."

"I won't."

"Do you want to come downstairs now, and join the others, and have some supper? If they've left any for us. . . ."

"I have to comb my hair and wash my face."

"In that case." He relinquished her hand with a little pat, got off the bed, and went to the door. She watched him go. As he left the room, he turned back for a final reassuring smile.

"Don't be too long, my duck."

CHRISTMAS EVE

Christmas Eve.

In this fickle northern climate, one woke each morning without any idea of what the elements were about to reveal, but today had dawned astonishingly pure and gentle, like a day stolen from spring. The thaw had melted the snow away from streets and fields, and only the hills still wore their white mantles, summits glittering in the light of the low sun streaming down from a cloudless sky. A sun that, because there was no breath of wind, even managed to engender a faint warmth. Birds sang from leafless trees, and in the Estate House garden a few early snowdrops pierced the rough, untended grass beneath the lilac bush.

At Corrydale, in Rose Miller's garden, stood a bird table laden with scraps and crusts, and with a bag of nuts dangling. Pigeons and starlings were out in full and greedy force, while tits and robins pecked at the nuts and the scraps of fat which Rose had threaded on a piece of string. They hovered, and paused, then flew off into the safety of a nearby hawthorn bush, so that its twiggy branches trembled and swayed with fluttering wings and feathered activity.

Because of the fine day, and the fact that the roads were clear, Elfrida and Oscar had come to Corrydale on their own, in Oscar's car. The others, Carrie, Sam, Lucy, and Rory Kennedy, were driving over later, because Carrie reckoned that she had to wait until after noon before getting on the telephone to her sister in Florida. She had already spoken to Dodie Sutton, holed up in her hotel bedroom in Bournemouth, and the conversation had gone more smoothly than any of them had dared to hope. Dodie was clearly much relieved to be shed of the sole responsibility for Lucy, and even spoke quite warmly of Elfrida's kindness and hospitality, conveniently forgetting that, at one time, she had not had a good word to say for her ex-husband's raffish, theatrical cousin.

"Oscar will come and see you in Bournemouth," Carrie had promised. "He says he would like to meet you, and if you want, talk things over." And Dodie had raised no objection to this suggestion either, and said that she would be pleased to stand him afternoon tea in the residents' lounge of the Palace Hotel.

So now, there was only Nicola to be dealt with, to be told of the tentative plans for her daughter, encouraged to fall in with them, and gently coaxed into agreement. Having listened to Carrie speaking to Dodie, all sweetness and understanding, Elfrida was pretty sure she would do as good a job on Nicola. Objections, should there be any, would be token. Nicola wouldn't care much what happened to anybody, provided her own chosen path lay smooth and free of any sort of angst.

As well, Carrie had volunteered to assemble and bring the picnic. Elfrida had started making suggestions about hot soup and ham rolls, but Carrie and Sam had shooed her out of the kitchen, and sent her and Oscar, feeling quite irresponsible and light-hearted, on their way.

So now, from the window of Rose Miller's sitting-room, Elfrida watched the birds. Rose's garden was empty of flowers and vegetables save for a few rotting Brussels sprouts, but the beds were neatly dug and the earth raked, all ready for planting time. The garden ran, a long and narrow plot, down the slope of the hill. At its foot was a wooden fence and some gnarled beech trees, and then, beyond, the sea-fields of Corrydale sweeping down to the blue firth and the hills on the farther shore. Elfrida was much interested in this prospect, because she knew that the view from Major Billicliffe's house would be almost identical. Today, with the clear winter air, the colours so sharp and brilliant, the lacy branches of trees so black, she could not imagine any outlook more beautiful.

Behind her, Oscar and Rose sat on either side of the fireplace, where burnt a glowing stack of peat, and drank the fresh coffee which Rose had made for them. Rose was talking. She had not done much else since Oscar and Elfrida had arrived, as arranged, at half past eleven.

". . . Of course, the poor chentleman let the house get in a terrible state. Betty Cowper, she's the tractor-man's wife, she did what she could for him after his wife died, but she has three children of her own and a man to care for, and she swore it was an uphill task. Once we'd heard he'd passed on, she and I went along and did our best to clear the place up. Most of his clothes were in a terrible state, fit for nothing but a bonfire, but there's a few things that would maybe do for the charity shop, and we packed them in suitcases. He didn't seem to own anything of value, but we left his ornaments and possessions and books and such where they were, so you'll be able to do what you want with them."

"That was good of you, Rose."

"Betty gave the place as good a clean as possible, scrubbed the kitchen floor and such, and the bathroom, which was in a terrible state. A disaster. Poor lonely man. It's sad to think of him dying alone, with no family. You said the funeral would maybe be at the end of the week? Will you let me know? I'd like to be there."

"Of course . . . and it's going to be a cremation. But we'll take you with us to Inverness, in the car."

"It wasn't his fault the wee place fell into such disrepair. But no doubt you'll be altering things for yourself, and if you get the builders in, they'll tear the place apart and make a lot of dust."

Oscar said, "We haven't finally decided if we're going to take up residence."

"And why should you not?" Rose sounded quite indignant. "Major

Billicliffe would never have left it to you in his will had he not thought that you would live there. Just imagine—the chance to come back and live at Corrydale again after all these years."

"It might not be large enough, Rose. You see, we may have another young person coming to live with us."

Rose let out a hoot of unexpectedly earthy laughter. "Don't tell me you're having a wee baby."

Oscar remained unfazed by this wild suggestion. "No. No, Rose, not that. But you remember, I told you we were expecting visitors for Christmas. Lucy is fourteen, but her mother has just remarried, in America, and rather than send her back to London, she's going to stay with Elfrida and me for a bit, and go to the school in Creagan."

"But that will be splendid. And good for us all to have another young person about the place. She can be friends with Betty Cowper's family. They're a bit younger, but a cheery bunch. And it's paradise for children here at Corrydale. They have the whole estate to themselves for bicycle riding, and no fear of being knocked to Kingdom Come by some great lorry."

Elfrida turned from watching the birds, and went to join Oscar and Rose to sit in an antique wheel-back chair and reach for her coffee-cup.

She said, "Perhaps we could make Major Billicliffe's house a little larger. Build on an extra room, or something. We'll have to see."

"You'll need to get the planning permission," Rose warned sagely. For all her years, she was up to all the tricks of the local authorities. "Tom Cowper put up a greenhouse without the permission, and as near as a whisker he just about had to tear it down again. And where is the little girl now?"

Elfrida explained. "They're driving over later. Lucy and her aunt, Carrie, who's a cousin of mine. And Rory Kennedy. And Sam Howard. Sam was an unexpected guest. He called in at the Estate House, and then got stuck there by the snow. Couldn't get back to Inverness."

"And who is *he*?"

"He's going to run McTaggarts in Buckly."

"Well, I never did! What a party you'll be for Christmas. When Oscar telephoned me to tell me you were coming today and bringing a picnic, I got the key from Betty and went along and laid a wee fire, in case the place was cold for you. But on a day like this, you could eat a picnic in the garden. It's as though the good Lord wanted you to see it at its best."

"Yes," said Elfrida. "It does seem a bit like that."

Rose was both old and tiny, but spry as a bird. She wore a tweed skirt, a blouse with a brooch at the collar, and a red Shetland cardigan; and her bright dark eyes seemed to see everything without the help of spectacles. Her hair, thin and white, was dragged back from her brow in a little bun, and the only apparent sign of ageing showed in her hands, which were worn and knuckled with arthritis. Her house was just as neat, colourful, and confident as she herself; polished tables stood awash with scraps of china, mementos, and snapshots, and over the fireplace was an enlarged photograph of Rose's brother in seaman's uniform, who had been drowned at sea when the *Ark Royal* was sunk during the Second World War. Rose had never married. Her whole life had been dedicated to Mrs. McLennan and to Corrydale House. But she was not in the least sentimental, and the fact that the house was now a hotel and no longer belonged to the family was one that she took entirely in her stride.

She said, "And what will you all be doing tomorrow?"

Elfrida laughed. "I'm not sure. Opening presents, I suppose. We've got the tree in the dining-room. And then we're going to have Christmas dinner in the evening."

"Christmas dinner! I remember Christmas dinner parties at Corrydale in the old days, with the long table set with all the lace mats and the candlesticks. There was always a house party, friends and cousins and relations, and everybody dressed up in dinner jackets and evening gowns. Christmas Eve, it was the same. Very formal. And then, after Christmas Eve dinner, all the house party would get into motors and drive to Creagan for Midnight Service in the church—

and there was a car, too, for the staff, and anyone who wanted to go. And what a sensation they created, walking into the church and down the aisle, all dressed up, and Mrs. McLennan, in long black taffeta sweeping the floor and her mink coat, leading the way. People liked to see that. So elegant and festive. And the men in their good overcoats and their black ties. You won't remember that, Oscar."

"No. I was never at Corrydale for a Christmas."

"When Hughie was here, all the old traditions went out the door. I don't think he ever went to the church, even on Christmas Eve. Sad, when you think about it. That he, such a fusionless creature, should be the one to take over the place, and let it all slip through his fingers." She shook her head and sighed at the iniquities of the hopeless Hughie. "But that's all in the past now. And how about you, Oscar? Will you be going to the Midnight Service? No need for a car. Just step across the street."

Elfrida did not look at Oscar. She had finished her coffee and now laid the empty cup and saucer down on the little table alongside her chair.

"No, Rose. I shan't be going. But maybe the others . . ."

Oh, Oscar, Elfrida thought sadly.

But she said nothing. His apartness, his withdrawal, was his own problem, and one which only he could deal with. It was a bit, she decided, as though he had had a disagreement, a row with an old friend. As though words had been spoken which could never be unspoken, and until one of them proffered the hand of friendship, the impasse remained. Perhaps by next year, she told herself. Another twelve months and he would feel himself strong enough to take this last hurdle.

She said, "*I* shall certainly go. The church at night is so beautiful, and as you say, it's just a step across the street. The others can do what they want, but I think Lucy will want to come, and certainly Carrie. How about you, Rose? Will you be there?"

"I wouldn't miss it for anything. My nephew Charlie said he'd drive me into Creagan."

"We'll see you, then."

Oscar remembered something. Or perhaps he just wanted to change the subject. "Rose, I had another small bequest from Major Billicliffe, but one about which I do not feel so enthusiastic. The dog."

"Did he leave you his dog? Brandy?"

"I'm afraid so."

"Do you not want her?"

"No. I don't think I do."

"In that case, Charlie will keep her. He likes the old girl, and she's company for him when he's working in the shed. And his children would be heart-broken to see her go."

"Are you sure? Hadn't we better speak to Charlie first?"

"*I'll* speak to Charlie," Rose told him, in tones which boded ill for nephew Charlie should he not fall in with her plans. "He'll keep the dog, all right. And now, how about another cup of coffee?"

But it was time to leave. They all got to their feet, and Rose took the key from inside an old flowered teapot which stood on the mantelpiece. This she gave to Oscar. Then she came to the door to see them out. "Why do you not leave your motor here, and walk to Major Billicliffe's house? It's only a step, and there's not much parking space."

"It won't be in your way?"

"And why should it be in my way?"

So they did as she suggested, only pausing to open the door of the car and let Horace out, because while they had been chatting with Rose, he had remained incarcerated, in case he chased a rabbit, or put up a pheasant, or otherwise misbehaved himself. He leaped lightly down, and was at once delighted by local smells.

"For a dog," observed Elfrida, "this must be a bit like being let loose in the perfume department of Harrods. *Eau d'autre chien*. He's going to buy a bottle and dab it behind his ears."

High above, rooks cawed from empty branches, and Elfrida, gazing skywards, saw the white, ruler-straight line of a jet stream being dragged across the blue sky by a four-engine passenger airplane. It was so high that she could scarcely see the plane, just the jet stream, but it was headed north-west, flying, she guessed, from Amsterdam.

"Do you ever think, Oscar, that in that tiny dot, people are eating nuts and reading magazines and ordering gin and tonics?"

"In truth, it never occurred to me."

"I wonder where they're going?"

"To California? Over the Pole."

"Over the North Pole for Christmas. I'm glad I'm not going to California for Christmas."

"Are you?"

"I'd rather be going to Major Billicliffe's house for a picnic. We must find a new name for it. We can't go on calling it Major Billicliffe's house now that he is no more."

"It used to be the forester's house. But I believe that in the fullness of time it will simply become Oscar Blundell's house. Doesn't that make sense?"

"Oscar, everything you say makes sense."

A few moments, and they had traversed the hundred yards or so that lay between the two cottages, and were there, standing in the open gateway of Oscar's new property. It was a twin of Rose's house, but not nearly so appealing, and the rusted car parked before the front door did nothing to enhance a first impression. Elfrida, with Oscar at her side, remembered that first dark evening when, exhausted after the long journey, they had finally run Major Billicliffe's abode to earth, and come to collect the key of the Estate House. So much had happened since then that she felt as though years had passed.

They walked up the driveway, the soles of their boots scrunching on sea-pebbles, and Oscar put the key in the lock, turned it, and then the brass knob. The door swung inwards, and she followed him, fingers crossed, indoors, and so into the little sitting-room.

It felt very cold, and a bit dank, but not nearly as bad as Elfrida had remembered and feared. The window at the back of the room let in a flood of sunshine, and Betty Cowper and Rose, between them, had scoured, cleaned, emptied ashtrays, shaken rugs, polished furniture, dispatched much rubbish, and scrubbed floors. Over all hung the smell of strong soap and carbolic disinfectant. The roll-top desk had been closed, and the trolley which Major Billicliffe had called his bar cleared of old bottles and used glasses. Even the dingy cotton curtains had been washed and ironed. In the fireplace were laid paper and sticks, all ready for kindling, and there was a brass bucket (polished) filled with coal, and a pile of dry logs on the hearth.

Oscar said, "First things first," removed his jacket, and knelt to set a match to the newspaper and to start the sticks crackling. At the back of the room stood the door against which poor Brandy, howling and frustrated, had, from time to time, flung herself, causing Elfrida to be frightened out of her wits. Now, she went, cautiously, to open this, and found herself in a mean and chill little kitchen, built of breeze-blocks and with utilitarian steel-framed windows. It had a clay sink, a wooden draining-board, a tiny refrigerator, and a gas cooker. A small table was spread with an oilcloth, and worn linoleum covered the floor. Not much else. A half-glassed door to her left led out onto a bit of paving, where stood a broken wheelbarrow, a digging fork, and a dried-out tub containing dead geraniums. There was no sign of a hot pipe or any sort of heating and it all felt cold as charity.

She went back to Oscar, who was piling coal onto flames. She watched him add a log or two. She said, "How did the Major keep himself warm?"

"Probably didn't. I don't know. We'll find out." He pulled himself to his feet, dusting off his hands on the seat of his corduroys. "Come. Let us go and explore."

It did not take very long. They went through the small lobby into the other room; Major Billicliffe's dining-room, where Oscar remembered the old man's drip-dry shirts draped over the backs of the chairs. But here, too, Betty and Rose had been busy, and all was cleaned and put to rights. The old cardboard boxes and piles of newspapers had disappeared; the table was decently polished and set about with four chairs.

From this room, stairs, very steep and narrow, led to the upper floor, and they ascended and inspected the two bedrooms. In Major Billicliffe's bedroom, only a couple of ancient leather suitcases, firmly closed, remained as evidence of the former occupant. They were, Elfrida guessed, packed with his more respectable clothes. The bed was covered with a fresh cotton counterpane, and rag rugs had been laundered.

"We could move in tomorrow," Elfrida observed. And then hastily added, in case Oscar should take her at her word, "If we wanted to."

"Dear girl, I don't think we want to do that."

The second bedroom was smaller, and the bathroom, if not exactly the disaster that Rose had predicted, spartan to a degree, and not conducive to long soaks in scented water. The bath, which stood on feet, was stained and rusted, the basin cracked, and the linoleum beginning to curl up at the corners. A clean, threadbare towel hung on a wooden towel-rail, and a bar of Lifebuoy soap sat on the basin.

The best thing about the bathroom, like the kitchen, was the view. Elfrida, with some difficulty, got the window open and hung out. It was very still and quiet, but she could hear the movements of the trees, like a whisper, in some mysterious, unfelt breeze. And then two curlews flew by, headed for the water, calling their sad and lonely cry. Below her, the garden lay untended and neglected. Rough grass, clumps of weed, two rusted wash-poles with a bit of rope suspended between them. Nothing, it seemed, had been done for years, and yet she did not feel either depressed or disheartened. The view, the same view that she had admired from Rose's window, was there. The sloping fields, the dazzling blue water, and the distant hills. And she thought that, for a house that was not exactly bursting with happy memories, it had a good feel to it. It had been neglected, but was not without hope. It simply needed, like any human being, a bit of laughter and some tender loving care, and it would leap into life again. The only thing was, they'd have to do something about keeping themselves warm.

From behind her, Oscar spoke. "I am going to go out of doors," he told her. "To inspect my policies."

"You do that. You'll burst with pride when you see your ragwort."

She heard him go downstairs, whistle for Horace. She waited. Presently, he appeared beneath her, having let himself and the dog out of the kitchen door. She watched him, foreshortened, stand in the sunshine and look about him. Then, with Horace at his heels, he set out to walk down the length of his plot, and, when he came to the end, and the sagging fence that was his boundary, he leaned an elbow on one of the posts and stood there, watching the sea-birds on the shore of the firth.

Elfrida thought, I must buy him a pair of field-glasses. And she thought that he looked comfortable, and at ease with himself. A countryman who had finally come home.

She smiled, shut the window, went out of the bathroom, and crossed the narrow passage into the smaller bedroom for a quick reassessment, because this would have to be for Lucy. She eyed it professionally, trying to decide if there would be space to put a desk for homework. Which there would, if they replaced the enormous fumed-oak double bed with a single divan. The only thing was, it faced north and so was a bit lightless. Maybe something could be contrived, on the western aspect. . . .

She heard the sound of the approaching car, and, going to peer through the window, saw Sam's Discovery bumping down the drive from the main road, swinging around the turn, and drawing to a stop at the open gate. The back door opened and Lucy tumbled out.

"Elfrida!"

She sounded joyous. As though everything, for once in her life, was going to work out. Feeling ridiculously hopeful and happy, Elfrida turned and went from the room and ran down the narrow stairway to fling open the front door and hold wide her arms. Lucy bolted into them and was already imparting information, in high excitement, before Elfrida could say a word.

"Oh, Elfrida, it's all right. Carrie got hold of Mummy, and she was frightfully surprised and had to have it all explained to her *twice* before she finally understood what we all want to do. And Carrie was marvellously persuasive, and told Nicola that she had to think about *herself* and *Randall,* and have a lovely honeymoon, and take her time before coming back to England. And Mummy said that they want to go to Hawaii for their honeymoon, and then go to Cleveland to see Randall's other house there, so she'll need masses of time. And she said it was very, very kind of you to have me, and I could stay with you."

Elfrida, relieved and delighted as she was, managed to remain practical. "What about school? School in London, I mean."

"Oh, Mummy's going to see to all that. Ring Miss Maxwell-Brown and explain, and ask Miss Maxwell-Brown to keep my place open for me next summer, just in case I want to go back then. And she wanted to speak to you, but Carrie said you were here, and Mummy said she'd ring back and speak to you another time. Elfrida, isn't this the sweetest house? What's the old car doing there?"

"Rusting."

"Where's *yours*?"

"At Rose's."

"We thought maybe you'd flogged it at a garage and bought that one instead."

"You never thought any such thing."

"Does it go?"

"I don't know."

"Rory will get it started. Oh, and Elfrida, he's had a letter. He's going to Nepal in the middle of the month. Isn't that exciting? The only thing is, he won't be here when *I'm* here, but he's coming back in August to be ready for University. Elfrida, is this the sitting-room? And look, you've already lit a fire! It's too cosy. Where's Oscar?"

"Out in the garden."

"How do I get to him?"

"Through the kitchen. Out the door . . ."

With no hanging about, Lucy went, galloping down the garden and calling Oscar's name. Then Carrie appeared, staggering through the door with a huge shopping basket, spouting thermos flasks and bottles slung over her arm.

"Here we all are. Sorry, I hope we haven't kept you waiting." She dumped the basket on the floor, then, straightening up, raised a clenched fist as a sign of victory. "Done it," she told Elfrida. "Got through to Nicola, talked her into a good mood, and everything's okay. Parental approval has been bestowed. Lucy can stay and go to school in Creagan, and Nicola says she'll be in touch about contributing a bit of cash to the household for board and lodging."

"I never thought of that," Elfrida admitted.

"No, I don't suppose you did. And, as well, she will honour you with her presence next time she comes back to this country. I suppose that means driving north in some fantastic car with Randall Fischer at the wheel, in order to flaunt her new-found riches and cast a beady eye over you and Oscar. . . ."

"Carrie, don't be unkind."

"She'll probably patronize."

"It doesn't matter. We've got our way. Oh, well done." They hugged in triumph. Then Carrie drew away, and her expression became serious. "Elfrida, you promise it's not going to be too much for you?"

Elfrida shook her head. "I don't think so."

"It's a lot you're taking on."

"Don't say that. Ever."

"What's the house like?"

"Cold. That's why we lit the fire."

"Can I nose around?"

"Of course."

"Is this the kitchen?"

"Isn't it gruesome?"

"But full of sunshine! Oh, look, there's Oscar. . . ." She drifted out into the garden by way of the kitchen door. *"Oscar!"*

Elfrida picked up the basket, humped it into the kitchen, and set it down on the table. As she did this, she was joined by Sam, hefting a grocery box close to his chest. It looked very heavy.

"Is this all picnic?" she asked in some amazement.

"A feast. Where shall I put it?"

"Here, by the basket. Where's Rory?"

"Trying to deal with Major Billicliffe's old car. It looks dreadful standing there. Have we got the ignition key?"

"I've no idea."

"We can take the brake off and shove it out of the way. It lowers the tone of your newly acquired property." He went to the window and stood looking down the garden to where Oscar, Carrie, and Lucy had started to walk back to the house. He said, "What an amazing view. It's a good house, Elfrida. It's got a good solid feel to it."

And she felt warmed, like a mother whose child is praised for its beauty. "That's what I think, too."

The Christmas Eve picnic at Corrydale, the first one they ever had there, was something of a movable feast. It started with a glass of wine by the fireside, in the warmth of the blazing logs, but slowly progressed out of doors, because the day was so beautiful that it seemed almost sacrilegious to be inside. Rory and Lucy were the first to make their way out into the garden, and the others, one by one, joined them, to perch on kitchen chairs, or cushions from the sofa, or the thick rug that Rory fetched from Sam's car. The air was cold, but the sun beamed down upon them, and in the shelter of the house there was no breath of wind.

Carrie and Sam had done a splendid job. They had brought hot soup laced with sherry, drunk from mugs; fresh rolls filled with thick slices of ham and English mustard; a bacon-and-egg quiche; chicken drumsticks; tomato salad; crisp green apples; and chunks of cheddar cheese. Finally a flask of fresh, boiling-hot coffee.

Elfrida, sitting on a cushion with her back against the wall, turned her face up to the sun and closed her eyes. "That was the best picnic ever. Thank you, Carrie. I feel quite stunned with wine. Maddened by drink. I could be in Majorca."

Oscar laughed. "Discount the fact that you're still wrapped up in your blanket coat."

Rory and Lucy, having finished their picnic and shared between them a large bag of potato crisps and a bar of chocolate, had disappeared, gone indoors to inspect the layout of the little house. Now, they appeared again.

"It's so nice, Oscar," Lucy told him.

"The only thing," said Rory bluntly, "is you're going to have to do something about the heating problem. It's arctic."

Carrie protested. "Rory, it's been standing empty, and there's been snow. Come on, it's December. Nothing's particularly warm in December."

"No," Oscar said firmly. "Rory's right. Heating will be our first priority. Where are you two off to now?"

"We thought we'd take Horace for a walk, down to the water and the beach."

Oscar tipped back the last of his coffee. "I shall come with you." He had eaten his picnic sitting on the step of the kitchen door. Now he set down the mug and held out a hand to Rory, who took it and pulled Oscar to his feet. "After that feast, I need exercise. Who's coming with us?"

"I shall," said Carrie.

"I shan't," said Elfrida firmly. "Why can't you all sit around, just for a moment? It's all so blissfully peaceful."

"If we do, it will be dark before we know it, and too late for a walk. What about you, Sam?"

"I shall stay with Elfrida. I would like to do a building inspection."

Showing Sam Howard around Major Billicliffe's house was quite different from looking at it with Oscar. With Oscar, Elfrida had simply gone from room to room, and ended up grateful that it was neither as poky nor as decrepit as they had feared. But Sam was infinitely more practical and meticulous, just as she had suspected he would be. He tapped walls, turned taps, inspected window frames and power points, and made no comment when she revealed to him the horrors of the breeze-block bathroom. Finally they were finished, and back in the sitting-room. The fire was dying, so she put another couple of logs on the embers and stirred it up with a poker. Sam had said so little, made so few observations, that she began to feel afraid that, mentally, he had condemned Oscar's inheritance, and was about to break the news that, in his opinion, it was unfit for human habitation.

"What do you think, Sam?" she asked nervously.

"I think it has great possibilities. And the location is out of this world . . . hang on a moment, I just have to fetch something from the car. Is there electricity? Could we have a light or two on? It's beginning to get a bit dark in here. . . ."

When he had gone, she turned on lights. A faint gleam emanated from an overhead shade. Was the bulb on its last legs, or was this simply another example of Major Billicliffe's parsimonious life-style? A lamp by the fireside, another on the desk. After that, things looked a bit better. When Sam returned she saw that he had brought with him a yellow scratch-pad and a ball-point pen.

They sat together on the sofa. "Now," said Sam, reaching into his pocket for his spectacles and putting them on, "let's talk turkey. Do you intend living in the place just as it is, or do you want to change a few things?"

"It depends," said Elfrida cautiously.

"On what?"

"How much it would cost?"

"Supposing . . ." He began to draw a plan on the scratch-pad. "Supposing to begin with, you demolished the existing kitchen and bathroom. They're ugly, impractical, and shut out the light from the south. And then, I think, you should demolish the wall dividing the living-room and the lobby . . . it's only plasterboard, and doesn't seem to support anything. Then you'd have one big, open-plan room. And my suggestion would be that you make the dining-room into a kitchen, and maybe build a small dining area out to the south. The south and west walls could be glassed . . . you'd get all the view and every ray of sun. And it would give you a sheltered corner for sitting out. A little terrace. Good for warm summer evenings."

"What would we do about the staircase?"

"Move it around to the back wall."

"And things like fridges and washing machines? Appliances, I think the word is."

"Incorporate them into a fitted kitchen. There's a chimney there already, so you could install an Aga or a Raeburn. Continual steady heat, winter and summer, and if you're visited by a heat wave, which isn't very likely in this part of the world, you just open all the doors and windows."

"Would that do instead of central heating?"

"I would reckon so; this house is so well-built, and of stone, that once you get it properly insulated, it'll stay warm. As well, you've got this fire in your sitting-room. As for the bedrooms, you could put in electric radiators, and heat your water by electricity as well. It's enormously efficient, and if you have a power cut, you've still got the Aga."

"Bathroom?"

"A new one." He sketched it in on his rough plan. "Over the dining room."

"Lucy would have to use it, too."

"No problem."

"The small bedroom, where she would sleep, is terribly dark."

"Once you've got rid of the old bathroom, and the passage, she'd have a southern wall for another window."

Elfrida gazed at his simple suggestions, all drawn out for her on the yellow scratch-pad, and was astonished that he had so quickly solved the dilemma. And as for a single open-plan living space, she rather liked it. She imagined herself and Oscar sitting, just as she was now, by the fire, with the comfort of a modern kitchen at the far end of the room.

"The lobby?" she ventured.

"Get rid of it. It's simply a draught trap. But double glazing and a new front door will keep the cold out."

Elfrida chewed her thumbnail. She said, "How much will all this cost?"

"Honestly, I don't know."

"Would it . . . would it cost more than eighty thousand pounds?"

He laughed, his face creasing up with amusement. "No, Elfrida. I don't think it would cost as much as that. You're not, after all, rebuilding. Simply adapting. The roof seems to be sound, which is the most important thing. No sign of damp. But I think you should get a surveyor in. And you'd be better off to have all the electricity rewired. Even so, eighty thousand should be more than adequate." He took off his spectacles and looked at her. "Have you *got* eighty thousand?"

"No. But I hope to have. Jamie Erskine-Earle is going to sell my little clock for me. We never told you, but apparently it is very rare. A collector's piece. Worth a lot of money. So I told him to sell it."

"Eighty thousand?"

"That's what he said. Top price, eighty-five."

"In that case you have no problems. I am delighted for you! Go for it, Elfrida."

"We'll have to get an architect. And planning permission. And things like that."

"How about the doctor's wife? Janet Sinclair. She's an architect. Give her the job. The bonus *there* is that she's local, and she'll know all the best builders and joiners and plumbers."

"How long will it take?"

"I suppose six months. I don't know."

"We'll have to stay in the Estate House until it's ready for us to move in."

"Of course."

"But *you*, Sam? *You* want the Estate House."

"I can wait. I'm certainly not about to throw you out onto the streets."

"But you'll be working in Buckly. So where will you live?"

"I'll be okay."

A brilliant idea occurred to Elfrida, and in her impulsive way, she immediately shared it with him. "You can live with us. At the Estate

House. You and Lucy and Oscar and me. You've already got a room there. You might just as well stay."

Again, Sam laughed. "Elfrida, these are the sort of suggestions you should think about very deeply."

"Why? Why should I think?"

"Because you may change your mind. And you must talk it over with Oscar. He may not like the idea at all."

"Oh, Oscar will love to have you. And so shall I. It will be a new job for me. Letting out lodgings. You know, I've been a lot of things in my time. An actress, albeit not a very good one. A waitress, when I wasn't working. A lady of not very respectable repute. A cushion stitcher. And now I shall become a landlady. Oh, please say yes. I feel the Estate House is already yours, in a strange way, even though you don't own it yet. As though you were always meant to come and live there. And that's where you should be."

"Thank you," said Sam. "In that case, I accept, subject, of course, to Oscar's approval."

The sun was beginning to dip down out of the sky by the time the walkers returned. Oscar and Carrie were first, with Horace, who was badly in need of a cooling drink.

"How was it?" Elfrida asked, searching a cupboard for a suitable bowl for a dog.

"Perfect," Carrie told her, unknotting her scarf. "Such a heavenly place. And all the birds down on the shore! Ducks and cormorants and gulls . . . how did you and Sam get on?"

"Sam is *brilliant*. He's practically drawn the plans. You must come and look, Oscar. We hardly have to do anything. Just knock bits down and build other bits, and get rid of a wall and find an Aga. Don't gape, Oscar, it's all very straightforward. And we'll ask Janet Sinclair to be our architect. And Sam says we must have it all surveyed and rewired, but he doesn't think there's a thing wrong *anywhere* . . . come and see. . . ."

It was half an hour before Rory and Lucy finally joined them, by which time Oscar had seen and listened to all Sam's ideas, been persuaded, and given his consent. Carrie approved as well. "You know, I've always loved the idea of an open-plan ground floor, specially in a small house. And with the new extension, it means you'll get masses more light. Sam, you are clever. You actually are *very* clever. How did you learn so much about knocking down walls and drawing plans?"

"For the last two months I've been living with plans and projects and elevations and architects' blueprints. I'd be pretty dumb if I hadn't absorbed a bit of know-how. . . ."

Now the light was fading. Carrie looked at her watch and said that it was time to go back to Creagan. Lucy still had to finish laying the table for Christmas dinner, and Carrie was going to cook a large and satisfying dish that they could eat that evening. "Are we going to Midnight Service, Elfrida?"

"I think so. Oscar doesn't want to come, but I'll go."

"Me, too. And Lucy and Sam are coming as well. We'll have a late meal, otherwise it's a very long evening."

Oscar said, "We'll play cards. I found some packs of cards in the bottom drawer of the bookcase. Who knows how to play three-pack Canasta?"

"Samba, you mean?" said Sam. "*I* know how. There was a great craze for it in New York when I was there."

"I can't play," said Lucy.

"Never mind," he told her. "You can play with me."

Eventually, having packed up the remains of the picnic, found hats and gloves, and generally sorted themselves out, the first party took their leave in Sam's car. Elfrida, Oscar, and Horace were left behind, to lock up and follow later, but they went out of doors to see the others off.

By now, at only four o'clock, the blue dusk had crept in, and a fine new moon, delicate as an eyelash, hung above them in the sapphire sky. The snow-capped hills became almost luminous in the strange half-light, and the ebbing tide was draining the firth, revealing sweeps of beach and sandbank. Curlews still flew, skimming the shore, but other birds were silent, their song finished for the day.

The big Discovery, tail-lights shining, disappeared up the drive. Oscar and Elfrida waited by the door until they could hear the sound of its engine no longer, and then turned and went back inside.

Elfrida said, "I don't want to go. I don't want to leave. I don't want today to end."

"Then we'll stay for a little."

"If I had any tea, I would make you a cup."

"We'll have one when we get back."

He sank tiredly down on the sofa, where, earlier, Sam Howard had sat. He had walked, with the young ones, farther than he intended, and felt weary. Elfrida put the last bit of wood on the fire and then sat opposite him, stretching her cold fingers to the blaze.

She said, "We will live here, won't we, Oscar?"

"If you want."

"I do. But do you?"

"Yes. I admit, I did have reservations, but now that I have seen it again, and Sam has come up with all these ideas and possibilities, I think it is exactly what we should do."

"It's exciting. A new start. Architects and builders, and everything made new. One of my most favourite smells is that of wet plaster. And the next most favourite is the smell of fresh paint."

"Furniture?"

"We can manage with what's here for the time being. Maybe look around, pick up some pretty bits at auction. The first priority is to get the place the way we want it. Warm and light and airy. With an Aga, and a good-looking kitchen. Warmth is the most important. I can't imagine how Major Billicliffe lived here for so long without dying of hypothermia."

"He was one of the old school. A thick tweed jacket and long woolly underfugs, and no nonsense about feeling the cold."

"You won't ever be like that, will you, Oscar? I couldn't bear it if you started wearing long woolly underfugs."

"No. With a bit of luck I won't ever do that."

The shadows lengthened. Beyond the window, the bare trees faded into the darkness. Elfrida sighed. "I suppose we should go. I mustn't leave everything to Carrie. . . ."

But Oscar said, "Wait. I want to talk."

"What about?"

"Us."

"But—" She had been about to say, *We've been talking about us all day,* but Oscar interrupted her.

"Just listen. Just listen to me." And his voice sounded so serious and intent that she got up from her chair and went to sit beside him, close, on the old sofa, and he put out his hand and laid it upon her own. And she remembered his doing this once before, as they sat at the kitchen table at the Grange, with Gloria and Francesca dead, and neither of them able to find the words to comfort each other.

"I'm listening," she told him.

"This is a new step we're going to take. Together. A real commitment. Doing up this house, spending serious money, and coming to live here. As well, for the foreseeable future, Lucy is coming, too. Don't you think perhaps the time has come for us to get married? To be man and wife? It's a formality, I know, because if we tried, we could scarcely be more married than we already are. But it would put a seal on our union . . . not in a moral sense, but an affirmation of our trust in the future."

Elfrida realized that her stupid eyes were filling with tears. "Oh, Oscar. . . ." She drew her hand away and began to search for her handkerchief. *Old people,* she had once told him, *look hideous when they cry.* ". . . You don't need to do this. It's only months since they died. So little time to grieve and recover. And you mustn't think of me . . . because I'm not that sort of person. I will stay with you happily for the rest of my life, but I don't want you to feel you have to marry me. . . ."

"I don't feel that. I love you and I honour you just the way things are, and I don't suppose either of us gives a jot what other people think or choose to say. All things being equal, I should happily settle for carrying on just the way things are. But we now have Lucy to consider."

"What difference does she make to how we live our lives?"

"Oh, my dearest Elfrida, just think. So far the people of Creagan have accepted us with great kindness, even forbearance. No questions. Not a single soul has cast a stone, not even a tiny pebble. But for Lucy it is different. She is going to the local school. Children are not always very kind. Rumours can be started, and even in this day and age, parents can be mean-spirited. I wouldn't want any of that sort of thing to rub off on Lucy. As well, we have Nicola's new husband to consider. We know nothing about him, and he's probably a perfectly decent chap, but he might turn out to be one of those high-minded individuals with a strong and unforgiving moral code. Sometime Nicola is bringing him to visit us. We don't want to give either of them a valid reason for spiriting Lucy off to Cleveland, Ohio, against her will."

"You mean, he wouldn't want to leave her with us, simply because we live in sin?"

"Exactly so."

"So for her sake, we should be married."

"Put baldly, yes."

"But Gloria . . ."

"Gloria, of all women, would understand."

"It's such a short time, Oscar."

"I know."

"You're sure?"

"Yes, I am sure. Because one thing is truly certain, and that is that you have helped me to start again, and it is you who have made a dark and painful time not only bearable and possible, but even joyful as well. I think you carry joy around with you. We can't go back. Life, for both of us, can never be the same as it was, but it can be different; and you have proved to me that it can be good. I told you a long time ago that you could always make me laugh. As well, you have made me love you. Now, I cannot imagine an existence without you. Please marry me. If I wasn't feeling so bloody stiff, I'd get down on one knee."

"I'd hate you to do that." Elfrida, having at last found her handkerchief, now blew her nose. "But I'd like to marry you very, very much. Thank you for asking me." She put her handkerchief away, and once more he took her hand.

"So. We are betrothed. Shall we break the news or keep it to ourselves?"

"Let's keep it to ourselves. Secretly relish. Just for the time being."

"You are right. There is so much going on. Let us get Christmas behind us, and then I shall take you to Kingsferry and buy you a diamond ring, and after that, we can announce our happiness to the world."

"I have to be truthful," Elfrida admitted. "I'm not all that mad on diamonds."

"Then what would you like me to buy you?"

"An Aquamarine?"

And Oscar laughed, and kissed her. And they might have sat on, in the gloaming, for the rest of the evening, but the last of the logs had burnt out, and the house, with the sun gone, grew cold again. It was time to leave. Outside, the air, so quickly, had chilled and it was winter again. A wind stirred from the north, shivering the leafless branches of the big beech tree that stood opposite their gate.

Elfrida, her hands deep in the pockets of her coat, looked about her. The moon was rising, the first star pricked.

"We'll be back," she said, to no one in particular.

"Of course." Oscar locked his front door, took her arm, and with Horace at their heels, they walked, in the deep-blue evening light, down the pebbled path.

Christmas Eve

It's nearly eight o'clock in the evening, and there's still masses to do. I must write everything down, otherwise it will be lost forever. So much has happened. The worst was Mummy ringing yesterday in the middle of Elfrida's party to say that she has married Randall Fischer. I think it was the worst thing that ever happened to me, because all I could think about was having to go and live in America, and lose all my friends, or else have to live with Gran in London on my own. And not fit in or be wanted in either place. It was really dire. I had horrible hysterics and made myself feel quite ill and was beastly to Carrie, but that's all over now.

Anyway, now it is all sorted out, and I'm going to stay here, in Creagan, with Elfrida and Oscar for the time being, and go to day-school in Creagan. Rory was the one who told everybody that I must do this, and I am so pleased that he and I had time to talk, when he was fixing the television. So that he knew exactly how I felt, even if nobody else did. I think he is really my best friend. He is going to Nepal in the middle of next month and is tremendously excited about it. I shall miss him, but will see him again, I am sure, when he gets back in August. Whatever has happened by then, I shall make a point of seeing him, and I shall be fifteen then. Fifteen sounds much older than fourteen.

So this morning I woke up and knew that everything was going to be all right, and it was like having a huge weight off my mind. Carrie rang Gran and told her about our plans, and she went along with them; and then later she rang Mummy in Florida, and with a bit of coaxing, persuaded her, too. Actually, it didn't take very long. And then I had a chat with Mummy, and managed not to sound too delighted, in case she took offence and changed her mind.

So then Rory appeared, and we got a picnic together, and Sam drove us over to Corrydale. I have always longed to go there and see it all. It is beautiful and it was a beautiful day, with no clouds or wind and really quite warm. Oscar's little house is too sweet, tucked away on the estate with a few other little houses in view, great big trees, and a long view of the water and over hills. It was tremendously quiet: only bird-song, and no sound of traffic or anything. The house isn't very big and is fairly shabby and dreadfully cold, but Oscar had lit a fire which made it look cosy. There are only two bedrooms, and the one I shall have is a bit gloomy, but Elfrida says it will be better when they have done a few alterations. Sam thought up lots of clever ideas, and when it is finished it will look really nice. It has a garden, a bit weedy, and a sort of little terrace where we all went out and ate our picnic. Elfrida says there are other children, called Cowper, who live nearby at the farm, and they go to the Creagan school, too; so maybe when term starts, I can get a lift in the mornings with them.

We all came back with Sam, and left Rory at the Manse and then came home. Carrie made a huge dish called an egg tortilla for us to have for supper: it has potatoes and leeks in it, and eggs, bacon, and heaps of other delicious things. While she did this, I finished laying the table for Christmas dinner, and put on the candles and the crackers and dishes of chocolate, and folded the napkins. There's a bowl of holly in the middle of the table and it looks really festive, and when we've lit the fire, will look exactly right, like a Christmas card. Carrie said all that was missing was a Jolly Cardinal.

Then we're going to play cards to fill in the long evening, and then we're all going to Midnight Service, except Oscar, who says he doesn't want to come.

I don't know how long it will be before they are able to move to Corrydale, because of all the work that has to be done there. I would love to be there in the summer, but Elfrida says we'll have to see. Meantime, it's lovely here. And Sam is going to come and be our lodger until everything is sorted out.

I can't believe that I could be so miserable and despairing one day, and so utterly happy the next.

The next time I write in my diary, Christmas will be over.

Elfrida endeavoured to fan out her enormous hand of cards, and at the same time decide what she was going to throw away. She had run out of twos and threes, and was now in the uncomfortable position of trying to work out whether or not Carrie had a pair in her hand, and if so, a pair of what? The discard pack was too large for comfort, they were nearing the end of the game, and if Carrie picked it up now, Elfrida and Sam would be defeated.

"Come along now, Elfrida." Oscar was getting tired of the long wait. "Be brave. Throw something you don't want."

So she gritted her teeth, threw the eight of hearts, and waited anxiously for Carrie to let out a shout of glee and pounce. But Carrie shook her head, and Elfrida relaxed with a sigh of relief.

"I can't stand the nerves! If I wasn't going to church, I should have another large drink."

It was now ten past eleven, and they were on the last hand. So far, Sam and Elfrida were ahead on points, but the tension would continue until the final card was turned. Elfrida had played Samba long ago, when Jimbo was still alive, and they had sometimes whiled away the evening with a couple of friends. But she had forgotten some of the rules, and it was not until she started playing again that the old tricks and shibboleths came back to her. Oscar and Sam were both old hands and up to all the nuances of the game, but Carrie and Lucy were starters. Carrie quickly picked it up, and Lucy played with Sam, who was kindly and patient about explaining; and by the end of the first hand he was allowing her to make the choices of discard, and not becoming annoyed when she made the wrong one.

Carrie picked up two cards, put them into her hand, and was then able to finish a Samba. Oscar let out a grunt of approval. She threw the four of spades. "If you pick that up, Sam, I shall strangle you with my bare hands."

"I can't."

Lucy said, "There are only four cards left."

"When they're finished, the game's done," Sam told her. "Pick two up, Lucy, and see what we've got. . . ."

From the landing, the telephone rang.

Oscar said, “That damned telephone. Who’s ringing us at this hour?”

Elfrida said, “I’ll go.”

But Oscar already had laid down his cards and was getting to his feet. He went out of the room, closing the door behind him. Elfrida heard him say, “Estate House.”

And then silence, as the caller spoke, and then a murmured reply. The next moment, he was back with them, settling down in his place on the window-seat, picking up his cards again.

Elfrida was curious. “Who was it?”

“Nothing much. A mistake.”

“You mean, wrong number?”

Oscar gazed at his cards.

Sam said, “If you’ve the wrong number, why did you answer the phone?” And Lucy giggled at the old joke, sitting with her head to one side, trying to decide what she should throw.

In the end, they ran out of cards, and nobody won. But Sam pulled the score-pad towards him, totted up all the figures, and announced that he and Elfrida were the overall winners, and that he hoped that Oscar was about to come up with a valuable prize.

“I am about to do no such thing,” Oscar informed him with dignity. “You were extremely lucky and held all the best cards; nothing to do with skill.” And with that, he laid his cards on the table and got to his feet. He said, “I’m going to take Horace for a walk.”

Elfrida stared at him in some astonishment. He often took Horace out into the garden last thing at night, but never for a walk.

“A walk? Where are you going? Down to the beach?”

“I don’t know. I just feel the need of some fresh air and to stretch my legs. Horace might as well come with me. I may not be back by the time you set off for church, but leave the door open, and I’ll still be up when you all return. Have a good time. Sing nicely, Lucy.”

“I will,” she promised him.

He left them, closing the door behind him.

Elfrida's expression was puzzled. "*Funny.* You'd have thought he'd had enough exercise today to last him for a week."

"Oh, leave him, Elfrida," said Carrie, gathering up all the cards and starting to sort them out into three separate packs, one blue, one red, and one flowered. "Help me, Lucy. You can do the flowered ones. I think that's a marvellous game. There comes a subtle moment when you stop playing Samba and start playing Canasta. The scoring's a bit complicated, though. You'll have to write it down for me, Sam, so that I don't forget."

"I'll do that."

The cards were sorted, stacked, and put away. Elfrida went around the room puffing up cushions and picking up newspapers from the floor. The fire was low, but she left it, and stood the guard in front of the smouldering wood ashes.

"We shouldn't be too long making our way, I think. There's bound to be a huge congregation, and we want to be able to get a seat."

"It's like going to the theatre," said Lucy. "Will it be cold in the church? Should I wear my red jacket?"

"Yes, definitely, and your warm boots."

Alone in her bedroom, Elfrida combed her hair, put on a bit more lipstick, and sprayed herself with scent. Then she took her blanket coat from the wardrobe, buttoned it up, and put on her tea-cosy hat. She sat on the bed and pulled on her fur-lined boots. Some money for the collection. A handkerchief in case she felt emotionally touched by carols, and a pair of gloves.

All ready. She surveyed her reflection in the long mirror. Elfrida Phipps, soon to become Mrs. Oscar Blundell. She thought that she looked terrific. *Here I come, God. And thanks.*

She went out of her room and downstairs to the kitchen, to check that all was in order for Christmas morning, and that she hadn't left the gas on, or the kettle boiling itself dry, which she quite often did. And in the kitchen, in his basket, she found Horace.

She frowned. "Horace, I thought Oscar had taken you for a walk."

He gazed at her and thumped his tail.

"Did he leave you behind?"

Horace closed his eyes.

"Where's he gone?"

Horace did not tell her.

She went upstairs again and into the sitting-room. "Oscar?" But the sitting-room was dark, empty, and all the lights switched off. No Oscar.

On the landing she found Sam, pulling on his good navy-blue overcoat. "Oscar's disappeared."

"He's walking Horace," Sam reminded her.

"No, Horace is back in the kitchen. In his basket. It's a mystery!"

Sam grinned. "Oscar's probably sneaked off to the pub."

"What a suggestion."

"Don't worry. He's a big boy now."

"I'm not worrying." And of course she wasn't. Just puzzled as to where Oscar could possibly have taken himself.

Lucy ran downstairs from her attic. "All ready, Elfrida. Do we need collection?"

"Yes. Have you got any?"

"Is a pound enough?"

"Fine. Where's Carrie?"

"She's still getting ready."

"Well, you and I will go, Lucy, and bag a pew for the four of us. . . . Sam, will you wait for Carrie, and come over with her?"

"Of course . . ."

Elfrida and Lucy ran downstairs. Sam heard them open and slam shut the big front door.

He stood there on the landing, in the emptied house, and waited for Carrie. Soft sounds came from behind her closed bedroom door: drawers being opened, a cupboard door shut. He felt no sense of impatience. He had waited, during the course of his life, for countless women to appear—sitting at bars, standing around in the foyers of theatres, whiling away the time at the table of some small Italian restaurant. He had waited, more times than he could remember, for

Deborah, who had never been punctual for anything. So now, in the house which would, one day, belong to him, he waited for Carrie.

"Oh, Sam." She came out of her room, slammed shut the door behind her, saw him there, and looked a bit abashed. "Are you waiting for me? I am sorry. I couldn't find my silk scarf." She wore her loden coat, her fur hat, her long, shining boots. The errant scarf, all pinks and blues, was softly wound around her slender throat, and although all of this was by now dearly familiar to him, he knew that he had never seen her more beautiful. "Where are the others? Have they already gone . . . ?"

He said, "Yes," and put his hands on her shoulders, drew her close, and kissed her. Something he had been longing to do ever since that first night, when she had opened the door to him, and found him standing on the doorstep in the falling snow. So, now, it took a long time. When at last they drew apart, he saw that she was smiling, and her dark eyes had never seemed so lustrous.

He said, "Happy Christmas."

"Happy Christmas, Sam. Time to go."

Elfrida and Lucy crossed the street. The square, lamplit, was already busy with cars arriving and people walking, converging on the church. There was, it was clear, going to be a huge congregation. Voices called out, country people greeting each other, falling into step as they made their way.

"Elfrida!"

They stopped and saw Tabitha, Rory and Clodagh behind them, having walked down the steep lane from the Manse.

"Hello! I thought we were early, but it seems we're not. I've never seen so many people. . . ."

"I know, it's fun, isn't it?" Tabitha wore a tartan coat and had wound a red muffler around her neck. "It's always like this. People come for miles. . . . The only thing is, we've had a bit of a setback. Alistair Heggie, the organist, has got flu, so we won't have any proper music."

Elfrida was horrified. "You mean, we've got to sing carols unaccompanied? I can't *bear* it. . . ."

"Not quite. Peter rang Bill Croft, the television man, and he's come to the rescue and set up a ghetto blaster, and we're going to use taped music. It's a bit of a come-down, but better than nothing."

"Oh, that is disappointing . . . poor Peter."

"Oh, it can't be helped. Come on, with a bit of luck we'll get a pew to ourselves."

They crossed the street to the wide gates and the path beyond, which led to the wide flight of stone steps and the double doors of the church. Tonight, these had been flung wide open. Light from inside streamed out onto the cobbles, and Elfrida could hear the taped music from within the church. A choir. Singing carols.

"God rest you, Merry Gentlemen,
Let nothing you dismay."

It sounded a bit mechanical and tinny. A bit, thought Elfrida, like a portable gramophone played on a picnic. Inappropriate and somehow inadequate.

"For Jesus Christ our—"

Silence. Either the tape player had broken down, or some person had inadvertently switched off the electricity.

"Oh, no!" said Rory. "Don't say the ghetto blaster's got flu."

And then it started. A great surge of sound from the organ. Huge chords and waves of music filled the church, overflowed out through the open doors, resounded up and out into the night.

Elfrida stopped dead. She looked at Tabitha, and Tabitha's eyes were wide and innocent. For a long moment, neither of them spoke. Then Elfrida said, "Did Peter ring Oscar? About a quarter past eleven?"

Tabitha shrugged. "No idea. Come on, kids, see if we can find somewhere to sit."

And she turned and ran up the steps, with her two children and Lucy at her heels.

After a moment, Elfrida followed. A nice man with a beard was waiting for her. He said, "Good evening, Mrs. Phipps," and handed her a hymn-book. She took it automatically, neither looking at him nor thanking him. She walked into the church and saw that it was already nearly filled, the congregation shuffling into their places, leaning to chat to neighbours or to others sitting behind them. The music thundered all about her, filling the huge void of the soaring arched ceiling, echoing down the long nave. She began to walk down the centre aisle, which was paved in red and blue. Walking in to the music was like stepping into a pounding sea of sound.

A hand touched her arm. She stopped. "Elfrida. Here." It was Lucy. "We're keeping seats for you and Sam and Carrie."

She took no notice. Did not move.

The Christmas tree, lavishly decorated and twinkling with lights, stood in the middle of the transept, between the pulpit and the lectern. Beyond this, against the north wall of the church, the organ pipes soared. The organist's seat was enclosed by an oaken stall, so that he was not visible to the seated assembly. But Elfrida was standing. And she was tall. An overhead spotlight shone down upon him, and she could clearly see his head, his profile, and the thick white hair, rendered unruly by the unselfconscious exuberance of his own performance.

Beethoven. "Ode to Joy."

And Oscar Blundell, playing his heart out. Reconciled. Returned. Back where he belonged.